Ana Huang is a #1 *New York Times, #1 USA Today, Sunday Times, Wall Street Journal*, and #1 Amazon bestselling author. Best known for her Twisted series, she writes New Adult and contemporary romance with deliciously alpha heroes, strong heroines, and plenty of steam, angst, and swoon.

Her books have been translated in thirty languages and featured in outlets such as Good Morning America, NPR, *Cosmopolitan*, and *PEOPLE* magazine.

A self-professed travel enthusiast, she loves incorporating beautiful destinations into her stories and will never say no to a good chai latte.

BOOKS BY ANA HUANG

GODS OF THE GAME

A series of interconnected standalones

The Striker

The Defender

KINGS OF SIN

A series of interconnected standalones

King of Wrath

King of Pride

King of Greed

King of Sloth

King of Envy

TWISTED

A series of interconnected standalones

Twisted Love

Twisted Games

Twisted Hate

Twisted Lies

IF LOVE

If We Ever Meet Again (Duet Book 1)

If the Sun Never Sets (Duet Book 2)

If Love Had a Price (Standalone)

If We Were Perfect (Standalone)

THE
STRIKER

THE MULTI-MILLION COPY BESTSELLING AUTHOR
ANA HUANG

PIATKUS

PIATKUS

First published in the US in 2024 by Bloom Books,
An imprint of Sourcebooks
Published in Great Britain in 2024 by Piatkus

1 3 5 7 9 10 8 6 4 2

Editor: Becca Hensley Mysoor at the Fairy Plotmother
Proofreader: Britt Tayler
Cover Designer: Cat Imb at TRC Designs
Formatter: Cat Imb at TRC Designs

A CIP catalogue record for this book
is available from the British Library.

ISBN 978-0-349-44225-9

Printed and bound in Great Britain by Clays Ltd, Elcograf S.p.A.

Papers used by Piatkus are from well-managed forests
and other responsible sources.

Piatkus
An imprint of
Little, Brown Book Group
Carmelite House
50 Victoria Embankment
London EC4Y 0DZ

An Hachette UK Company
www.hachette.co.uk
www.littlebrown.co.uk

To loving every version of yourself,
even the ones you want to leave behind.

PLAYLIST

🖤 **So High School**
Taylor Swift

🖤 **Applause**
Lady Gaga

🖤 **Smooth Operator**
Sade

🖤 **London Boy**
Taylor Swift

🖤 **Who Do You Think You Are**
Spice Girls

🖤 **Piece of Me**
Britney Spears

🖤 **Paparazzi**
Lady Gaga

🖤 **Delicate**
Taylor Swift

🖤 **Can't Get You Out of My Head**
Glimmer of Blooms

🖤 **It's Gonna Be Me**
*NSYNC

🖤 **Into You**
Ariana Grande

🖤 **Love Letter to Japan**
The Bird and the Bee

🖤 **Unstoppable**
Sia

🖤 **Iris**
The Goo Goo Dolls

🖤 **Let Me Down Slowly**
Alec Benjamin

🖤 **Sweet Caroline**
Neil Diamond

CONTENT NOTES

This story contains explicit sexual content, profanity, and topics that may be sensitive to some readers.

For a detailed list, please visit anahuang.com/content-warnings

AUTHOR'S NOTE

This story takes place in London, so it uses the British term "football" instead of soccer.

Unless otherwise stated, football as it's used here always refers to soccer, not American football.

Please also note that certain details about the Premier League schedule have been modified for story purposes, and the word for posterior will remain in its American instead of British form (apologies to the word "arse." It's not you, it's me).

CHAPTER 1

ASHER

I DIDN'T GET PERFORMANCE ANXIETY, BUT THERE WAS nothing like seventy thousand people watching you get fucked that really put a guy on edge.

Sweat dripped into my eyes as I received the ball from the left-winger. The crowd's cheers reached a fever pitch, and a tiny prickle of trepidation snaked through my gut.

Usually, the fans' enthusiasm revved me up. After all, I'd *dreamed* of moments like this growing up. Playing on a professional pitch, hearing thousands chant my name, being the one who took my team to glory.

Moments like this meant I'd made it and proved my critics wrong—which I had, many times over.

After all, I was Asher Fucking Donovan.

But today, in the last minute of the final game of the Premier League season, I felt like just Asher, the newest and most controversial transfer to Blackcastle.

It was my first season with the team, the match was tied, and we were second on the league table behind Holchester United.

We *needed* a win to take home the trophy, but so far, the match had been a clusterfuck of disasters.

An intercepted ball here, a missed penalty there. We were all over the place, and I could practically see the victory slipping through my fingers.

Frustration mounted as I tried to maneuver past the swarm of Holchester defenders. Bocci, Lyle, Kanu—I knew their tricks well, but they also knew mine.

That was the problem with playing against your old team; there was nowhere to hide.

With no way out, I passed the ball to another forward and tried to ignore the time ticking down.

Forty seconds.

Thirty-nine.

Thirty-eight.

The ball bounced between players until, through a stroke of equally good and bad luck, Vincent gained possession through a counter-attack.

The cheers dulled to a low roar beneath the weight of my anticipation.

Seventeen.

Sixteen.

Fifteen.

I was in the perfect position to receive the ball. I had a clear shot at the goal, but I could see Vincent's eyes searching the pitch for someone, *anyone* else to pass it to.

My pulse hammered in rhythm with the ticking clock.

Come on, you bastard.

There *was* no one else. I was the only player on our team who could feasibly score at this point. Vincent must've come to the same conclusion because, with a noticeable clench of his jaw, he finally kicked the ball to me.

The crowd's excitement pitched high, but it was too late.

Vincent's precious few seconds of hesitation gave Holchester an opening, and they stole the ball before I could connect with it.

A collective groan rippled over the pitch.

I blinked away the sweat and tried to focus, but my old team's taunting stares and the blaze of bright lights disoriented me in a way I hadn't felt since *that* match many moons ago.

Five.

An attempt to steal the ball back failed.

Four.

Flashes of news headlines and TV snippets blared in my head. *Traitor. Judas. Sellout.* Was I worth the record 250-million-pound transfer, or was I the most expensive mistake in Premier League history?

Three.

By some miracle, I got the ball on the second attempt.

Two.

No time to think.

One.

I kicked.

The ball went wide to the shrill of the final whistle, and the stadium fell so silent I could hear the rush of blood in my ears.

All around me, my team stood, stunned, while the Holchester players jumped and whooped in celebration.

It was over.

We'd lost.

My first season with Blackcastle—the one where everyone

expected me to bring home a trophy—was over, and we'd *lost*.

My surroundings blurred into a muffled stream of noise and movement, and I barely felt the soreness of my muscles or a teammate's consoling slap on my back.

I barely felt anything at all.

No one spoke during our walk to the changing room, but the dread was palpable.

The only thing worse than losing a match was facing Coach afterward, and he barely gave us a chance to sit before he went off.

Frank Armstrong was a legend in the football world. As a player, he was famous for his string of hat tricks in the nineties; as a manager, he was famous for his innovative approach to leadership and his hair-trigger temper, the latter of which was on full display as he laid into us.

"Are those the standards you play with?" he demanded. "Are those the fucking standards? Because I'll tell you, they're nowhere *near* Premier League level. They are fucking shit!"

Lack of focus, terrible teamwork, no cohesion—he touched on all the issues that had plagued us since I transferred in mid-season, and it didn't take a genius to know why.

Even as Coach berated us, heads swiveled between me and Vincent, who sat on the opposite side of the room.

Team dynamics had been fucked since I joined. Part of that was the natural consequence of incorporating a new member into a tight-knit club; a larger part boiled down to the fact that I, the league's top scorer, and Vincent, the club's star defender and captain, despised each other.

We played different positions, but our rivalry was infamous. He was the only true competition I had for press, status, and sponsorships—important things in our world—but the biggest source of our contention was what happened at the last World Cup.

The dive. The fight. The red card.

I tried not to think about it. If I did, I might punch him in the face, and I doubted Coach would appreciate me doing that in the middle of his rant about teamwork.

"DuBois! Donovan!"

My head snapped up at the sound of my name, and Vincent's did the same.

Coach had apparently ended his speech because the rest of the team was shuffling off to change while he glared at us.

"My office. *Now*."

We obeyed without argument. We weren't stupid.

"Do you want to take a guess as to why I called the two of you, specifically, in here?" Coach didn't wait for the door to fully close before launching into part two of his rant.

Vincent and I remained silent.

"I asked you a question."

"Because we lost," I said. My stomach tightened at the word *lost*.

Everyone hated losing, but today's loss stung particularly hard for me when I knew there were people actively rooting for me to fuck up at Blackcastle—namely, Holchester United fans who hated me for transferring to their biggest rival.

I'd had plenty of naysayers growing up—teachers who thought I'd never amount to anything, football fans who thought I was a flash in the pan, press who dug for dirt in every aspect of my life—and I couldn't stand proving my critics right.

"No. It's not because we lost," Coach snapped. "It's because you two are the ones the rest of the team looks up to the most, but you've let your stupid rivalry affect your game. Worst of all, it's affecting morale."

We slunk lower in our seats beneath his glare.

"I knew there would be a transition period, but I thought you would get over it and work things out because you're adults. However, it seems like I'm dealing with children because here we are, post-season, and we have nothing to show for it except a host of mistakes that could've been easily avoided if you'd learned how to *bloody work together*!" Coach's voice rose with each word until it was loud enough to seep through the walls.

The muted chatter from the locker room noticeably died down, and a flush of shame crawled across my face.

Coach's disappointment was almost as unbearable as not winning the league. I'd idolized him growing up, and the opportunity to work with him had been a major factor behind me handing in my transfer request.

This had *not* been how I'd envisioned ending our first season together.

Vincent shifted beside me. "Coach, I—"

"Don't get me started with you." Coach cut him off. "What the hell was that in the last twenty seconds? Donovan was *right there*. You should've passed him the bloody ball when you had the chance. See opening, pass ball. It's football 101!"

Vincent's mouth tightened. He couldn't say what we all knew: he hadn't passed the ball immediately because he hadn't wanted me to score the winning goal. The press would've replayed that kick over and over, and I would've received all the glory that came with it. Vincent wouldn't have been able to stand it.

Selfish prick. I didn't dwell on whether I would've done the same had I been in his place.

Coach's stare sharpened. He'd been a club manager long enough to figure out Vincent's motivations without him verbalizing it.

"Since you want to act like children, I'll treat you like children," he said. "Normally, I leave off-season training up to the individual players, but not this summer. This summer, you're both cross-training at the Royal Academy of Ballet. Together."

"*What*?"

Vincent and I exploded at the same time.

My sense of self-preservation couldn't override my shock at Coach's edict. Clubs almost *never* dictated the specifics of how we spent our off-season. Players hailed from all over the world, which meant summer was their chance to go home, see their families, and train as they saw fit.

"I already spoke with RAB's director. She's on board," Coach said. "I didn't say anything before because I wanted to see if you two could pull it together by the last match and fucking win. You couldn't, so you'll be taking private lessons with the *same* instructor for the summer. She's one of their best, and she has an intimate knowledge of football. You'll be in good hands."

I didn't want to be in any fucking hands except my own. I had nothing against ballet. Though I'd never cross-trained using its techniques, I knew players who had, and they sang its praises for improving their strength, flexibility, and footwork techniques.

However, I'd already created my training plan. I didn't need a stranger jumping in and telling me what to do.

Vincent straightened, his face taking on a ghostly pallor. "Don't tell me she's…"

"Your instructor will be Scarlett DuBois." Coach offered a mirthless smile. "You're welcome."

DuBois? As in...

"Vincent's sister?" I sputtered. "You're joking. That's a conflict of interest!"

I'd never seen or met Vincent's sister, though I'd heard him talk about her. The two were close, which was just my luck. I didn't need the DuBois siblings conspiring against me together.

"I don't want to train with my sister," Vincent said. "That's not... *no.*"

"It's a good thing neither of you has a say in the matter." The volume of Coach's voice dropped back to normal levels, though it was no less cutting. "The director assured me she's the right person for the job and that she won't let personal ties affect her work. I believe her. That means you two *will* train with Scarlett and you *will* take it seriously. And gentlemen?" He pinned us with a warning glare. "When you return, you'd better convince me you're goddamn capable of working together instead of against each other, or you'll be riding the bench. I don't give a shit if you're the captain or the top scorer on the team. Understand?"

"Yes, sir," we muttered.

Coach's mind was made up. There was nothing we could do or say to get out of it, which meant I was stuck with the DuBois siblings for an entire fucking summer.

My jaw tightened.

I didn't know much about Scarlett DuBois, but given she was related to Vincent, I knew one thing: I wasn't going to like her.

At all.

CHAPTER 2

SCARLETT

"NOW WE GO A LITTLE QUICKER. BACK, SIDE, BACK, SIDE."
I walked through the studio, correcting the students' posture and
alignment. "Don't overcross to the back. Now demi-plié…"

My leg ached, but I ignored it. It was manageable compared to
true flare-ups, which could last days or weeks or months, and there
were only ten minutes left until class ended. I'd deal with it then.

The studio was quiet except for the sound of my voice and the
piano music keeping pace with the movements. I taught the advanced
and masterclasses, and at this level the students were so focused, a
nuclear bomb could go off and they wouldn't notice.

I used to be one of those students, and as much as I loved teaching,
I wished I could rewind time so I was on the other side of these lessons.
Things had been so different then, and—

Stop it. No more self-pity, remember?

I shook my head and refocused on the task at hand.

"Faster with the beat, Jenna. Up and stay…" I faltered when my
aches intensified but quickly recovered. "Good. Open the supporting

side a little more."

I'd lived with more or less constant pain and fatigue for the past five years, so I pushed through to the end without incident.

Nevertheless, it took all my willpower not to rush my students out after class so I could get off my feet and sit in silence.

Just for a minute. Just so I could breathe.

"Excuse me, Miss DuBois?"

I glanced up. Emma stood before me, her hands fiddling first with her skirt and then the neckline of her leotard.

"I'm sorry to bother you, but I have some news." Her excitement shone through her usual reserve. "Remember when I auditioned for *The Nutcracker* last week? They released the cast list today. I'll be playing the Sugar Plum Fairy!"

"Oh my God." My hand flew to my mouth. "Congratulations! Emma, that's amazing."

It wasn't the most professional response, but Emma had been my student for years, and while we technically weren't supposed to play favorites, she was secretly my favorite. She worked hard, she had a great attitude, and she wasn't catty or competitive with her peers.

The Nutcracker was her favorite ballet. If anyone deserved its most prestigious role, it was her.

I'd been one of the audition judges, but none of us knew the final cast until the director announced it. I hadn't checked my emails yet, so I'd missed it.

"Thank you. I still can't believe it," Emma said breathlessly. "It's such a dream come true, and I couldn't have done it without you. I'd love...I mean, if you're not busy, I'd love for you to come to the opening night. I know it's only May and opening night isn't until December, and I know you usually don't attend the school showcases, but I thought I'd ask anyway." Rose colored her cheeks. "It'll be at the Westbury Theatre again."

Westbury Theatre.

The name punched a hole through my gut, and my excitement leaked out like water through a sieve.

Emma was right. I never attended school showcases because they were *always* held at Westbury.

I wanted to support my students, but the thought of going anywhere near the theatre caused panic to swell.

"You don't have to," Emma said, obviously picking up on my mood shift. She drew her bottom lip between her teeth. "It's during the holidays, so I understand—"

"No, it's not that." I forced a smile. "I'd love to attend, but I might be out of town. I'm not sure yet. I'll let you know."

I hated lying to her, but it was better than saying I would rather stab myself in the leg than step foot in Westbury.

There were too many memories there. Too many ghosts of what I'd loved and lost.

"Okay." Emma's face regained some of its glow. "I'll see you next class, then?"

"Of course. Congratulations again." My smile was more genuine this time. "Sugar Plum Fairy is a huge role. You should be proud."

I waited until the door shut and Emma was gone before I released a shaky breath and sank onto the floor.

The ache in my leg sharpened into a bright, pointed pain, as if the mere mention of Westbury had awakened the worst parts of my condition.

In, one, two, three.

Out, one, two, three.

I hated taking medication, so I breathed through the discomfort instead of reaching for the emergency packet I'd stashed in my bag.

Luckily, my symptoms had improved a lot over the years, thanks to lifestyle changes and careful stress management. It wasn't like the months immediately following my accident, when I could barely get out of bed, but it wasn't a walk in the park either.

I never knew when pain or fatigue would strike. I had to be on guard all the time, but I'd more or less learned to live with it. It was either adapt or wallow, and I'd done enough wallowing to last a lifetime.

My phone rang. I picked it up without checking the caller ID; there was only one person in my contacts who had that ringtone.

"Lavinia wants to see you in her office," Carina said without preamble. "Don't worry, it's nothing bad." A pause. "I think."

The shock was enough to take my mind off my leg for a second. "Wait. Seriously?"

Lavinia was the director of RAB and quite possibly the most intimidating person I'd ever met. I'd worked at the academy for four years, and I'd never heard of her calling an unscheduled meeting.

This can't be good.

"Yes." Carina's voice dropped to a whisper. "I tried to find out more but she's being *super* hush-hush about it. She just told me to tell you to see her as soon as class is over."

"Right." I swallowed. "Oh God, I'm getting sacked."

Was it because I refused to attend the school showcases? Did she think I was a bad team player? I mean, I wasn't the *best* team player, but that was because people were so—

"No! Of course not. If she sacks you, she'll have to sack me too," Carina said. "We're a package deal, and we both know she can't afford to lose her top instructor *and* her trusty assistant. I hold the keys to all her PDFs."

A small laugh rippled across the surface of my anxiety. She always knew how to make me feel better.

I'd lost a lot of "friends" after the accident, but I'd met Carina three years ago, when she joined RAB as Lavinia's executive assistant. We'd bonded her first day over our mutual love for trashy reality TV and jigsaw puzzles, and we'd been best friends since.

"I'm coming," I said. "See you soon."

I stood with a wince, but the pain gradually faded into a manageable ache again. Or maybe it was all in my head and manageable only relative to my sky-high anxiety over the surprise meeting.

Carina was on the phone when I arrived, but she mouthed *good luck* and flashed me a thumbs-up as I knocked on the director's door.

"Come in."

I stepped inside with the caution of someone approaching an aggravated rattlesnake.

Lavinia's office was as neat and polished as the woman herself. Giant windows overlooked the academy grounds, and an artfully arranged gallery of photos dominated the wall opposite the door. They captured the famous former prima ballerina in every stage of her career, from blossoming ingenue to international star to retired legend.

Lavinia herself sat behind her desk, her hair pulled back into a bun, her glasses perched on her elegant nose as she flipped through some papers.

"Please, sit." She gestured at the chair opposite her.

I obliged, trying to tame my rampage of nerves and failing miserably.

"We're both busy, so I'll cut to the chase." Lavinia was never one for beating around the bush. "We've partnered with the Blackcastle football club on a special training program this summer. I want you to run point on it."

My mouth parted. Out of everything I'd imagined she'd say, a football cross-training program ranked in the bottom five.

Granted, I'd run similar programs in the past, but they were usually for League One or Two teams, not for the freaking Premier League.

"By run point, you mean…"

"You'll be training them. You're one of my best instructors, and you're familiar with football," Lavinia said. "I trust you'll do a good job."

I bit back a knee-jerk rejection. I knew exactly what she meant when she said I was "familiar with football." After all, my brother was the captain of Blackcastle.

However, as much as I loved him and the club, I did *not* want to train him or his teammates. Most footballers were arrogant, insufferable, and selfish.

I should know—I used to date one.

Vincent was the only exception to my anti-footballer sentiments, and that was because he was family.

"I'm honored," I said carefully. "But I have a full schedule this summer, and I think there are instructors who would be better suited for the role. Less conflict of interest."

Lavinia's brows rose a fraction of an inch. "Are you saying you can't put aside personal feelings for the sake of professionalism?"

Dammit. I'd walked straight into a trap I should've seen coming.

"No, of course not. I'm simply pre-empting problems based on other people's potential perception." I gave the first excuse I could think of. "I don't want to be accused of favoritism."

"I'll deal with any problems that might arise." Lavinia looked unimpressed by my explanation. "If it makes you feel better, you'll only be training two players, not the entire club."

I blinked, blindsided twice in the space of five minutes. That had to be a record.

I'd thought it was strange Blackcastle would require its players to stay in London for the off-season, but given their performance yesterday, I'd figured it was some sort of special exception.

The two-player development was both a relief and a concern.

"I assume my brother is one of the two players," I said. Otherwise, Lavinia would've denied the conflict-of-interest issue. "Who's the other?"

There was a short pause before she answered. "Asher Donovan."

My stomach dropped. "*Asher Donovan*?" I couldn't have contained my outburst if I'd tried. "You want me to train Vincent and Asher in private lessons for an entire summer? They'll kill each other!"

I'd lost count of the number of times I'd had to listen to Vincent rant about Asher, and the internet was constantly debating who was the better player. I thought the comparisons were unfair considering they played different positions, but people loved to pit the two against each other.

It started years ago when an innocent online *Match* poll asked people to choose the best up-and-coming footballer. Asher won by one point over Vincent, which had my brother fuming. Since then, their rivalry had escalated to encompass who got paid more (Asher), who had the most brand sponsorships (Vincent), and who won the most Ballon d'Ors (Asher, though they'd received an equal number of nominations). It came to a head at the last World Cup, when Asher's red card turned their feud into something even more bitter.

"Part of your job is to ensure they *don't* kill each other." Lavinia's face softened a smidge. "I realize it's unfair of me to spring this on you with so little notice, but when Frank reached out to me, we agreed to keep the arrangement under wraps for as long as possible in order to prevent leaks." Frank was Blackcastle's manager. "He also hadn't committed to his decision until after yesterday's match."

I understood the reasoning, but that didn't mean I had to like it. In fact, the more I thought about it, the worse my gut churned.

It was easy to figure out why Frank Armstrong was singling out my brother and Asher. Their animosity had led to plenty of issues and resulted in Blackcastle losing this year's league. Things between them were bitter on a good day, and Frank obviously wanted them to patch things up by forcing them to train together.

That was all well and good, but unfortunately, that meant I was now caught in the middle.

Asher Donovan. Of all the people in the world, the other player *had* to be him. He was most women's celebrity crush, and he might've been mine too had it not been for my loyalty to Vincent, my strict No Footballers rule, and his questionable reputation.

Asher was generally regarded as the world's greatest footballer. The striker who played as impressively as he looked, the savior whose goals had brought his team back from the brink of defeat countless times. But for all his talent on the pitch, he was mired in controversy off it. The car crashes, the parties, the revolving door of women—all tabloid fodder that the public ate up like sweets at a children's party.

I'd never met the man, but if other players had a god complex, I could only imagine how massive his was.

"Is there anything I can say to get out of this?" I asked hopefully.

Lavinia's brows rose another half an inch.

I held back a sigh. *That's what I figured.*

"Lessons start next Monday," she said. "You've cross-trained footballers before, so small tweaks to your previous regimens should be sufficient. I've also taken a look at your summer schedule and adjusted it accordingly. Are there any more questions?"

It was a subtle dismissal.

"No," I said. "I'll have a final training plan ready by Monday."

"Good." Lavinia returned to her papers. "Thank you, Scarlett."

Okay, that was a *clear* dismissal.

When I exited her office, Carina was already waiting for me with her bag in hand. It was six thirty-five, which meant it was officially after work hours.

She grimaced when she saw me. "That bad?" She could read my expressions better than anyone.

"I'll tell you about it over drinks," I said. "I need one. Badly."

CHAPTER 3

ASHER

"A HUNDRED QUID SAYS YOU OR DUBOIS WILL PUNCH THE other before the month is over," Adil declared. "Wilson, you taking that bet?"

"Absolutely not," Noah said, his tone dry. "Leave me out of your bets. They never end well."

"I have no idea what you mean, and I'm offended that's how you're sending me off for the summer." Adil clutched his chest. "When I'm on the flight home, I'll remember your words. They'll hurt."

"Good. Maybe you'll stop stirring up shit next season."

"Is that any way to talk to your teammate? What type of example are you setting for your daughter?"

"Yes, it is, and my daughter's not here," Noah said.

I shook my head.

Noah, Adil, and I were at the Angry Boar, our favorite pub, for a last get-together before they flew home to the US and Morocco, respectively. It was the day after our disastrous loss against Holchester, but they'd already heard all about Coach forcing Vincent and me to train together for the summer.

I'd invited them out hoping for sympathy and distraction, but I should've known better. Adil thought my situation was hilarious, and Noah was stoic as a rock.

Wankers.

"I'm going to order us another round," I said. "I'll be right back."

Adil had moved on to needling Noah about his nonexistent love life, and Noah was too busy ignoring him to do more than nod at my words.

I made my way toward the bar. I got a few glares and snide mutters, but no one openly pushed for a confrontation.

There was a reason why footballers loved the Angry Boar, which served strong drinks, cheap food, and no bullshit. It had a strict no-cameras, no-autographs, and no-brawls policy, enforced by triplet bouncers the size of mountains and the meanest owner this side of the Thames.

The last person who'd violated its rules had gotten tossed out on his ass (literally) and banned for life.

I ordered at the bar and glanced around the pub. A group of women blatantly stared at me from the corner and giggled to each other behind their hands while a passing couple did a double take. The girl opened her mouth, but she didn't get a chance to speak before her boyfriend dragged her off and shot me a dirty look over his shoulder.

I took it all in stride. Stares and whispers came with the territory, and at least there were no paparazzi here hoping to trip me up.

"Here ya go." Mac, the owner, shoved two pints (for me and Noah) and one Coke (for Adil) across the counter. "Don't fucking spill it this time."

"C'mon, Mac, you still mad about the other week? We didn't actually break the jukebox."

The Angry Boar was one of the few pubs with a jukebox, and Mac took great pride in it.

He glared at me, his grizzled face wreathed with a scowl. He didn't give a shit about celebrities and was as likely to chew out a film star as he was the average Joe. It was why we loved him.

I grinned. "No spilling. Got it."

I balanced the three glasses with both hands, turned—and promptly spilled one of them all over the person behind me.

In my defense, she hadn't been there a second earlier, and she was standing so close, I couldn't have avoided her in time unless I had eyes in the back of my head.

"Jesus Christ!" Mac exploded behind me while the girl let out a string of curses colorful enough to make a sailor blush.

I never would've thought someone so delicate-looking could string together those particular words in those particular ways. It was impressive.

"Shit, I'm sorry." I set the glasses down, grabbed a handful of napkins, and attempted to help her clean her shirt. "I didn't see you there."

"I figured. I—" She glanced up, and the expression that crossed her face would've been comical had it not been aimed at me. "*You*."

My eyebrows popped up. I was used to eliciting various reactions from the opposite sex, but horror typically wasn't one of them.

"Have we met before?" I asked. The *you* sounded a little personal.

I was almost positive we hadn't. If we'd crossed paths, I would've remembered her.

She was objectively, unequivocally stunning. Glossy black hair, creamy skin, light gray eyes fringed with thick lashes—she looked like a classic Hollywood star in the mold of Ava Gardner and Hedy Lamarr.

—

However, it was more than her looks. I met a lot of beautiful women in my line of work, but there was something about this girl... even in a beer-stained shirt and jeans, she exuded an elegance that couldn't be bought or learned. You had to be born with it.

"No, we haven't," she said. "But I know who you are." Her tone indicated that wasn't necessarily a good thing.

Interesting. Maybe she was a Holchester fan.

I hope not.

"Well, then, it seems a bit unfair that you know my name and I don't know yours," I teased.

I didn't date. If I wanted to be the greatest footballer in the world, I couldn't waste time or energy on a serious relationship. Many would argue I was *already* the greatest footballer, but I hadn't won a World Cup yet, and until I did, I couldn't assume that title.

That being said, there was nothing wrong with a little flirting—or a *lot* of flirting, if it involved this mystery girl.

"Life isn't always fair," she said, looking amused.

The woman standing beside her muttered something under her breath. It sounded suspiciously like *"He'll figure it out soon,"* but I couldn't be certain.

Honestly, I'd been so captivated I hadn't realized she was with a friend until that moment.

"In that case, I'll settle for your number." I nodded at her shirt. "I owe you a new top."

"Oh, you'll *settle* for my number?" The glint of amusement in her eyes brightened.

"Yep. It'll be anonymous if you want. No name, just a number— so I can buy you a new shirt or pay for dry cleaning, of course."

"Of course. I'm sure that's all you'll use the number for."

I shrugged, a smile playing around the corners of my mouth. I hadn't felt this lighthearted since yesterday's match. Coming out to the pub had been a good idea after all.

"I can't guarantee things won't change in the future, but for now, my intentions are pure." I held up a hand. "I promise."

I really did intend on buying her a new top, so I wasn't lying. Technically.

"As much faith as I have in promises made by *players*..." Her emphasis on the last word made it clear she wasn't talking about my job title. "I have to respectfully decline. I can afford my own dry cleaning, and I don't like handing out private information to strangers." She cocked an eyebrow. "Try not to spill any more beer on unsuspecting passersby. It's a waste of good ale."

I stared, stunned, as she walked away. Her friend followed, half-laughing and half-sneaking peeks at me on her way to the exit.

What the hell just happened?

I couldn't remember the last time I'd been rejected. Surprisingly, I wasn't upset about it; I was...intrigued.

Jesus. The guy who could get any girl he wanted was fascinated by the one girl who wasn't impressed. I was a walking cliché.

"Oof. Shut down *hard*." Adil's voice shook me out of my stupor. I hadn't even noticed his and Noah's approach. He grabbed his soda from the counter and smirked at me. "She must've watched yesterday's match and thought you played like shit too."

"Shut up." But I wasn't paying attention to him.

I was too focused on the flash of dark hair and blue jeans as she disappeared through the door.

I'd never seen Mystery Girl before, but for some reason, I had a feeling this wouldn't be the last time we ran into each other.

I spent the next week enjoying relative freedom. I hung out with friends, watched reruns of old shows, and took my favorite sports cars out for a spin or three. Football fired me up, but driving calmed me, and I'd amassed an enviable collection of luxury vehicles that I used for everyday errands or racing.

However, I chose a nondescript car for my first session at the Royal Academy of Ballet. Paparazzi were a problem, and I didn't need a bright red Ferrari announcing my every move.

When I arrived at RAB, I felt a pinch of satisfaction at the absence of Vincent's Lamborghini. He didn't drive decoy cars, so I knew he wasn't here yet.

I parked close to the entrance, my thoughts split between the dreaded cross-training session and the girl I'd bumped into last week.

I didn't know why I was still thinking about her. We'd exchanged only a handful of words, and I didn't know a single thing about her other than the fact she could pay for her own dry cleaning and that she didn't like "handing out private information to strangers."

My mouth curved at the memory.

I didn't wish for much outside the realm of football, but I'd give up one of my cars to see her again.

Maybe.

Possibly.

Definitely.

Perhaps it was a good thing she hadn't given me her name and number. I didn't need that big a distraction in my life.

I entered RAB, checked in with the starry-eyed receptionist at the front desk, and followed her instructions to the training studio.

Housed in a mansion that looked like something straight off a Regency movie set, the Royal Academy of Ballet was worlds away from the sweaty, utilitarian grounds of Blackcastle's training facility.

There were paintings of ballerinas, photos of ballerinas, bronze statues of ballerinas...basically, ballerinas everywhere.

I guess subtlety wasn't their strong point.

Then again, Blackcastle's facilities had our team logo stamped on every possible surface so I shouldn't throw stones.

I arrived at the studio just in time to see students from the previous class trickling out.

I was early, so I hung back, waiting for the last person to turn the corner before I slipped inside. Thankfully, neither of the DuBois siblings was here yet, and I took the opportunity to examine my surroundings.

I'd never attended a ballet performance before, much less been inside a studio, but it looked exactly as I'd imagined.

A wall of mirrors reflected a row of giant arched windows, which overlooked the academy's manicured grounds. A wooden barre stretched the length of the room, and the floors gleamed so brightly I could almost see my reflection in them.

The only out-of-place object was the giant tote wobbling on the edge of the corner table. It was stuffed with what looked like a jumper, a book, and...whatever else people stashed in their totes.

The weight of its contents must've been too much for the overworked bag because, after a valiant effort to stay upright, it tipped over and spilled half its items across the floor with a raucous clatter.

The book thudded to the ground. Pens rolled this way and that while a scarf drifted dreamily on top of a small box.

I half-expected someone to run in and check on the disruption, but no one did.

Should I pick up the stray items or wait for their owner to return? Would it be an invasion of privacy if I chose the former?

Screw it. It would be weirder if she walked in to find me staring at her scattered belongings without doing a thing about it.

I walked over and started scooping the contents back in their bag.

Jumper, book, pens, makeup, keys, water bottle, tights, hairspray, canvas slippers, medication, sweat towel, heat pack, sewing kit, *another* book...Jesus, it was like Mary Poppins's magic bag. How the hell did she fit all of that inside one tote?

I wedged a protein bar between her sunglasses and resistance bands. I didn't know how I'd get the—

"What are you doing?"

I glanced up, and my reply died an instant death.

No. It can't be.

She'd tied her hair up instead of leaving it down, and she wore a leotard, leg warmers over tights, and a wrap skirt instead of a shirt and jeans, but it was unmistakably *her*.

The girl from the pub.

She had the same midnight hair, the same red lips, the same piercing gray eyes that were currently boring a hole through my face.

If it weren't for the tangible heat of her stare, I would've thought I'd conjured her through the mere force of my thoughts.

"I'm not snooping." I recovered from my shock and raised my hands in a gesture of surrender. "The bag fell, and I was simply picking up the items."

She responded with a wary stare as she walked toward me—or rather, toward her bag.

I should've known she was a dancer. Even at the pub, she'd moved with the grace of one, her posture perfect, her movements smooth and fluid. But whereas I'd picked up on a touch of apprehension at the Angry Boar, here, she carried herself with the ease of someone who was completely in her element.

"Do you go here?" I asked.

I guessed she was in her mid-twenties, which seemed outside RAB's target age range, but maybe she was here for professional training.

A small smirk crossed her mouth. "You could say that."

"Then this is a sign. What are the chances we'd run into each other twice?" I hoped our schedules overlapped this summer. Seeing her might make my forced training sessions a bit more bearable. "Now you have to tell me your name. It's only polite."

"Oh, I'm sure you'll find out soon enough," she said dryly.

She bent to retrieve her scarf while I picked up the remaining book on the floor. The worn yellow-and-green cover sparked a flare of recognition.

"Leo Agnelli," I said appreciatively. "Good taste."

Our hands brushed when she reached for the outstretched book, and a frisson of electricity shot up my arm. It was so sharp, so unexpected, that I almost dropped the paperback.

What the hell?

She stiffened, making me wonder if she'd felt it too, but her expression was unreadable. "You read Leo Agnelli." Her tone contained a heavy dose of skepticism.

"Occasionally." The little jolt must've been static from our clothing. That was the only feasible explanation. "Try not to act so surprised, Chloe. I promise I'll live up to your 'dumb athlete' preconception of me in other ways."

A small laugh escaped. She quickly covered it up, but it was too late. I'd heard it, she knew I'd heard it, and my ability to draw that smile out of her might just be the highlight of my shitty week.

"My name isn't Chloe," she said.

"I didn't think so, but since you refuse to tell me what it actually is, I'll have to keep guessing until I get it right, Alice."

"That's going to get old *real* fast."

"Luckily, there's an easy solution to the problem."

I was being pushier than normal, but I would've backed off if I'd picked up on any signs of discomfort from her.

However, the gleam of laughter in her eyes told me she wasn't as annoyed as she pretended to be...*and* she hadn't pulled her hand away yet.

We must've come to the same realization because our gazes dropped to our hands at the same time.

The air crackled with sudden tension, and another electric spark streaked through me.

The first had been bright and brief, like lightning in a cloudless sky. This one was slower, more potent, and the heat from it made me feel like I was running laps in Markovic Stadium instead of standing frozen in an air-conditioned dance studio.

Mystery Girl swallowed, and even the steady hum of the AC wasn't enough to drown out my roaring pulse.

I tried to think of something else to say, but I couldn't remember what we were talking about or why I was here.

I hadn't been this out of sorts around a girl since my ill-fated childhood crush on Hailey Brompton (she'd moved to Brighton during Year Five and broke my heart).

The thrill of seeing Mystery Girl again faded into trepidation.

How did she have such a strong effect on me when I barely knew her? Maybe our close proximity wasn't a good thing after all. If I were smart, I'd stay away and focus on my goals: a league championship with Blackcastle, followed by the Euro Cup and the World Cup.

My inexplicable fascination with this girl did not factor *anywhere* into the equation.

Flirting was one thing; losing focus was another.

"Let's get this over with." A familiar, unwelcome voice cut through the tension.

Vincent strode in, wearing sunglasses inside like a douche.

The girl finally yanked her hand away and shoved her book into her bag.

I dropped my arm as well, though the shadow of a tingle remained.

"It's about time you showed up," she said, her cheeks noticeably redder than before. "I thought I'd have to call and remind you about today's session."

"There was traffic, and I'm technically right on time. It's not my fault you show up early everywhere." Vincent ignored me to focus on her. "You ready to get started?"

Despite my misgivings about the girl and losing focus, a twinge of jealousy snaked through my gut at their easy banter.

"Do you know each other?" I asked as casually as possible.

She didn't seem like the type who'd go for Vincent, but stranger things have happened. In hell.

She opened her mouth, but Vincent beat her to it.

"Of course." He looked at me like I was stupid. "She's my sister."

CHAPTER 4

SCARLETT

I WISH I COULD'VE SNAPPED A PHOTO OF ASHER'S FACE when Vincent announced I was his sister. If his jaw had dropped any lower, he'd have to reattach it.

I shouldn't have led him on by keeping my name to myself, but part of me had been amused at seeing *the* Asher Donovan flabbergasted by my refusal to fall at his feet like every other woman in the world.

I wasn't above fangirling or celebrity crushes. For example, if I ever met Nate Reynolds, my favorite actor, I'd probably scream and pass out. I just didn't fangirl over footballers; being related to one really took the shine out of their glory.

"Your sister?" Asher finally found his words. His gaze traveled between me and Vincent.

I understood why he was so shocked. Our parents couldn't have natural-born children, so they'd adopted us when we were babies. Vincent's dark eyes and light brown skin were the polar opposites of my gray eyes and pale complexion, but even though we weren't biologically related, he was my brother in every other sense of the word.

Not a lot of people knew we were adopted, though, and it was always amusing to see their reactions when they found out we were siblings.

"Scarlett DuBois," I said with a hint of apology. I really should've said something earlier. "Your new trainer."

Asher cut a glance in my direction, and an unsettling spark of electricity danced over my skin.

Anti-footballer biases aside, the man was gorgeous. As in, gave-Nate-Reynolds-a-run-for-his-money, movie-star gorgeous.

Thick dark hair flopped over his forehead, framing sculpted cheekbones and a sensual mouth. Unfairly long lashes fringed the greenest eyes I'd ever seen, and every inch of his body was chiseled to high-performance perfection.

But the attraction wasn't even really about his looks, though they were objectively flawless. It was the charisma, the utter ease with which he moved in the spotlight that made it impossible to look away. Asher was one of the most famous athletes in the world, yet he possessed the down-to-earth charm of the boy next door.

Raw masculinity wrapped in cool confidence. The combination was so magnetic, even my antagonism toward footballers couldn't dull it. If he weren't my brother's teammate and rival, I would be swooning big-time.

Except he is, so you need to get it together.

"Anyway." I cleared my throat, my skin still tingling from our brief touch earlier. It must be the static from my clothes; that was what I got for wearing wool in May. "Let's start. The focus of our training will be strength, stamina, and flexibility. We'll start with warm-ups, then move to footwork."

I gradually relaxed as the session got underway and my unease over Asher's proximity faded beneath my desire to do a good job. I hadn't wanted this role, but now that I had it, I was going to excel, dammit.

"Let's move into some deep stretches," I said after we finished basic warm-ups. "We're going to lift our right leg onto the barre, breathe, and lower our chest to our leg. Go slowly, take your time…"

I demonstrated the movement for them, luxuriating in the stretch and the gentle music playing in the background. This was the most calming part of—

"Dammit!"

My head jerked up at Vincent's curse. I lowered my leg and turned to see him struggling to get his foot up on the barre. Football didn't naturally develop flexibility the way dance and gymnastics did, so some stretches were difficult for the players.

However, Asher was already in the correct position and reveling in my brother's difficulties.

"It's a simple stretch, DuBois," he drawled. "But it's okay if you can't do it. We can't all have natural talent."

Vincent's face flushed. He *hated* being second best, especially to Asher. I never said it out loud, but I suspected that was the reason why he did what he did in the last World Cup.

If he'd been up against anyone else, he wouldn't have faked that injury. He despised diving, but his rivalry with Asher often made him do stupid things.

"I'm not surprised you have such a low bar for what you consider talent," Vincent snapped. "Newsflash, Donovan, tricks and flashy goals don't mean you're better than other people."

"That's not what the Ballon d'Or jurors thought when they presented me with my fourth award last year." Asher had won the prestigious award for best player of the season four times; Vincent had won it twice. "Besides, it appears that for you, the barre isn't low *enough*." Asher smirked at Vincent's form.

My brother's knuckles whitened around the barre. "You—"

"Enough!" I said sharply. "Let's get back to work. If you want to argue, do it on your own time."

They lapsed into mulish silence, but to their credit, they didn't attempt to pick a fight with each other again during the session.

I modified some of the stretches for Vincent, and we spent the next hour drilling into different footwork techniques, which was where football and ballet had the biggest crossover.

Neither of them had cross-trained with dance before, so I took it easy on them the first day. Even so, by the time our session ended, everyone was exhausted and dripping with sweat.

"I take back everything I said about football being more strenuous than ballet." Vincent guzzled a bottle of water. His face gleamed with perspiration. "I can't believe you did this for fun for half your life."

"It wasn't just for fun. It was my job," I reminded him. A pang hit me at the word *was*, as in former, as in it was no longer my job. Not the professional dance part, anyway.

And yes, I *had* found ballet fun when I was younger. I'd loved the discipline, the choreography, and the costumes, but most of all, I'd loved discovering something I had a natural talent for. While my peers stressed about what they were going to do after graduation, I already had my future locked in.

Then a rainy summer night stole that future away, and I was left with the pieces of what could've been.

A wave of prickles swarmed my skin. I turned and wiped down the barre, hoping Vincent didn't pick up on my mood shift.

I loved that he didn't tiptoe around my past the way our parents did, but sometimes, I wasn't in the right mental space to talk about it.

"If the sessions are too hard for you, you could quit," Asher said. He grabbed a wipe to help me clean the barre, and this time, the tingles suffusing my body had nothing to do with the ghosts of my past. "I'm sure Coach would understand."

Vincent's eyes sharpened. "Oh, I'll be fine. I'm more worried about you." He tossed his empty bottle into his duffel bag. "After all, only one person in this room has a World Cup to their name, and it's not you."

The temperature plummeted to subarctic levels.

Asher's face hardened as I suppressed a wince. Even I knew bringing up the World Cup was a no-no around him, and I barely knew the man.

"Perhaps not, but at least I don't have to cheat to win."

"Cheating according to whom? Not the ref. Not the—"

"Stop it!" My interjection sliced through their argument for the second time that day. "I let your earlier spat slide, but I won't do that again. This is a training session, not a cage fight. I don't know how you operate in your club, but in my studio, you *will* behave like adults and you *will* act like professionals. If you can't or won't do that, then I'm happy to relay that message to your manager because I did not sign up to be your babysitter, mediator, or therapist. Is that clear?"

Asher and Vincent gaped at me, their brewing fight forgotten.

I rarely yelled, but between my unwanted reactions to Asher and the prospect of dealing with their bickering for an entire summer, I'd just about had it.

"Is that clear?" I repeated.

"Crystal." Asher responded first, his earlier scowl melting into something akin to appreciation as he examined me.

I almost preferred the scowl.

"You got it, sis." Vincent offered a cheeky smile when I glared at him, but he didn't attempt to provoke Asher again. Well, Asher had provoked him first, but he'd escalated it by bringing up the World Cup. "I'll see you for dinner Thursday?"

I wasn't fooled. He wanted to remind Asher that he was the odd man out in this trio, but if he thought I'd show him favoritism just because he was my brother, he was sorely mistaken.

Nevertheless, I nodded. "Remember, it's your turn to choose."

Vincent and I had a standing Thursday night sibling dinner every week (barring travel and club obligations). I'd stayed in London with our mother while he'd moved to Paris with our father after our parents' divorce, so we only saw each other during holidays growing up.

After he transferred to Blackcastle a few years ago, we tried to make up for lost time. Nothing beat family, especially when you were surrounded by as many wannabe freeloaders and starfuckers as Vincent was.

"I have a *Match* interview in an hour, so I'll see you later." He shot a warning glare at Asher before leaving.

I shook my head. The *Match* mention was obviously aimed at Asher. The two competed for press and sponsorships off the pitch as much as they did for glory *on* the pitch. Everything was a dick measuring contest to them, and they were constantly trying to one-up the other.

"So," Asher said as I packed up and got ready to leave, too. Their session was my last of the day, and I was looking forward to a nice, long bath at home. It helped with the aches and pains. Plus, I liked the bubbles. "I finally know your name."

"Did it live up to your expectations?" I quipped.

"Half of it did. You look like a Scarlett." His gaze briefly touched my mouth, and my skin warmed yet again.

"Ah, but the DuBois threw you off."

"You could say that." The careless grin he threw my way shouldn't have made my pulse race, but it did. "However, I have to commend you on achieving something that I thought was impossible."

"What's that?"

"Making me *like* someone with the last name DuBois."

I rolled my eyes even as I fought an exasperated laugh. "You are an incorrigible flirt."

"Flirt? Yes. Incorrigible? That's a matter of opinion." Asher followed me into the hall, his long legs keeping easy pace with my brisk stride. "Besides, I have to be extra nice to you now that I know you're Vincent's sister. You've suffered enough."

My laugh finally broke free, and his answering smile soothed my sting of guilt over laughing at Vincent's expense.

I truly wasn't prepared for how charismatic Asher was in person. I'd glimpsed it at the pub last week, but the effect had been muted by the beer spill and our crowded surroundings.

Being alone with him after seeing him in action during training and bearing the full weight of his attention when there was no one else around...that was a whole other matter.

He commanded attention the way no one else did. It was dangerous.

"Are you two stepsiblings?" Asher asked when I didn't respond.

"Adopted." It wasn't a secret, though we didn't go around screaming about it. "Before you say anything else, this..." I gestured between us. "Ends now."

Amusement slid across his infuriatingly perfect face. "What's *this*?"

"The flirting. It's unprofessional."

"I'm afraid flirting is part of my nature, darling."

Ugh. It should be illegal for any word to sound as delicious as *darling* did in Asher's deep, silky voice.

"Well, change it or suppress it."

"That's not how nature works."

"It is at RAB." I spotted my salvation at the end of the hall. "Carina! There you are." I sped up my pace. Finally, someone who could act as a buffer. "I was looking for you."

She glanced up from the sheaf of papers in her hands. "You were? I mean, of course you were." Her eyes fell on Asher, and I swore I heard a dreamy sigh. *Oh, no. Not you too.* "Hi."

"Hey." His grin could only be described as panty-melting. "I saw you at the pub last week with Scarlett, right? I'm Asher."

He held out his hand, which she grabbed with far too much enthusiasm. "Carina. It's so nice to officially meet you. I'm a *huge* fan."

Asher upped the wattage of his smile. "Thanks. Perhaps you can help convince Scarlett I'm not the devil then?" He dropped his voice to a conspiratorial whisper. "I don't think she likes me very much."

"Oh, she doesn't like anyone very much, but don't worry. She'll come around. Eventually."

"Excuse me." I crossed my arms. "I'm standing *right here*."

"Yes, I know," my traitor of a friend said. She tacked one of the papers to the bulletin board. "Let me finish putting this up, then we can leave."

Asher examined the sheet. "'Staff showcase auditions,'" he read aloud. "'This year's featured performance will be *Lorena*.' I've never heard of that ballet."

"It's a newer piece," Carina explained. "Contemporary, not classic."

"Which role are you auditioning for?" he asked me. "I'd love to see you onstage. Show me how the professionals do it."

This time, even his smile wasn't enough to unknot the twist in my gut.

"None," I said. "I don't participate in showcases."

"Why not?"

"Because." I avoided Carina's sympathetic stare. Besides Vincent, she was the only person who knew my hang-ups around performing. "I don't have time."

"The showcase is a lot of work," she added, backing me up. "Staff participation isn't mandatory."

"That's too bad." Asher appeared genuinely disappointed.

He wasn't the only one. If I could snap my fingers and get one wish, I'd wish for the ability to dance onstage again, but life didn't work that way.

"We have to go, or we'll miss our train." I hooked my arm through Carina's and dragged her down the hall before he drew us deeper into conversation. "I'll see you Wednesday for our next session," I added, glancing back over my shoulder.

His mouth tilted up like he knew exactly why I was rushing off. "Looking forward to it, Scarlett."

A breathless shiver slipped down my spine.

If the way he said *darling* was illegal, the velvety intimacy with which he uttered my name was downright sinful.

I didn't look back, but the warmth of his gaze lingered long after we'd turned the corner.

"Wow," Carina said once we were out of earshot.

She didn't have to elaborate.

For better or worse, I knew exactly what she meant.

CHAPTER 5

ASHER

MYSTERY GIRL WAS SCARLETT.

Scarlett was Vincent's sister.

Vincent's sister was our new trainer.

I'd had two days to wrap my head around those mindfucks, and I still couldn't pinpoint how I felt about them.

Scarlett was nothing like how I'd imagined Vincent's sister would be. She was quieter, wittier, and pricklier in the most charming way. I'd shown up at RAB on Monday, prepared to tolerate her at best, and now I found out the girl I couldn't stop thinking about was related to my biggest rival.

The universe had a sick sense of humor.

I paused in the studio's doorway. Scarlett was already in there setting up, but something kept me from entering right away.

I'd told myself I would stay away from her before I found out who she was. Obviously, I didn't have that option anymore.

But you do *have the option of not showing up extra early in order to spend more alone time with her,* an annoying voice pointed out in my head.

My jaw tensed. *Oh, shut up.*

Arguing with myself. Never a good sign.

Scarlett turned. Our gazes collided, and a streak of awareness ran down the length of my spine.

"You're early." She didn't move from her spot near the barre, nor did I move from the doorway.

"I'm just that type of student."

"You mean a teacher's pet?"

"Darling, if you want to call me pet, I won't stop you."

My mouth curled into a tiny grin at the pink tint creeping over her neck and face.

She blushed so easily. It was adorable, especially when it contradicted the words coming out of her mouth.

"Two new rules," she said. "One, no flirting with me. Ever."

"Ah, we're back to that again. *Ever*'s a long time." I finally abandoned my post in the doorway and entered the studio. "Also, I wasn't flirting. I was telling the truth."

"Two," she continued, ignoring me. "Don't call me darling."

"What about honeybun?"

"No."

"Madame?"

"*No.*"

"Tinkerbell?"

"Only if you want me to kick you in the tinkerbell between your legs."

A burst of laughter erupted from my chest. "Here I thought ballerinas were supposed to be soft and elegant."

"Oh, we are." Scarlett cocked an eyebrow. "We're also, pound for pound, some of the strongest athletes in the world. So believe me when I say I *will* kick you and it *will* hurt."

"I believe you." I couldn't stop smiling. "No flirting, no darling. Understood."

Our repartee died down when Vincent showed up a minute later. *Typical*. He always ruined things.

However, Scarlett's warning from our last session was fresh in my mind, so I kept my mouth shut and ignored him the best I could.

That probably wasn't what Coach had in mind when he forced us to train together, but he wasn't here. What he didn't know wouldn't hurt him.

We didn't have much time for "bonding" regardless. People underestimated the rigor of ballet because it looked so ethereal, but in reality, the training was *brutal*—and we were still in the beginner's stage.

Scarlett's delicate appearance was a red herring; she ran her studio like a bloody drill sergeant. Even Coach would be impressed.

"One, two, three, four. Repeat, two, three, four. Good. Again. I—" Scarlett stopped short, the color draining from her face.

Vincent and I faltered.

"Are you okay?" I asked at the same time he said, "Is it—"

"No. I'm okay." She flashed a tight smile. "I just have to...use the loo. Keep going. I'll be right back."

My gaze followed her out of the room. Her walk seemed off, like she was favoring one leg over the other, but that might've been a trick of the eye.

She's fine. She had no reason to lie, and even if she wasn't feeling well, she was capable of taking care of herself.

So why did I feel worried?

"Don't even think about it." Vincent's sharp tone brought my attention back to him. "I saw the way you were looking at her," he said when I raised a questioning brow. "Touch my sister, and you're dead."

"Drop the overprotective brother bit, DuBois. It's cliché."

"I'm just giving you a friendly warning." There wasn't an ounce of friendliness in his expression. "Scarlett is off limits."

"Scarlett can speak for herself."

"Yes, but she's too nice to creeps who want to take advantage."

I wasn't sure if we'd met the same Scarlett, since the one I knew seemed perfectly content putting me in my place.

I didn't bother acknowledging the *creeps who want to take advantage* part of his comment. I knew my intentions and boundaries; Vincent could think whatever the hell he liked.

"Not that you'd succeed even if you tried getting with her. She won't date a footballer again." Vincent shrugged. "Tough luck."

Again? Which player had she dated before? How long had they dated? Was it an old fling or recent breakup?

I tamped down the irrational desire to grill him about her ex. I wouldn't give him the satisfaction.

Scarlett returned, cutting our conversation short. Some of the color had returned to her cheeks, but her voice lacked the strength from the first half of our session.

Vincent said something in French. She responded in kind and gave him a pointed look. Whatever he was saying, she didn't want him saying it in front of me, even if it was in another language.

We were nearly finished with the session when his phone went off.

"I know, I know. I'm sorry." He jogged to his duffel bag in the corner. "But that's Dad's emergency ringtone."

Scarlett's frown melted into visible worry as Vincent picked up. He listened and said a few brusque words in French before ending the call.

"What happened?" she asked.

"Dad had an accident." More rapid-fire French, followed by a nod from Scarlett and a sideways glare from Vincent.

What the hell did *I* do?

"I'm sorry about the interruption," Scarlett said as Vincent shouldered his bag. "This is highly unusual, but..."

"It's fine. I get it." We only had ten minutes left of training anyway, and my muscles could use an early break. "Is your dad okay?"

"I think so. Vincent's going to deal with it. Dad's...particular about the people who handle his personal affairs."

"I'll call you later with an update." Vincent pinned me with a hard stare on his way out. "Remember what I said earlier."

The Nobel Peace Prize committee should note that I chose the high road and didn't respond with snark. His father was injured, after all. I wasn't a monster.

"Apologies again." Scarlett smoothed an unsteady hand over her bun. "This is only our second session, so I don't want to give the wrong impression. There's usually never this many disruptions."

"By disruptions, you mean using the loo and a family emergency?" I leaned against the barre and crossed my arms. "How unprofessional. You should quit now."

Her mouth twitched. "When you put it that way, I guess it's not so bad."

"It never is."

Thunder boomed in the distance and drew our startled gazes to the window. I'd been so caught up in what was happening in the studio that I hadn't noticed the transition from beautiful spring afternoon to raging storm.

"Don't tell me you're taking the tube in this weather," I said as Scarlett packed up her belongings.

It was a fifteen-minute walk to the nearest tube station, and it sounded like the apocalypse out there.

"People take the tube when it's raining all the time."

"Only when they don't have another choice. Let me drive you home." I followed her out the door and down the hall. "Carina left early, so you don't have to wait for her."

Scarlett slid a glance my way. "Are you stalking her?"

"I ran into her on my way to the studio. She told me she had a doctor's appointment this afternoon."

"Why would she...never mind." Scarlett shook her head. "She's the queen of oversharing."

"Think about it," I said as we neared the exit. "Would you rather ride the tube with a bunch of wet, grumpy commuters or enjoy the passenger seat of a brand-new Mercedes?"

"The tube. I've heard stories about the way you drive, and I want no part in it."

I should let it go. I shouldn't even be talking to her outside training—no distractions and all that—but she had a way of making me forget reason.

"It's a saloon car, not a sports car." The Mercedes was my anti-paparazzi decoy. "I won't go a single mile over the speed limit. I promise."

"No thanks." Scarlett opened the door. "I'll take my—"

"*Asher*! Asher, is this your new girlfriend?"

"How do you feel about losing the league during your first season with Blackcastle?"

"Is it true you and Vincent are training together this summer?"

An onslaught of questions and camera flashes exploded like a bomb amidst RAB's otherwise tranquil sanctuary.

Paparazzi swamped us, their raincoats slick with water, their cameras shoved in our faces as I was stunned into momentary silence.

How the hell did they find me? Everyone at RAB had to sign NDAs, and I was always careful driving from my house to the school. Most importantly, how the *hell* did they get past the security gates?

"Did you see people are burning your shirts in Holchester?"

"How does it feel to be hated by the fans that used to love you?"

The clamor escalated. With their hoods up and giant black lenses obscuring their faces, they resembled a pack of vultures frothing for scraps.

My heart rate ratcheted up. The shouts and flashes blurred into white noise while my gut twisted with familiar overwhelm.

I didn't hate the media per se. We had a symbiotic relationship, but only when the engagement was mutual.

I hated *this*—the ambushes, the invasions of privacy, the gross attempts at getting a rise out of me so they could sell my reaction for a buck. That was why I refused to give them one.

The rain fell in fat, heavy drops, soaking me to the bone. Claps of thunder rolled overhead and added to the chaos as I recovered my faculties and tried to push my way through the crowd.

I'd worry about how they found me later. Right now, I needed to get to my car and get us the hell out of here.

Us. Scarlett.

I turned, my heart giving a panicked thump when I saw her frozen at the top of the steps, her eyes wide and her face pale. I'd assumed she was right behind me, but she appeared to be in shock.

One of the paps said something that got lost in the storm and grabbed her arm.

A switch flipped, and my determination to keep my mouth shut washed away beneath a haze of red.

"Hey!" I doubled back and shoved him off her. "Don't touch

her!"

The camera flashes burst into a fresh frenzy.

"Are you sleeping together?"

"Is she your trainer?"

"What's your relationship?"

"Asher?"

"*Asher!*"

My voice and the renewed shouts shook Scarlett out of her stupor. She grabbed my outstretched hand and ran with me to my car.

I barreled through the paparazzi without care, and we somehow made it to my car without further incident.

She gave me her address, but neither of us spoke again until I'd cleared RAB's grounds and the cameras were a distant horde.

"Are you okay?" I asked. That seemed to be the question of the day.

"Yeah. I just…" Scarlett blinked, lingering traces of shock evident in the tremor of her words. "Is it always like that for you?"

"Not always, but most of the time."

It was one of the many reasons I didn't date. Any relationship would crumble beneath the combined weight of my football obligations, public scrutiny, and intrusive paparazzi. Everyone wanted to date a celebrity until they came home one day to find people rummaging through their trash for paydirt.

"God." Scarlett slumped in her seat. "How did they find you?"

"Either someone broke their NDA, or they tailed me from my house and I didn't notice."

I needed to call my publicist and see if she could deal with the photos before they got published. Paparazzi often played fast and loose with the rules, but Sloane had a history of bending them to her will. I didn't want Scarlett to deal with the absolute mess that would occur if her face got splashed all over the tabloids.

"Thank you for helping me back there," she said quietly. "You didn't have to do that. They probably got a money shot of you pushing that guy."

"He deserved it." My muscles coiled again at the memory of that asshole's hands on her. "He shouldn't have touched you."

Scarlett swallowed hard.

"I'm surprised you haven't had similar run-ins before," I said after another bout of silence. "Because of your brother."

"He keeps me shielded from that kind of stuff. Besides, he lives in Paris during the off-season, and when he *is* here, we hang out at each other's houses, not in public."

"So you two are close."

"Yes. We grew up in different cities, but we talked often. I didn't have a lot of friends as a kid because of my ballet schedule, and he had the same issue because of football. We were the closest the other had to a confidante."

It was weird. The topic of Vincent usually aggravated me, but I could listen to Scarlett talk all day and not get tired.

Then again, it had less to do with the subject and more to do with *her*. She was so reserved that any glimpses into her personal life fascinated me.

I stopped at a red light and glanced over at her. Scarlett stared straight ahead, her brows knitted together in thought. I read people pretty well, but she could be contemplating my words, her life, or what she wanted for dinner. I had no idea.

My gaze traced the elegant curve of her profile, searching for something I couldn't name. Water droplets clung to her lashes and coated the strands of hair slicked back into a dancer's bun. The elegant slope of her nose gave way to a lush mouth and delicate chin, both of which firmed into a stubborn line.

"Stop doing that," she said without looking at me.

"Doing what?"

"Staring at me."

"Training's going to be difficult if I'm not allowed to look at you."

"Looking at me for training is fine. Staring at me like *this* is not." She finally tore her eyes away from the road to gesture between us.

"How, exactly, am I looking at you?" I asked, amused.

"Like you..." Scarlett faltered, and the air suddenly condensed into something thicker, almost tangible.

Her eyes didn't quite meet mine, but the steady drip, drip, drip of water against the windows matched the spike in my pulse.

"Like I what?"

The question floated between us, soft enough not to disturb the tension coating the interior of the car.

Her lips parted for a breath before she lifted her chin, her face hardening. "Like you're flirting with me. That's not allowed, remember? It's one of the rules."

"Do you have many of those?"

"What?"

"Rules."

"I'm a ballerina. I live by rules."

"That's too bad." The light finally turned green, and I broke eye contact to focus on the road. "You'd have more fun without them."

Scarlett's gaze warmed my cheek before she, too, faced forward again.

The tension didn't dissipate in the resulting silence so much as rearrange itself, charging the air with a steady hum and making me hyperaware of her presence even when I wasn't looking directly at her.

The subtle shift of her leg. The dip of her chin. The shallow rise and fall of her chest.

Fuck. My fingers tightened around the steering wheel.

The twenty-minute drive to Scarlett's flat seemed both far too long and far too short, and when she finally climbed out of the car with a murmured *thanks*, I couldn't muster more than a nod.

I waited until she made it safely inside before I drove away, but the scent of her lingered.

Scarlett is off limits. Vincent's warning echoed in my head.

I was inclined to heed it—not because I was afraid of him, but because I was afraid of what getting close to Scarlett might do to me if I didn't.

CHAPTER 6

SCARLETT

"WHO DROVE YOU HOME?"

"What makes you think someone drove me home?" I unpacked our Chinese takeaway and avoided my brother's eyes. "I always take the tube."

It wasn't Thursday, but he showed up at my flat an hour ago after he finished dealing with our father's situation. I took one look at his face, let him in, and ordered us food.

Sometimes, sibling intuition trumped explanations.

"It's a long walk to the tube station, and you don't have an umbrella drying in the hall. Therefore, you didn't take the tube." Vincent shrugged. We were seated at my kitchen table in our usual spots—me next to the window, him next to the fridge. "Elementary, my dear Watson."

"Wow, I have Sherlock Holmes in my kitchen. Someone call BBC One and tell them they need another reboot."

"Ha ha." Vincent snagged a spring roll from its container. "It wasn't Carina, was it? Because I haven't forgotten the time she drove my Lambo into the curb."

"She's apologized multiple times for that," I said, suppressing a laugh at the memory of Vincent's face when he saw the scratch on his precious car. Carina was like a second sister to him, which was the only reason he'd let her behind the wheel. "And no, it wasn't her. It was someone else from the academy."

Asher was training there and therefore a temporary member of the academy, so I wasn't lying. Technically.

I hadn't *wanted* to get into a car with him. I didn't deal well with new-to-me drivers after the accident, which was why I rarely took taxis, but the paparazzi ambush had left me no choice.

"So it's another staff member." For some reason, Vincent looked relieved. Maybe a paranoid part of him had feared *Asher* was the one who drove me home. "Good."

I didn't correct him and prove his paranoia right.

Looking back, I should've been terrified given Asher's reputation for reckless driving. However, he'd driven safe and slow, and our conversation had kept me from spiraling.

For someone whose mere presence put me on edge, he had a way of also easing my anxiety—namely by distracting me so much I didn't have time to think about anything else.

A twist of unease tightened inside me. I didn't like my contradictory reactions to Asher. I preferred to sort my emotions into separate boxes—black and white, good and bad, alphabetized and color-coded. But when I looked at him, I was a muddled canvas of gray.

I *hated* gray.

"So, are we going to talk about what happened?" I asked, switching subjects. Asher and I hadn't done anything wrong, but I didn't want Vincent to freak out and go on a tangent about me consorting with the enemy. "How's Dad?"

All I knew was he'd had an accident. He had a lot of those now that he was retired and constantly puttering around, but they usually involved him hitting his head or slamming the door on his hand. Nevertheless, he made it sound like he was dying every time.

Vincent wasn't the only drama queen in the family.

Still, he was our father, so it was our duty to check in anyway, hence why Vincent gave him an emergency ringtone.

"He fell and broke his hip. He's fine," he said when I opened my mouth. "He doesn't need surgery. But, uh, he asked me to come home and stay with him until the season starts or he's fully healed."

I narrowed my eyes as Vincent wolfed down his spring roll. "You can't hire a home nurse? It has to be you, specifically?"

"I *did* hire a nurse, which is why he wants me to stay with him. You know he hates being alone with strangers."

Fair enough, but…"Vince, you can't even make a proper bowl of soup. What are you going to do while you're there?"

I couldn't picture my wonderful, athletic, yet deeply out of touch brother taking care of anything that didn't involve a football, a video game, or a party.

"Good thing soup has nothing to do with it," he countered. "I just have to keep Dad company and make him feel better about having the nurse around twenty-four-seven. If I'm not there, he's liable to drive her to murder."

"How long will recovery take?"

"It's hard to say. The doctors estimate anywhere from three to four months."

"Hmm." I studied him with a hint of suspicion. "You're not doing this to get out of training with Asher, are you?"

"Of course not," he snapped. "Trust me, Lettie, I'd rather stay in London. I don't want you dealing with Asher alone, especially when he…"

I stiffened. "Especially when he what?"

He knows about the ride home. He knows Asher has been flirting with you and, despite what you say, a part of you likes it.

"Especially when he's such a dick," Vincent said after a beat of hesitation. "Don't fall for the charmer act he puts on with girls. It's just that. An act. I've seen it a million times. We should've never signed him," he added with a grumble. "You see how he is. He's more trouble than he's worth."

Relief loosened the knot in my lungs. *He doesn't know.*

"I'm not stupid. Besides, I have a strict no-footballer rule. Asher Donovan is not on my romantic radar, and he never will be."

Attraction didn't count as romance. That was an involuntary, hormonal thing. My body may not agree, but my brain was firmly on board and my heart was safely locked away.

However, a seed of guilt remained lodged in my chest. No matter how I rationalized the car ride, it *felt* like a betrayal, and I hated doing anything that might jeopardize my relationship with Vincent. Besides Carina, he was the only person I fully trusted.

"Good." Despite his response, Vincent's frown deepened. "On second thought, maybe I can talk to Dad and convince him his home nurse won't, I don't know, stab him in his sleep when I'm not there. I can be here during the week for training and take the train to Paris on the weekends. The more I think about it, the more I don't fucking trust Donovan."

"That's ridiculous. You're going to travel to Paris *every* weekend?" I shook my head. "There's no convincing Dad. He'll lose his shit and you know it."

"But—"

"Stop treating me like a kid." I pointed my fork at him. "I'll be fine. Anyway, didn't the Boss make you guys train with me because he wanted you to work together? If you're not here, that defeats the purpose. There's a good chance he'll call off the program altogether and Asher can go back to training on his own."

Vincent stared at me for a long beat before his shoulders relaxed.

"You're right." Relief shrouded his words. "If the Boss okays my leave, which he basically has to, he's not going to make Donovan stay with you. It would be stupid."

I hoped that was the case. Otherwise, it meant Asher and I would be forced into one-on-one lessons. Three times a week, every week for the remainder of the summer.

An errant flutter disrupted my stomach. *Disappointment or anticipation?* I couldn't tell, which was alarming.

"Exactly." I hoped I sounded confident and not like I was trying to reassure myself. "There's no way he would do that."

"The sessions continue. I've already spoken to Frank. Vincent's absence doesn't change anything for you and Asher," Lavinia said, seemingly oblivious or indifferent to my squeak of surprise.

Vincent was leaving for Paris tomorrow with the Boss's permission. Frank was probably suspicious of his conveniently timed family emergency, but there wasn't much he could do about it. My brother was officially off the hook for our trainings.

I'd requested a meeting with Lavinia that morning to see if his departure would affect my summer obligations.

Apparently, it didn't.

"I don't understand." A swirl of anxiety pooled in my gut. "The goal of the sessions was for Vincent and Asher to learn how to work together. If Vincent isn't here, then..."

"That was *one* of the goals. However, they still need to train like normal athletes. We've already signed a contract with Blackcastle, and they've paid through the summer. There's no use undoing all of that simply because of one departure."

"Right." I forced a smile. *Damn contracts.*

"That means you'll be working with Asher one-on-one." Lavinia peered at me over the rim of her glasses. "Will that be a problem?"

"I—no. Of course not."

Personal sessions with Asher. That was fine.

Totally. Fine.

Did Vincent know? He'd left our dinner convinced that the Boss would cut the training program short. If he didn't, he was going to be livid when he found out, but he couldn't do anything about it at this point. There was no way our father would let him come back until the nurse was out of his house.

Like it or not, I was stuck with Asher for the rest of the summer.

"Is there something else you'd like to discuss?" Lavinia asked pointedly.

My *no* reached the tip of my tongue just as my eyes rested on the photo behind Lavinia. It featured the cast after last year's staff showcase. Every instructor was present except for me and Barden, who'd been on his honeymoon.

Which role are you auditioning for? I'd love to see you onstage.

A shard of ice pierced my gut.

I'd lied about being too busy for the showcase. The truth was, I *missed* being onstage. I missed the glide of smooth wood beneath my feet, the pulse-pounding crescendos during pivotal scenes, the feeling of transcendence when it was just me and the music.

When I was onstage, I didn't overthink; I simply moved.

But my desire to perform again didn't outweigh my fears. I hadn't truly danced onstage in five years. If I tried, would I aggravate old wounds or, worse, fail altogether?

Scarlett DuBois. She was the next big star; now look at her. She can't even audition for a school showcase.

The shard of ice slid deeper behind my rib cage.

"No," I said in response to Lavinia's question. "Nothing else."

I left her office and shook my head at Carina's questioning stare. I'd explain things to her later.

For the rest of the day, I attempted not to think about Asher or the showcase. Instead, I answered Emma's questions about how to prep for a big show, listened to Carina regale me with wild tales about the students' parents over lunch (dance moms were a terrifying breed), checked in with my father during a break, and ignored my mother's voicemail about setting me up on a blind date.

"Scarlett, love, call me back when you get the chance," she said. "I have the most *marvelous* prospect for you. He's a res—"

"You changed your outfit."

My phone slipped out of my hand and clattered to the studio floor. "Jesus! Don't sneak up on people like that."

Asher leaned against the doorframe, the picture of effortless devastation in jeans and a gray shirt.

Ugh. How was it possible for someone to look *that* good in such a basic outfit?

I frowned, irrationally annoyed.

God definitely had favorites, and Asher was one of them.

"I didn't sneak up on you," he said, laughter coloring his voice. "You were just too busy to notice me."

I swiped my phone off the floor. At least my mother's voicemail had ended, so he didn't have to overhear whatever scheme she'd concocted to "liven up" my "tragically nonexistent" love life.

"What are you doing here anyway?" I asked. "We don't have anything scheduled today."

It was Thursday, and our sessions were every Monday, Wednesday, and Friday.

Asher offered a casual shrug. "I was in the area and thought I'd drop by."

"For?"

"No reason. Just felt like it."

"You're telling me *the* Asher Donovan has nothing better to do with his time than drop by a ballet academy?"

A shadow flickered in those crystalline green eyes. "I have other things I could do," he said. "I wouldn't say they're better."

Warm air breezed through the open windows and brushed the nape of my neck. It traveled the length of my spine all the way down to my toes, making my skin tingle from the inside out.

Then Asher blinked, and the moment dissolved like honey in a sun-kissed ocean.

"Actually, I did have something to tell you," he said. "I spoke with my publicist. She took care of the paparazzi from yesterday. They were trespassing on private property, and we were able to scare them into agreeing not to publish any of the photos."

"Oh." I scrambled to orient myself to his crisp new tone. It was like he'd flipped the switch from playful to professional. "That's good. Do you know how they found you?"

"They followed Vincent." His features tautened. "It's not hard to spot that ridiculous orange Lamborghini of his."

I resisted pointing out that Asher owned his fair share of "ridiculous" sports cars; *Football World* did a whole feature on his multimillion-dollar collection.

"He didn't mention them when we talked yesterday." I'd been so distracted by our father's accident that I hadn't asked Vincent whether he'd run into paparazzi on his way out. "He would've if he'd seen them."

"I think they were still hiding when he left but found a way to sneak in afterward." Asher examined me, his eyes inscrutable compared to their earlier warmth. "I heard he's going back to Paris for the summer."

"Yes. To take care of our father." An ache settled into my knee joints.

"So training will be just the two of us going forward."

I shifted my weight, hoping to ease the pressure. It didn't work. "That's what Lavinia said. There's no point complicating things when Blackcastle already paid for the summer."

"I suppose you're right." Asher didn't move from his spot in the doorway. His response was cooler than I'd expected, which was a *good* thing. I was the one who'd established our no-flirting rule; I couldn't get mad at him for following it.

The ache shot up my thigh to my hips.

I sucked in a sharp breath and exhaled, Asher's curious change in attitude forgotten. I'd gone months without a flare-up, but the past week had been a nightmare. Stress, hormones, weather changes—there wasn't always a rhyme or reason to my pain.

Before I could muster a reply, he suddenly straightened and jerked his head to the left.

"Hey!" Suspicion serrated his voice. "Do you work here?"

I didn't hear a response, but a second later, pounding footsteps echoed through the hall.

Asher took off after them, and I instinctively followed despite my body's scream of protest. My pulse rocketed with trepidation.

Was it the paps again? That was the only reason I could think of for his reaction. If it was, how did they get *inside* the school when security was already on alert from the first incident?

I rushed into the corridor, but in my haste, I banged my hip against the doorframe. Most people could easily shake off the hit, but for me, in my current state, it was the equivalent of a bomb going off inside me.

A cry of pain escaped before I could stop it.

Asher halted his chase and whirled around. Worry seeped into the planes of his face.

"Scarlett?" His voice sounded far-off, like I was sinking underwater while he watched from the shore.

Blood roared in my ears. The hall tilted as every ounce of attention coalesced around my legs, and the ache throbbed with the force of an sledgehammer battering its way through a wall.

Breathe.

In, one, two, three. Out, one—

Another lightning bolt of agony ripped through me, so sharp and excruciating it felt like someone was tearing me in half from the inside out.

If my earlier ache was a hammer, this was a thousand spikes piercing the most tender points of my body.

My vision filled with static, and I maintained lucidity just long enough to see Asher sprint toward me before the ground rushed up and everything turned black.

CHAPTER 7

SCARLETT

EVERYTHING HURT.

My bones, my joints, the simple act of breathing. Every drag of air resembled a steel claw raking through my lungs, making me wish for oblivion again.

I was dimly aware that I *should* open my eyes and take stock of my surroundings. It didn't smell right. Instead of lemony cleaner or lavender diffuser, I detected antiseptic and...aftershave? Something spicy with a hint of citrus.

So. I wasn't in the studio or my bedroom.

Where the hell am I? Hopefully not some random one-night stand's house. One-night stands were never a good idea, even if they smelled delicious.

"Need anything else..."

"When she comes around..."

The faint murmur of voices dragged my mind off the mysterious aftershave and onto my current predicament again.

Strange room. Pain. *Right.*

At least my joints didn't hurt quite as much as when I first regained consciousness. I still wanted to curl into a ball and pray for sleep, but I could push through it.

I always did.

I cracked my eyes open, half-afraid I'd find myself in some dingy man cave with weeks-old takeaway and topless posters plastered all over the walls.

Instead, a pair of green eyes stared down at me beneath furrowed brows.

Chiseled cheekbones. Sculpted mouth. An annoyingly attractive flop of dark hair.

Asher.

"You're awake." The furrow smoothed, though his eyes remained worried. "How are you feeling?"

"Like I got hit by a truck that reversed and ran me over again." My response scratched its way up my throat. "So I feel great."

Asher snorted. "Your sarcasm is intact, so it can't be that bad."

Nevertheless, he scanned me with the brisk thoroughness of someone who needed to confirm the other was all right without making a big production out of it.

There was nothing remotely sexual about it, but my skin prickled with awareness anyway.

To distract myself from his scrutiny, I glanced around the room. Whoever he'd been talking to was gone, leaving us alone in the school's infirmary. No wonder I hadn't recognized it by scent alone; I rarely came here, preferring to deal with my flare-ups alone.

"You want to tell me what happened?" Asher's gaze met mine again. "You took quite the fall back there."

He sounded both concerned and commanding, a rare combo that made warmth curl low inside me.

Still, I defaulted to an excuse instead of the truth. "I forgot to eat lunch and got dizzy."

I didn't like talking about my chronic pain. It often made people uncomfortable, which made *me* uncomfortable. They were sympathetic, of course, but there was always a beat of pity, an unspoken *poor you* that had me biting my tongue.

"That wasn't dizziness. You were in pain." Asher's eyes darkened. "Are you *still* in pain?"

A rough edge ran beneath his voice, and I had to swallow to ease my suddenly dry throat.

"A little." *A lot.* Not enough to pass out again, but enough that the prospect of getting up seemed more daunting than climbing Mount Everest.

He cursed under his breath. "Let me get the nurse—"

"No!" I grabbed his arm before he could leave. "There's nothing she can do. I just have to wait for it to pass."

Anything that required asking other people for help made me squirrelly, which was why I'd had such a difficult time coping after my accident. The transition from fully self-sufficient to reliant on others was a difficult one to endure.

Asher's features sharpened. "Wait for what to pass?"

"My flare-up. I don't get them often anymore, but when I do, they can be...debilitating."

Resignation pulled the truth out of me. If we were going to spend the summer together, I might as well tell him, especially since my flare-ups were growing in frequency.

It was one thing to hide it from my other, younger students; it was another trying to conceal it from a professional athlete who understood the body's tells as much as I did.

"I got into a car accident five years ago," I said. Asher went deathly still, his intake of breath the only sign of life as I continued my story. "I was on my way to a performance when the other person ran a red light and collided with the taxi I was in. I woke up in the hospital with a punctured lung, dislocated hip, and a dozen other issues. That was the end of my career, and the start of this." I gestured at myself. "The doctors said my chronic pain is a result of nerve damage."

The piercing pain had dulled into a general tenderness, but my recounting of that night caused a different kind of ache to blossom.

I hadn't told anyone about the accident since Carina. It'd made waves when it happened, but that was long enough ago that no one outside the ballet world would remember. Car accidents happened every day; they weren't memorable unless you knew someone personally involved.

It was funny how a life-changing moment for one person was nothing more than a blip on the news for someone else.

"Is there anything I can do to help?" Asher didn't tell me how sorry he was or pry for more details. He simply focused on me with those steady, sympathetic eyes, and the ache behind my rib cage thickened into an unidentifiable emotion.

"Sure." I managed a wan smile. "Tell me how you got us here."

My studio was on the first floor, the infirmary was on the fourth, and the lift was currently under maintenance.

"I carried you." He answered so matter-of-factly it took a minute for his words to sink in.

"You *carried* me up three flights of stairs?"

Broad shoulders lifted in a shrug. "It was my strength training for the day."

A vague recollection of strong arms and pounding footsteps floated through my brain but vanished as quickly as it surfaced. I couldn't tell if it was an actual memory or a fantasy brought about by his words.

Either way, it made the room feel just a little bit less cold.

"Wow, I'm good at my job," I said with small laugh. "Unconscious and I still made you work."

"You're a tough taskmaster." Asher's mouth tipped up before softening again. "If it still hurts, I can ask the nurse for a heating pad or pain meds."

The curl of warmth returned, spreading from my stomach and down my legs to my toes.

I shook my head. "I just want to go home." Pilates, sleep, and a warm bath were my go-tos for managing flare-ups, and the infirmary's cot wasn't a great place for any of those things.

Normally, I would've never confessed something so vulnerable out loud. I followed a chin-up, suck-it-up philosophy, but fatigue had set in, loosening my inhibitions, and Asher's presence was oddly comforting.

"We can make that happen." Asher's gaze dipped, and to my horror, I realized I'd been holding onto him this entire time.

I dropped his arm immediately, fire crawling up the back of my neck. *Why didn't he say anything earlier?*

My palm tingled in the absence of his warmth, and I wiped it against the side of my leg, hoping that would help.

It didn't. It only succeeded in aggravating the tenderness of my muscles.

I winced. *Smart move, Scarlett. Truly Mensa-worthy.*

A brief frown touched Asher's face before he looked away. "A warning, though," he said. "The press is back. The guy I was chasing earlier? He was a young pap disguised as a prospective student. That was how he got in."

My chest swam with disbelief. "Seriously?" That was *unhinged*. What story could they sell with photos of Asher at RAB anyway? Him cross-training at a dance studio wasn't scandalous in any way.

I was all for people making a living how they could, but I firmly believed paparazzi deserved a special place in hell next to the telemarketers and corrupt politicians.

"That's going to be a problem," I said.

I didn't want to worry about candid pictures of me ending up in some sleazy tabloid every time I came to work. Asher was their target, but as his trainer, I had a high likelihood of getting caught in the crossfire.

"I agree, but I've been thinking about it since our first run-in with them, and I might have a solution," Asher said. "Can you send me a list of everything we need for training? Equipment, supplies, room dimensions. Everything."

"Why?"

"Trust me."

I must've looked skeptical because a small smile quirked at the corner of his lips.

"It'll be a surprise. The paps will continue to be an issue because they *know* where I'll be every other day. We have to throw them off our scent. Trust me," he repeated. "I know what I'm doing."

I didn't have the energy to argue.

I also didn't make a habit of trusting anyone outside my family and Carina, but in that moment, it was hard to remember why I should keep Asher at arm's length.

He wasn't my brother's nemesis or my trainee—he was the person who'd carried me up three flights of stairs, stayed with me until I regained consciousness, and didn't make me feel like an object of pity when I told him about my accident.

And that's exactly why he's dangerous.

CHAPTER 8

ASHER

I DEVELOPED A NEW MANTRA OVER THE NEXT TWO weeks: *Keep it professional and stop thinking about her.*

It was a bit long for a mantra, but it was smart, clear, and actionable. I was quite proud of it.

Unfortunately, it also proved that mantras were bullshit because fourteen days later, Scarlett still haunted my thoughts like a smart-mouthed, entirely-too-beautiful ghost.

When I woke up, I anticipated our next session together.

When I got behind the wheel, I remembered the night I drove her home in the rain.

When I entered her studio, I relived my sheer panic at seeing her collapse and my utter relief when she woke up.

Despite what I'd told her, I'd dropped by RAB that day to discuss the paparazzi issue with Lavinia. That was it. And yet, my feet had steered me to her studio instead of the director's office, and my determination to keep her at arm's length had snapped the second I saw her in pain.

I was convinced we were the subjects of some universal conspiracy at this point. I just couldn't prove it.

"Are you listening to me?" My father's irritation pierced through my unwanted thoughts.

I leaned back in my chair and refocused on his frown. We sat opposite each other at my childhood dining table, which still bore traces of the permanent marker stick figures I'd doodled of famous footballers when I was a kid. Despite my best efforts to move my parents to a newer, bigger place, they'd insisted on staying at their old split-level in southwest Holchester.

Luckily, they'd consented to a new security system after several run-ins with the press, but I was still uneasy about how accessible they were to anyone with an internet connection and the barest modicum of sleuthing skills.

"I'm listening," I said, even though I'd tuned him out twenty minutes ago.

We always talked about the same things: what I did wrong in my last match and how I could improve for the next one. My father watched more replays of my matches than Coach, which was saying something.

"You lacked focus the entire season," he said. "Where was the cohesion? Where was the *fire*?"

"Oh, come off it, Ron," my mother said from her spot by the counter. She picked up two mugs of tea and set them on the table, casting a glare at my father along the way. "I think he played wonderfully. You were the league's highest scorer this season, weren't you, darling?"

My father cut me off before I could respond. "Highest scorer yet no trophy." The weathered planes of his face drew deeper into a scowl. "Should've stuck to Holchester like I told you. You know I can barely show my face at the pub these days? We've always been a red-and-white household. Then you had to go and...and do *this*."

He gestured at the newspaper splayed open on the table. A photo of me, clearly devastated after the Holchester match, took up half the first page of the sports section.

Not only had I lost, but I was wearing Blackcastle's signature purple and white.

If my father was the head of the Holchester United Church, I was its greatest heretic.

"You know why I did it." I was tired of rehashing the same thing over and over again. Every time I visited, my father inevitably brought up my "traitorous transfer" to Holchester's biggest rival, which was why I rarely came home anymore. I was only here this weekend because of Teddy's birthday.

"Money, Frank Armstrong, and a bloody loss on your record. How's *that* treating you?" My father made a disgusted noise.

Money and working with Frank Armstrong. They were the reasons I gave him, but they weren't the *only* reasons. I would never tell him what the third was, though.

When I didn't respond, he shoved his chair back and stormed off, his tea forgotten.

"Don't take what he says to heart." My mother patted my shoulder. "You know how fanatical he is about that team. It'll take time, but he'll get over it."

He'd had half a year to get over it. Then again, he'd refused to talk to me for a month after he found out about the transfer, so the fact we were on speaking terms at all was an improvement.

"I'm heading out to see Teddy." I stood and placed my half-empty mug in the sink. "I'll be back in time for dinner."

Her face softened. "Okay. Don't be too hard on yourself, okay?

All this—the matches, the press, the pressure—it's temporary. It doesn't define you."

I kept my smile even as my gut clenched.

She meant what she said in a comforting way, but the temporary nature of my career *was* the reason why I pushed myself so hard. I only had a set number of years to achieve everything I wanted, and that was assuming I didn't suffer an injury that would cut the number down further.

Besides, she was wrong. Football did define me. It was the only thing I'd ever excelled at. What would I be without it?

Nothing.

However, I didn't voice any of those thoughts as I kissed her on the cheek and left.

My mother dealt with enough problems in her job as a teacher. I didn't want to add mine to the heap.

My parents lived in a quiet part of Holchester so there was rarely traffic, and it took me less than ten minutes to reach Teddy.

The grounds smelled like damp earth and moss. Sunlight peeked through spindly branches, and bursts of flowers added color to the otherwise staid landscape. Workers kept the place well-tended, but there was only so much cheer one could expect in a cemetery.

I trod the familiar path to Teddy's resting site. Guilt wormed through my chest when I saw how bare it looked.

His mother had died years ago, and his father had remarried and moved across the country. I was the only person who visited regularly anymore; even so, my visits had dwindled since I moved to London.

I placed a birthday card on my best friend's grave and sat there until sunset beckoned.

Besides my mother, Teddy was the only person who remembered me as Asher before I became Asher Donovan.

Sometimes, I needed that reminder too.

SCARLETT

"If you're dragging me to your secret lair so you can butcher me, I'm going to be deeply upset," I said. "I have plans to see a West End show tonight."

"It's alarming that that was the first thought that popped into your head, but no, I am not dragging you to my secret lair. All my lairs are public."

"Cute." I glanced at our driver and tried not to calculate the million different ways we could die if he sped up, slowed down, or took the wrong turn. *It's fine. You'll be fine.* "Seriously, where are we going? Where's the new studio?"

"You'll find out soon enough." Asher sat next to me in the backseat, his posture relaxed and indifferent compared to my white knuckles and rigid back.

He'd asked me to meet him down the road from RAB today so we could avoid the paparazzi, who still camped out near the school grounds every day hoping for a money pic of Asher.

When I'd shown up, too curious about his "paparazzi solution" to stay away, I'd been greeted by an armored Range Rover, a black-suited man the size of the Hulk, and Asher.

"I'm not driving today. Earl is," he'd said, nodding at the Hulk 2.0. "We're going to our new studio."

I should've insisted he tell me where the studio was before I (reluctantly) climbed into the car, but again, curiosity got the better of me.

Well, that and Asher's reassurance that Earl was the safest, most skilled driver in the London metro area. Apparently, he'd been a chauffeur for Downing Street for twenty years, followed by a stint with an extremely wealthy, extremely reclusive billionaire.

I still hated getting into cars with strangers, but I believed Asher, and he was right. Earl had been great so far.

"Which West End show are you seeing tonight?" Asher asked.

I named a new musical that had been garnering rave reviews.

"Friday night date. Should be a fun time," he said.

I threw a sharp glance in his direction. He was the picture of carelessness, his profile outlined in sunlit gold against the window, but an edge ran beneath his otherwise casual drawl.

Our relationship the past three weeks had been perfectly cordial. He showed up to the studio, we trained, he left. Still charming but absent the flirtatiousness of our early encounters.

It was easy. Simple. *Professional.* Exactly what I'd asked for.

"Yes." For some reason, I declined to mention that Carina was my hot Friday night date. "It should be very fun."

A muscle ticked in Asher's jaw before his expression smoothed. "Good."

Good.

The terseness of his response ran the length of my spine, followed by a strange thrill.

He'd uttered one word, and my mind was tearing it apart, searching for hidden meanings that didn't exist—like whether that was jealousy behind his *good* or sincerity.

I crossed and uncrossed my legs, restless amidst the mushrooming silence. Asher's gaze flicked down before sliding toward the window again.

Clearly, today's abrupt change of plans had addled my brain if I was worrying over what he thought about my "date."

Why didn't you tell him you were going with Carina instead of some hypothetical guy you met on an overrated dating app?

Because it's none of his business.

Sure. That's why.

Shut up.

Earl turned the corner, and my oh-so-delightful conversation with myself died a quick death.

I wasn't a stranger to luxury. Vincent lived in a multimillion-pound mansion that once belonged to a famous rock star, and during my career prime, I'd attended parties at venues that would make even the most jaded jaws drop.

But the estate before me...wow.

It boasted the usual features one would expect from a house in one of the poshest neighborhoods outside London—intimidating iron gates, marble fountains, a sprawling green lawn.

That wasn't what made it exceptional. What made it exceptional was how *unexpected* it was.

I would've pictured Asher's house (and I was almost positive this was Asher's house) as some modern monstrosity made of glass, concrete, and no soul, per the standard bachelor pad design package.

Instead, three stories of pale stone soared over the perfectly manicured grounds, its walls thick with ivy and its arched windows bright beneath the sunlight. A marble swan adorned the fountain anchoring a circular drive, and everywhere I looked, flowers flourished in all their summertime glory. Peonies, roses, geraniums...

A snort of laughter escaped when I noticed a pair of hedges sculpted into the shape of a football and a championship trophy, respectively. They were so obviously satire that I could only shake my head.

"Subtle," I said as Earl parked in the drive and we exited the car. "If you added your squad number, you'd have the trifecta on your lawn."

"That's a great suggestion," Asher said with all seriousness. "I'll call my landscaper and let him know."

"Will you pay me a consulting fee for the idea?"

"Only if you take it in the form of pizza and ice cream."

"Veggie and pistachio?"

"Pepperoni and Rocky Road."

"Deal."

A smile tugged on Asher's mouth. Our earlier awkwardness dissolved, replaced with a heady new tension. It crawled beneath my skin and spurred my pulse into a gallop.

I'd always prided myself on my ability to think clearly.

When my parents divorced, I'd drawn up a thirty-point logistical plan of action for all four members of our household.

When a pipe burst last year, flooding my flat and destroying half my belongings, I'd calmly turned off the main water supply, opened the faucets to drain any remaining cold water, and called the plumber.

And when I found out I'd never dance professionally again, I hadn't shed a single tear. Devastation was a private thing, to be confined within the walls of my mind and soul.

So no, I wasn't prone to emotion-led decisions. I kept my thoughts as rational as possible.

But sometimes, when I was around Asher, I found it hard to think much at all.

My mind blurred around the edges. I was roasting in my leotard and tights. I couldn't tell whether that was because of the weather or—

Earl cleared his throat. The sound had the same effect as dumping ice water over a roaring fire.

My mental haze vanished, and Asher and I took a simultaneous step away from each other.

Earl didn't say a word, but I swore I saw a smirk slip across his mouth.

"Let's go inside." Asher turned his back to me and unlocked the front door. "It's too hot out here."

A hush blanketed us again during our walk through his house.

"Pizza and ice cream. Not the diet I'd expect from a top footballer," I said. I was beating a dead horse at this point, but I needed to fill the silence.

"I don't make a habit of it." Asher's arm grazed mine as we turned the corner. "But sometimes, I'm in the mood for something sweet."

A faint roughness ran beneath his words, turning what should've been an innocent response into anything but.

Heat warmed the back of my neck. A brief image of Asher enjoying *something sweet* flashed through my mind before I crushed it with a determined fist.

I took another, deliberate step away from him as we walked deeper into the house. It didn't stop the bolt of awareness streaking through my blood, but at least I was actively fighting back against my hormones.

Those traitors. I could never trust them.

Asher gave me an abbreviated tour of the mansion, which was even larger than it looked from the outside.

Original Picassos hung next to framed shirts signed by retired football legends; a state-of-the-art entertainment center faced a display case filled with trophies, medals, and sentimental items like the boots he wore in his first ever Premier League match. A forty-person screening room with a genuine concession stand occupied the same hall as an indoor bowling alley, and natural light spilled through dozens of giant windows overlooking the grounds.

It straddled that perfect line between cozy and luxurious, and I loved it.

"The basement is dedicated to all things fitness. It's actually level with the lower tier of the back garden—the first floor of the house leads to the main tier—so there's plenty of light," Asher said, leading me down the stairs. "The sauna, steam room, and indoor pool are to the left. Gym and massage room are to the right."

"So you basically have an at-home spa." I twisted my neck to get a better look at the infrared sauna. I'd *love* a personal sauna. They helped a lot with my pain.

"Basically." We stopped in front of a closed door. "You ready to see the latest addition to Spa Donovan?"

"I suppose." I feigned a yawn to mask my curiosity. "Hopefully the inside is more inspired than the name."

Asher rewarded me with a quick grin. "Hey, that's why I'm a footballer, not a hospitality mogul. That being said..." He opened the door with a flourish. "Welcome to our new training center."

I didn't know what I'd expected. A standard room with mirrors, maybe, or gray concrete and a barre.

I should've known better; Asher Donovan didn't do things halfway.

Instead of a basic workout area, I walked into a full-blown professional ballet studio.

Correction: it wasn't *a* ballet studio; it was *the* ballet studio. As in, the ballet studio of my dreams, only even better.

RAB hadn't spared any expense with its facilities, but this...this was everything I'd dreamed of.

A gleaming expanse of hardwood stretched across the vast space, its surface so polished it appeared to undulate with sunlight. It was a sprung floor, which meant it was designed to offer optimal shock absorption and minimize the stress on bones and joints.

Golden warmth poured through a wall of windows that opened onto an attached outdoor gym, and a double row of barres lined the perimeter of the room. They appeared to have been custom-built to accommodate for my and Asher's different heights. A black Steinway piano and state-of-the-art sound system dominated one corner while potted plants added a welcome pop of greenery throughout the studio.

The floor-to-ceiling mirrors reflected my shock back at me.

"I had it built according to the list you gave me about our training essentials, but I added a few flourishes." Asher nodded at the outdoor gym. "If I missed anything, let me know."

"How did you..." I spun slowly, taking in the details that elevated the studio from professional to exquisite. The line paintings of dancers by famed artist Marina Escrol; the unobtrusive camera setup that would allow us to film our sessions and monitor progress over time; the adaptive smart home resistance training system. He hadn't missed a single thing. "It's only been three weeks!"

"Money is a great motivator." Mischief sparked in Asher's eyes. "I may also have added VIP season tickets for the entire crew as an incentive if they got it done in under a month."

Of course the contractors were football fans.

However, as much as I loved the studio and newfound privacy, there was one problem.

"It took us almost an hour to get here by car," I pointed out. "The tube doesn't run here, which means I'd have to take a cab, and we meet three times a week. That's not sustainable."

My schedule didn't leave room for such a long commute. I had other classes I needed to teach.

"You don't have to take the tube. Earl will be your chauffeur," Asher said. "I had him drive us today so you can get a sense of his style. If you're comfortable with him, I'll cover the cost since I'm the reason we're in this predicament in the first place." He shrugged. "The car is basically a tank, so you don't have to worry about safety either."

A knot of emotion formed in my throat.

The most unexpected thing I'd encountered today wasn't our impromptu trip to Asher's house or the contents of the new studio; it was his thoughtfulness.

Careful. Remember what happened the last time you got sucked in by a handsome face and "thoughtfulness."

"And my schedule?" I asked. "I have a class right before our sessions."

"I'm fine pushing our sessions back, and I'm sure Lavinia won't object to a schedule change."

Our sessions already took place late in the afternoon. If we pushed them back any further, they'd veer dangerously close to evening time.

Being alone in a beautiful, private studio with Asher after the sun set?

Apprehension fluttered through my body like a thousand tiny butterflies.

Absolutely not.

"Fine." I turned to retrieve a resistance band from its rack. The warmth from Asher's gaze burned between my shoulder blades, and the flutters multiplied into an unruly swarm. "Let's get started, shall we? We've wasted enough time."

CHAPTER 9

ASHER

ADIL

I'm bored

ADIL

New bet. Hundred quid says Donovan gets caught in another scandal by summer's end

What do you mean ANOTHER scandal?

I feel targeted

ADIL

Remember what happened with your Lambo?

That wasn't a scandal. That was a tragedy

ADIL

A tragic scandal.

ADIL

I think they finally rebuilt that wall you destroyed

It was overdue for a renovation anyway. I did them a favor

ADIL

> Ask the National Historic Society if they agree

NOAH

> Stop texting me

NOAH

> I went to the gym and came back to 86 new messages

ADIL

> This is a group chat. Texting is literally the point

NOAH WILSON LEFT THE CONVERSATION.

ADIL CHAKIR ADDED NOAH WILSON TO THE CONVERSATION.

NOAH

> I'm blocking you

ADIL

> That's very un-Nice Single Dad of you. You have an image to protect, you know

ADIL

> Noah

ADIL

> Hello?

ADIL

> You didn't actually block me, did you?

ADIL

> Wilson!!

I shook my head. If Noah had his way, he'd show up to work, do his job, then immediately go home to his daughter, but Adil had somehow dragged him into our Blackcastle Baddies group chat (yes, that was really the name, and no, Adil wouldn't change it).

We had another chat with the entire team, but I rarely posted there. The other guys were nice enough on their own, but Adil and Noah were the only ones who didn't treat me differently when Vincent was around.

An incoming call disrupted Adil's spiral over being blocked.

"Hey, boss." I tucked my phone between my ear and shoulder as I flipped through the post. Every week, I received bags of items to sign for my official fan club. Some players ignored their fan mail altogether, but I tried to sign when I had the time. It didn't require much effort, and it made people happy. "I haven't crashed any cars yet, but I promise I'm working on it."

"You do that, and I will personally fly to London to slap some sense into you," Sloane said without a trace of humor.

I suppressed a laugh.

Coach was the boss on the pitch, but as my publicist, Sloane Kensington was in charge of everything related to my image (much to her chagrin). I paid her a boatload of money for dealing with me, but honestly, I was surprised she hadn't quit yet.

Then again, Sloane and "quit" didn't belong in the same sentence. She'd soldier through a trench of paparazzi bottom-feeders and internet trolls before she gave up.

"If you're finished with your unamusing jokes, I'd like to remind you of your *Sports UK* interview on Thursday," she said. "I'll connect you to the reporter at noon sharp. Also, I spoke with Leon about Aoki Watches. They're renewing your brand ambassador contract. I'll send you details for the Japanese press tour once they're confirmed."

"Perfect." Leon was my business manager, and Aoki Watches was my most lucrative brand sponsorship. "You're worth your weight in gold."

"Instead of gold, pay me by staying out of trouble. I mean it, Asher. I don't want to see you *near* a street race unless the internet and media collectively implode and I won't have to deal with the resulting headlines."

"Does that mean if I comply, I won't have to pay your monthly retainer? I just bought a new Bugatti. Cash is a little tight." It wasn't, but I was curious as to how she'd respond.

She hung up on me.

Well, then. There was my answer.

I didn't have any urgent mail, so I set it aside for the moment and walked to my garage. The custom-built space was the size of an airplane hangar, and it housed all fifteen of my cars, including my favorite vintage Jaguar convertible and the Bugatti in question.

The striking all-black model was so rare, there were only three in existence. Quad-turbo 8.0-liter W16 engine, six exhaust tips, seven-speed dual-clutch transmission, custom headlights—it was a thing of beauty.

I ran a loving hand over the hood before I climbed in and switched on the ignition. The powerful growl of the engine roared to life, and an electric thrill zipped down my spine.

Besides football, driving was the only thing that truly made me feel alive. In the dead of night, when the streets were quieter and the music was blasting, I could clear my head and *think*.

For the next few hours, that was exactly what I did as I pulled out of the garage and took my new car out for a spin.

However, instead of vibing to the music and brainstorming strategies for the next season, my mind kept conjuring images of dark hair and gray eyes.

I shoved them aside.

They came back.

Jesus.

I rubbed a hand over my face and tried to steer my thoughts

toward something, anything, other than a certain ex-ballerina.

Focus on the Sports UK *interview. What questions will they ask?*

Definitely something about my first season with Blackcastle, how I felt losing to my old team, and maybe my summer training regimen.

Summer.

Training.

Scarlett.

My groan of frustration cut through the music. *Why* did everything route back to her? We met a month ago, and I still couldn't pinpoint why she had such a hold on me.

Was it because she was beautiful? I'd met plenty of beautiful women, including movie stars, supermodels, and two Miss Universes. I hadn't given them more than a passing thought.

Because she was witty and talented? They were great qualities to have, but they weren't enough to explain why she haunted me the way she did.

Because she was off limits and seemingly uninterested in me? I liked a challenge, but her connection to Vincent was a detractor more than anything else.

So if it wasn't any of those things that drew me to her, what the hell was it?

My frown deepened.

I needed to decipher the source of her magic so I could negate it and refocus on what was important—my game. A summer distraction was all well and good, but I couldn't afford a wandering mind after the next season started.

Since I transferred mid-season this year, I technically had some leeway when it came to our performance, but if I screwed up my first *full* season with Blackcastle, there'd be no going back. It would always be a black mark on my record.

I turned up the music and entered central London. I passed the illuminated buildings of Parliament Square and Buckingham Palace before I eventually found myself in the bowels of the West End.

I tapped my fingers against the center console.

Scarlett had gone on a date here two nights ago. I hadn't asked for details because I didn't *care*, necessarily, but what if she got so distracted with her beau that it affected her work in the studio?

The question unleashed an onslaught of new ones.

Who'd been her date? How did she meet him? Was he an athlete, accountant, or shit, I didn't know, an aerospace engineer or something?

She won't date a footballer again. Vincent's declaration echoed through my head. I hadn't figured out her ex's identity yet, though admittedly I hadn't dug that hard. It was best if I didn't wade too deep into her love life.

Unfortunately, that resolution didn't stop the questions about her mystery date.

Had Friday night been their first date, or had they been seeing each other for a while? Had they kissed? Gone back to one of their places after the show?

A quick burst of discomfort jolted up my arm. When I looked down, my knuckles had whitened around the wheel.

I immediately loosened my grip, but an unpleasant sensation continued to slither through my veins.

The Bugatti drew plenty of stares, but as the hour wore on, the streets gradually emptied. Billboards and lights gave way to brick and concrete; the bustle of central London quieted into a residential calm.

A familiar pastel building loomed in the distance, and I almost slammed on the brakes when I realized where I was.

I had somehow, unthinkingly, unintentionally driven to Scarlett's flat.

Way to go. That's not creepy or anything.

I didn't linger. I already felt like a stalker, and my car was too distinctive to escape notice should she happen to wake up and look outside her window.

Nevertheless, a small part of me wondered what would happen if I cut the engine, walked up to her flat, and knocked on the door.

Nothing will happen because you're both smarter than that, and she is Off Limits. Capital O, capital L.

I'd reminded myself of that so often I never wanted to hear the term "off limits" again, but I'd still repeat it a thousand times until it sank in.

If Vincent and I had issues now, they were nothing compared to the war that'd break out if I got involved with Scarlett. Coach would lose his shit, and I could kiss my my chances of winning the league and possibly my spot on the team goodbye.

No girl was worth giving up my career for.

I tore my eyes away from her building and drove home, letting the music drown out any thoughts to the contrary.

CHAPTER 10

SCARLETT

I HATED TO ADMIT IT, BUT MOVING OUR TRAINING TO Asher's house was a genius idea. The facilities were better, there was more privacy, and I didn't have to take the hot, jam-packed tube home every day.

The armored car did ease my anxieties, and Earl was an excellent driver. By our third day together, I was comfortable enough to release my death grip on my seat.

That was also the day Asher and I experimented with outdoor drills for the first time. We trained in the open-air gym for a while before he offered to show me the grounds during our break.

I'd agreed, thinking it would be a quick walk. I was wrong.

I knew his estate was big, but I hadn't realized how *massive* it truly was until we reached the southwest corner.

"You built a football pitch in your back garden?" I stared at the sea of perfectly cut grass. White lines marked the most important playing areas, and nets anchored both ends of the pitch. "That's *mad*."

"It's not an official pitch." Asher lifted his shirt to wipe the sweat off his face. "It's a mini pitch."

"A pitch is a pitch." I kept my eyes glued to his backyard and *not* on the flash of chiseled abs and tanned skin.

Admittedly, calling this place a back garden was like calling Versailles a house. Besides the football pitch—sorry, *mini* pitch—it boasted an Olympic-size pool with a waterfall and attached Jacuzzi, heated cabanas, two clay tennis courts, a wisteria walkway, and an outdoor dining area.

I couldn't imagine how much Asher shelled out for landscaping every year; the flowers alone must've cost tens of thousands of pounds.

"Fair enough. You play?" Asher grabbed a football from the ground and tossed it lazily in the air. He caught it with his toe, flipped it to one knee, and bounced it to his other knee.

"No." I grabbed the ball, halting his impromptu show. "Show-off."

His eyes gleamed with laughter. "Not even a little? You must've kicked a ball around once or twice."

"Kicking a ball around isn't the same as playing."

"Let's see." He snatched the ball back and dribbled it onto the pitch. "First person to score a goal wins bragging rights and a pint of ice cream."

"That's stupid. There's no goalkeeper!" I yelled. Unguarded football nets were so large a toddler could score if they got close enough, which meant the challenge was retaining possession of the ball and, well, getting close enough.

Asher's laughter drifted across the pitch.

Oh, screw it. My competitive drive kicked into high gear, and I sprinted after him.

My muscles protested immediately. I'd avoided high-impact activities like running since my accident, but I gritted my teeth and focused on the satisfaction of scoring on Asher.

I caught up to him surprisingly fast. I suspected he'd held back for my sake. Even so, it was frustratingly difficult to steal the ball from him. I succeeded twice, but he stole it back almost as quickly as he lost it.

"You're better than you let on." He wasn't even breathing hard, the bastard. "Come on. Put that fancy footwork of yours to the test."

I issued a little growl that earned me another laugh. Then we were off again, and my mind blacked out everything except for the need to score.

I may have been better than I let on, but there was a reason Asher was the top-paid footballer in the world. Playing against him, even in an unserious two-person match, was like pitting David against Goliath (if David lost). Nothing could've prepared me for it.

I'd watched him play before, of course. There wasn't a single person in the UK who didn't remember his legendary halfway line goal against Liverpool or his spectacular header in the quarter-finals of the last World Cup.

Asher was incredible onscreen, but up close, in person? He was magic.

He matched me turn for turn, feint for feint. He intuited what I'd do before I did it, and he was barely trying.

Sweat poured down my face and neck, but sheer stubbornness held me together.

One goal. I just needed one goal.

A wheezing cough rattled my lungs. I should've warmed up or drank more water before I came out here.

Asher slowed, concern sliding over his face. I took the opportunity and attempted a steal. To my shock, it worked.

However, my triumph was short-lived. Asher reacted so fast, he almost regained possession immediately, but I wasn't letting go that easily this time.

Back and forth, left and right. Somewhere during our tussle, our legs tangled.

I hit the grass with jarring force, and I didn't have time to move before Asher fell too. He braced himself against the ground so he didn't totally crush me, but he was still there—right on top of me.

We froze in simultaneous shock. If someone were to come across us at that moment, I imagined we'd pass for stone statues in Medusa's garden, entangled and unmoving.

My heart rate slowed to a crawl. Despite his braced position, his body pressed against mine enough for me to feel every ridge and plane.

All that muscle pinning me to the ground *should've* been uncomfortable. Instead, it was oddly comforting, like a shield against the outside world.

An extremely well-toned, sculpted shield.

I tried and failed to swallow past the dryness in my throat. *I really should've drank more water earlier.*

My tongue darted out, wetting my lips unconsciously. Asher's eyes dipped to my mouth, and the remaining oxygen in the air snuffed out with a near audible puff.

Move. Breathe. Push him off. Do something.

My brain fired commands at me, and I didn't heed a single one. I couldn't. I was stuck, trapped by the heat of his body and the soft rise and fall of his chest against mine.

I was tingling all over. Either my muscles were shutting down from overexertion or it was an involuntary reaction to Asher's proximity. Or both. Either way, the stutter in my chest when his gaze drifted up and met mine again couldn't be healthy.

Did he always have those golden flecks in his eyes? They were absurdly beautiful, like splashes of sunlight on a verdant hill.

A hint of aftershave and sweat teased my nostrils. Instead of smelling gross, it smelled earthy and masculine and utterly addicting.

Leave it to Asher Donovan to make sweating sexy.

His chin lowered. If I tilted mine up, we would—

The soft but distinct whirr of a shutter snapping smashed into the moment with the grace of a wrecking ball.

Our heads jerked toward the sound, and my jaw dropped when I saw a man peeking out at us from over the greenery.

"What the *fuck*?"

Asher's outburst mirrored my feelings exactly. The cameraman had somehow *climbed over* the twelve-foot-hedge bordering the grounds and was capturing our interaction with a super zoom lens.

Now that he'd been spotted, he didn't waste time. He lowered his camera, tucked tail, and ran right as Asher pushed off me and bolted after him.

After a beat, I followed suit.

Our impromptu football match earlier (if one could call it that) had sucked away most of my energy. My entire body ached, especially my legs, which burned with each step. A fresh surge of adrenaline was the only thing propping me up.

Luckily, there was a shortcut through the hedges to the driveway, so I didn't have to traverse the entire mansion.

By the time I turned the corner, Asher had already caught and restrained the pap by pinning his arms behind his back. A fancy Nikon lay in several pieces next to them.

"You broke my camera!" the man howled. His bulbous nose reddened. "That's an eight-thousand-pound lens!"

"Your lens?" Asher twisted his arms harder, and the man let out a pained yelp. "You trespassed on *my* property. Took photos of us during *my* personal time." His eyes glittered like emerald knives. "I put up with your bullshit when I'm in public, but make no mistake. If I ever catch you *anywhere* near either of us again, I'll break more than your camera. Understand?"

The man's mouth flattened into a mulish line.

I didn't recognize him. He wasn't one of the regulars who'd hung around RAB when we trained there, and the ease with which Asher caught him suggested he was new to the job. If so, he'd made a terrible new enemy.

"I said, do you understand?" Asher twisted his arms again, and the man's stubbornness dissolved into a pathetic cry.

"*Yes.*"

"Good. Now get the fuck off my property before I change my mind."

"I can't believe you caught him," I said once the pap left. He must've had at least a minute head start on Asher. "And I can't believe you broke his camera."

"He got off easy with the broken camera." The cords in Asher's neck bunched with tension.

I'd never seen him so furious. I didn't know it was possible for him to *be* furious. He was always so good-natured, but right now, with his body coiled and his face creased in a scowl, he was the picture of pure, unadulterated anger.

However, with the pap gone and air quiet once more, the anger slowly drained, leaving visible frustration behind.

"I need to upgrade my security." Asher rubbed a hand over his face. He sounded tired, and a needle of sympathy pierced my gut. "I didn't want to turn this place into a bloody surveillance state, but I can't have people sneaking in like that. If we hadn't caught him in time..."

A chill rippled over my skin. In one month, we'd had two close calls with the paparazzi. How long until our luck ran out?

"How did he get in?"

Breaking onto school grounds was one thing; breaking onto someone's private property was another.

"My landscaping crew was in and out while we were training. He must've slipped in with them." Asher's jaw clenched. "People like him are fucking vultures, sniffing around for any scraps they can find."

The needle of sympathy dug deeper. "Being in the public eye like that must be awful."

Vincent dealt with the same thing to a certain degree, but no athlete sold headlines like Asher. The scrutiny and invasions of privacy he faced were on another level.

"I could handle it if they were just coming after me. I know what I signed up for," Asher said. "But you're getting caught up in this mess, and that's not fucking okay."

His words pulsed in my veins, filling them with uncomfortable warmth. "Oh. I..." I stumbled for a second before I regained my composure. "You don't have to worry about me. I'm a big girl. I can handle an out-of-shape pap."

That brought forth a small curve in his lips. "Says the person panting like she just ran a marathon."

"Give me a break. It's been years since I ran like that." My jelly-like legs confirmed my long break with cardio.

The hint of a smile vanished. "Shit. I forgot how high-impact running is. It's not good for chronic pain, is it?"

The warmth in my veins melted into honey. Hell, *everything* melted. At this rate, they'd have to scrape me off the driveway with a spatula. "You looked up chronic pain?"

A wash of dull red colored Asher's cheekbones. "Out of curiosity, that's all," he said. "I didn't know much about it, so I figured I should learn the basics. Obviously."

"Obviously."

Was it normal for a human heart to beat this fast? I had my annual checkup a few weeks ago. The doctor said everything looked normal, but maybe I needed a second opinion because *something* strange was going on inside my chest.

Asher's eyes flickered with an array of emotions I couldn't decipher. "Do you want to take a bath?"

The abrupt switch in subjects was so absurd, it jolted me back into normality. "Excuse me?"

"A bath. For inflammation. I take one after a particularly intense workout. It helps with recovery."

"Inflammation. Right." *Of course he wasn't asking if you wanted to take a bath with him, idiot.* "It's okay. I can take one at home."

Except a bath *did* sound wonderful, and home was at least an hour away if I factored in afternoon traffic.

The remaining adrenaline drained from my limbs. I wanted to lie down on the driveway and let the sunbaked stone take away my soreness.

"Are you sure? I have a million guest baths. It's not a big deal." Asher's frown suggested he'd picked up on my dip in energy. "Traffic is a nightmare at this time of day. If you're not feeling well, I don't want things getting worse while you're stuck in Piccadilly."

No. It would be too weird for me to take a bath at a trainee's house, especially when said trainee was Asher Donovan.

I should absolutely, positively, 100 percent *not* accept his offer.

Except I was so tired, and my body hurt, and if I didn't sit down right now, I might pass out for the second time in front of him and wouldn't *that* be embarrassing?

"I..." *Don't do it. Suck it up. Wait until you're home.* "Okay. If you don't mind."

CHAPTER 11

SCARLETT

THIS WAS THE BEST WORST DECISION OF MY LIFE.

I sank deeper into the marble tub, certain the water here contained some sort of magic. Warm baths always soothed my pain, but the ones at home never worked this quickly or effectively.

I'd only been in here for—I checked my phone—seven minutes, and I already felt like a new person.

Maybe Asher imported his bathwater directly from a secret French mountain village and had it blessed by virgin nuns before he allowed it to pour out of the faucets. Or maybe his Epsom salts were higher quality than mine.

Whatever it was, I wasn't complaining.

I leaned my head against the cushioned headrest and closed my eyes. The water jets, the classical music piping through hidden speakers, the scent of lavender and chamomile…my flat's dinky little tub and the screams from the on-again, off-again couple next door seemed worlds away.

I didn't care if bathing in Asher's house was weird. I could stay in this tub forever.

Scarlett DuBois: the woman who sold her convictions for Epsom salts and a Jacuzzi bathtub.

Damn right I did. And it was worth it.

The only downside to my current situation was the lack of distractions. No distractions meant more time to think. More time to think meant my thoughts inevitably drifted toward a certain footballer. Trying to rein them in was like a novice trying to rein in a wild stallion—useless.

You looked up chronic pain?

Out of curiosity, that's all.

Tiny wings fluttered to life again throughout my body.

How sad was it that Asher had done more for me in one month than my now-ex-boyfriend did in the year following my accident?

Pretty damn sad.

I stayed in the tub until the water ran cold. Afterward, I tossed on a fluffy guest robe and slippers and padded into the hallway. Asher had offered to run my grass-stained clothes through the laundry while I was in the bath, so I just needed to grab them before I left.

It was getting late, and I'd already overstayed my welcome.

Nevertheless, I took my time wandering through the private wing of his house. I didn't want to snoop, but I was fascinated by the little peeks into Asher's personal life.

I paused by the wall of photos outside the primary suite (the cracked-open door revealed enough personal effects to mark it as his bedroom and not a guest room). The photos were arranged in chronological order, documenting his life from adorable baby to adult superstardom.

My lips curved at a picture of toddler Asher wearing a birthday hat and a chocolate-smudged grin. A few frames down, a slightly older version of him sported a Holchester United kit and the same (albeit sans chocolate) grin. A stern-looking older man stood next to him with one hand on his shoulder. He must've been Asher's father—they shared the exact same eyes and bone structure.

"My fifth birthday." Asher's voice pulled my attention away from the adorable photos. He walked out of his bedroom and nodded at the gallery. "My father gifted me my first Holchester kit, and I was so excited I put it on straight away. We ended up playing football the rest of the afternoon, much to my mother's exasperation."

Heat curled around my neck and ears. "I'm sorry. I didn't mean to be nosy."

"It's fine. If I didn't want people seeing the pictures, I wouldn't have put them out here." Asher shrugged. He must've taken a shower while I was bathing. His hair was damp, and he'd changed out of his workout clothes into a gray T-shirt and shorts.

"They're cute pictures. I assume your father is a big Holchester fan?"

"Die hard," he confirmed. "I grew up in Holchester, and he took me to every home match when I was a kid. Some away matches too. When I signed with them, he was over the moon. Even forgave me for my stint with Man U before that."

"And Blackcastle? How does he feel about that?" I asked. Holchester fans didn't like Man U, but Blackcastle was even worse. They were Holchester's number-one rival.

"Less thrilled." Asher's tone verged on matter-of-fact, but the shuttering of his expression suggested there was more to the story.

I swallowed my curiosity. If he wanted to elaborate, he would.

Instead, I pivoted to another question that'd been nagging at me for a while. "Why did you transfer? You were doing so well at Holchester."

"Two hundred fifty million pounds is a lot of money."

"It is, but I don't think that's the only reason."

"Why not?"

"You don't strike me as someone who'd do something solely for a paycheck." For all his flash and show, Asher possessed an honest, tangible reverence for the sport. It came through in his training, his interviews, his collection of mementos featuring other football greats, not just himself.

Players like that didn't make huge decisions based on money alone. Besides, he'd already been mind-bogglingly rich before the transfer.

A small smile touched his face. "A DuBois saying something nice about my character? Someone check the temperature in hell."

"I'm not my brother." I'd been biased against Asher for reasons that had nothing to do with Vincent, but the more time we spent together, the harder it was to hold on to that initial animosity.

"No." Asher's gaze held mine for a fraction longer than was customary. "You're definitely not."

His words floated softly between us. My skin buzzed to life, and I was suddenly hyperaware of the fact that we'd been naked in the same house—*his* house—less than an hour ago. Me in my bath, him in his shower.

That shouldn't feel so intimate. But it did.

Asher's mouth parted. Anticipation ricocheted through my chest, but before he could speak, a boom of thunder rocked the house. The unmistakable sound of pouring rain followed, drawing my attention to the window at the end of the hall.

I'd been so caught up in this—whatever *this* was—that I hadn't noticed the shift from beautiful summer afternoon to sudden downpour.

"Shit," Asher said. Our earlier moment was gone, shattered by the distraction and our gradual return to our senses. At least, that applied to me; I had no idea what he was thinking. "We should get you home before the rain gets worse. I'll call Earl and check on your laundry. It should be done."

I'd forgotten I was only wearing a bathrobe.

My cheeks flamed. Nevertheless, I followed him to the laundry room, where my clothes were still spinning in the dryer.

"Four minutes left," Asher reported. He appeared to be avoiding my eyes, though that might be my paranoia talking. "Not too long. We'll have you out of here in no—"

A shrill alert emanated from both our phones.

Interruptions seem to be the theme of the day. First the pap, then the thunder, now this.

However, my annoyance soon morphed into alarm when I read the accompanying emergency text.

> A flash flood warning is in effect for this area until 8:00 a.m. BST. This is a dangerous and life-threatening situation. Do not attempt to travel unless you are fleeing an area subject to flooding or under an evacuation order.

8:00 a.m. BST. That was tomorrow *morning*, which meant...

Asher and I lifted our heads and stared at each other in horror.

Which meant I was stuck here for the night.

CHAPTER 12

ASHER

THIS WAS A NIGHTMARE.

The Met Office had warned of possible severe thunderstorms today, but the morning and afternoon had been so beautiful, I'd dismissed their concerns.

Now, all of a sudden, I was trapped with the one person I didn't want—or *shouldn't* want—to spend the night with.

I glanced at Scarlett, who'd finally changed out of her bathrobe and into her freshly dried clothes.

Thank God. The robe had been distracting, to say the least, which was irritating because it'd been *my* bloody guest robe.

Note to self: Buy more full-coverage robes in case of similar future occurrences. Preferably full-length with a turtleneck and so many layers you can't tell if it's a human body or a concrete block under there.

Certainly nothing that revealed endless dancer's legs or a shadow of cleavage. Nothing that exposed miles of smooth skin or tempted the imagination.

"Absolutely not. I refuse," she said, crossing her arms. "Anything but that."

My pulse leapt before I realized she was talking about my movie choice and not the traitorous thoughts she'd somehow divined from my face.

"It's a movie. It's not real." I tossed out a teasing smile to mask the balloon of relief in my chest.

It'd been hours since we received the emergency weather alert, and the storm showed no signs of abating. For lack of anything better to do, we'd settled in the theatre with popcorn and an agreement to alternate movie choices.

Scarlett chose the first film, a heist comedy about sorority sisters who had to steal a rare diamond necklace after getting caught up with a Vegas mob boss. It wasn't to my usual taste, but I hadn't complained, and the movie had turned out to be pretty good.

It seemed a bit unfair, then, for her to renege on her part of the deal.

"It's a horror movie," she said. "I don't watch horror."

"Too scared?"

"As a matter of fact, yes. Horror movies give me nightmares, and unless you want me screaming the house down at three in the morning, I recommend we switch to literally any other genre."

"Oh, come on. It's not that bad. This isn't even the original Japanese version."

Japanese versions were always ten times scarier than their American counterparts. It was a universal fact.

"I couldn't even handle *Scream*, and that was satire." Scarlett grimaced. "No, thank you. Pick another movie, please."

"That's not part of our deal."

"Pretty please?"

"Don't bat your lashes at me. It's not going to work." I cocked an eyebrow. "Come on. What happened to facing your fears and overcoming them?"

"I never said I would do that. I'm perfectly happy locking my fears in the closet and pretending they don't exist."

"Ah, denial. The best way to go through life."

"Slap it on a T-shirt and call me Egypt."

Laughter burst from my chest at her unexpected pun. I'd heard it before, but it was better coming from her.

Everything was better coming from her.

Her knee grazed mine as she shifted in her seat. My smile vanished, and it took all my willpower not to jerk my leg away.

I'd done a decent job of keeping things professional the past few weeks (minus my unplanned detour to her place on Sunday). The occasional flirtatious remark slipped out here or there, but they were harmless.

However, it was easier to stay professional when we were in the studio. It was a hell of a lot harder when we were sitting next to each other in a dark, private theatre.

Every time we moved, we risked brushing against each other. The anticipation of those light touches was more stressful than the jump scares in a horror film. Plus, the faint coconut scent of her shampoo— *my* guest shampoo—lingered hours later. It made me want to bury my face and hands in her hair, which would be deeply *un*professional.

Second note to self: Restock guest toiletries with unscented products. Or better yet, with Lynx. My father had worn Lynx exclusively since I was born, and it was the ultimate attraction killer.

Who wanted to kiss someone that smelled like their dad? No one.

"Let's make a deal," I said. "You watch this with me, and I'll forfeit the rest of my choices for the night. We can watch as many heist comedies as you want."

"Nice try. By the time it's over, it'll be time for bed." Scarlett shook her head. "No deal."

Dammit. I was hoping she'd overlook that.

"Fine. I'll fetch you pistachio ice cream from the kitchen."

"You don't have pistachio ice cream. I checked."

"When did you…? Never mind." I mentally flipped through my other options. "Okay. If you watch the *entire* movie with me tonight, I'll give you a pass for a future favor. Any favor you want." I held out my hand. "Pinky promise."

Scarlett rolled her eyes. "What are we, eight?"

But she was thinking about it. I could tell by the furrow between her brows as she looked up to the left.

Left meant she was pondering something. Right meant she was lying.

It was alarming how well I could read her after only a month.

"Any favor?"

I held back a triumphant grin. "Any favor as long as it's not illegal." I paused. "Well, depending on the activity, I could be persuaded even if it is illegal."

"Good to know your morals, Donovan." Scarlett tapped her fingers against the armrest before she hooked her pinky around mine. "You have a deal."

Whatever favor I'd have to grant in the future was worth it for the sheer entertainment value of seeing her overreact to every tiny thing for the next ninety-five minutes.

"Oh my God." Scarlett peeked out from between her fingers, her eyes huge. Onscreen, the scared-but-determined-looking housewife inched upstairs, the wood creaking menacingly beneath her feet. "*Why* is she going to the attic? It makes no sense! If I heard strange noises coming from my house, the last thing I'd do is investigate alone."

"Maybe she's braver than you."

"You mean stupider."

"Every brave act is stupid until it succeeds."

"You—*aaah*!"

The scene's ominous soundtrack crescendoed. Scarlett screamed and dove for me, burying her face in my shoulder and clutching my arm so hard I swore my circulation cut off.

"What happened? Did she die? *What's going on?*"

Her muffled panic was drowned out by my laughter. I couldn't help it. Scarlett was usually so reserved and put together that seeing her lose it over a cheesy horror film was almost better than winning a match.

Almost.

Once the music calmed and it turned out there was nothing in the attic except for a creepy old chest, Scarlett lifted her head to glare at me.

"Stop laughing."

"Your scream," I choked out, my shoulders shaking. "I should've recorded it. Priceless."

She shoved my arm in retaliation, but I barely felt it. Apparently, amusement was the greatest insulator against pain.

"You're a terrible host," she huffed. "Polite hosts don't— *aaahhhhhh*!"

This time, there *was* a jump scare onscreen. Scarlett shoved her face into my shoulder again, and my laughter escalated into full-blown guffaws.

She spent the remainder of the movie attached to my side, peeking out occasionally when the sounds were calm and using my torso as a shield when they weren't.

"This does not count as watching the movie," I said. "You might as well be listening to an audiobook instead."

Despite my words, I didn't mind. Her hands were warm against my skin, and I liked the way she curled into me.

"Is it over?" she asked when the closing credits started rolling.

"Yes, you coward. You can come out from your hiding spot now. And by hiding spot, I mean the area between the seat and my back."

Scarlett detached herself from me with great dignity, or as much dignity as one could muster with tousled hair and red cheeks.

"Great." She straightened her top, the picture of prim elegance once more. "Tell anyone about this, and I will…"

"Scream some more?" I grinned. At this point, I was immune to her glares. "You weren't kidding when you said you were a wuss when it comes to horror. I assume you've never performed in any spooky ballets."

"Actually, I performed in *The Cage* for a season, but that's different."

I had no clue what *The Cage* was, but it sounded appropriately unsettling.

"What was your favorite ballet?" I asked.

It was late, the movie was over, and we *should* be heading to bed—separately. That would be the smart thing to do.

Unfortunately, my decisions and *smart* didn't belong in the same sentence where Scarlett was concerned. My brain screamed at me to leave before I did something stupid, but I wasn't ready to say good night yet.

Besides, it wasn't like I was grabbing her and kissing her. I was engaging her in friendly conversation. What could it hurt?

"Favorite ballet." A furrow dug between her brows again. "That's hard. For choreography, probably *Petite Mort*. For a classic, *Giselle*.

That was the first show my mother took me to, so I guess there's sentimental value."

"Did you know you wanted to dance professionally since you were young?"

"Yeah." Scarlett's face softened. "My mother put me in pre-ballet classes when I was four. Some of my classmates were only there because they were forced to be there, but I looked forward to the lessons every week. It was…I don't know. It was nice being part of something so structured. I get anxious when there's too much uncertainty. Also…" A small smile peeked out. "The costumes were pretty."

That smile shouldn't have snuck through me the way it did, like a burglar breaking into a vault at night.

Dangerous, a voice whispered. *Stay away*.

"I was good at it too, which helped. I think I have too much pride to love something that doesn't love me back." Scarlett let out a small laugh.

If her smile was a burglar, her laugh was a fucking thief because I was pretty sure she just stole a piece of my heart from right out under me.

Stop being dramatic. No one stole anything. It's a laugh. Get over it.

Except it wasn't just her laugh. This was the first time she'd opened up to me. Sure, her childhood dance lessons weren't exactly deep, dark secrets, but they were *something*.

She was letting her guard down, and I'd be damned if I did anything to ruin that.

"What about you?" she asked. "When did you know you wanted to be a footballer?"

"Probably around the same time you knew you wanted to be a ballerina." I settled deeper into my seat. "I told you earlier my father bought me my first Holchester kit when I was five, but he'd been prepping me since I was in the womb. My mother said that instead of music, he'd play his favorite post-match analyses for me. I think he hoped Fetus Me would soak up all that strategy and pop out ready for the Premier League."

Scarlett laughed again. "Your mother must've loved that."

"Oh, she let him get away with it for a week before she threatened to toss all his Holchester memorabilia if he so much as uttered the word 'football' near her again during the pregnancy." I smiled, imagining my mother's ire and my father's protests. "He wasn't stupid enough to call her bluff, but the minute I was old enough to kick a ball, that was it. My future was set."

That was hyperbole, to an extent. No one could guarantee a career in professional football. There'd been aspiring players who'd worked equally as hard but never made it close to the big leagues. Luck and timing mattered.

I'd benefited from both. Teddy hadn't.

A rock lodged in my throat. I forced myself to swallow past it. Now wasn't the time to dwell on the past.

"What would you want to be if you hadn't gone into football?" Scarlett asked, unknowingly throwing me a lifeline before I drowned in a sea of *what-ifs*.

"I have no idea," I said. "Football is the only thing I've ever been good at."

I'd hated school. I'd spent my classes daydreaming about football, which was probably why my grades had been abysmal. My teachers hadn't known what to do with me. Most eventually gave up, and some had outright laughed when I said I'd be the next Beckham or Armstrong.

I'd proved them wrong, but a small part of me had held on to their words. Their dismissals had etched deep into my psyche, fueling me with spite but also agonizing me with fears that they'd been telling the truth.

That I was where I was merely because I'd gotten lucky, and that the luck could be snatched from me at any second.

"Maybe I'd be a race car driver," I said as an afterthought. "Or another sport."

It was a lie. There *was* no other sport. There was only football. However, that was too sad to admit, so I made something up.

"Barring that, I'd go off the rails with something wild, like a dog surfing instructor or professional cuddler or something."

"Professional cuddler is not a thing."

"It most definitely is. Google it." I waved my phone in the air. "Not to brag, but I'm great at cuddling. I can demonstrate."

Scarlett rolled her eyes, but a small smile peeked through. "No, thanks. I'll take your word for it."

We lapsed into a comfortable silence. It seemed Scarlett wanted to stay as much as I did, despite the yawns she tried to hide.

Guilt pressed on my shoulders. I shouldn't have pushed her to play earlier. I'd read that intense exercise could aggravate chronic pain symptoms, but the weather had been so beautiful, and I hadn't been thinking. I'd enjoyed seeing her let loose too much, and she moved with a dancer's grace that was apparent even to an untrained eye.

"Would you want to dance again?" I asked. "If you had the opportunity."

Scarlett stilled for a second before she shook her head. "It doesn't matter what I want," she said, her face devoid of emotion. "I *can't*. I've had surgeries, physical therapy, you name it. I'm much better now, but I lost a lot of mobility and flexibility because of my hip injuries. I'll never perform at the level I used to."

"But you miss dancing," I said gently.

There was a long pause before she answered. "Yeah." The word contained a world of wistfulness. "I do."

An answering ball of emotion knotted in my chest. I couldn't imagine waking up one day and losing the ability to play football. The end of her career was all the more devastating because it'd been so unexpected. I'd looked up the accident after she told me about it. She'd been on her way to a performance when the other car hit them.

The universe could be fucking cruel, and I hated seeing the sadness in her eyes.

"Not all dances have to be at the Royal Opera House or Westbury." I thought I saw her flinch at the mention of Westbury, but I might've imagined it. "Can you do it for fun instead? Maybe there are roles that are less physically taxing."

"I don't know. I haven't tried." Scarlett's curt response suggested she wanted to end the conversation as soon as possible.

I didn't want to push her too far, nor did I want to judge, but I couldn't stop a jolt of shock at the fact that she hadn't tried to dance since her accident.

I would've understood if she'd left that world behind, but she was still teaching ballet and she said herself that she missed it.

"The RAB staff showcase seems like a good opportunity to try." I broached the subject with caution. "Low stakes, familiar audience."

"No."

One word. That was all it took for the gates to slam down.

Scarlett's face closed, her eyes shuttering and her mouth flattening into a stubborn line. The openness that had brightened our conversation earlier dimmed, leaving an awkward tension in its wake.

Her reasons for not participating were none of my business (even though I hadn't bought the "I'm too busy" excuse she gave me when

I'd first asked her about it. Everyone at RAB was busy). The aftermath of her accident was a rightfully sensitive subject; if I were in her shoes, I'd be livid at me for prying.

Nevertheless, the longing in her eyes when I'd mentioned dancing again had imprinted itself on my consciousness, and I couldn't let it go.

I'm perfectly happy locking my fears in the closet and pretending they don't exist.

"What are you afraid of, Scarlett?" The question slipped out, quiet yet filled with certainty.

Her physical limitations weren't her biggest obstacles; her fears were.

I'd known someone who'd let his fears control him. I couldn't get through to him, and he took those fears to his grave.

There were nights when I'd lie awake and wonder what would've happened had I pushed him more. Tried harder instead of being caught up in the dreams of my own success. Would it have made a difference? Would he still be alive?

Those regrets kept me from backing down even as Scarlett turned rigid.

I didn't care if she was livid with me. I'd let someone I cared about down once; I wasn't going to do it again.

Scarlett wasn't my best friend, girlfriend, or family, but I didn't need a label to know that I *did* care about her.

I'd expected her to lash out after my question. Instead, the stoniness slowly fizzled from her face, and her shoulders sagged with a resigned sigh.

"The last time I performed, I was in my prime," she said. "The next great prima ballerina. That was what the press called me. I opened *Swan Lake* at the Westbury and killed it. Standing ovation, rave reviews. But I'm not that dancer anymore, and I want people to remember me as I was. Healthy. Talented." Her voice cracked on the next word. "Whole."

"Bullshit." My response cracked like a whip through the air.

Scarlett startled, her face creasing with equal parts shock and affront.

"You're not broken, so don't give me that 'whole' BS," I said. "And I bet you can still run circles around the majority of the general population when it comes to ballet, so don't try to feed me that untalented line either." I paused, replaying my words. "Okay, maybe 'run' wasn't the right verb to use, but you know what I mean."

The faintest curve touched her lips.

"The point is, your injuries don't define who you are. Maybe you're not the same dancer anymore, but who says you have to be? Growth isn't always linear, and I've seen you in the studio. I think you're still pretty damn incredible."

Scarlett's mouth parted. She stared at me, her eyes wide, as my mini motivational speech settled between us.

I wasn't a big speech person, but I had to get that out there. Sometimes, we needed someone else to point out what was right in front of us.

"Where the hell did that come from?" she asked. There was an odd note in her voice, but I couldn't pinpoint what it was.

"It's the truth. I didn't have to look too hard for it."

Scarlett closed her mouth, opened it, then closed it again. A full minute passed before she spoke. "What if I flop? It's been five years. I'm out of practice, and I've never performed *Lorena* before. I know a staff showcase isn't the same as a Royal Opera ballet, but those are my colleagues. My students. If I screw up, I'll have to face them every day afterward, and I don't know if I can do it."

By the time she finished, her words were nearly inaudible.

A raw, unfamiliar ache settled in my chest. I hated how despondent she looked, but I understood how she felt.

Ballet, football. Both careers that came with preset expiration dates.

We weren't like writers or lawyers who could theoretically keep their job until they died. We entered our fields knowing that one day, no matter how hard we tried, our bodies would simply be incapable of performing at the level necessary to sustain our dreams.

Our careers burned brief yet bright, and they were subject to the whims of the universe—one accident, one stroke of bad luck could end everything earlier than we'd expected.

I recognized it; Scarlett had lived it.

So maybe I was stepping over the line with what I had to say next, but I wouldn't be a friend if I didn't point it out—and I did consider her a friend, even if that sentiment wasn't reciprocated.

"I think you're capable of more than you give yourself credit for," I said. "But at the end of the day, you have to ask yourself what you'd regret more—trying and failing, or not trying at all?"

CHAPTER 13

SCARLETT

THE STORM CONTINUED TO RAGE OUTSIDE. RAIN pounded against the windows, and flashes of lightning chased away the shadows on the ceilings every other minute.

It was a white-noise dream. People paid for this kind of bedtime ambiance, yet I couldn't sleep a wink.

Instead, I'd been lying in bed for two hours, replaying the day's events on an endless loop.

The weight of Asher's body on mine.

The chase for the pap.

The moment we realized I'd have to stay the night.

And most of all, our conversation in the theatre, which had unearthed insecurities that I would rather have kept buried.

I hadn't meant to unload them on Asher. I'd always kept my deepest (and shallowest) fears locked inside me, hidden from even Vincent and Carina. Because what was more shallow than refusing to step onstage in case I looked like a fool, like a has-been desperately clinging to her former glory?

Yet there was something about Asher that made me *want* to confide in him. He'd listened without a trace of judgment, and as an athlete, he probably understood my dilemma as much as any non-dancer could.

I should be angrier about him pushing me so hard, but maybe he was right. Was trying and failing better than not trying at all? Twenty, forty, sixty years from now, would I regret not reaching for a second chance when I could?

Ugh. Late-night existential crises were the worst.

I closed my eyes, listening to the claps of thunder roll through the room. My body was exhausted after the day's exertion, but my mind was wide awake.

Asher had placed me down the hall, as far from his room as possible, despite the many empty guest suites between us.

I didn't know whether to be relieved or insulted. Did he think I was going to break into his room and ravish him or something? Either that, or he was worried about what *he'd* do if I was too close.

Orrrr...hear me out...maybe it was a random assignment and you're overthinking things. Not everything is about you, Scarlett.

Fine. My inner consciousness got me there. Thinking Asher Donovan was so attracted to me, he'd lose control if we slept across the hall from each other was the height of arrogance.

Still, an ember of heat flickered to life at the mental image of him in bed. Was he awake? If so, what was he thinking about? Did he sleep in boxers or a T-shirt and sweats or nothing at all?

I groaned and buried my face in the pillow. Why was I suddenly picturing him naked? What was *wrong* with me?

I attempted to focus on something else. Unfortunately, the only other thing grabbing my attention was how hungry I was.

My stomach growled in resentment.

"Shut up."

The second growl overpowered the thunder. Clearly, my muffled command had only served to antagonize the hunger monsters more.

Oh, screw it.

I tossed my covers to the side and tiptoed into the hall.

It was almost three o'clock, the devil's hour, and a shiver snaked down my spine. The house transformed into a different entity at night, when twisted shadows danced on the walls and the silence took on a menacing weight.

I couldn't shake the feeling that I'd been cast as the unsuspecting lead in a horror flick, unknowingly walking to her gruesome death when she should've stayed safe and warm in bed.

Stupid Asher. I blamed my paranoia on him. Did he really think a story about a countryside manor haunted by sinister spirits was the best movie to watch before bed?

Maybe *that* was why I couldn't sleep. My subconscious was protecting me from potential nightmares. It had nothing to do with anyone initialed A.D.

I made it downstairs and through the living room with the help of my trusty mantra.

Ghosts don't exist. Ghosts don't exist. Ghosts don't—

I turned the corner and stopped dead in my tracks. Pale light spilled through the kitchen doorway, alerting me to the fact that someone—or some*thing*— was already inside.

I finally understood how the characters in horror films felt because while self-preservation screamed at me to run away, morbid curiosity propelled me forward.

Apologies to every stupid character I've ever lambasted for making poor decisions. It turns out I, too, am a stupid character who makes poor decisions.

I peeked around the doorway, my heart jackrabbiting in my chest. A tall, dark figure stood near the open fridge, wielding a knife.

I couldn't help it.

I screamed.

"Aaaahhh!!"

"Aaaahhh!!"

The figure whirled around. His knife clattered to the floor as our simultaneous screams shredded the silence.

I didn't think. I simply darted inside, grabbed a nearby frying pan, and swung it toward his head before he recovered from his surprise.

He ducked just in time. I swung again, but he grabbed my arm mid-arc and sent us both tumbling to the ground.

He hit the tile first with an audible groan. I straddled him and brought the frying pan over my head.

I was acting on pure instinct at this point. If I stopped moving, fear would take over, and I couldn't allow that to happen. Someone was going to get hurt, and it wasn't going to be me. *Not today, Satan.*

I was about to swing the pan down when a familiar voice pierced my cloud of adrenaline.

"Scarlett, stop!"

Wait. Was that...

I blinked, my mindless haze parting to reveal a sharp jaw and emerald eyes. "Asher?"

"Obviously," he grumbled. "Who did you *think* I was?"

"I thought you were an intruder." My heart continued to race as it scrambled to catch up with this new development.

"Why would you think that?" Asher eyed my white-knuckled grip on the pan with wariness.

Oh my God. I'd almost bashed Asher Donovan's face in with cookware.

I flushed and quickly set the pan on the floor. "I came downstairs for a snack and saw the light from the kitchen. I didn't realize…"

"That I might've gotten the same idea?" he finished, his tone dry.

The flush spread to my neck and chest.

My mind had somehow leapfrogged over the most logical answer and straight to the worst-case scenario.

I wanted the floor to open me up and swallow me whole. Free falling into hell couldn't be worse than assaulting my host with surgical-grade stainless steel.

"I was being cautious. If you *had* been an intruder…" I trailed off. *Don't make it worse.* "Anyway, I apologize." I should get that out before my face exploded from mortification. "I didn't mean to, um, almost kill you."

"Apology accepted."

Relief ballooned at the twinge of amusement in his response.

Good. He wasn't *that* upset.

Getting hauled off on attempted murder charges would've put a serious damper on my weekend.

The hum of the fridge crept between us. He hadn't closed the door before I swung at him, and the blast of cold air sent goose bumps rippling up and down my arms. Asher's body was the only source of warmth.

My eyes drifted down of their own accord. A soft green T-shirt molded to his shoulders and chest, not too tight but just enough to hint at the sculpted eight-pack underneath. Unlike the bright, piercing hue of his eyes, the shirt was so faded it was almost gray. It'd ridden up during our altercation, revealing a strip of tanned skin above the waistband of his sweats.

So this was what he wore to sleep.

It was so casual yet intimate, like he'd unwittingly offered me a peek at his most private—

"Scarlett."

"Hmm?"

"I hate to interrupt your ogling, but can you please get up? As much as I love having you on top of me, this tile wasn't designed for comfort."

My gaze snapped up to his as realization dawned for the second time that night.

I was still straddling him.

Asher's eyes creased with mirth as I shoved off his chest and scrambled to my feet.

Forget malicious spirits. If I died tonight, I only had myself to blame.

Here lies Scarlett DuBois, a victim of self-inflicted humiliation.

"I wasn't ogling you," I lied, drawing the tatters of my dignity around me in a last-ditch shield.

"Sure, and rain isn't wet." Asher stood, looking remarkably put together for a quarter past three in the morning. Further proof the universe didn't play fair. "It's alright, darling. I won't hold it against you."

"What did I say about calling me 'darling'?"

"I'd say I get a pass considering you almost rearranged my face with my own cookware."

He—well, okay, he had a point. "You're never going to let that go, are you?"

"Never is a long time." A wicked grin stole across his face. "However, I'd expect frequent mentions of this night for the next fifty years or so."

"Bold and erroneous of you to assume we'd still be talking in fifty years."

"Stranger things have happened. If you're lucky, it might even be seventy."

I pictured wrinkled, white-haired versions of ourselves bickering in a nursing home somewhere.

The image didn't repulse me as much as it should've.

Another gust of arctic air billowed from the open fridge door.

Asher's gaze slid from my face down to my neck and chest. His smile faded, and an electric shiver rippled down my spine.

Neither of us moved to close the door.

Tension swallowed our earlier levity, and I was suddenly conscious of how little I was wearing.

I hadn't wanted to sleep in my workout clothes, so Asher had lent me one of his shirts. The vintage black tee hit mid-thigh. Underneath it, I wore my favorite lace knickers—and that was it.

No bra.

My nipples hardened to painful points beneath Asher's scrutiny. His eyes darkened, and an answering pulse throbbed to life between my legs.

I wasn't a casual fling person. I'd tried. They didn't do much for me, so my vibrator and I had developed a close relationship over the years. Usually, it was enough, but right now, it wasn't the thought of my Maximus 3000 Ultra that made my body sing with heat.

It was the thought of what Asher could do with his hands and mouth when his gaze alone turned me on.

It was the fantasy of me straddling him again—only this time, we were both naked.

It was the simmering attraction that had been building between us since we met, the one I'd done everything in my power to destroy, only to have it revive again and again like a phoenix from the ashes.

I wasn't saying I wanted to date him or marry him, but I *wanted* him, and judging by the way his breathing shallowed, he wanted me too.

He took a step toward me. "Scarlett—"

The husky rasp of my name slapped me back to reality.

What the hell am I doing?

"Sorry again about the attempted murder, but I...I have to go back to sleep," I blurted. "Early morning tomorrow. Talk to you later."

I turned and beelined out of the kitchen before he could stop me.

It wasn't until I'd safely locked the door and burrowed beneath the duvet that I realized I hadn't grabbed a single thing to eat.

Good news: I was no longer hungry.

Bad news: My craving for food had morphed into a craving for something else.

After five minutes of tossing and turning, I gave in and pushed the covers to the side. The throb between my legs had intensified into a painful ache, and when I slipped a hand into my underwear, it was instantly soaked with my arousal.

I closed my eyes, lost to the pleasure and the montage of scenes unfolding in my head.

Asher opening the door and finding me like this, legs spread and fingers rubbing shamelessly over my clit.

Him climbing on top of me, his face half-shadowed by the relentless storm.

The weight of him pinning me down, the delicious stretch when he first enters me, the steel grip on my hips as he fucks me with long, hard strokes.

Oh God. My breath shallowed into pants. I rubbed faster, my skin slicked with sweat, but it wasn't enough.

My other hand reached up to play with my nipple, and I kept my thumb on my clit while I pushed two fingers inside me.

A loud moan escaped. *Fuck*, that felt good.

It'd been so long since I got myself off manually, and the fact that I was doing it here, in my should-be enemy's house, only made it hotter.

The slippery sounds of my fingers pumping in and out intermingled with the booms of thunder.

My pants came faster.

I was so close.

I could practically taste him on my tongue, a cocktail of sweetness and earthiness that made my head spin. I imagined it was his hand squeezing my breast, his fingers filling me up so well. The thunder was the slam of the headboard against the wall, and the blasts of cool air were his breaths on my skin.

It was wrong to imagine those things, but fantasies ran wild beneath the cover of night, and once they broke free, there was no holding them back.

My orgasm hit with blinding ferocity. White lights burst behind my eyes, and I was falling, falling into an abyss where there was only warmth and pleasure and an unbearable sensation of lightness.

I lay there, sweaty and breathless, until the world eventually returned in bits and pieces.

I'd taken the edge off, but as I finally drifted off to sleep, a pang of unfulfilled need remained, filling my dreams with images of dark hair and green eyes.

CHAPTER 14

SCARLETT

I SNUCK OUT OF THE HOUSE THE NEXT MORNING LIKE A coward.

When I woke up, the storm had passed and Asher was (presumably) still asleep, so I changed, placed his shirt in the laundry, and texted him a *thank you* before I hauled ass out of there.

I couldn't face him knowing I'd gotten off to fantasies about him mere hours ago. With my luck, he probably possessed some superpower that allowed him to pick up on any orgasms he'd had a hand in (literally and figuratively).

I couldn't risk it. I needed time to gather myself and figure out what I was going to do about our situation because it was unsustainable.

It took me almost an hour to get home. After another shower and change of clothes, I texted Carina to meet me at our local café.

"Thanks for coming on such short notice," I said. "I had to get out of the house. It's one of those days."

"Not a problem. I'll never turn down tea and pastries." Carina broke off a piece of her scone. "Plus, I needed an excuse to get out of the house too. My parents are visiting."

My eyebrows skyrocketed. "They're in town? They were just here for Easter."

"Yep. It was a surprise visit. I love them but, well, you know."

I did, indeed, know.

Carina's parents lived in Liverpool, where her father owned a thriving pho shop and her mother taught chemistry at the local university. They were super sweet, but she was their only daughter and they had strong opinions about her job, clothes, boyfriends, friendships, hobbies, and basically every other aspect of her life. It was the reason she moved to London and never looked back.

"There's all this family drama because my aunt ran off with her accountant and sold our ancestral house in Vietnam without telling anyone," she said. "My mom is beside herself."

"Selling an ancestral home seems like something an accountant would advise against."

"I don't think he was very good at his job." Carina shrugged, oblivious to the appreciative glances from a passing group of men.

With her gleaming black hair and flawless bone structure, she could easily make a killing as a model, but she hated being photographed. We'd been friends for three years, and there were maybe five pictures of us total.

"Anyway, enough about me," she said. "What's up with you? You look weirdly flushed."

I relayed what happened yesterday minus the masturbation part. Some things were better kept secret.

"Wait, you slept over at *Asher Donovan's* house and I'm just finding out now?" Her mouth hung open. "And you watched a horror movie? *And* you attacked him with a frying pan? Scarlett DuBois, who are you? It's like I don't know you anymore."

"I didn't *attack* him," I grumbled. "It was self-defense. I thought he was an intruder."

"You thought he was an intruder in his own house?"

"I told you I didn't see his face before my fight-or-flight kicked in." My reaction seemed even more ridiculous in broad daylight than it had last night, but weren't best friends supposed to have your back no matter what? "Whose side are you on anyway?"

"I didn't realize there were sides," Carina said between bouts of laughter. "But if there are, I'm on yours, obviously. That being said, what happened was clearly a sign."

"A sign that I need better judgment?"

"No, a sign that you need to sleep with him." Carina ignored my sputter of protest and ticked off the reasons on her fingers. "He accidentally landed on top of you. You accidentally landed on top of him. You were forced to spend the night together because of a freak storm. You went downstairs for a snack *at the same time*. I know when the universe is playing matchmaker, and it is totally shipping you two right now."

She loved the woo-woo universe stuff as much as she hated photos. It was charming when it wasn't directed at me.

Thank God I hadn't told her about what I did when I returned to my room.

"I can't sleep with him," I hissed. I cast a furtive glance around in case anyone was eavesdropping. "How would that look?"

"Like a rocking good time. Did you see that story a few years ago about the soap star who hooked up with him? She said he does this incredible thing with his tongue—"

"*Carina.*"

"I'm just saying, there's documented proof that the man is a god in bed."

"Which is another reason why I'll never sleep with him. Even if I weren't training him and he wasn't Vincent's nemesis, I could never hook up with another footballer. They're fuckboys, and the few that aren't are already taken."

My ex hadn't cheated on me, but it'd taken him less than a month to move on after our long-term relationship—among other things.

Carina's brows dipped. She examined me over the rim of her mug for a moment before she set it down with a soft sigh.

"You can't let one bad ex ruin your opinion of the opposite sex forever," she said gently. "Don't let him have that power over you."

"It's not the opposite sex. It's the profession."

She pinned me with her signature don't-you-bullshit-me look. I countered with my we've-talked-about-this-so-don't-you-push-me stare.

I used to roll my eyes at the clichéd characters who could "never love again" because some asshole broke their heart. Everyone suffered heartbreak at least once in their life, right? Get over it and move on.

It wasn't until I experienced it myself that I understood how they felt. Once you've been betrayed by someone you trusted completely, it was hard to let your guard down again.

I saw potential heartbreak everywhere now, and I'd rather nip it in the bud than regret it later.

My feelings toward Asher were complicated. Complicated was *never* good.

Nevertheless, something he said last night nagged at me.

"Can I ask you something?" I asked after my stare down with Carina dissolved into a silent truce.

"Always."

"Do you think I should try for the staff showcase this year?"

Her expression shifted into one of neutrality. "It depends," she said after a telling beat. "Is that something you're interested in?"

I picked at my toast. "Maybe."

"Have you talked to your doctor about dancing again?"

"No." I shredded my poor toast into further pieces. "Do you think I should?"

Carina had supported my decision to abstain all these years, but she'd never offered her personal opinion on the matter.

She raised her mug to her lips again. "I think the fact you're even considering it is your answer."

Carina and Asher's words played in my mind the rest of the weekend.

On Sunday night, I booked a virtual appointment with my doctor.

On Monday morning, I met with Lavinia during her office hours and broached the possibility of joining the staff showcase before I lost my nerve.

As it turned out, I needn't have bothered.

"Auditions closed last week."

A sharp intake of breath betrayed my surprise.

I didn't have my doctor's sign-off yet. There was also a chance my newfound motivation would fizzle, and I'd regret my decision by the time the showcase rolled out.

But if that were the case, why did I feel so disappointed?

Lavinia studied me, her eyes sharp and knowing behind her glasses. "Is there a reason why you're so interested in this showcase? You've declined to participate every other year."

"I like *Lorena*'s choreography?" It came out more like a question than an answer.

The subtle arch of Lavinia's brow displayed her skepticism.

I couldn't get anything past her so, despite the rock lodged in my gut, I explained my reasoning and focused on my desire to take the stage again, if only for a night. Hopefully, she didn't pick up on my skyrocketing anxiety when I talked about the performance.

I should've thought this through before talking to Lavinia, but I was in too deep to back out now.

This is what spontaneity gets me. A speech begging for something I'm not sure I even want.

Except the more I spoke, the more I started to believe what I was saying.

I wanted to prove I could do it.

I wanted to feel the exhilaration of dancing again.

I wanted one last show on *my* terms, not the universe's. That was one of the hardest things I had to accept—that my career had ended due to something as unpredictable as a car accident.

If I'd known, I would've better appreciated my last moments onstage. I would've had more closure.

"I see." Lavinia leaned back and steepled her fingers. Her lips thinned into a slash of red against porcelain skin. At sixty, she possessed a better complexion than most women my age. "You've worked here for four years, Scarlett. You know I believe rules exist for a reason and that willful disregard for said rules leads to disorder. I despise disorder."

The rock in my gut expanded, dragging my heart and hopes to the ground. "I understand."

I should've checked the audition deadline before I wasted her time. I'd been so afraid I would lose my nerve if I waited that I'd barged in and made a fool of myself instead.

I resisted the urge to slide down in my seat and hide.

"That being said, I'm aware yours is a special circumstance," Lavinia said. "You've been a valuable member of the RAB family for a while now. If we can't provide a measure of flexibility for one of our own, then how can I expect loyalty in return?"

A tiny sprig of hope sprouted past my misgivings.

"I can't promise you'll be onstage. We've assigned all the roles already," she said. The sprig wilted. "However..." The spring perked up again. "We still need an understudy for Yvette, who's playing Lorena. If you're interested, the position is yours. It's not what you asked for, but it's all I can offer—pending final approval from your doctor, of course."

"Of course." *Fingers crossed Dr. Stein has good news for me.* "I would love to be the understudy. Thank you. I really appreciate it."

"Don't thank me yet," Lavinia said dryly. "Let's see if you feel the same way in a few months."

Being an understudy was one of the most difficult jobs in ballet. They had to learn the choreography, the musicality, and every spot of the performance without stepping on the principal's toes, figuratively speaking, and they were expected to do all that *without* the promise of a turn in the spotlight.

Since the showcase was only one night, my chances of performing were low, but it felt good to *do* something again.

A pinprick of excitement buzzed through me. I hadn't shaken off my hang-ups about reentering the world of ballet, but it'd be nice to fall back into a headspace where anything was possible and nothing could stop me.

That wasn't true anymore, but a girl could dream. Sometimes, dreams were all we had.

The rest of the afternoon flew by. My students must've picked up on my energy because several cast curious glances my way.

Emma was one of the few brave enough to ask me about it outright. "Did you have a good weekend, Miss DuBois?" Her eyes sparkled. "You look happy."

"Instructors shouldn't discuss their personal lives with students. It's inappropriate," I said sternly. Her face fell. "But since you asked…" My mouth twitched. "I got some good news this morning."

Her smile returned to full wattage.

We had a quick chat about her *Nutcracker* rehearsals before I packed up and met Earl in front of the school.

My stomach fluttered during our drive to Asher's house. He'd responded to my thank-you text with a simple *you're welcome*. Other than that, we hadn't talked since I snuck out Saturday morning.

Enough time had passed for me to pretend my, er, self-care session never happened. That was the only way I could look him in the eyes.

I was also oddly excited to tell him about the understudy role. He was the one who'd encouraged me to leave my comfort zone; he deserved to be the first to know.

Earl pulled into the circular driveway and opened my door. "Have a good session, Ms. DuBois."

"Thank you, Earl."

I walked up the front steps and tried the doorknob. It was unlocked, but Asher was nowhere in sight.

Weird. He usually greeted me at the entrance so we could walk to the studio together. Maybe he was running late from an interview or other prior commitment.

I let myself into the house and tread the familiar path to the studio. I'd been here so many times I no longer looked twice at the original Rembrandts or the state-of-the-art gadgets.

I passed the living room. Stopped. Then doubled back.

Was that…?

It was.

My good mood evaporated like a puddle in the sun. A strange ringing filled my ears.

Now I knew why Asher hadn't been there to greet me. He had a guest over. A very blond, very leggy guest in an outfit that probably cost more than my monthly rent—and they were kissing.

CHAPTER 15

ASHER

THE KISS CAME OUT OF NOWHERE.

One minute, I was trying to get Polina out of the house as quickly and politely as possible. The next, she'd tossed her arms around my neck and crushed her mouth on mine.

"Jesus!" I pushed her off and wiped my mouth with my forearm. "What the fuck, Pol?"

"What?" She blinked at me with those baby doe eyes that'd turned her into one of the biggest supermodels in the world. "It's just a kiss. We've done *so* much more than that."

"Not since last year."

There'd been a time when the kiss would've led us straight into the bedroom, hot tub, or any nearby place with a semblance of privacy. That time had long passed because Current Me didn't feel a single twinge of pleasure or arousal.

"We should remedy that." Polina propped a hip against the couch. "I miss you. You never call anymore."

"Because we're not together anymore." My patience frayed with each passing second.

We went on a few dates last spring. It took one date for the shine to wear off, two dates for me to realize we had nothing in common, and three dates for me to officially call it quits.

I didn't hate her. She was nice enough (surprise kisses aside). She just wasn't for me, and we'd ended things amicably. At the time, there'd been a filthy-rich oil magnate courting her on the side, so she hadn't exactly been heartbroken.

Things with the oil magnate must've gone south, because after a year of radio silence, she'd shown up at my door half an hour ago claiming she wanted to "catch up."

"But we could be." Polina sounded unfazed by the reminder.

"No, we can't." I snuck a peek at the clock. *Shit*. I was late for training, so I needed to get Polina out of here fast.

I hadn't talked to Scarlett since her thank-you text, and I wanted...I didn't know. I wanted to see her, I guess.

That sounded pathetic even in my thoughts. *Good thing no one can hear them.*

"Listen, Pol—"

"Why not?" She tilted her head. "Are you dating someone?"

"No. I'm not dating *anyone* right now."

Liar, a voice whispered.

I ignored it.

"As much as I've enjoyed our catch-up, I have training right now," I said. "I'm already late, so—"

"Training, schmaining." Polina rolled her eyes. "You're always so concerned about *training*, but fine, I'll go. Before I do, I have a favor to ask."

"What is it?" I asked warily.

"Vuk Markovic is hosting a fashion gala at the end of the summer.

I was hoping you could be my date."

My eyebrows popped up. Vuk Markovic owned the Blackcastle football club and our home grounds, aptly named Markovic Stadium. The Serbian American billionaire was a notorious recluse, and the idea of him hosting any sort of gala was absurd to the point of laughable.

However, Polina's sources when it came to single, powerful men were enough to make MI6 weep. If she said Vuk was hosting a gala, he was hosting a gala.

A sudden burst of clarity hit me.

"Let me guess," I said. "You want me to come and make him jealous."

Polina had gravitated toward me because I was young, famous, and good-looking, but her real goal was to snag a billionaire. Everyone in our circles knew that.

She shrugged, not bothering to deny it. "Yes, but we can have fun before then, no? We were so good together."

"I'd love to help, but I can't. Too busy with training." I ushered her out of the living room and toward the door. "However, I'm sure you can find someone much better than me. You're too beautiful not to," I added to soften the sting of rejection.

It worked.

Polina's pout transformed into a preen. "Of course, you are right. I thought you would be the perfect date since you play for Blackcastle, but maybe...hmm. I wonder if Xavier Castillo is available."

Why did that name sound so familiar? *Right.* He was also Sloane's client. I was pretty sure he annoyed her more than I did, which was a commendable feat.

"You should call him and check." I all but shoved Polina out the door. "Good luck!"

Thankfully, she left without further protest.

Once she was gone, Earl stopped buffing his car and raised an eyebrow at me.

"Don't look at me like that," I said. "I didn't know she—you know what? I don't have to explain myself to you. Where's Scarlett?"

"Inside." He resumed his task. "We arrived a while ago."

I left him and his unwarranted judgment in the driveway and sprinted to the studio.

This was the one time I cursed the size of my house. Why did it take so bloody long to get from one end to the other?

When I arrived at the studio, Scarlett had already set up our cross-training equipment and was scrolling on her phone.

"Hey. Sorry I'm late," I said breathlessly. "A, uh, friend dropped by, and our conversation ran over."

"It's fine."

I frowned at her distant tone. She hadn't been this standoffish since our first few sessions, and the chilliness seemed especially incongruous given our movie bonding time on Friday night.

Granted, she'd left without saying goodbye the next morning, but I'd slept in. I couldn't expect her to wait around for me.

"Are we good?" I asked as she dropped her phone in her bag and walked to the sound system without looking at me once.

I didn't like it. I didn't like it all.

"Yes. Why wouldn't we be?" She fiddled with the controls. "Let's start with warm-ups. We—"

"Fuck that. We're not starting anything until you tell me why you're acting so strange." I crossed my arms. "Is this about Friday night?"

Scarlett's back turned rigid.

I'd kept my wording vague, but we both knew I wasn't talking about the frying pan incident.

Three days later, the memory of our kitchen encounter was burned into my mind.

Scarlett straddling me.

The heat in her eyes.

The sight of those perfect fucking nipples poking through *my* shirt. Seeing her wear my clothes was hands down one of the hottest things I'd ever experienced. It made almost getting bashed in the face worth it.

I'd needed an ice-cold shower and a date with my right hand after that. Even now, just thinking about it made me uncomfortably warm.

Scarlett looked as tense as I felt. "No," she said. "This is *not* about Friday night. However, since we're on the subject, you could've mentioned your girlfriend before I—while we were in the theatre."

My frown deepened. "I don't have a girlfriend."

"Fine. Your hookup, fling, whatever you want to call it."

What the hell was she talking about?

"I don't…" *Earl's judgment. Scarlett waiting in the studio. The only woman she could've possibly seen me with since Friday.* The puzzle pieces slotted together with perfect clarity. "You're talking about Polina."

"If Polina is the blond with legs longer than a giraffe, then yes." Scarlett finally whirled around and faced me. "You were having quite a snog fest in the living room. I didn't want to interrupt you, so I came downstairs and waited for you to finish."

"It wasn't a snog fest session," I growled. "*She* kissed *me*."

"Sure."

Irrational anger simmered in my veins. "I guess you didn't stay long enough to see me push her off," I said. "Polina and I went on a few dates last year. That's it. She came by because she wanted me to help her make someone else jealous, and she thought seducing me first would make it easier." I nodded at her bag. "If you don't believe me, I'll give you her number and you can confirm with her."

Scarlett faltered. "Oh."

"Yes, oh." I kept my eyes trained on hers as I carefully picked my next words. "Even if we *were* making out, I don't understand why you'd be mad."

"I'm not mad. I'm annoyed about your tardiness."

"That wasn't annoyance I heard."

"Then you're hearing things that don't exist."

"Maybe. Maybe not." I took in her stiff posture and the rosy flush darkening her cheeks. A slow smile spread across my face. "Wait. Scarlett, darling…are you jealous?"

"You wish."

I'd been half joking, but her answer came too quickly, too aggressively to ring true.

My smile vanished beneath an unsteady thump of my heart. "Maybe I do."

The confession drifted between us like confetti in the wind, blowing this way and that, uncertain of where to land.

It was the closest either of us had come to acknowledging our attraction—and there *was* attraction. A quiet, smoldering, mutual one. Of that, I was sure.

If she'd stayed in the kitchen a minute longer the other night, I would've kissed her, and she would've let me.

Scarlett's throat moved with a small swallow. "You shouldn't."

I drew in a deep breath and exhaled. The invisible confetti fluttered, finally coming to rest on the far side of the room. So tangible yet untouchable.

"Those rules of yours again, huh?"

"Yeah," she said softly. "Those rules of mine."

We didn't discuss Polina or Friday night again for the rest of our session. They weren't the real issues at hand.

No, the *real* issue lay dormant, as patient and incendiary as a ticking bomb.

It was only a matter of time before it exploded.

CHAPTER 16

SCARLETT

"WHEN DO REHEARSALS START?" CARINA ASKED.

"On Tuesday. They're only once a week, so it shouldn't be too bad."

Since it was a one-night school showcase and the staff members were seasoned professionals, the rehearsal schedule was less grueling than that of a normal dance company performance.

My stomach flip-flopped. It was Saturday, five days since Lavinia appointed me understudy, and my excitement had bled into nerves.

Luckily, *Lorena*'s choreography didn't involve a lot of moves that would aggravate my old injuries. My doctor had given me her tentative approval pending a full physical (to make sure nothing had changed since our last checkup) and my promise that I would commit only to one performance.

"Don't overexert yourself," she'd told me yesterday. "Your body can handle performing again up to a certain point, but once you pass that point, you'll be undoing a lot of progress. If you feel any abnormal discomfort at all, call me and your PT immediately."

She didn't have to worry about that; I had her and my physical therapist on speed dial.

"Perfect. So we'll still have time for shopping and trolling for good-looking men with a stable job, decent personality and no significant other," Carina joked, drawing my attention back to her.

We were having drinks at the Angry Boar, which was packed with happy hour patrons and a handful of lost-looking tourists. I usually steered clear of this pub because it was a magnet for footballers, but it had great weekend drink specials and the number of athletes usually thinned out during the off-season.

"Good-looking, single, employed, *and* not a prat? In *London*? You're asking for way too much," I said.

Carina grinned. "A girl can dream. Speaking of dreams..." She raised her glass. "Here's to the best understudy for Lorena in all of RAB."

"I'm the *only* understudy for the role at RAB."

"Exactly."

I laughed and clinked my glass against hers. "How's the second job search going?" I asked. "Any luck?"

"No." Her shoulders slumped. "Not unless I want to strip or bartend, both of which I'd be terrible at. If some drunken finance bro tries to grab my ass while I'm working, they'll have to haul me off to jail."

"It's okay. You have time," I said optimistically. "You're only twenty-six, and Antarctica will always be there."

Well, unless climate change did us all in, but I kept that caveat to myself.

"I hope so." Carina shook her head. "This is so stupid. I can't believe I'm looking for a second job to fund a *holiday*."

"It's not stupid. It's a childhood dream." I nudged her leg with my foot. "We don't downplay those, remember?"

Carina's top bucket-list item was to visit Antarctica before she got married. It may sound random to anyone who didn't know her, but she'd watched a documentary about penguins when she was a kid and fell in love with them. Ten-year-old Carina got it in her head that she *had* to visit them in Antarctica when she grew up, and it'd been a goal for her since. As for the married part, she said a husband would cramp her style.

Unfortunately, visiting one of the most remote locations on earth was *expensive*. An executive assistant salary barely covered the cost of rent in London, much less a sojourn to the South Pole, hence her desire for a second job.

I told her once that penguins existed in less expensive, more accessible countries like South Africa. The glare she gave me almost sent me six feet under, so Antarctica it was.

"I guess not." She sighed. "It's okay. I'll figure it out. There are definitely more important things in the world to focus on. How's your dad?"

"He's doing well. Vincent says he's finally warming up to his nurse, which is a good sign. Apparently, they bonded over their favorite wine."

"How very French," Carina said dryly. "Did you tell Vincent about Asher?"

I paused mid-sip before swallowing. A wave of prickles swarmed my skin. "He knows we're training together. There's nothing else to tell."

Vincent wasn't happy about me and Asher still training together, but that was the Boss's decision, not ours. We all had to make the best of it.

"Hmm."

I narrowed my eyes. "What was that?"

"What?" she asked, the picture of innocence.

"That sound."

"What sound?"

"That *hmm* you just made."

She tapped her nails on the table as a neighboring group of guys went wild over the cricket match on TV. "You and Asher have been talking a lot. That's all."

"We see each other three times a week. It would be weird if we *didn't* talk."

"Oh, I'm sorry, I didn't realize movie nights were essential to your training regimen." Carina laughed and ducked when I pelted her with a crisp. "Admit it. You want to shag him." When I didn't answer, her smile morphed into open-mouthed shock. "Wait. Do you *really*?"

"No." I reached for my glass again, but it was empty.

"Scarlett DuBois, don't you dare lie to me." Carina gasped. "Oh my God. Did something happen when you stayed at his house during the storm?"

"*No.*" The prickling sensation intensified. "But it almost did? I'm not sure."

Her face sobered. "I know I joke about it, but if you hook up with Asher, Vincent will lose his shit. As in, 'potentially sabotage Blackcastle's chances of winning by taking his anger out on Asher during a match' lose his shit.'"

"I know." Vincent had always been protective of me, but he'd gotten worse since my accident and breakup with Rafe.

"On the other hand, you're an adult and Vincent needs to get a life, so he'll have to suck it up."

I allowed myself a small laugh. "Nothing has actually happened between us."

"Yet."

Yet. Funny how one three-letter word contained a world of possibilities.

Every time I thought about Asher, I felt like I was trapped on a runaway train, the wind whipping through my lungs as we barreled toward the edge of a cliff. I knew how the story would end, but for a few precious moments, the sheer exhilaration overshadowed our inevitable doom.

Scarlett, darling, are you jealous?

You wish.

Maybe I do.

The memory blew through me, spiking my pulse and scattering my concentration.

The truth was, I *had* been jealous. A vicious dose of green poison had burned through me at the sight of him kissing someone else, and I hated it.

"So." Carina arched a perfectly shaped brow. "Back to what you said earlier. Define *almost did*. What *almost did* happen?"

I groaned. "I was hoping you'd overlook that."

"Me? Overlook a potentially juicy carrot of information? I'm not even going to dignify that insult with a response."

"Okay." I took a deep breath. I might as well spill the beans. She was going to find out eventually (I was convinced Carina had some secret mind-reading capability she didn't tell me about), and I was desperate to talk to someone about what happened. "If I tell you, will you promise not to read too much into it?"

She held up her right hand. "Cross my heart."

I told her.

"Wait. You did *what* in the guest room?" She covered her mouth with one hand, but it wasn't enough to hide her grin. "Babe, I am so fucking proud of you right now."

"It's not something to be proud of," I grumbled, my face hot. "It was inappropriate."

"Most fun things are." Carina's eyes sparkled. "Does this mean you're rethinking your anti-footballer stance?"

"No. There's a difference between fantasy and reality." My response came off less resolute than I would've liked.

I'd promised myself I'd never fall for another footballer, but I hadn't been this consumed by a guy since Rafe, and it terrified me. Asher wasn't my ex; he was smarter, funnier, more thoughtful.

It was awful.

Because smart, funny, thoughtful men were my weakness, and I didn't have the option of avoiding him until my attraction petered out. I was literally forced to see him multiple times a week.

If only Vincent were here. He would've acted as our buffer, and we wouldn't be in this situation.

The chimes over the door jingled. A gust of warm air swept over me, and the pub noticeably quieted as every head swiveled toward the entrance, mine included.

My entire body tensed. *Oh, you have* got *to be kidding me.*

Whichever evil fate was responsible for throwing us together this summer struck again as Asher walked in. Even with his wind-tousled hair and worn white T-shirt, he was breathtaking enough to cause several audible sighs.

"Speak of the devil." A mischievous glint entered Carina's eyes as she raised her arm.

"*Don't you dare,*" I hissed, but it was too late.

"Asher!" She waved, her bangles gleaming beneath the lights. His gaze slid across the room and rested on us. "Over here."

That traitor. I was putting Carina on my shit list next to my hormones, the UK weather, and the inventor of horror films.

I prayed Asher was meeting someone else here, but no, that would be too easy.

Instead of declining Carina's invitation or acknowledging my strong stay-away vibes, he pivoted in our direction and slid onto the empty stool across from me with infuriating ease.

"Two run-ins in five weeks," he drawled, flashing a smile that left my *ex*-best friend starry-eyed. "This must be my lucky spot."

He addressed Carina, but his eyes were locked onto mine.

I lifted my chin and met them head-on. I hoped he couldn't hear the sudden roar of my pulse.

"Must be," Carina echoed. Her eyes ping-ponged between us before she stood and cleared her throat. "Excuse me. I have to, uh, use the loo. I'll be right back."

Oh, I was going to *kill* her. Forget the penguins; she'd be lucky if she lived long enough to see the inside of her flat tonight.

A beat of awkward silence passed.

"Are you meeting someone here?" I asked, hoping a miracle would call him away from this table, in this corner, *this* close to me.

"Nah. I was in the area and decided to drop by." Asher's smile could've melted the knickers off a nun. "Good thing I did, or I wouldn't have run into you."

Those were absolutely *not* butterflies winging through my chest. They were something far less appealing, like…flying cockroaches. Or angry wasps.

Luckily, I was saved from answering when someone bumped into Asher with his shoulder. Hard.

The guy's mouth moved. I couldn't hear what he said, but judging by the way Asher's smile vanished, it wasn't an apology.

I wasn't a confrontational person. The prospect of making a

scene in public made me want to crawl under the table, but there was something about their interaction—the smug smirk on the guy's face as he turned away, the angry yet resigned set of Asher's jaw—that raised my hackles.

"Hey!" The rebuke slipped out before I knew what I was doing. "You bumped into him, and you're just going to walk away? Apologize."

Asher's shocked gaze snapped toward me while the guy's eyes narrowed. He looked like he was in his mid-to-late-forties, with graying hair and a blue shirt that stretched over his paunch.

"Whatcha gonna do if I don't, little girl?"

"Well." I offered a sweet smile. "While I can't physically make you apologize because I'm such a *dainty* little girl, I *can* call your employer and tell them one of their officers has been harassing a civilian." I nodded at the Holchester Police logo on his shirt. "I'm sure they won't be too thrilled about that, especially when they find out the civilian is Asher Donovan."

"Bumping into someone ain't harassment," he growled.

"Maybe not outside this pub, but premeditated physical aggression is strictly prohibited at the Angry Boar." I tipped my head toward the bar, where Mac was slinging drinks with his signature scowl. "If you don't believe me, we can call Mac over and see if he agrees."

The man's mouth thinned. Everyone knew Mac had a subzero tolerance for any type of provocation in his establishment. He'd once banned someone for intentionally stepping on another's foot without apologizing.

"Or," I said, "you can apologize and we'll forget this happened. Your choice."

A long, tense beat passed before he spoke again. "I'm sorry," he gritted out.

"For what?"

If looks could kill, my lifeless body would be floating in the Thames. Luckily, they didn't, and he had no choice but to amend his apology. "I'm sorry for bumping into you."

"It happens," Asher drawled. "Not everyone is born with grace, coordination, or manners."

"You—" The man cut off with a small growl when I flicked my eyes toward the bar again.

He stormed off without another word, leaving the stench of cheap aftershave and indignation in his wake.

Asher turned his full attention toward me. His mask of amusement faded, softening the furrow between his brows and the hard set of his mouth. "You didn't have to do that."

"Maybe not, but he deserved it." My heart raced in the aftermath of the confrontation, but it wasn't from nerves. It was from exhilaration. I felt like I could take on the world and win. "He was a wanker."

"There're plenty of wankers in the world, unfortunately. I've learned to pick my battles. Besides…" Asher flashed a crooked smile. "I have to watch myself here. Mac's still upset with me for spilling beer on his beloved jukebox earlier this year."

I wasn't fooled by his devil-may-care attitude. "What did that guy say to you?"

"Nothing I haven't heard before."

"Asher."

His smile devolved into a sigh. "The usual B.S. about me being a traitor and getting what I deserved in that final match against Holchester. It's boring at this point, though I have to commend his commitment to his hatred while he's on holiday."

My brows pulled together. Asher got a lot of hate from Holchester fans when he transferred to Blackcastle, but it'd been months. I couldn't believe people were still hung up on it when transfers happened all the time.

Then again, football fans were nothing if not passionate (to put it mildly), and the rivalry between Holchester and Blackcastle was particularly bitter.

"Well, I hope his beer is always warm, his food is always cold, and he stubs his toe every time he gets out of bed for the rest of his trip," I said. "Imagine being so hateful on holiday. That's bad karma."

Asher's laugh coated my arms and chest with warmth. "The ballerina has claws. I didn't expect that from you," he teased.

I shrugged. "I don't like it when people act like wankers."

"Either way, thank you again. I was going to ignore him. I can't give every arsehole the attention they seek, but a little bump was worth seeing that side of you."

"Don't get used to it. I can't always be around to protect you," I said, but I couldn't resist a small smile in return.

His eyes crinkled deeper at the corners. "Noted."

A long, languorous beat passed between us.

Every time I thought I knew where I stood when it came to him, something happened that threw me off-kilter.

There was no steady ground with Asher Donovan. It was a constant sea of change—frustrating, terrifying, and, as much as I hated to admit it, exhilarating.

All the banked heat we shouldn't acknowledge thrummed across the tiny high-top table. We—

"Sorry that took so long." Carina's breathless apology doused the moment in ice water. *Sorry, my ass*. She'd left us alone on purpose, and her grin indicated as much. "The queue took forever." She slid onto her stool and regarded us with naked interest. "What did I miss?"

"Not much," I said when Asher remained quiet. His run-in with the man wasn't my story to tell. "We were just chatting about football."

"Oh, okay." Carina seemed oblivious to the tension smoldering around us. "Before I forget, I want to tell you I can't make it Tuesday. I got a call from my parents while I was in the queue. They made us dinner reservations at Babko that night, so I won't be able to watch your first rehearsal. I'm so sorry." Genuine remorse crossed her face. "I really wanted to be there for the first one."

"It's okay," I reassured her. "You won't be missing much."

Asher's brow wrinkled. "What rehearsal?"

Carina flicked a quick glance at me.

Shit. I hadn't told him about the showcase yet. It wasn't a secret, and he wasn't *entitled* to know, but a stab of guilt pierced my chest anyway.

"I changed my mind about not participating in the RAB showcase," I admitted. "I spoke with Lavinia, and I'm now the understudy for the lead role in *Lorena*."

"The lead role?" His eyes sparked with admiration, and an answering warmth drifted through my veins. "That's brilliant!"

"It's not a big deal. Like I said, I'm the understudy." I tucked a strand of hair behind my ear, feeling oddly self-conscious. "Chances are, I won't get to perform. I'm just there in case the lead gets sick or injured."

"It's still exciting. When did you find out?"

The guilt deepened. "Monday."

Asher's expression didn't change, but the barest hint of a pause indicated his confusion.

"I was going to tell you earlier," I added. "But I, um, forgot."

I'd wanted to tell him during Monday's training. But after seeing him with Polina and our subsequent moment in the studio, sharing such an important milestone with him first seemed too dangerous.

Too intimate.

So I hadn't.

Nevertheless, a pinprick of guilt pierced my skin at the hurt in his eyes. Not only had I not told him, but I probably wouldn't have brought it up at all had Carina not mentioned rehearsals.

"That's okay." Asher smiled, the flash of hurt smoothing into one of indifference. The boulder sank deeper to my toes. "I'm just glad you're participating." He checked his watch. "I have to run. I have an online interview in an hour." He stood and slid a fifty-pound note onto the table. "Next round's on me. As a thank-you for letting me crash your girls' night."

"That's way too much for drinks here," Carina protested.

"Three rounds then," Asher said easily. He glanced at me.

I remained quiet, trying to reason away my niggle of disappointment at his departure. I hadn't wanted him to join us, so why was I upset about him leaving?

He hesitated, then added, "My friend's throwing a party in Neon's VIP lounge later tonight. If you guys are free, you should drop by."

"We're not big clubbers," I said before Carina committed us to something neither of us wanted.

The last time we clubbed, I'd spent half the night holding her hair back while she puked up four shots worth of tequila. Afterward, it took us fifteen minutes to reach the exit because it'd been so packed.

Would I like to repeat that experience? No, thank you.

"Sadly, it's true." Carina sighed. "I wish we were fun club people."

The tiniest hint of amusement tugged on Asher's lips. "I'll add your names to the list anyway in case you change your minds." His gaze slid back to me with a brief, inscrutable flicker before he left.

The crowd parted without him uttering a word and closed just as easily once he was gone.

"Yeah, screw what Vincent thinks," Carina said after Asher was out of earshot. "He's *so* into you, and he checks all your criteria. Good-looking, single, employed, and not a prat? Hello, perfect match."

"Those are your criteria, not mine, and let's not forget his playboy reputation."

"Oh, so you wouldn't mind if I went after him?" Carina smirked at whatever she saw on my face. "Exactly. Your death glare just gave you away."

"I did not give you a death glare, and he's not into me. Not really," I said. "Maybe he *thinks* he is because I'm the only woman he's seeing on a regular basis this summer."

I wasn't trying to be self-deprecating; it was the truth. He was a famous footballer. What were the chances he was actually, truly interested in me?

Carina shook her head but didn't press the issue. "Jokes aside, are you really going to skip the party tonight? I know we're not club people, but it's an *Asher Donovan* invite. Can you imagine the VIPs who'll be there?" She let out a dreamy sigh. "Sadly, my parents are staying with me, so I can't go even if I wanted to. I don't want to deal with their lectures about 'drugs and debauchery.'"

Whenever her parents visited, they stayed with her for at least two weeks. I couldn't imagine staying with my mother for that long as an adult—we'd kill each other by day three—but it was a cultural thing. Asian daughters simply did not banish their elders to a hotel when they had a perfectly serviceable flat.

"If you change your mind and you *do* go, you have to tell me every detail after," Carina said. "I'm living vicariously through you at this point."

I shook my head. "Sorry, but tonight's a book-and-bed type of night," I said. "Trust me. There's no way I'm going to that party."

CHAPTER 17

SCARLETT

IN MY DEFENSE, I HADN'T *PLANNED* ON CHANGING MY mind.

After Carina and I left the Angry Boar, we parted ways—her to meet her parents for a West End show, me to my flat and my comforting Saturday night routine of tea, reading, and pajamas.

However, I couldn't focus on Isabella Valencia's latest thriller for the life of me. I usually loved her books, but I found myself zoning out every other paragraph.

Instead of following the sociopathic detective's adventures in hunting down another sociopath, my concentration kept scattering into images of a trendy nightclub and green eyes.

After I reread the same line four times without comprehending a single word, I gave up and closed the book with a frustrated sigh.

I was a single twenty-six-year-old living in London, and this was how I spent my weekends: alone with fictional sociopaths.

It'd never bothered me before, so why did I feel so restless now?

After all, there was nothing *wrong* with staying in. A book and tea were far superior to battling drunken strangers for breathing room in a sweaty nightclub. Right?

It's not about the club. It's about who's there.

I groaned and sank deeper into my armchair, covering my face with my book as I did so. I was too ashamed to look at my reflection in the dark telly screen.

The smart thing to do would be to stay home and unravel the mystery of the mountain town murders.

The stupid thing to do would be to brave a taxi ride and London nightlife simply because Asher invited me to a party hosted by someone I didn't even know.

Silence pressed in from all sides.

The clock ticked, counting down the minutes to eleven.

And my mind continued conjuring flashes of neon lights and sweaty bodies.

"Scarlett DuBois, you are an idiot," I said.

My self-condemnation lingered before dissolving into air.

Then I got up, walked to my room, and rifled through my closet for an appropriate outfit to wear to the city's most exclusive nightclub.

What am I doing here?

I stared at the scene before me, my heels cutting into my feet, my skin sticky with summer heat and regrets.

I'd forgotten how chaotic London clubs were. Neon's deceptively simple exterior, fronted by a brick wall and a black metal door, didn't deter everyone under the age of thirty from wanting that magic entry stamp on their hand.

I was tempted to take the next taxi home and crawl back into bed, but I'd spent an hour getting ready and shelled out an exorbitant sum for taxi fare. I didn't want that to go to waste.

Asher said he'd put my and Carina's names on the list, but did he mean the list for the club or the list for the party *inside* the club? Or both?

I eyed the queue snaking down the pavement and around the corner. The thought of waiting an hour or more in heels made me want to die, but how humiliating would it be if I walked up to the bouncer and my name wasn't on the list? I'd get banished to the back of the queue while dozens of strangers judged me during my walk of shame.

If Carina were here, she'd charge up to the door and check for us. Since she wasn't, I was forced to text Asher for clarification. I should've done so on my way here, but I hadn't been thinking.

> Hi! I changed my mind about the party after all! Can you confirm whether I'm on the list for the club or the party inside? Ty!

I winced at the overly peppy tone (so many exclamation marks!), but I hit send anyway. The sooner he responded, the sooner I could move from my awkward spot by the curb.

I felt like everyone at the front of the queue was staring at me— *what is that loser doing standing there by herself?*—so I scrolled through my phone in an attempt to look busy.

My regrets compounded by the second. I *really* should've stayed home. This was what I got for trying to pretend I had a "normal" social life instead of one wonderful but currently busy best friend and an overreliance on fictional worlds.

Five minutes later, my inbox remained empty. Perhaps I should join the queue while—

"You *bitch*!"

My head snapped up and to the left. A guy was doubled over, his face red and his hands clutching his groin, while a petite blond stared down at him with satisfaction.

They were in the alley around the corner from the club, so security couldn't see them.

"Next time, don't grab a woman's ass without their consent," she said. "Be glad I kneed you instead of kicking you with my heel. *That* would've hurt."

I would've smiled at her gumption—the guy was at least double her size—had it not been for the second interloper sneaking up behind her.

The areas around nightclubs were always hotspots for pickpocketing and petty crime. Distracted crowds, heavy alcohol, and lowered inhibitions meant big paydays for those looking to score some extra cash, like the skinny teenager reaching for the blond's clutch.

"Hey!" I shouted. "Look out behind you!"

The blond had the fastest reflexes I'd ever seen because the words had barely left my mouth before she whirled and smacked the wannabe thief right in the face with her bag.

He cursed and scampered off, obviously not looking for a real fight, but the man she'd kneed had recovered enough to lurch toward her.

My instincts kicked into action before reason did. I ran over (even though these heels were *not* made for running) and pushed him before he made contact. The distraction gave the blond enough time to turn and realize what was happening.

She raised her bag again. Like the thief, the guy was too much of a coward to confront her face-to-face, especially now that she had backup. He ran off, leaving a trail of shouted insults in his wake.

"Ugh." The blond blew out a sigh and stared at his retreating back. "I wish I'd gotten *one* good hit in first. How disappointing."

A surprised laugh bubbled up my throat.

For someone who'd gotten harassed and almost mugged, she appeared remarkably unfazed.

She faced me, her frown melting into a grateful smile. "Thanks for your help. You totally didn't have to do that." She stuck out her hand. I shook it, bemused by her formality. "I'm Brooklyn."

Her accent sounded American, but there was just enough of a British lilt to throw me off.

"Scarlett. And you're welcome. Both those wankers had it coming."

Between the Angry Boar and this, I was on a roll. I hardly recognized myself, but I didn't hate the person I was today (minus my questionable decision to come out in the first place).

"They did, didn't they?" The blond's grin widened. She was lean and athletic-looking, with hair the color of a lion's mane and the healthy tan of someone who spent most of their days outdoors. A faint constellation of freckles dotted her nose and cheeks. "Are you here by yourself?"

"I'm meeting a friend inside," I said.

"Great. Me too." Brooklyn hooked her arm through mine. "Come on."

Before I could protest, she pulled me around the corner and straight to the entrance. "Hey, Timmy. How's it going?"

Timmy? This giant's name was *Timmy*?

His scowl broke out into a toothy smile. "Hey, Brookie. Good to see ya. How's your dad doin'?"

"Great, if you overlook his stress and unwillingness to take his vitamins."

The boom of Timmy's laughter sounded like boulders rolling down the side of a mountain. "Sounds like him." He unhooked the velvet rope and waved us through without checking our IDs. "Have fun."

We swanned past, eliciting a chorus of grumbles from the queue. Timmy silenced them with another scowl.

"Next!" he barked. "Where's your ID?"

The door closed behind us, enveloping us in neon-splashed darkness and thumping music.

"Brookie, huh?" I shouted over the noise.

She laughed. "Family friend!" she yelled back. "Speaking of friend, you want me to help you find yours?"

"It's okay. You go have fun." I gestured toward the dance floor. "I don't want to keep you, and you've helped enough."

"You sure?"

I nodded.

"Give me your phone anyway." Brooklyn took my mobile and entered her number. "Here, I texted myself, so I have your number too. You need anything, give me a shout. It was nice meeting you, Scarlett!"

"You too!"

Normally, I would never exchange numbers with a virtual stranger, but Brooklyn gave me good vibes. Plus, I needed more friends. I hadn't realized how small my social circle really was until tonight, when I couldn't think of anyone else to invite out besides Carina.

I stared at the undulating crowd, took a deep breath, and plunged in.

Luckily, it didn't take me long to find the VIP lounge. It was located on the top floor, and the relative quiet here compared to the chaos of the main rooms was almost jarring.

A security guard and a woman in a dazzling silver sequined dress stood at the base of the stairs leading into the lounge. She carried a clipboard and walkie-talkie and arched her eyebrows at my approach.

"Hi. I'm here for the private party."

Asher still hadn't responded to my text, but he *had* to be here. Right?

The hostess flicked her eyes over my outfit. I was wearing my nicest black dress and heels accessorized with a designer clutch Vincent bought for my twenty-fourth birthday. It wasn't cutting-edge fashion, but judging by her grimace, you'd think I'd shown up in a potato sack and Crocs.

"And who are you?" Her tone indicated she already knew the answer.

No one.

I stiffened, my self-consciousness ceding ground to indignation. "Scarlett DuBois." I tried my best to project confidence. "I'm on the list."

"I'm sorry, I don't see your name." She couldn't have sounded less sorry if she'd tried.

"You didn't check!"

"I don't need to. This is a *VIP* party." She tapped her nails against her clipboard. "I'm afraid your hundred-quid dress and two-year-old bag don't meet our criteria. Now, if you'll excuse me…" She turned to greet a trio of newcomers.

The swanlike models brushed past me, all legs and thousand-dollar minis. They provided their names, the hostess checked them off with a smile, and they disappeared up the stairs in a flurry of giggles and clacking heels. None of them spared me a glance.

The hostess's smile disappeared when she faced me again. "Miss, I'm going to have to ask you to leave. Otherwise, Roscoe will escort you out."

The security guard next to her glared down at me.

My teeth clenched, but I had no choice other than to turn and exit with as much dignity as I could scrape together.

I'd made enough scenes for today. Besides, what was I going to do? Snatch the clipboard from her and search the list myself? Roscoe would tackle me before I got past the A's.

Exhaustion burned behind my eyes. I turned the corner and jabbed the button for the lift.

I couldn't wait to go home. This entire night was a—

The doors opened with a *ping* and a whiff of familiar aftershave.

"Scarlett?"

There was a treacherous quickening in my chest.

"You made it." The shadows fell away, revealing the slant of Asher's cheekbones and chiseled jawline. His gaze trailed the length of my dress and legs. "You look…" A small pause allowed the muffled beats from the lounge to creep between us. *Thud. Thud. Thud.* "Good."

A brief sizzle of electricity sang through my arms and legs.

"Thank you." I forced a smile, my encounter with the hostess too fresh to forget despite the relief of running into Asher. "But apparently not good enough."

"What do you mean?"

I told him what happened.

Asher's eyes darkened with each word until they resembled storm clouds on the horizon.

"Come with me."

He didn't wait for a response. He placed a hand on the small of my back and guided me firmly toward the lounge's entrance, where the hostess was chatting with security.

The guard tipped his chin toward us. She turned, her face lighting up at the sight of Asher.

"Mr. Donovan!" She straightened and smoothed a hand over her hair. "How lovely..." Her voice trailed off when she noticed me walking with him.

I wasn't a petty person (most of the time), but I would be lying if I said her shock didn't give me immense satisfaction.

"Asher Donovan and Scarlett DuBois," he said smoothly, his hand still on my back. "My date."

A second ticked past.

The hostess looked like she'd just swallowed a bucket of live maggots, but she eventually forced a smile and stepped aside.

"Of course." She unhooked the rope, her shoulders stiff. "Please enjoy the party."

"Thank you. Oh, one more thing." Asher paused and looked her straight in the eye. "Disrespect her again, and I'll make sure this is the last event you'll ever work in London."

The hostess's face flushed crimson.

Surprise flashed through me, quick as lightning, followed by an irrepressible warmth as we entered the lounge and left her sputters behind.

"I'm sorry about that," he said. "The door people can go on a power trip sometimes."

"It's okay." I slid a sideways glance at him. "Your date, huh?"

"It sounded better than *friend* in the moment. Besides, it was worth it to see the look on her face."

"Oh, I agree." My grin matched his. "I thought she was going to go into cardiac arrest right then and there."

"So are we?" Asher guided me through the crowded room. His palm burned through the fabric of my dress, leaving me slightly flushed.

"Are we what?"

"Friends."

"I extracted an apology for you from a police officer and you put the hostess in her place for me, so I suppose we are." We passed by a familiar-looking beauty with long legs and high cheekbones. I did a double take when I realized it was the supermodel Ayana. I *loved* her latest *Vogue* cover; Carina was going to die. "Whose party did you say this was?"

"Poppy Hart."

I came to an abrupt halt. "Wait. This is a *Poppy Hart* party?"

Asher's mouth tipped up. "You've heard of her?"

"I'm going to pretend that's a rhetorical question," I said, earning myself a deep laugh.

Everyone knew who Poppy Hart was. The model, socialite, and style icon sat in the front row of every major fashion show, headlined the VIP list of every major event, and chaired the board of every major charity. She was London's latest It Girl and the ultimate arbiter of what was cool and what was not.

She was also famous for her ultra-exclusive parties, one of which I was attending *right now.*

Surreal.

"Fair enough." Humor transformed Asher's face into a softer version of itself. "I should tell you she has strict rules for her parties. No cameras, no harassment, and no fights—exactly like the Angry Boar, except fancier."

That was an understatement. In the past five minutes, I'd spotted fire-eaters, dancers dressed as the seven deadly sins, and a world-famous DJ from Iceland in the sound booth.

Velvet banquettes lined the perimeter of the walls; crystals formed hanging sculptures in the shapes of stars and flowers and waterfalls. Haloes of LED light drenched the seating alcoves in futuristic purple while a bar stocked with only top-shelf spirits took up an entire wall.

I hadn't seen Poppy yet, but the room was bursting with celebrities, socialites, and other varieties of young, rich, beautiful, and famous.

Asher and I stopped at the bar. He ordered us two house specials, whatever those were, and handed me one.

"So." He examined me over his glass. "You changed your mind about coming."

"Only because I didn't have anything better to do." I took a tentative sip. Whiskey mixed with something rich and sweet. It burned smoother than any drink I'd had before. "Don't read too much into it. My appearance tonight is strictly platonic."

"Good, because my invitation was strictly platonic."

"Good."

"Good."

Our seemingly banal exchange didn't curb the wild current charging around us, drawing our eyes together like magnets and forming a bubble against the noise and movement from the rest of the club.

My earlier insecurities, exhaustion, frustration...they all fell away as my body came alive with anticipation.

This was why I'd changed my mind. This heady sense of possibility. The exhilaration of dipping my toe into something forbidden.

Whatever happened tonight, the rush of this moment was worth it.

The combination of alcohol and the heat in Asher's gaze scorched through my veins. Either the drink was stronger than it seemed, or I was treading into dangerous territory.

Not treading into. You're already there.

"Asher!"

The bubble popped. Noise swept in on a deluge, and I almost stumbled from the force of it.

Poppy Hart swanned up to us, a vision in green and gold. She greeted Asher with a cheek kiss before turning her attention to me. "Who's this?" Unlike the hostess, her question contained only friendly curiosity.

"Scarlett. She's a…friend." The timbre of Asher's voice dipped on the word *friend*, and my toes instinctively curled.

"Not that kind of friend," I added quickly.

His amusement warmed my cheeks while Poppy laughed. With her cinnamon-colored hair and alabaster skin, she gave every woman here a run for her money.

"I like you already. It's nice to meet you, Scarlett." She didn't introduce herself; she didn't need to. If it were anyone else, it would come off arrogant, but since it was Poppy, it simply came off natural.

After a few minutes of friendly small talk, she made an apologetic face. "Do you mind if I steal Asher away for a minute? I have a friend visiting from New York and she's a *huge* fan. She'll absolutely murder me if I don't introduce her." She dropped her voice to a stage whisper. "I told her Asher isn't all he's cracked up to be in real life, but she refused to listen."

"I don't mind. It's something they have to learn for themselves," I agreed with mock solemnity.

"Thank you both. I appreciate you talking shit about me while I'm standing right here," Asher said dryly.

"Any time." Poppy patted his arm. "Scarlett, don't worry. I'll have him back in a jiffy." Her plummy voice somehow made *jiffy* sound cool.

"I won't be long." Asher's arm brushed mine on his way past, leaving a trail of tingles in its wake. "Don't get into too much trouble while I'm gone."

"I'll try my best, but no guarantees."

The way his answering smile made my stomach flip should be illegal.

I stuck by the bar and finished my drink while I took in my surroundings. I felt self-conscious about being the only solo person here, but it soon became apparent that everyone was too wrapped up in their own world to notice me standing awkwardly by myself.

If it weren't a private party, I'd ask Brooklyn to come up. She seemed like the type who would appreciate the fire-eaters' performances.

Was that allowed in a nightclub? Didn't it violate some sort of fire code?

If it did, no one seemed concerned.

"Bit intimidating, innit?" A boyishly good-looking blond came up beside me. He had shoulders the width of a football pitch and a tiny, endearing mole above his lip that shifted with his smile.

"A bit," I admitted. "I'm here with a friend, but they got called away."

Asher used the term. I might as well too.

"Boyfriend? Girlfriend?"

I smiled at the obvious fishing. "Platonic friend."

Besides *friend*, *platonic* was in the running for the word of the night.

"Good for me, then," the blond said. "Though if I were your friend, I wouldn't leave you alone with the wolves." He nodded at the crowd around us. "Don't let their expensive clothes and champagne fool you. They're a vicious bunch. If they smell weakness, they'll pounce."

I laughed. "I'm glad I have you then. Safety in numbers, right?"

"Right." His grin widened. He extended his hand. "I'm Clive."

"Scarlett." I'd introduced myself more in the past hour than I had in months, but surprisingly, I didn't mind.

I guess it was easier to make friends when I actually left the house. *Imagine that.*

Clive ordered us another round of drinks, and we fell into an easy conversation. I learned that he was a rugby player and Poppy's cousin, hence his appearance tonight.

"I don't like these parties either, but I've skipped out on her past three soirees. If I missed this one, she'd clobber me with one of her hideously expensive handbags," he said with a sheepish smile.

I laughed again. Clive wasn't my type, but it was nice to flirt harmlessly with a cute guy at a club. It'd been far too long.

I was telling him about my job at RAB when the temperature suddenly plunged to subarctic levels.

Goose bumps coated my arms, and I trailed off mid-sentence when Asher reappeared. He looked decidedly less pleased than when he'd left.

"Finished with your fan club already?" I quipped.

He stared back at me, unsmiling. Poppy was nowhere in sight.

Okay. What crawled up his ass and died?

Across from me, Clive's expression turned amused. "Donovan. I take it you know Scarlett."

"Hart." The curt reply served as both greeting and affirmation. "Do you mind if I steal Scarlett away? We need to discuss something."

My eyebrows winged up. *We do?* That was news to me.

"Sure. Before you leave…" Clive borrowed a pen from the bartender and scribbled his number on a cocktail napkin. He handed it to me with a wink. "In case you ever need safety in numbers again."

A muscle ticked in Asher's jaw, but he didn't say a word until the rugby player disappeared into the crowd—nor did he say anything as he led us to an alcove near the back of the lounge.

Floor-to-ceiling velvet drapes separated it from the main floor. One tug on the tasseled ties, and we were ensconced in our own world.

I crossed my arms, unsure whether to be nervous, annoyed, or intrigued. I settled for a combination of all three.

"What's so important that you had to drag me away from my conversation?"

"I leave you alone for five minutes and you pick up the captain of England's national rugby team," he said. "Impressive."

Seriously? *That* was what he wanted to talk about?

Men. Everything was a dick-measuring contest to them.

"I didn't 'pick up' Clive," I said. "He approached me. What was I supposed to do? Twiddle my thumbs while I wait for you to return from your meet-and-greet?"

"You could've talked to anyone *except* Clive bloody Hart," Asher growled. "Don't you know his reputation?"

"Not really." I didn't follow rugby, so England's entire national team could walk in, and I wouldn't know a thing.

"Right." Asher's jaw flexed again. "Don't be fooled by his nice-guy act. He's a notorious fuckboy."

I stared at him for a stunned beat before I burst into laughter. "Did you just use the word *fuckboy* unironically?"

He didn't seem to share an ounce of my amusement. "It's the right term for him. He's slept with half the women at this party."

"Good thing I wasn't planning on sleeping with him. We were just talking." I crossed my arms. "Also, hypocritical much? You're not exactly celibate, if the tabloids are to be believed."

"The tabloids are never to be believed."

"So you didn't have a threesome in Ibiza last year?"

Asher didn't dignify me with a response. "Are you going to throw his number away?"

Yes. "No. Why would I? It could come in handy one day."

I was playing with fire. I knew that. But instead of deterring me, the heat beckoned, urging me closer and closer until I eventually got burned.

"I sure as hell hope not," Asher snapped. "I've seen what happens to girls who get 'handy' with him. It usually ends with tears and tissues."

"So what if it does? That's my problem, not yours." I cocked an eyebrow, drunk off potent whiskey and the danger swirling in the air. "Why are you so interested in what I do with Clive, Asher? Are you jealous?" I threw his question from Monday back at him.

"What if I am?"

The air stilled. Asher's quiet response cut through the music like a knife through silk. It lodged somewhere between my heart and throat, where my pulse beat with the frantic rhythm of a hummingbird's wings.

"What happened to platonic?" I asked. Equally quiet. Equally dangerous.

It was a last-ditch attempt to cling to *normal*, though my definition of the word had warped since I met Asher.

None of this was normal. Not us standing here. Not the way he was looking at me. Not the way my heart thrummed in reply.

It was enough to make me believe that normal was overrated.

Asher closed the distance between us with two deliberate steps.

My back pressed against the wall. I had nowhere to run; even if I had, I wouldn't have gone anywhere.

I'd known, from the minute I left my house, that this might

happen. Part of me had expected it.

The back and forth, the give and take, the denial and attraction—every piece of choreography had led us to this moment.

"Platonic." The warmth of Asher's breath brushed against my skin. "Does this feel platonic to you?"

I couldn't think, couldn't move, couldn't *breathe* as his hand trailed up my arm and over the bare curve of my shoulder. I burned everywhere he touched, my skin nothing more than a map of little fires that consumed whatever oxygen was left in my lungs.

Every muscle was strung tighter than a bowstring. When his palm reached the nape of my neck, my body instinctively arched, just enough to make his eyes flare with heat.

His hand curled, anchoring me in place. "I asked you a question, Scarlett."

A breathless shiver ran from my head to the tips of my toes.

Does this feel platonic to you?

"No," I whispered. "It doesn't."

Another breath shuddered from his chest.

That was the last warning I got before he pulled me toward him and slanted his mouth over mine.

CHAPTER 18

SCARLETT

THE WORLD BURST INTO A KALEIDOSCOPE OF SENSATION.

I gasped, shocked by the sudden onslaught. Asher used the opportunity to deepen the kiss, sliding his tongue inside and exploring my mouth with such lazy sensuality that any resistance I might've had simply floated away.

Some men were gentle; others were aggressive. Everyone had their own technique, and Asher kissed the way he played—skilled, dominant, and so thorough in his approach that it left me dizzy.

I pressed tighter against him, eager for more.

Every second of the kiss unraveled another inch of me. The glide of his tongue. The firm hold on my neck. The delicious escalation in pressure—soft at first, then harder, more demanding.

I was falling apart, and he was the only thing holding me together.

I slid my hands over his back and across his shoulders before I dug my fingers into his hair.

He groaned, and another wave of pleasure rippled down my spine.

Time lost all meaning. We could've been there for minutes, hours, or days, but as always, physics prevailed.

Oxygen grew scarce, and when it finally ran out, we broke apart gasping.

Our ragged breaths filled the enclosed space as we stared at each other, our chests heaving.

Gradually, the world seeped back into my consciousness—a flash of movement outside the curtain here, a lyric underlaid with bass there.

My mouth was still swollen from our kiss when the fog fully dissipated and left me with the cold, hard reality of what we did.

In a nightclub.

Surrounded by people who would be all too happy to snitch to the tabloids about Asher Donovan and his mystery girl, a.k.a me.

Anxiety flooded my bloodstream and chased away the dregs of lust.

Oh God. What had I been *thinking*?

Asher must've picked up on the shift in mood because his face turned somber. He had a tiny cut on his bottom lip from where I'd nipped it, and embarrassment swirled at the evidence of what I'd done. "Scarlett—"

"I have to go." I pushed past him and hurried toward the exit, head bent, heart in my throat.

He didn't stop me, and I didn't look back until I was free of Neon's seductive darkness.

The queue outside still stretched around the corner. I ignored the stares from the waiting clubgoers and climbed into the first available cab, my mind spinning from how quickly the day had spun out of control.

It'd started with innocent drinks at the Angry Boar and ended with me running away after kissing Asher Donovan.

I came out tonight hoping for excitement. Well, I got it—a little too much of it.

I gave the driver my address and was about to text Carina when my phone rang.

Vincent.

My heart stalled. It was two in the morning in Paris. Why was he calling at this hour?

He couldn't know about the kiss. It happened literally minutes ago.

The party had a no-cameras policy, but what if someone saw us go into the alcove and texted him?

I am so stupid. I hadn't thought about the Vincent angle to our relationship in weeks. I should've, considering he was one of the reasons I'd stayed away from Asher for so long, but his physical absence made it easy to forget.

My earlier drinks climbed back up my throat as I answered his call. "Hello?"

"You're up." I heard the whistle of a kettle in the background. "I was expecting your voicemail."

He didn't know. Otherwise, he wouldn't have expected my voicemail.

Relief loosened the knot in my lungs.

"Nope. No voicemail." A nervous laugh leaked out. "Just me."

"Where are you? It sounds like you're in a car."

"I went out with a friend, but I'm on my way home." Technically not a lie. "What's up? Is Dad okay?"

"He's fine. Complaining about the government and state of modern cinema, per usual," Vincent said. "But he's recovering well, and Bernadette, our nurse, has a good handle on things. Enough that I can leave the house without him worrying that she'll murder him with arsenic when his back is turned."

I snorted. Our father was eccentric, but I suspected he went on his rants because he liked to complain, not because he believed what he was saying.

"Anyway, I'm going to be in London next weekend. I have a promo video to shoot for Nike. You free for dinner one of those nights?"

"Hmm. I do have a riveting date with my latest thriller, but I suppose I could make time for you." I strove for a normal, sarcastic tone. If I was too quiet or accommodating, he'd know something was wrong.

"Your generosity knows no bounds," Vincent said wryly. "It'll be good to catch up. How are things going with Donovan? He's not giving you a hard time, is he?" His tone darkened at the mention of his teammate.

My pulse sped up again.

"No," I squeaked. *Quite the opposite, actually.* "He's fine. Very, um, professional during training." I let the *during training* part do the heavy lifting.

"Good. I hate that you have to spend a whole summer with him." I could practically see Vincent gritting his teeth. "Be careful, Lettie."

I mumbled some semblance of a response.

"If he so much as lays a hand on you or makes you uncomfortable, let me know immediately," Vincent said. "I'll kill him."

"You're so dramatic." I forced another laugh. It sounded like I'd inhaled a tank of helium. "I can take care of myself. Hey, I just got home so I'm going to call it a night. Text me when you get in next weekend, okay?"

I could tell he wanted to say more, but he settled for a simple,

"Yep. See you soon."

I hung up and leaned my head against the headrest, too exhausted to fret over the taxi ride.

Asher and I had completely upended our relationship within the span of five minutes.

My brother was visiting next weekend.

And I was stuck in the backseat of a cab, wondering how, exactly, I'd fucked myself so thoroughly.

CHAPTER 19

ASHER

FIVE TILL FIVE.

Scarlett was due to arrive at any minute.

I ran a hand through my hair. Fiddled with the volume controls on the sound system. Straightened the dumbbells on the rack.

None of it dislodged the phantom touch of her lips against mine.

It'd haunted me since Saturday night, when I finally gave in to the damn *need* inside me and kissed her.

That fucking kiss. If Scarlett had plagued my thoughts before, the kiss had built her a permanent home there and invited her in for tea. She was the only thing I could think about before sleeping, after waking up, while showering, and basically during any activity I used to try and forget her.

It drove me up the wall. And yet, I didn't regret what happened.

That alone terrified me more than any consequences. My career had always been my number one. It anchored my world, and the fact that I was willing to risk it, no matter how indirectly, for a woman...

I rubbed a hand over my face, but I didn't get a chance to pursue that train of thought before soft footsteps scattered my concentration.

I looked up. My heartbeat slowed when Scarlett entered, her black hair scraped back into a dancer's bun and her lithe frame clad in a leotard, jumper, and ballet skirt.

I hadn't chased after her on Saturday because we'd both needed space to think, but seeing her again after two days proved that space didn't do shit.

I was as twisted up about her now as I'd been at Neon.

"Hey." I aimed for casual and landed somewhere north of cautious.

"Hi." She shrugged off her jumper and hung it on a hook by the door. "So we're focusing on agility today. I suggest moving outside so we—"

"Scarlett."

"Yes?" The rigid set of her shoulders belied her cool tone.

"We should talk about Saturday night." I wasn't going to let her pretend nothing happened. We were beyond those games.

"There's nothing to talk about."

Or maybe we're not. Irritation simmered low in my blood.

"I disagree," I said silkily. If she wanted to play that game, we'd play on my terms. "We have plenty to talk about. For example, the way you taste or the way you sighed when I pressed you against the wall. Or maybe we should talk about how your hair feels wrapped around my—"

"*Stop.*" Flags of color scorched the crests of her cheekbones. "It was a kiss. We were drunk, and we got caught up in the moment. It didn't mean anything."

The ember of irritation ignited into anger.

"Bullshit." I closed the distance between us. She lifted her chin, her expression stubborn, but I detected a faint quickening in the rise and fall of her chest. "I knew you were a coward when it came to movies. I didn't expect that from you in real life too."

Scarlett's nostrils flared with a sharp inhale.

I tamped down a swell of regret. I'd said what needed to be said. She couldn't run from the hard stuff forever.

This was the same girl who'd reamed out a police officer for bumping into me, who'd survived a horrible accident and came out stronger on the other side. She was so bold and resilient in so many ways that it killed me to see her fears win.

"Fine. Let's say the kiss did mean something," she said. "What then? Do we date? Have a summer fling? Call things off when the season starts? There are *always* people watching you, Asher. It'd be impossible to keep a relationship secret." Her jaw hardened. "You lost the league last season because you and Vincent didn't work together! Imagine how much worse it'll get if he finds out something happened between us. Imagine how your coach will react. You'll both ruin your careers, and I will *not* allow that to happen, nor will I play a part in it."

My bubble of anger deflated.

Of course I'd considered the obstacles she'd laid out. Hell, they were the reason I'd fought my attraction for so long. But the more time we spent together, the hazier those obstacles seemed.

Her clinical breakdown of the situation threw them right back into focus.

I wasn't surprised by the Vincent and career angle, but the issue with the paps...I hadn't paid as much attention to that as I should've. Most of the women I'd dated in the past were public figures themselves, so they were used to the attention. Scarlett wasn't.

If anything happened between us, they'd harass her to the ends of the earth. They'd follow her, dig through her trash, talk to her old friends and classmates. Anything and everything to make a buck.

There were ways around it. I knew players who made things work with their "civilian" partners, but at the risk of sounding arrogant, they didn't have as visible a profile as I did. The tabloids would eat Scarlett alive.

I'd let the privacy of our studio and the respite of summer lull me into a false sense of security. It didn't matter how much I wanted her or how much I wished things between us could work; if *she* didn't want it, and she wasn't prepared for it, then that was it. Case closed.

The post-kiss fantasies that'd consumed me all weekend cleared, leaving a tang of bitterness in their wake.

"You're right." The words sounded hollow despite the thickness in my throat. "I don't know what I was thinking. We'll pretend the kiss never happened and never discuss it again."

"Great." Scarlett swallowed. "I'm glad we're on the same page."

"Me too."

We didn't speak about anything non-workout-related for the rest of the session.

She'd given us both the wake-up call we needed, so I ignored the cramp in my chest and carried on with my training.

Later that night, I drove my Bugatti to a borough in north London. Its seclusion, wide-open roads, and indifferent law enforcement made it a hotspot for local high rollers who liked to indulge in a bit of street racing without the complications of other car scenes—namely: leaks, paps, and drugs.

There wasn't a race scheduled this week, but people usually showed up anyway to brag about their latest vehicle or indulge in friendly competition.

Tonight was no exception.

A half dozen cars were already parked in the meetup lot when I arrived. My headlights sliced a bright swath through the group before I cut the engine and joined them.

I recognized everyone there. A footballer from Chelsea, a B-list actor with a supporting role in a major fantasy series, several rugby players...including Clive.

A wave of something unpleasant burned through my veins.

"Donovan." Simon, the footballer, greeted me first. "Haven't seen you in a while."

"Been busy. You know how it is." I returned his one-armed hug and slapped him on the back before saying hi to the others.

I stopped at Clive and gave him a cool nod.

The image of him and Scarlett flirting at Neon rose, unbidden, in my mind, and a wave of something unpleasant hurtled through my veins.

Clive leaned against his car, his self-deprecating demeanor stripped in the absence of potential bed partners. He was a regular at these meetups. I hadn't lied when I said I'd met him through Poppy, but we saw each other here more often than at her parties.

"Surprised you're not with your girl," he drawled. I wasn't the only one thinking of Scarlett. The mere evidence that she existed somewhere in his filthy mind made my muscles coil. "Never seen the great Asher Donovan that possessive over someone. Must be serious."

The others' ears visibly perked up. Society painted women as gossips, but truthfully, no one talked more shit than a group of blokes.

"I don't know what you're on about." If I displayed an ounce of genuine interest in Scarlett, Clive would swoop in like a fucking bird of prey. He liked stealing others' partners just to prove he could.

"No?" His smile told me he didn't believe a word I said. "Damn. You're even more into her than I thought. Since you want to play dumb, I'll refresh your memory. Black hair, great ass, looks like a young Liz Taylor? I was about to close the deal with her before you interrupted."

"I hate to break it to you, but you weren't about to close anything." My pleasant tone belied the dangerous thrum in my chest. "She actually has good taste."

"Yeah, and she was eating my shit up. All the girls do."

"Yeah? Has she contacted that number you gave her?"

That wiped the grin off his face. "I liked her, you know," he said, his narrow gaze assessing. "She's fit, she's funny, she can carry a conversation. I get why you're so twisted up about her."

Prior to Saturday, I didn't have a problem with Clive. Like I told Scarlett, he was a fuckboy and a bit of a tool, but those things were par for the course when it came to professional athletes.

After Saturday, I'd die happily if I could smash his face in before I croaked.

His acute observation about my feelings toward Scarlett raised several alarms—he'd only seen us interact once, so the fact he'd hit the nail on the head didn't bode well for me—but I ignored the warning bells for now.

It wasn't like the three of us would ever inhabit the same space again.

"So, is she a good shag?" he asked. "If she is, I might take her for a ride once you're done with—"

I moved before he had a chance to blink.

His sentence cut off with a surprised grunt and the slam of muscle against metal. The rest of the group, who'd been following our exchange like avid spectators watching a tennis rally, broke out into a chorus of *oohs*.

Anger muffled their jeers and narrowed my focus on Clive. The air sparked against my skin like a live wire; my blood pumped with the ferocity of a charging bull.

I imagined slamming him against the car again.

Imagined my fist in his face.

My knee in his groin.

I wasn't a violent person, but when it came to Scarlett being hurt, my values unraveled.

I get why you're so twisted up about her.

If he only knew.

"Don't talk about her like that again," I said, soft enough for Clive's ears only, steely enough for him to hear the implicit threat.

He raised his hands in surrender. "I guess I have my answer." His tone contained equal hints of triumph and unease.

With one reckless move, I'd shredded my neutrality. He knew exactly how I felt about Scarlett—but wiping that smug look off his face had been worth it.

Yet it still wasn't enough.

A physical fight would provide short-term satisfaction, but I wanted to hit Clive where it would really hurt.

"How about a friendly wager?" My smile didn't match my words. "Fifty grand says my Bugatti beats your McLaren."

Clive's eyes narrowed. I loved my cars, but he had an unhealthy obsession with his McLaren. It was his pride and joy, and if he could marry it, he probably would.

He also had an ego the size of Jupiter and a reputation for being a sore loser. Rugby, racing, it didn't matter. He needed to be number one.

"Double it and make it a hundred," he said.

So predictable. "Done."

With my brand sponsorships and transfer money, I made significantly more than Clive did in a year, but he had family money to back up his professional salary. However, the word on the street was that most of his inheritance was locked in a trust, so his doubling of my initial challenge was driven by pure ego.

Our spontaneous race lacked the bells and whistles of a planned competition. There were no cheering crowds, no drinks and music.

There was only us, our cars, and the road—just the way I liked it.

Simon volunteered to count us down. We drove to the main road, and he took his position in front of us, using his shirt as the starter flag.

Three.

The powerful growl of the engine vibrated through me, sharpening the edges of my anticipation.

Two.

I tightened my grip on the wheel. *Almost there.*

One.

The flag came down, my foot hit the pedal, and the screech of tires filled the air as we rocketed forward with reckless abandon.

Darkened buildings and empty lots whizzed by in a blur. My heart rate kept pace with the car as we flew through the streets.

This. *This* was what I'd needed. I'd been in a foul mood since training, and nothing helped me vent like a good race.

The first corner approached. I braced myself, my body tense as I calculated the perfect angle for a clean turn. Beside me, Clive appeared to do the same.

We zoomed toward the bend in near parallel streaks.

Not yet...

The guardrail loomed. Its rusted metal glowed with menace

beneath our glaring headlights.

Not yet...

The world narrowed to that one stretch of pavement.

Now!

With a quick flick of the wheel, I punched the car into a sharp turn. The tires squealed, but a controlled switch between the brake and accelerator smoothed the shift.

I was clear—and I'd pulled ahead of Clive.

However, my grin of triumph faded when the glint of his headlights filled my side mirror again. He'd recovered faster than I'd expected.

Motherfucker.

He inched in front of me by a hair.

I caught up a second later.

On and on, we traded leads until the finish line came into view. Simon stood by the roadside, shirt in hand.

Clive and I were still neck and neck. I could take one of two strategies. Either I pushed now, or...

Fuck it.

I went with my gut and eased my foot off the throttle a centimeter, just enough to let Clive speed past.

I ignored his gloating stare even as my blood drummed to the beats of competition and adrenaline.

Are you going to throw his number away?

No. Why would I?

It was a kiss...It didn't mean anything.

I get why you're so twisted up about her.

Is she a good shag? If she is, I might take her for a ride...

I slammed my foot on the pedal in the home stretch. It was my first time going full speed, no holds barred in this car, and the Bugatti shot forward like a bullet tearing through the night.

My body hurtled forward while my organs remained behind. The amount of g-force I'd unleashed proved *exactly* what several million pounds' worth of vehicular optimization could do, so I held on and didn't fucking breathe as the scenery outside morphed into an indistinguishable blur.

I imagined this was what astronauts experienced during a rocket launch—acceleration so powerful, it pressed them into their seats through sheer force.

Thank God I hadn't eaten before I left the house.

But my temporary light-headedness soon gave way to relief and the sweet, sweet taste of victory as I flew past the finish line half a second before Clive.

Gravel sprayed as we skidded to a stop.

"*Fuck!*"

I heard his shout of frustration loud and clear through the glass, and I didn't bother hiding my smirk as I exited my car.

Clive slammed his door shut and spat on the ground. One of his rugby buddies tried to console him with a pat on the back, but he shrugged him off with a scowl.

I walked over and held out my hand. Part common courtesy, part acknowledgment that I'd won.

After a moment of audible teeth grinding, he took it.

I squeezed. Dark satisfaction coasted through my chest when discomfort shaped the contours of his grimace.

"I trust the hundred grand will be in my account tomorrow?" I drawled.

Clive's eye twitched. "I'm good for it."

I believed him. He wouldn't go back on his word, not when we had witnesses. He'd lose too much street cred.

"Good." I released his hand and pretended not to notice as he discreetly shook it out. Simon and the rest of the guys watched us, their faces rapt with fascination. "And Clive? Don't ever talk about Scarlett again, or losing a hundred grand will be the least of your problems."

I walked away, his glare of resentment scorching my back. He was probably plotting how to get back at me, but I didn't care. He could plot and sulk all he wanted. I'd made my point, and I'd taken the edge off my frustration, which was what I came here to do.

Two birds with one stone.

However, the high from winning faded quicker than I would've liked. I only made it halfway home before a swarm of unwanted thoughts buzzed through my head again.

I drove because it calmed me; I raced because it exhilarated me in a way no drug could touch. Racing made me feel in control. Alive.

Tonight, I'd needed that more than most nights. Yes, I'd wanted to teach Clive a lesson, but I'd also wanted to forget about my kiss with Scarlett.

For fifteen glorious minutes, I had.

But now that Clive was gone and the race was behind me, my thoughts returned to where they always went.

Back to *her*.

And there was nothing I could do to stop it.

CHAPTER 20

SCARLETT

"THAT ENOUGH POPCORN FOR YOU, OR SHOULD I BUY you another bucket?" I asked.

Vincent grabbed the bucket from the counter and arched an eyebrow at me. "I'm preparing for you to steal half my snacks the way you always do."

I gasped. "*Do not.*"

"Do too." He pitched his voice higher. "*No, thanks, I'm not hungry.* Ten minutes later: *Vince, can I have some of your chips?*"

"Oh, shut up. Like you don't steal my stuff *all the time*. Remember when you stole my limited-edition Adele vinyl one summer because she was your crush's favorite singer and you wanted to impress her? Then you *scratched* it and tried to make it up to me by taking me to Nando's."

"First of all, Nando's is great. Second of all, that was ten years ago. You *have* to let it go."

"Never." I followed him to our assigned theatre. "That's what little sisters are for. To remind you of your transgressions for the rest of your life."

Vincent rolled his eyes. "I should've rescheduled my promo video and stayed in Paris. I'm clearly not appreciated here."

"Wrong. I appreciate you opening your wallet." He'd covered our movie tickets and snacks today. "I'm so lucky to have such a generous ATM by my side."

He snorted out a laugh and ruffled my hair with his free hand. "Brat."

"Stop! You're messing up my hair." I pushed his hand away, but I couldn't resist a laugh.

Despite his overprotectiveness, inflated ego, and totally slanderous lies about my food stealing habits, he was a great brother, which was why my kiss with Asher felt like a betrayal even though I hadn't meant it as one.

A needle of guilt wormed through my gut.

Don't think about it. Today was about sibling bonding and the latest Nate Reynolds movie. There was no room for anything else in this theatre.

Vincent and I secured our favorite middle row seats with ease. It was Saturday afternoon, well before the evening rush, and we were at our favorite little cinema on the outskirts of London.

He'd also dressed down in one of his ridiculous disguises—baseball cap, sunglasses, hoodie with the hood pulled up. I kept telling him that wearing sunglasses inside made him look like a wanker, which in turn made *me* look like someone who'd be friends with a wanker, but he wouldn't listen.

While Vincent settled in to watch the trailers, I checked my phone.

I'd texted Brooklyn last Sunday to thank her again for getting me into Neon queue-free, and we'd been talking like longtime friends since. I had a new message from her inviting me to brunch one day (answer: Of course! I'd love to join), as well as one from Carina asking if I thought cricket drop shipping was a viable side gig (answer: No, not for her, since she hated insects).

Other than that, I had no other messages.

Not that I was expecting or desiring any, especially not from anyone I was training.

My studio time with Asher had been cordial and professional all week. I showed up, we worked out, I left. Not a single hint of flirting in sight.

I grabbed a handful of popcorn from Vincent's bucket and stuffed it in my mouth.

"Ha! See?" He sent an accusing glare my way. "*Stealing*."

I ignored him and reached for more.

All the reasons I gave Asher for why we wouldn't work were true, and I refused to be one of those people who got mad when others did what they asked.

I told him to pretend the kiss never happened, and he had.

So why did I feel like crap about it?

"DuBois. That you?"

Vincent and I looked up at the same time.

Blond hair. Hazel eyes. Boyish grin.

My heart sank to my toes.

Clive.

"Hart. What's up, man?" Vincent slapped hands with him while I sank deeper into my seat.

If I hadn't been convinced the universe was fucking with me before, I was a true believer now. The chances of us running into Clive in this dinky cinema were so slim, they were near impossible, yet here he was.

If I were a more paranoid person, I'd find his appearance suspicious, but it was a huge movie opening and I didn't have a monopoly on this cinema. Besides, I wasn't vain or self-centered enough to think a guy would stalk me after meeting me once.

After he greeted Vincent, Clive's attention flipped to me. His eyes widened, and a slow smile spread across his face.

"Scarlett. Wow. I didn't expect…" His gaze slid to Vincent again. "Are you on a date?"

Full-body shudders ran through me and Vincent at the same time.

"Abso-fucking-lutely not," Vincent said. "She's my sister."

"*Sister?*" Clive's gaze darted back and forth, obviously trying to make sense of our contrasting looks.

"Adopted." Vincent's brows drew together. "Wait. How do *you* know her?"

Oh, fuck. My fingers curled around the edge of my seat. If Clive mentioned Neon, that was a step away from mentioning Asher, and *that* was a step away from total disaster.

"We met at a party last weekend. She—"

"The one I told you about," I added quickly. "Remember, Vince? I was there with *Carina*, and you called me on my way home."

Clive's eyebrows rose at the emphasis I placed on Carina's name. He knew I hadn't shown up with a girlfriend, and I could practically see the wheels turning in his head.

Please be smart enough to pick up on what I'm putting out.

"Where was the party? You didn't say." Suspicion leaked into Vincent's voice.

I didn't blame him. Carina and I weren't big partiers, and we certainly weren't the types who usually attended the same events as someone like Clive.

"Some club. I forgot the name," I said. "The night was kind of a blur."

"Hart? You remember?" Vincent asked. The suspicion grew from a seed into a sapling.

I saw the instant the pieces clicked for Clive. I was Vincent's sister. I'd lied about being at the party with Carina so I didn't have to mention who I was *really* with (Asher). Like 98 percent of the planet, Clive probably knew Asher and Vincent didn't get along.

It didn't take a genius to put two and two together.

"Peony, Legends, MYX...it could've been any or none of those," Clive said. "Honestly, I was pretty smashed. Don't remember much beyond meeting Scarlett."

"Huh." Vincent's eyes narrowed. "What happened after you met?"

"We talked for a few minutes. Then I took Carina to the loo because she, uh, got sick and threw up all over the bar." *I'm so sorry, Car. I'll donate extra to your penguin fund to make up for the slander.*

My brother grimaced.

Thankfully, we were saved from further interrogation when the lights dimmed and a prerecorded voice announced the film was about to start.

"How do you know Clive?" I whispered after the rugby player left and took his seat several rows behind us.

My nerves were still in knots from the close call. I needed to know how often Vincent talked to Clive in case the latter slipped up about Asher.

"We have a few mutual friends, but we're not that close." Vincent finally took his sunglasses off and dropped them in the cup holder. "Stay away from him. He's a fuckboy."

Interesting. Asher had said the exact same thing.

The opening credits rolled. The ensuing action sequences and up-close shots of Nate Reynolds's face temporarily alleviated my worries, but my bladder caught up with me an hour in.

I snuck out during a lull and quickly used the loo. I didn't want to miss anything important.

I exited the toilet and nearly bumped into Clive, who was leaving the men's room at the same time.

"Hey!" He smiled. "Third run-in in a week. I'm starting to think the universe is trying to tell us something."

The universe has been trying to tell me a lot of things lately. I wished it would keep its mouth shut, but it had a tendency to butt in where it wasn't welcome.

"Perhaps, though I'm not sure the cinema and the cinema toilet count as two separate instances." Just because I had beef with an immortal, amorphous force didn't mean I had to bring innocent bystanders into it.

Clive laughed. "I guess not."

"Thank you for not blowing my cover earlier," I added. "Vincent can be a little overprotective, and I didn't want him knowing that, um…"

"You and Donovan have a thing going on?" It might've been a trick of the light, but I thought I saw Clive's eyes flicker at the mention of Asher.

"We don't have a thing going on." If I could bold, highlight, and underline that sentiment three times, I would. "We're just…" *Friends? Colleagues? Acquaintances?* None of those terms felt right. "Platonic."

I was starting to hate that word, but it was the most accurate description I could come up with.

Platonic people don't kiss each other, my inner voice sang in an apparent bid to outdo the universe as my most hated incorporeal entity.

"Platonic, huh?" Clive's eyebrows winged up. "Does Donovan know that? I thought he was going to punch me when I gave you my number."

"I don't know." I forced a flippant smile. "You'll have to ask him. From my end, we're platonic." The words tasted strangely like betrayal, but I swallowed nonetheless.

"That's good to know." Clive rubbed a thumb over his bottom lip. "In that case, would you like to get dinner sometime?"

"Are you asking me on a date?" I should've seen where this was going, but that didn't stop surprise from bleeding into my tone.

"Yes." He offered a crooked smile. When Asher did it, it seemed genuine, but for some reason, Clive's looked a little put on. "I didn't get a chance on Saturday, and I figure this is the universe's way of giving me a second shot. I promise I'll take you somewhere nicer than this." He gestured around us.

I drew my bottom lip between my teeth. The conversation had already dragged on too long—I'd missed a good chunk of the film while we were chatting—but I was torn.

Asher and Vincent had both warned me away from Clive. What did they say? That he was a "fuckboy?" Then again, they were biased, and what good-looking professional athlete *didn't* go through a player phase?

The important thing was, Clive wasn't Asher. His smile didn't make my heart flutter, his flirting didn't get under my skin, and a dinner with him had no consequences beyond a few potentially wasted hours. If the date went south, I wouldn't have to see him ever again.

Clive was still waiting with an expectant expression.

"In that case, yes," I said. "I'd love to go out to dinner with you."

I told Asher about my run-in with Clive and the story I'd concocted for Vincent during our next session. I doubted the party would come up between him and Vincent, but in case it did, I wanted to make sure our stories were aligned.

However, Asher seemed less concerned about my brother finding out we were at Poppy's party together and more concerned about Clive.

"He just so *happened* to show up at the cinema you and Vincent frequent?" His nostrils flared. "That doesn't strike you as suspicious?"

"We don't own the place. He has as much right to be there as we do."

"Have you ever seen him there before?"

"No," I admitted. "Not that I remember. But that doesn't mean anything." He could've been in the area and dropped in, or we could've crossed paths there before but I didn't notice.

No one paid attention to the random people they passed unless there was a good reason to. Asher was being paranoid.

"I don't like it," he said flatly. "You slipped through his fingers at Neon, and now he sees you as a challenge. I wouldn't be surprised if he somehow figured out you liked that cinema and planned the 'accidental' run-in."

I didn't get a chance on Saturday, and I figure this is the universe's way of giving me a second shot. Clive's words echoed for a beat before logic took over.

"Okay, you need to ease off the thrillers because you're entering conspiracy territory." I crossed my arms. "Maybe he's a player, but I doubt he's a stalker. How would he know the exact date, time, and movie Vincent and I were going to see? It's not like we broadcast that information online."

Asher opened his mouth, then shut it without replying.

"Exactly. As for the other part..." I gripped the barre. "Do you think the only reason someone could possibly like me is if they see me as a 'challenge'?"

Was that why he'd been so persistent in his flirting? To stick it to Vincent?

The prospect made bile rise in my throat. It was ridiculous. By now, I knew Asher well enough to know he wouldn't do something so mean-spirited, but once the seed had been planted, it was hard to dig it out.

His mouth thinned. "That's not what I meant, and you know it."

"Actually, I don't." I should've left it at that, but my mouth kept running of its own accord. "Also, player or not, I like Clive. He's nice."

"That's what he wants you to think."

I ignored the snark. "As a matter of fact, he asked me out on a date, and I said yes."

The words fell into a pool of TNT-laced tension. Asher's jaw ticked, and I instinctively braced myself for an explosion.

It never came.

After a beat of silence, he turned and jabbed the power button for the sound system. The faint strains of a classical hip-hop instrumental filled the room "Good for you," he said, his tone unreadable. "Have fun."

"I will." *Stop talking.* But I couldn't. It was like my mouth had a mind of its own. "He's taking me to the Golden Wharf this Friday. It's supposed to be one of the best restaurants in the city."

"Great."

"Afterward, we might head to this secret cocktail bar that—"

"I get it," Asher bit out. He faced me again, his expression stamped with irritation. "Can we start training, or will you continue to regale me with unsolicited details about your love life?"

I suppressed a flinch, but he was right. Why was I provoking him? We should be working, not engaging in this ridiculous back and forth.

However, things had been so coldly *civil* between us that it was nice to see sparks fly again.

"I guess things didn't work out with your West End suitor," Asher said, more calmly this time.

My brows knitted. "West End suitor?"

"The guy you went to see a West End show with earlier this summer."

What is he—ohhhh. He was talking about my girls' night with Carina. We'd watched a musical and gotten smashed on blueberry cocktails afterward.

I hadn't outright *said* it was a date, but I'd led Asher to believe it was a romantic outing. Even back then, I'd unconsciously been trying to make him jealous.

The realization struck with the force of an anvil. I swallowed, wishing I had a pair of magic scissors so I could snip my way out of this tangled mess.

When it came to Asher, *should* and *want* battled for dominance over my decisions, and the winner changed by the hour.

I hated myself for how wishy-washy that made me. I kissed him, then I ran away. I told him to pretend the kiss never happened, then I tried to provoke him by discussing my upcoming date with Clive. I wanted to make him jealous, but I wanted him to leave me alone.

I was turning into the type of person I hated, the kind who couldn't make up her mind and flip-flopped between what she said and what she did.

The problem was, I didn't know how to stop it.

"No," I said in response to Asher's statement. "It didn't work out romantically. We decided we're better off as friends."

It was the truth…if I stretched the truth out and dipped it in a bowl of lie-by-omission sauce.

"I see." Asher's jaw ticked again. "It's funny you mentioned the Golden Wharf. I have a date there this Friday too."

I couldn't hold back a snort. "Oh, please."

"You think I'm lying?"

"What are the chances you have a date at the same restaurant on the same night as me right after I tell you about it?"

"What are the chances you run into Clive at some hole-in-the-wall cinema a week after meeting him when you've never seen him there before?" he countered.

Dammit. He got me there.

"Who's your date?" I asked, still suspicious.

"Someone I met over the weekend. She's cute, funny, and loves football. I'm excited to take her out."

The fact he was clearly trying to make me jealous didn't stop me from feeling, well, jealous. "Great."

"It is."

More silence, punctured only by the instrumentals soaring in the background.

"We should go on a double date," Asher said after ten long, tense seconds.

I burst into laughter, but it tapered off when he didn't join me.

He couldn't be serious.

"Are you daft?" I demanded. "What makes you think that'll be a good idea? You don't even like Clive!"

"I don't have to like him to double date with him."

"That's the stupidest thing I've ever heard."

"No, it's not. Think about it. First dates are awkward. It's a small restaurant, and we'll both be there anyway. This is the perfect way for us to get to know the other person without the pressure of a one-on-one."

"Asher, darling, if you don't have faith in your first-date skills, you should've just said so," I said, deliberately throwing his nickname for me back at him.

His smirk indicated he'd caught it. "My dating skills aren't the ones I'm worried about."

"Are you implying I'm a bad date?"

Asher shrugged. "I wouldn't know. But I know *I'm* not a bad date."

"Please. I'll have Clive eating out of my hand before the main course." I hadn't been on a date in a while, but I could turn on the charm when I wanted.

"He's a guy," Asher said. "He'll eat anything you put in front of him."

"Way to insinuate my date has no standards."

"You're the one who said it, not me."

"You shouldn't talk. You depend on your looks and money to do the heavy lifting." I jabbed my finger at his chest. It was like poking a brick wall. "I bet you can't carry a dinner's worth of conversation to save your life. Your date will be bored to tears."

"You want to bet on it?" Asher's eyes glinted with challenge. "Let's see who ends the night with a second date lined up. Winner gets bragging rights. Loser suffers eternal shame."

"A bet? What are we, teenagers?" I scoffed. A beat passed. "What happens if we both get a second date?"

"Then we can sleep soundly knowing we've made it to adulthood with the proper social skills."

It was a trap. A double date with Asher was the worst idea in the history of worst ideas, and my self-preservation instincts were screaming at me not to take the bait.

But if I backed down, he'd say I was afraid. That I wasn't up for the task. And that was unacceptable.

"Fine. I accept your bet." Even if we weren't betting on anything material, I had no intention of walking away from Friday night's dinner without a second date locked in. "May the best man or woman win."

CHAPTER 21

ASHER

I SHOULDN'T HAVE SUGGESTED A DOUBLE DATE.

I didn't know what Monday Afternoon Asher had been smoking, but Friday Night Asher knew he was in deep shit the minute he arrived at the Golden Wharf.

"Wow." Ivy took in the flowering plants and gilded doors, her eyes wide. "This place is amazing."

"It's one of the best," I said, distracted.

It took one call for me to secure a table for four at the most exclusive restaurant in town. That wasn't the problem.

Neither was finding a date. Contrary to what I'd told Scarlett, I'd spent last weekend at home. I hadn't met anyone anywhere, but Ivy was a friend who'd been on board with a free meal and entertainment. She wasn't interested in me romantically, so it was perfect. I didn't want the complication of bringing someone who thought the date meant something.

I'd briefed her on how and when we supposedly met, so that wasn't the problem either.

No, the problem was walking toward us right now, and she looked good enough to make me regret every decision that led me to this point in time.

I'd seen Scarlett in workout clothes.

I'd seen her in my bathrobe and my shirt (the latter remained one of the hottest sights of my life).

I'd even seen her dolled up for a night out at Neon.

But I'd never seen her like *this*.

Her simple black dress stopped just above her knee and hugged her in all the right places, highlighting her delicate curves and long, slender legs. Silver heels added three inches to her height, and her hair cascaded past her shoulders in soft waves. It looked so touchable, I almost reached for her before I stopped myself.

I didn't know what she did with her makeup, but it defined her features in a way that made them pop without being overwhelming.

Huge dark eyes. Soft red lips. *Perfection*.

Nevertheless, I couldn't pinpoint what, exactly, was different about her appearance tonight. She was always beautiful, and her outfit, though elegant, wasn't extraordinary in its uniqueness.

But as she neared, I realized it wasn't her clothes or hair or makeup. It was *her*. It was the way she moved, her hips swaying with a combination of confidence and sultriness that she kept hidden when we were in the studio. It was the soft gleam lighting up her eyes. It was the glow in her face and the smile on her lips.

Up until this point, I'd been dealing with Professional Scarlett. Even when we'd flirted and kissed, she'd clung to pieces of that mask with determined fingers.

The Scarlett that was walking toward me? She wasn't wearing a mask. This was the Scarlett I'd see if we were dating—if I picked her up at her flat, flowers in hand; if we walked down the street, our fingers intertwined; if we woke up in the morning, her head on my chest.

This was what Scarlett would look like if she were mine.

The chatter from the restaurant fell away. I swallowed past the sudden dryness in my throat and wished I had a strong whiskey on hand.

I needed it. Desperately.

Scarlett stopped in front of us. Her eyes held mine for a fraction of a beat too long before sliding to Ivy. "Hi."

"Hi." A trace of roughness ran beneath my voice. "You look…" *Breathtaking.* "Nice."

"Thank you." Her mouth curved, but I could see the mask sliding back into place, hiding the momentary softness in her eyes. "So do you. Both. I mean, both of you look good."

I almost smiled at her adorable verbal stumble when a possessive hand touched her arm.

White shirt. Blue tie.

Clive.

My mood plummeted like a dead fly into a vat of acid.

I'd been so focused on Scarlett I'd overlooked his presence by her side. He'd followed the restaurant's dress code to a T, but his shirt stretched a little too tight across his chest and his watch gleamed a little too bright beneath the lights.

I'd bet another hundred thousand quid that he deliberately wore a shirt that was half a size too small so his muscles looked bigger.

One point for ego, zero for style.

And he was *still* holding onto Scarlett's arm. That fucker.

Clive flashed a tiny smirk in my direction.

Anger simmered in my veins. He'd sought her out on purpose at the cinema. I didn't know how, but he had. He was furious about losing the race, and he was using her to get to me.

I couldn't say anything without looking bitter and paranoid, so I kept my mouth shut. For now.

Play smarter, not harder.

However, my anger gave way to confusion when Clive's smirk fell. He stared at my date, his mouth agape.

"Ivy?"

"Clive?" Ivy sounded as stunned as he looked.

Color climbed high on her cheekbones, and I got the distinct impression that she would rather melt into the sidewalk than stand here with us.

Scarlett broke the silence first. "Do you two know each other?"

"Yes. We..." Clive cleared his throat. "We used to date."

"A long time ago," Ivy added quickly. "At uni."

Holy shit. I supposed it made sense. I'd met Ivy through Poppy, and Clive was Poppy's cousin. That entire circle attended the same schools and functions growing up.

That being said, the chances of my date and Scarlett's date being exes were so slim it was laughable. It almost made me believe Clive running into Scarlett at the movies *was* just another bizarre twist of coincidence.

Almost.

"Wow." Scarlett blinked. "It really is a small world."

There was strained laughter all around. After a quick introduction between Scarlett and Ivy, we entered the restaurant. The cloud of tension followed us like a swarm of buzzing gnats.

The Golden Wharf's patrons were used to famous faces, so we took our seats near the privacy-tinted windows with minimal fuss.

"So how did you and Asher meet?" Scarlett asked after we placed our orders.

In an odd seating shuffle, I'd ended up across from her and next to Ivy. Clive and I sat as far from each other as possible, though that didn't mean much for a four-top in an intimate dining room. We were still close—and he was *definitely* too fucking close to Scarlett, who was hemmed in between him and the wall.

Ivy flicked a quick glance at me before answering. "We met at a wine bar last weekend," she said. "He bought me a drink, we hit it off, and the rest is history."

Perfect. Exactly like we'd rehearsed.

Unfortunately, our rehearsal hadn't accounted for an ex-boyfriend with a steel-trap memory.

"I thought you hated wine," Clive said. "You stopped drinking it after Milly Blair's party fiasco."

"Uh..." Mild panic crossed Ivy's face. "I got over it. It's been years and, um, I've developed a new appreciation for it."

Clive's brows dipped. "What was the name of the wine bar again?"

"It's an underground spot in Shoreditch," I interjected smoothly. If I gave him a name, I wouldn't put it past him to check and see if I was actually there Saturday night. "Only those in the know would've heard of it."

"And this underground spot doesn't have a name?"

"Can't share it with people outside the inner circle. Bar rules." There were plenty of exclusive, hidden bars in London with similarly draconian rules, so my lie wasn't out of the realm of possibility.

"How convenient."

"What about you?" I turned the tables on him. "Scarlett said she ran into you at the movies. Quite a coincidence."

"I live near that cinema," Clive said. "I go there all the time."

"Really? What was the last film you saw there before last

weekend?"

A beat of hesitation passed. "The horror one with Riley K. I forgot the name."

"*House of Snakes*?"

"Yeah. That one."

"Funny." I leaned back, my pose deceptively casual. "My friend was a producer on that film. It had a limited release in the UK. Only shown in a handful of cinemas—all of them in central London. I believe the one you went to was in north London, wasn't it?"

Ivy and Scarlett's heads swiveled back and forth like spectators at a sporting event.

I wasn't going to let Clive get away with whatever shit he was trying to pull. Coming after me was one thing; dragging Scarlett into it was another.

"Then I remembered wrong," he said coolly. "Maybe I watched *House of Snakes* somewhere else. Either way, I'm glad I went to the cinema last weekend. Otherwise, I wouldn't have run into Scarlett, and we wouldn't be here." He smiled and draped his arm over the back of Scarlett's chair.

Ivy shifted with discomfort while I waited for Scarlett to tell him off. She wouldn't let someone take such liberties this early into a first date.

"Exactly." She leaned into him with an answering smile. "I'm glad I ran into you too."

Clive's teeth gleamed like little white targets for my fist.

What the actual fuck? She couldn't possibly like—

The bet. It hit me like a freight train. I'd forgotten about our wager, but it made sense why she was indulging Clive's delusions.

Ivy and I weren't on a real date, so I didn't have to worry about scoring a second one; I could just say I had. Meanwhile, Scarlett was under the impression that she needed to work for hers.

At least, that was what I told myself because the alternative explanation was too nauseating to contemplate.

Since she didn't know Ivy was a cover, I had to make an effort to "win" or she'd get suspicious.

"Did I mention that Ivy is studying environmental law at the University of London?" I said. "She's brilliant."

"You got a lawyer to go out with you? Impressive," Scarlett said. It was lighthearted enough to pass as a joke but pointed enough for me to know it wasn't.

I narrowed my eyes while Clive smirked.

"Law student," Ivy corrected with a laugh. "I mean, it's Asher Donovan. Who *wouldn't* want to go out with him?"

Clive's smirk disappeared.

A wisp of discomfort coasted through my stomach, but I washed it away with more wine.

Ivy was playing her part. I couldn't fault her for that. Still, I wished she would've called me Asher instead of *Asher Donovan*. I shouldn't complain, considering how many doors the latter opened for me, but sometimes it felt a little dehumanizing, like I was a walking brand instead of a person.

Scarlett's brow creased with a small frown. She slid a glance at me, her gaze oddly questioning, before she turned back to Ivy. "So, environmental law. Do you have a specialty?" she asked.

Ivy lit up for the first time since she saw Clive. "Marine protection, but I'm interested in the management of hazardous substances and wastes too."

For the next half hour, she regaled us with details about her courses while we ate our appetizers—Scarlett silent, Clive scowling, and me interjecting with the occasional *mmm* and *wow*.

I was all for saving the environment, but truthfully, listening to the intricacies of the UN's High Seas Treaty while we ate gourmet crab cakes wasn't my idea of a good time.

Ivy seemed oblivious to the growing tension. Thankfully, the server brought out our main courses and interrupted her before she could go into more detail about exploited fish stocks.

"This lobster is delicious." Scarlett speared a piece with her fork and held it out to Clive. "Here, try."

"Thanks, babe." Clive shot me a smug look and ate the lobster tail straight off her fork.

Scarlett and I reacted with simultaneous grimaces, but when I focused on her, her face had already smoothed into a smile.

"Tell us about rugby," she said. "I've always wanted to learn more about it."

She cast the bait, and he fell for it hook, line, and sinker. If there was one thing men loved, it was talking about themselves.

While Clive extolled the virtues of rugby and his "importance" on the pitch, Ivy poked at her pasta with a frown.

"Ivy, darling, would you like more wine?" I asked solicitously.

The word *darling* tasted strange when aimed at someone who wasn't Scarlett, but I swallowed my misgivings. We were halfway through dinner, and it was time to take things up a notch.

Scarlett's seeming fascination with Clive's rugby rant faltered.

"Yes, please." Ivy pushed her glass toward me. She might've hated wine at uni, but perhaps she *had* developed a new appreciation for it because she gulped it down like a desperate woman who'd finally stumbled upon an oasis in the desert.

The dinner dragged on.

If I hadn't regretted the double-date idea before, I sure as hell did now. Listening to Clive talk was insufferable. Seeing Scarlett stroke his ego with questions and encouraging nods was worse.

I tossed back my drink and glared as she laughed at his stupid joke about a priest taking up rugby. *Anyone* could've seen the conversions punchline coming.

"Excuse me." Ivy's chair scraped back with a rasp of wood against the carpet. "I don't feel too well. I'll be right back."

Concern leaked through my irritation. I'd been so focused on Scarlett and Clive, I'd neglected Ivy. Her face did look paler than when we'd arrived, but she hurried off before I could respond.

Her departure cast an immediate pall over the table.

Clive stared after her, then tossed his napkin on the table and stood. "I have to use the loo, too. I'll be right back."

Five seconds later, he disappeared into the hall housing the toilets.

Yeah. Not suspicious at all.

I didn't know why Ivy and Clive broke up, but judging by their reactions to each other, the attraction wasn't dead.

I couldn't have planned it better myself. Maybe they'd rekindle their flame and Clive could leave Scarlett the fuck alone. Ivy was too good for that wanker, but if she was into that, then it was none of my business.

Scarlett and I sat in silence, the specter of our dates and a thousand unspoken words hanging over us.

"Ivy seems nice," she finally said.

"She is. And Clive seems...present."

She snorted, an undignified sound that was at odds with her elegant appearance.

The corner of my mouth tilted up. I loved her reactions. They were so real, so *her*. No artifice, no ass-kissing. Pure Scarlett.

"I can't believe they used to date," she said. "What a plot twist."

"Maybe it's a sign."

"Of what?"

"That we're on dates with the wrong people."

My words stole the last semblance of pretense between us. They hissed and crackled like a blaze in a hearth, warming my skin and bringing a tint of red to Scarlett's cheeks.

"That's not something you should say when we're still *on* our dates." She glanced in the direction of the toilets.

No Ivy or Clive yet.

"Perhaps, but am I wrong?" I challenged. "Don't tell me you can endure Clive's grandstanding about rugby. *Rugby*." I made a noise of disgust. "It's violence disguised as a sport. All brawn, no finesse."

"You are such a snob. Other sports exist besides football, you know."

"Not good ones."

A hint of a smile crossed her face. "You're insufferable."

"But more sufferable than Clive Hart. Be honest." My gaze burned into hers. "Are you enjoying your date with him, or do you simply want to win our bet?"

The smile disappeared. "Why wouldn't I enjoy the date? He's good-looking, successful, and funny. The total package."

Funny? Sure, Clive was funny the way syphilis was funny, and his "total package" included a strong whiff of bullshit.

The same bullshit I heard in Scarlett's response.

"That's not what I asked," I said softly.

Scarlett's eyes flickered in the candlelight. They were the color of silver moonbeams, at times clear, at times obscured by wisps of clouds.

Sometimes, finding her true feelings amongst the mist was impossible. Tonight, I saw right through it.

"No." The clouds parted, revealing a glimmer of vulnerability.

"Not really."

Her answer was as close to an admission as she would allow, in this moment where our dates were gone and we could spin an illusion of normality.

My heart pattered to an uneven beat.

"Are you enjoying your date with Ivy?" she asked.

"No." I held her gaze. "Not really."

The clatter of plates and silverware retreated into the background. Scarlett's lips parted, and I felt it in my bones—a moment of perfect tension, stretched taut between our previous promises and our present desires.

Two weeks since our kiss.

Two weeks since we agreed to pretend it never happened.

And yet, beneath the surface of our otherwise innocent conversation, the rolling thunder of attraction drummed on.

Her reasons for disregarding the kiss were still valid. The consequences of not doing so were still threats.

But it was easier to choose logic during daylight, when work and distractions formed a barrier between the head and heart.

At night, that barrier dwindled, leaving us open to the possibility that consequences paled next to our wants.

"You called her *darling*." Scarlett's voice was smoke and velvet, threaded with a tinge of hurt. "You must be enjoying the date more than you admit unless you use that endearment with everyone. Does it always work for you?"

"I wouldn't know." The satisfaction of getting under her skin with that tactic was minute compared to my exhaustion. I was tired of our games. "I've only called one woman that and meant it."

Scarlett's soft inhale was nearly my undoing.

I didn't want to be in a crowded restaurant, on a double date, surrounded by strangers and cosplaying indifference.

I wanted to be anywhere else, as long as I was alone with her.

"Hey. I'm sorry that took so long." Ivy's apology jarred us out of our trance.

Our gazes jerked away from each other, and the soft honesty of the moment disappeared in a puff of smoke.

I pasted on a smile, trying not to look too annoyed as Ivy slid into her seat. "I think the wine doesn't agree with me," she said. "I'm still a little nauseous."

I frowned. Her skin looked even more waxen than before, minus the dark flush crawling over her neck and chest.

"Do you want to call it a night?" I asked. "I can drive you home. I don't want you to stay if you're not feeling well."

We weren't on a real date, but that didn't mean I was going to be a dick and leave her to fend for herself.

She nodded, her expression miserable. "I'm sorry. I don't want to ruin everyone's night, but..."

"Don't worry about it. I'll get the check." A tingle of relief loosened the fist around my heart. Leaving the date meant leaving Scarlett, but at least I didn't have to pretend anymore.

Before I could flag down our server, Clive reappeared. "What's going on?"

Scarlett explained the situation.

He didn't seem surprised, and I was reminded again of their suspicious timing. They'd left for the toilets and returned at almost the exact same time.

I doubted they'd hooked up while they were gone—though that would explain Ivy's growing nausea, in my opinion—but *something* must've happened.

Instead of staying and pursuing his vendetta against me via

Scarlett, he shocked the hell out of us by saying, "I'll take Ivy home. It's on my way anyway." He cast a sheepish glance at Scarlett. "I'm sorry for bailing early, but I have an emergency at home. Rain check?"

The fact that no one called him out on the contradiction of driving Ivy home when he had an "emergency" was a testament to how off the rails the date had gotten.

"Sure." I could've sworn that was relief in Scarlett's voice. "I understand."

"I'll take Scarlett home," I said before Clive offered to drive her as well. I wouldn't put it past the bastard to attempt a threesome or something similar. "Dinner's on me. I had a big payday earlier this week."

He didn't miss the subtle dig referencing the money he'd lost at the race. Resentment flared anew in his eyes, but he kept his mouth shut.

I wasn't under the illusion I'd seen or heard the last of him. I'd lucked out with the Ivy situation tonight, but Clive was petty enough to keep coming back until I knocked him out for good.

I'd deal with that tomorrow. For now, I allowed myself a measure of relaxation as he disappeared through the doors with Ivy, who went along with the change of plans silently.

"Well, this didn't turn out the way I'd expected," Scarlett said after I'd paid and we'd made it to my car. I'd had half a glass of wine, but I was clearheaded and sober enough to drive. "Do you think they…"

"Oh yeah." I pulled out of the car park. "The old flame is not dead."

She huffed out a laugh. "I should be insulted, but I'm not."

"Trust me, anything that takes Clive's attention off you is a good thing."

"He's really not that bad."

"That's what the Victorians said about adding boric acid to milk."

Another, startled laugh filled the car. "Asher Donovan, a scholar of the Victorian era? Color me surprised."

"I wouldn't say scholar." I flashed a quick grin. "But I did watch several YouTube videos about it."

Five minutes of lighthearted conversation, and I was already having a better time than I'd had at dinner.

"I hope no one recognized us at the restaurant," Scarlett said. "And by us, I mean you."

"Some definitely did, but as long as they're not paps, it should be fine. Most people have common decency."

I was recognized all the time on the streets. Sometimes, fans stopped me for autographs and pictures. However, I'd never had a stranger post a private moment of me online without my consent.

The tabloids were the issue, not the average citizen.

"I hope so." Scarlett ran a hand over the sleek leather interior. I'd picked a low-key black Porsche for tonight. It was my go-to car for when I wanted something nice but not too flashy. "I don't understand guys' fascination with cars. Why do you need so many?"

"Some women collect shoes and bags. Some men collect cars." I shrugged. "I'm one of them."

"Hmm. Can't relate."

Laughter rumbled past my throat. "It's not for everyone." I tapped my fingers on the wheel, debating whether to release the question sitting at the tip of my tongue. *Screw it.* "Have you thought about getting your own? I know you don't like taxis…"

I trailed off, letting her fill in the gaps. It was a sensitive topic, but we weren't strangers to those.

Luckily, Scarlett didn't appear offended. "I thought about it, but..." She shook her head. "No. I'd rather take the tube. Besides, city traffic is a nightmare."

"Fair enough." I didn't push the issue. "I'm happy you're doing the showcase. It should be a good time."

"Me too." Her face softened. "It's nice to sit in on rehearsals again, even if I'm only watching. It feels...I don't know. It feels like I'm part of something bigger than myself, and I haven't felt that way in a long time."

"I know what you mean."

It was one of the reasons why I loved football instead of, say, golf or tennis. Every team had its top performers, but at the end of the day, winning was a group effort. It was a brotherhood—at least, it was supposed to be, when it wasn't weakened by perpetual infighting.

Goddamn Vincent.

The indirect reminder of Scarlett's brother put an instant damper on my mood. If it weren't for him, we wouldn't be stuck on this merry-go-round of emotions. Hell, I probably wouldn't have met Scarlett in the first place. Life would be much simpler.

However, the thought of never meeting her sent an unpleasant chill through my chest. We'd known each other for two months, yet I couldn't imagine a world where she didn't exist in my orbit.

Even when caution kept us at arm's length, seeing her was the highlight of my week.

I snuck a peek at Scarlett as we entered her street. She stared out the window, her brow furrowed, her expression seemingly lost in thought.

I'd give Clive his hundred grand back in exchange for the ability to read her thoughts right now. The night had been a roller coaster of surprises, but the elephant in the room—the quiet admissions we'd allowed ourselves before Ivy's return at dinner—remained undiscussed.

"I guess neither of us won the wager," I said, breaking the silence.

"I guess not." Scarlett pulled her attention away from the window as I pulled up in front of her flat. "But I'm sure Ivy will agree to a second date if you call her up. You're *the* Asher Donovan."

Her tone contained lighthearted teasing, but her smile didn't reach her eyes. She was still distracted by something.

"I'm not sure she will," I said. "And I'm not sure I want her to."

The engine cut off, bathing us in silence.

Moonlight poured through the windows and highlighted the emotions fluttering across her face.

The elephant grew larger, pressing against the windows and into my lungs until it was hard to breathe.

If there was ever a moment to rethink our pact, it was now.

Come on, darling.

Just when I thought Scarlett would give in to the haze thickening the air, she tore her gaze away from mine.

"Thank you for the lift," she said, her voice steady but her fingers shaking slightly as she unbuckled her seat belt. "And for dinner. It's been…an interesting night."

My eyes lingered on her for an extra beat before I faced forward again, my jaw tight. "You're welcome."

I didn't offer to walk her to her door, and she didn't look back as she scrambled out of the car and into the building like the hounds of hell were nipping at her feet.

However, I did wait for the lights to switch on in her flat before I left.

Frustration chafed beneath my skin. I couldn't marshal my thoughts into any semblance of order. They scattered all over the place, ping-ponging between reason and emotion, practicality and desire.

I wish I had someone to talk to about this. My old teammates at Holchester weren't speaking to me, and Adil and Noah were on holiday with their families. Even if they weren't, I didn't know my teammates well enough yet to unload on them about my love life.

That was one of the downsides of fame that no one talked about—the more success you gained, the fewer friends you had.

It hadn't been a problem before. I'd never met a woman who made me question what I wanted the way Scarlett did, but now...

I swiped a hand over my face as indecision took root inside me.

Does this feel platonic to you?

We'll pretend the kiss never happened.

Are you enjoying your date with him?

You called her darling.

I'm not sure she will. And I'm not sure I want to.

I made it halfway down the street before I came to an abrupt halt. Thankfully, there were no cars behind me.

What the fuck am I doing?

I didn't know whether it was the empty roads or the quiet night, but clarity unfolded with sudden, blazing sharpness.

I wanted Scarlett. She wanted me. Yes, our relationship would have obstacles, and yes, overcoming them seemed impossible, but fuck it, how would we know unless we tried? Impossible things happened every day.

Look at Eldorra's royal couple. They overcame a centuries-old *law* to be together.

Even my rise to stardom would've been deemed unfathomable—the solidly working-class boy from a working-class town, whose teachers were so certain he'd amount to nothing, growing up to become the highest paid player in the Premier League.

Every problem had a solution. I was determined to find ours.

But in the meantime…

I switched gears and pulled a sharp U-turn. My heart thundered in my throat as I parked in front of Scarlett's flat, cut the engine, and ran upstairs. The main door was unlocked, which couldn't be safe, but I chose not to look a gift horse in the mouth.

Please don't be asleep yet.

If she wasn't up and I waited to say what I had to say, I might lose my nerve and we would end up right back in limbo. That couldn't happen.

I knocked on her door.

Once. Twice.

My pulse was a relentless anvil against my veins, and the hammering worsened when Scarlett answered the door.

She was still wearing her dress from dinner, but she was barefoot and makeup free.

Her eyes widened. "Asher? What are you—"

She didn't get a chance to finish her question before I stepped forward, grabbed the back of her neck, and crushed her mouth to mine.

Her gasp of surprise traveled into my lungs, and there was a taut, suspended moment when I thought she might push me away.

But then her gasp turned into a moan, and her lips parted for mine, and I knew nothing would be the same ever again.

CHAPTER 22

SCARLETT

THE SECOND ASHER'S LIPS TOUCHED MINE, I WAS LOST.

Every argument for why I should push him away, every piece of logic that'd kept us at arm's length for the past two months crumbled like a sandcastle beneath a tidal wave.

We stumbled into my flat, our hands tearing at each other's clothes, our mouths hot and desperate with want.

It was nothing like our first kiss.

Our first kiss had been an exploration, a dip into the world of *what if*. What if we gave into our attraction? What if we said fuck it and did what we wanted, consequences be damned?

This kiss...this kiss was an explosion. Every guardrail I'd constructed, every promise I'd made to myself, incinerated with one touch.

I heard the dim thud of my door slamming shut, but it was so far outside my realm of focus that it might as well have occurred galaxies away.

Asher's hands burned a path down my back to the curve of my

ass, and another gasp escaped when he lifted me with the ease of someone picking up a rag doll.

Electric shivers rippled down my spine, and I instinctively wrapped my arms and legs around him as he carried me to my room without breaking our kiss.

My flat had one bedroom and the door was open, so he didn't have to guess where to go. Every step added to the need building between my legs; by the time we passed through the doorway, I was nothing more than a bundle of anticipatory pleasure strung together with lust.

Asher pulled his mouth away from mine. I let out an involuntary whimper of protest, which elicited a soft chuckle as he laid me on the bed with exquisite, agonizing care.

"Don't worry, darling." The words feathered over my skin like tiny caresses. "We haven't even started yet."

My entire body tightened at the dark promise in his voice. I watched, blood thrumming, as he shed his trousers and boxer briefs.

We'd lost my dress and his shirt somewhere between the living room and bedroom. I was clad in my black lace bra and thong set—the one I always wore for first dates—and Asher was...well, he was naked.

The most glorious, mouthwatering type of naked a girl could dream of.

If I hadn't been lying down, my knees might've buckled from the sheer visual pleasure standing before me.

Broad shoulders. Tapered waist. Abs like chiseled marble. And those *thighs*. They looked like they could crush a freaking watermelon.

My belly fluttered with a fresh wave of need.

I'd never admit it, but I'd always thought footballers had the best physique out of any athletes. Slim yet muscular, light yet powerful.

Asher proved all my theories right.

My eyes tracked a light dusting of hair—down, down, past the ridges of his abs all the way to his arousal.

The air evaporated from my lungs. *My God.* Even his cock was beautiful. Long and thick, perfectly proportioned to his body, its tip already leaking pre-cum.

Another soft laugh interrupted my greedy perusal.

"Close your mouth, sweetheart," Asher drawled. "There's plenty of time for that later."

A flush worked its way from my face to my toes at the insinuation. However, my embarrassment faded when he approached me, his eyes dark with a mixture of heat, amusement, and something else that slotted between my rib cage like a key into a lock.

It wasn't my first time having sex, but the lead-up had never felt like this—like I was teetering on the precipice of something that could upend my entire world if I let it.

And I *wanted* to let it. That was the scariest part.

I'd tried so hard to prevent myself from getting to this point. Every time I gave in over the past two months, I immediately pulled back, but one side had to win the tug-of-war between my heart and mind.

Right now, the heart was leading bigtime.

The mattress dipped beneath Asher's weight. He hadn't touched me yet, but the warmth of his body curled around me in sensual tendrils as he dragged his gaze up my legs, over my stomach, and to my face.

I instinctively tensed. Self-consciousness coiled around me in a defensive shield, but unlike previous hookups, he didn't stop to gawk at the surgery scars on my hip and stomach or struggle to hide a flash of revulsion.

When his eyes met mine, they were filled with nothing except pure, appreciation-fueled desire, and it was that, more than anything else, that ended the war inside me.

Heart: one. Mind: zero.

No one had ever looked at me like that, like they could see past all my shields and pretenses to the imperfections I fought to hide. Like those imperfections didn't matter, and not only did they not matter, but they were a *reason* for appreciation instead of an obstacle.

It was the first time anyone had seen me for *me*.

Emotion tangled in my throat as Asher's lips brushed mine before he trailed a series of slow, excruciatingly gentle kisses down my throat and chest. He unclasped my bra with deft fingers along the way, and I bit back a moan when he turned his attention to my breasts.

Every inch of skin flamed like it was fire and he was oxygen. The heat spread, slowly at first, then gathering speed as he reached the aching center between my thighs.

My mind was so muddled, I didn't know when or how he'd slipped my underwear off, but I had enough faculties left to ask the question that'd plagued me since he showed up at my door.

"Why did you come back?" The words slipped out somewhere between nerves and anticipation.

I had an inkling, but I wanted to hear him say it. I needed to know that if we opened Pandora's box, we would brave the consequences together.

Asher paused, his breath soft against my parted thighs. The moonlight carved valleys and shadows across his face, but when he looked up, I saw the answer before he said it.

"I came back for you."

Simple. Honest. *Raw*.

Then he dove in and drove every other thought out of my mind.

There was no time to reflect on his answer or the way it made my heart fold in on itself. There was only the silkiness of his tongue, and the pleasure pouring through my veins, and the sharp, undiluted *need* to be as close to him as possible.

If I thought Asher was thorough with his kisses, it was nothing compared to the way he gave oral.

He left no inch of flesh unattended, no piece of want unfulfilled as he ate me out like I was his last meal. When I craved more pressure, he added it; when I wished for more attention on a certain spot, he moved there. It was like he had a crystal-clear look inside my mind, and my defenses were no match for his targeted onslaught.

"Please," I gasped. I grasped his hair, desperate for any hold that would keep me from slipping too far too fast. "I can't...I...oh *fuck*."

He dragged his teeth across my clit, and only the steel grip of his hands on my hips kept me from shooting off the bed.

Electricity shot through me, causing tears to pool at the corners of my eyes. My words devolved into unintelligible moans as Asher soothed me with gentler laps of his tongue.

"Fuck, sweetheart, you're so wet." He groaned, the sound rumbling through me like a match to gasoline.

I was still shivering from the aftereffects when he sucked my already swollen clit into his mouth, and the world splintered again.

I cried out, my back arching up again. But no matter how hard I bucked or how many times I instinctively tried to scoot away, he dragged me back, his mouth and tongue and teeth working in tandem as he continued his brutal, delicious assault against my senses.

My mind was fracturing, its hold on reality slipping with every lick and suck. I was so soaked, I almost didn't notice when he pushed two fingers inside me. They slid in with little resistance, but when he curled them just so, pressing against my most sensitive spot, my orgasm tore through me with blinding ferocity.

Another sharp cry clawed up my throat, but it was drowned out by pleasure so intense it seemed to unravel straight from my core. Wave after wave rushed through me, stealing the breath from my lungs and filling my vision with bursts of light.

I dimly heard the rustle of clothes and the rip of foil. Fireworks were still exploding behind my eyes when Asher tucked a pillow under my hips and pressed the tip of his cock against my pussy. The orgasm had wrung me out, but that didn't stop a whimper from escaping.

As good as the oral had been, I needed *more*. I needed something to fill the empty ache inside me.

Asher's lips grazed my ear. "Hold on tight."

My anticipation pulled tight into a painful knot, but I didn't get a chance to respond before he pushed inside me with a smooth thrust.

This time, my gasp only made it out halfway. It cut off into a half-moan, half-squeal that would've embarrassed the hell out of me had I had enough presence of mind to *be* embarrassed.

Since I didn't, I could only cling to him for dear life as he settled into a hard, relentless rhythm, my nails digging into his shoulders, my hips rising to meet his. The headboard slammed against the wall every thrust, and the sound of flesh slapping flesh mingled with our harsh breaths and cries.

I was sure I'd get a nasty note about the noise from my neighbor tomorrow, but I was so lost in the moment that I didn't care.

My condition meant sex could be difficult and painful if I wasn't in the right position or my partner didn't know what they were doing. However, the wine from dinner and my orgasm had loosened my limbs, and Asher managed to hit my sweet spot every single time.

Our bodies moved in sync like they were made for each other. I couldn't remember the last time I'd felt this connected to someone during sex, and it had less to do with the physicality of the act than it did with the emotions behind it.

For once, I didn't feel the need to perform. I could simply bask in the sensations, and the result was so overwhelming that part of me was afraid I'd never be the same after this.

Asher captured my mouth in a kiss. "God, you feel good," he murmured. "Your pussy takes my cock so fucking well, sweetheart. I could fuck you all day and night and you would still be wet and ready for me, wouldn't you?"

Heat pulsated in my core at the image he painted. "Yes," I panted. My nails sank deeper into his skin. "*Please.*"

He groaned again. Tension corded the muscles of his neck and shoulders. His hands dug into my hips, and I could tell he was on the verge of breaking.

That knowledge, combined with the taste of myself on his tongue and the deep strokes of his cock, set me off for the second time that night.

This time, my orgasm was less like a wave and more like a tsunami. It started in the pit of my stomach and slammed through the rest of my body with such force, my toes literally curled.

A scream ripped from my throat. My body bowed from the intensity as Asher increased his speed, and I felt his cock throb inside me before he came with a guttural cry.

He collapsed next to me, and we lay there during the come down, our bodies flushed with sweat, our chests heaving for oxygen as I tried to recover from what was hands down the best sex of my life.

"Your neighbor is going to hate us," he said after what could've been a minute or an hour.

I'd lost sense of time. I was still floating on a high, my limbs weightless with exhaustion, but a laugh bubbled from my chest, nonetheless. "I thought the same thing earlier."

Asher turned his head to look at me. "You were thinking of your neighbor while we were having sex?"

My laugh intensified at the insulted look on his face. "Only for a moment. I didn't think she'd appreciate the headboard slamming." I leaned over and gave him a quick kiss. "Don't worry. I was focused on you the majority of the time."

"Thanks," he said dryly. "You really know how to stroke a guy's ego."

But a glitter of amusement lit his eyes, and I couldn't hold back a grin of my own.

After-sex conversations were often so awkward, but I could lie here and talk to him all night.

"I'm not going to make a dirty joke," I said. "You set it up too easily for me."

"Exactly. I love dirty jokes." Asher shifted onto his side, and I sucked in a surprised breath at what I felt against my leg. "Among other things."

"How are you hard again *already?*" I demanded, even as a tingle of renewed lust shot through me. "You just came!"

Laughter vibrated through the room. "Stamina. It comes with the territory." His voice softened into smoke. "Now be a good girl and suck my cock clean."

It was like he'd flipped a switch with those ten words.

The levity instantly vanished, replaced by thick, heady tension. A flame ignited in my core as his earlier words surged up in my consciousness.

Close your mouth, sweetheart. There's plenty of time for that later.

Oxygen thinned, and I swallowed at the thought of taking him in my mouth. He wasn't fully hard yet, but he was still intimidating enough that my thighs clenched.

Nevertheless, I didn't take my eyes off his as I rose onto my knees and straddled him. I hadn't gotten to where I was in life without a boatload of determination and a certain taste for challenges.

Asher's expression didn't change as I grasped him with both hands and stroked him to full length, but his breathing visibly quickened when I rubbed my thumb across the pre-cum gathered at his tip. He was still slick from our previous activities, but I used the pre-cum as additional lube.

I twisted and squeezed, pumping him with long, firm strokes until his hips bucked and he let out a strangled noise.

The thrill of pulling that reaction from him pooled between my thighs. The squelch of my hands sliding over his cock, the way he fisted the sheets in an attempt to maintain control, the sheer *heat* and size of him...

"Enough teasing." Asher's steely voice halted my movements. "Suck my cock, Scarlett."

Oh God.

My clit throbbed at the harsh command, and I didn't bother protesting. Not when I was dying to taste him as much as he'd tasted me earlier.

My breaths left me in little pants as I eagerly swirled my tongue around his cock head. I whimpered with need at the taste, and my body buzzed to life at the sound of his groans. I kept my hands wrapped around him as I bobbed my head up and down and alternated between licking and sucking.

I smiled with satisfaction when his hands finally tangled in my hair. I worked him deeper down my throat, but I eventually hit a point where my gag reflex kicked in.

Fresh tears sprung to my eyes, and drool leaked from the corners of my mouth as I choked on half his length.

Asher's grip loosened, giving me an out, but I paused only long enough to catch my breath before I dove in again.

Like I said, determination and challenges. I thrived on both.

"*Fuck*, that's it." Asher tightened his hold again when I sucked harder. I didn't manage to take all of him, but he filled my throat so completely that my moan came out as a needy hum. "You drive me so fucking wild," he groaned. "And you don't even know it."

My muffled response got lost beneath a loud curse and grunt when his orgasm hit. His hips slammed up, and I choked again as bursts of cum hit the back of my throat.

My vision blurred, but I swallowed hungrily, trying to keep up as he came and came until he finally sagged, and I let his cock slip from my lips.

I pushed myself up and wiped my mouth, another smile flickering to life at Asher's expression of postcoital bliss.

"You look pleased with yourself," he said, an answering smile in his voice.

"So do you." I arched an eyebrow at his groin and earned myself a full-throated belly laugh.

We cleaned ourselves up, sliding from lust to comfort with an ease that made my chest glow. When we finished, I curled up next to him, utterly exhausted but satiated in a way I hadn't been for a long, long time.

A companionable silence filled the room. Drowsiness tugged at my eyelids, but I didn't want to sleep. Not yet.

Asher pressed a kiss on my forehead. "How are you feeling?" he murmured. "You need anything?"

My chest clenched. It was a casual question, but it was the casualness that made it so intimate. He wasn't trying to care; he simply did.

I'd been too wound up to appreciate it at the time, but I suddenly remembered how he'd placed the pillow beneath me earlier. It'd gotten shoved to the side during my ministrations, but it helped with the pain that sometimes accompanied sex.

Even in the throes of desire, he'd been thoughtful enough to think of my comfort.

My chest squeezed harder.

"No," I said honestly. "I feel great."

I might not in the morning. I hadn't had sex in ages, so who knew how my body would react later. But that was a problem for another day.

I also had enough wits left to understand there was no turning back after tonight. A kiss was one thing; sex was another, especially the kind of sex we'd just had.

We'd discarded our inhibitions, and we'd have to face the consequences tomorrow.

But right now, as Asher curled his arm around my shoulders and I tucked my head against his chest, I found it hard to care.

Tomorrow would always be there.

Tonight, it was just us, and I was going to enjoy every second of it while it lasted.

CHAPTER 23

SCARLETT

I AWOKE TO AN EMPTY BED AND THE SCENT OF SIZZLING bacon.

The former was normal; the latter was unusual enough to rouse me from the dregs of sleep.

I rarely slept over at anyone's house, and I rarely let anyone sleep at *my* house, so where did the bacon come from?

I reluctantly cracked my eyes open. Sunshine streamed through the curtains, gilding the pile of clothes on the floor and the glass of water on the nightstand. The space beside me was still warm, and the sheets smelled like sex and a trace of aftershave.

Sex. Aftershave. Asher.

Fragments of last night finally broke through my early-morning mental fog. The double date with Clive and Ivy, Asher showing up at my door after he'd already dropped me off, and then…

A smile spread before I could stop it.

It was the morning after, aka the day of reckoning. I should be worried, but all I felt were little champagne bubbles of euphoria fizzing in my blood.

I was still in bed, which meant my day *technically* hadn't started yet, though bacon and Asher were both tempting draws.

I stretched my limbs. I was sore all over, both in a delicious way and a I'm-going-to-need-extra-Epsom-salts-for-this type of way, but it wasn't bad enough to take precedence over my hunger.

After a minute of luxuriating in the quiet, I climbed out of bed and threw on the first oversize tee I found. I ducked into the bathroom to brush my teeth and make sure I didn't look like a gremlin before I padded barefoot to the kitchen.

I stopped in the doorway, my stomach flipping at the sight before me.

Asher manned the stove clad in only boxer briefs. The muscles in his back flexed as he plated the bacon, and my stomach flips morphed into full somersaults.

Forget porn. *This* was what women wanted.

I soaked in the sight of his tousled hair and tanned skin for an extra beat before I made my presence known.

"Making yourself at home, I see," I teased. I entered the kitchen and slid onto one of the island counter stools.

Asher turned, his face breaking into a smile when he saw me. "I figured you'd be less likely to kick me out if I bribed you with bacon, eggs, and sausage."

A hint of sleep roughened his voice, which really added to the ambiance, in my opinion. I could get used to waking up like this.

He slid a plate and silverware toward me. I accepted it gratefully, my mouth watering at the heap of food. He'd cooked the bacon exactly the way I liked it—crispy but not *too* crispy, with just enough fat to stave off unappealing dryness. The strips glistened next to two pieces of perfectly seared sausage and a small mound of scrambled eggs.

"If you hadn't forgotten the tea, I would've thought you were psychic," I quipped. "You cooked everything perfectly. Thank you."

"Ah, the tea." Asher snapped his fingers. "How could I forget the drink of the gods?"

He grabbed a mug off the counter and placed it in front of me. Black tea with a dash of milk and sugar on the side. Perfect.

"Never mind. You *are* psychic." I reached for the mug but stopped when he stared at me, his brow furrowing. Self-consciousness prickled my skin. "What?"

Had my bleary eyes deceived me in the bathroom mirror? Did I have a giant pillow crease marring my cheek or a line of dried drool at the corner of my mouth?

"Your shirt." Asher's mouth twitched. "Are you talking about the planet or the dog?"

I glanced down, confused, until I realized I was wearing my Justice for Pluto T-shirt. Carina had gifted it to me after I bought her a stuffed penguin from the Bronx Zoo Store during my holiday in New York.

My shoulders relaxed. "The planet. You see?" I pointed my fork at him, my breakfast temporarily forgotten. "You called it a planet. That's because it *is* a planet. I'll never forgive the IAU for demoting Pluto to a dwarf planet."

"Isn't a dwarf planet also a planet?"

"It's not the same! It's like moving from the Premier League to the EFL."

British football was divided into several leagues. The Premier League was at the top. The EFL, or the English Football League, occupied the next level down.

"I see." Another tiny smile came and went. "I didn't realize you were so, uh, passionate about Pluto."

"It's my favorite planet." The smallest, the most overlooked. It was the underdog of the solar system, and it deserved a little love. Why should Earth and Mars get all the glory? "I did an entire school presentation on it back when it was still the ninth planet from the sun. I had photos. I stayed up all night painting Styrofoam balls. My science teacher said it was the best planetary presentation she'd seen in years. Then you know what happened?"

Asher shook his head, looking alarmed.

"The very next year, the IAU *demoted it*. They said it wasn't a planet anymore." My indignation swelled at the injustice. "Can you believe that? Structures exist for a reason. Growing up, I was taught that there were nine planets. Then one day, they just went ahead and changed it to eight. How is that fair? It's not. Pluto deserves better, hence Justice for Pluto." I gestured at my shirt. "I don't like it when people arbitrarily change long-standing rules."

"I don't know if planetary classifications are necessarily *rules*..." Asher held up his hands when I glowered at him. "I mean, you're right. Justice for Pluto."

"Thank you."

"Remind me never to argue with you about astronomy or rule books. You're quite terrifying when you get rolling on those subjects." He said this with a straight face, but his eyes twinkled the tiniest bit.

Blood rose to my neck and cheeks. It occurred to me that we'd had sex for the first time last night, and I'd just spent a full five minutes ranting about planets.

"I like seeing this side of you." Asher brought another plate over and sat next to me. His knee touched mine, and he looked so at home in my kitchen that little bursts of warmth flickered in my veins.

"The nerdy rambling side?" I asked.

"The unguarded side." The corner of his mouth lifted. "You can ramble about Pluto all you'd like. I won't judge—too much."

I fought a smile and lost.

We were floating on the last wisps of postcoital bliss. Soon, our feet would have to touch the ground, and we'd have to face reality.

For now, as we ate breakfast side by side with the sun streaming through the windows and the air redolent with the aromas of home-cooked food, we were content.

I hadn't brought a guy home since I broke up with my ex, and Asher's presence was almost overwhelming. His muscled frame filled the room, sucking up all the oxygen and making it impossible to breathe without inhaling him into my lungs.

I didn't expect to like it as much as I did. I was a private person, and I guarded my personal space fiercely. But instead of rankling me, Asher's company made my bachelorette flat feel just a little less lonely.

"What are your plans for the day?" I asked, taking what I hoped was a casual sip of tea.

"Hanging out with you," Asher said easily. "If you want me to, of course."

Oh, he was good. Not only that, he was *genuine*, which made it that much worse for my poor heart.

"I *suppose* I could keep you company for a bit," I said with feigned reluctance. "My reading will have to wait."

His eyes crinkled at the corners. "I appreciate your magnanimity."

Since "hanging out" was the vaguest activity in existence, and he didn't offer ideas for what we should do after breakfast, I gave him a quick tour of the flat.

There wasn't much to see. Besides the kitchen, living room, bathroom, and bedroom (which he was already intimately familiar with), the only place of note was the box room I'd converted into a mini library. I didn't have a lot of space, so I only bought physical copies from my favorite authors or books I'd already read and loved on Kindle.

"This is the neatest house I've ever seen." Asher stared at my painstakingly organized collection of books. They were alphabetized by the author's last name, followed by the book height and then color.

"Um, have you seen your place? It's spotless."

"Yeah, but I have people who help. This is all you." He swiped his thumb over a shelf. It came away dust free. "Incredible."

"I like cleaning," I said, half-embarrassed, half-pleased. I tended my library the way some people tended their gardens. "It's soothing. It makes me feel like...I don't know. Like I'm in control."

I couldn't control the messes in my life, but I *could* clean them up at home. Spilled milk? Several swipes of a towel and it was gone. Muddy footprints? Nothing a good mop wouldn't fix. I could snap my fingers, figuratively speaking, and return things to the way they were.

That power provided a small measure of comfort in a world where chaos was the only certainty.

"I get it," Asher said. He touched the spine of one of my Leo Agnelli books—the same one he'd picked up and handed to me before our first training session. God, that seemed like a lifetime ago. "That's how I feel about driving."

I read the tabloids often enough to know he had a penchant for street racing. Several high-profile crashes had earned him a reputation for recklessness, though it hadn't stopped Blackcastle from paying an arm and a leg for him anyway.

I hadn't seen news of any crashes or street races he'd been involved in recently, so maybe he wasn't part of that scene anymore.

I hoped so. Before we met, I hadn't cared. If he wanted to race, then he'd race. It was his life he was gambling with. Now, dread curdled in my gut at the thought of anything happening to him.

Theoretically, his checkered history with cars and speeding should've turned me off given my hang-ups about those issues. But I couldn't reconcile that rash, daredevil tabloid version of him with the thoughtful, caring man who'd researched chronic pain after I told him about my accident and who'd hired the *same* chauffeur to take me to and from our training sessions because I wasn't comfortable with strange drivers.

I'd been a passenger in Asher's car multiple times, and he'd always followed the rules to a tee. I'd never felt uncomfortable or scared, which was saying a lot because even the smallest things set me on edge.

The tabloids weren't the most trustworthy source. Maybe there was more to Asher's racing than met the eye—or maybe I was naive.

I was cycling through ways I could ask him about it when he picked up a photo from the top of my bookshelf. "Is this your mum?"

Five-year-old me was dressed as a fairy princess, tiara and all. My mother stood next to me, her face glowing with pride.

"Yes. That was taken before my first ballet recital." My face softened at the memory. "She was so proud that she took me out for ice cream after. If you knew my mother, you'd know what a big deal that was. She is *not* a dairy or junk food fan. At all."

Asher examined the photo more carefully. "You were adorable."

"*Were*?" I teased.

He set the photo down and faced me again. "I think you've graduated from adorable to something else."

Warm honey filled my veins.

The low pitch of his reply chased away our lighthearted morning and resurfaced memories of what we did last night. The things he made me feel and the uncertainty we'd unleashed.

We'd tiptoed around the elephant in the room all morning. Neither one of us wanted to break the spell, but we had to leave our bubble eventually.

Before I could think of a witty reply or a tactful way to bring up our relationship (friendship? situationship?), Asher's phone rang.

"Excuse me," he said after he checked the caller ID. "I have to take this."

The tension cracked, giving me space to breathe more freely. "No worries. I'll be here."

He answered the call in the next room while I worried my lip between my teeth.

I'd never had a morning-after talk. I usually went in knowing what to expect or slipped out before the other person woke up, so what should I say when Asher came back?

Should I Google it? Did the internet have useful advice, or was it going to lead me astray like the time it told me shrimp was impossible to overcook? (Spoiler: it was, in fact, very possible to overcook shrimp).

Asher returned, and all my half-baked conversation starters died in my throat when I noticed how pale he was.

"What's wrong?" I asked.

"It's my dad." He swallowed, his expression dazed. "He had a heart attack."

CHAPTER 24

ASHER

I DIDN'T PROTEST WHEN SCARLETT INSISTED ON COMING with me to Holchester.

Normally, I wouldn't subject anyone to a three-hour drive with the worst, most anxious version of myself, especially when I was sure they were offering out of politeness and not a genuine desire to give up their Saturday for someone else's family emergency.

But when she'd offered, she'd done so with such sincerity I couldn't say no, and I didn't want to make the three-hour drive alone.

So I accepted.

We didn't talk much during the ride, but her presence helped calm some of the thoughts raging in my head.

My father, who'd never been sick for more than a few days in his life, had had a heart attack.

We hadn't spoken since my last visit to Holchester, when he'd stormed out of the kitchen and I'd left without making amends.

Regret rattled through me.

My mother hadn't provided many details over the phone. She'd only said he was in the hospital, but what if our last words to each other were said out of anger? What if he was gone by the time I got there?

My knuckles turned white around the wheel.

"You can drive faster if you want," Scarlett said, breaking the silence. "I'll be fine. I promise."

I shook my head. "We're almost there. It'll be slower if I sped and got pulled over."

I was already going faster than I normally would when she was in the car. She said she'd be fine, but I didn't want to stress her out, and getting a ticket from some traffic officer on a power trip wouldn't do anyone any good.

Scarlett's worried stare bore a hole in my cheek, but she didn't bring up the issue again. She did, however, call ahead and speak to someone at the hospital so that when we arrived, we were escorted directly to my father's floor without causing a commotion—or tipping off the paparazzi.

My mother sat in the hall, twisting her hands in her lap.

She jumped up when she saw me. Red rimmed her eyes, and she wore her pyjamas with a coat thrown on top. She must've gone straight to the hospital without changing first.

"Oh, Asher." She swept me up into a hug. I'd always considered her a strong person, but her body felt unbearably frail in the fluorescent-lit hallway. "Thank you for coming so quickly."

"Of course." I squeezed her, my heart in my throat. "How is he?"

"He's stable, thank the Lord." My mother pulled back, her eyes glossy. "We were having breakfast like usual. I made him a spot of tea, and we were talking about going to France for holiday. I turned for a second to check on the kettle and heard a crash. When I turned back again, he was on the floor. He...I..."

I hugged her again, my own chest tight. "It's okay. He'll be okay."

Guilt lodged in my gut for not living closer and abandoning her for London. I had my reasons, but what if something happened to my parents and I couldn't make it back in time? I was their only child, and the rest of our family lived elsewhere in the UK or abroad. Besides each other, I was all they had.

I didn't hate my father; I just wished our relationship was different. Plus, my parents had been married for over thirty years. If one of them was gone, I wasn't sure the other would survive.

My mother drew in a deep breath and straightened her shoulders. She was a strong believer in maintaining a stiff upper lip, and her tears visibly subsided as she locked down her emotions again.

"You're right. He'll be okay," she said. "Of course he will. He's already out of the woods. The doctor said they're keeping him for monitoring just in case, but he should be home within a day or two." She sniffled and wiped her cheeks with the back of her hand. "Forgive me. I don't know *what* came over me, crying in public like that. My Lord."

Now that she was in control once more, she realized we weren't alone. She glanced past me at Scarlett, who stood a respectful distance away. Surprise flashed across her face before her earlier weepiness morphed into intrigue.

"I'm sorry, I don't believe we've met," she said. "I'm Pippa, Asher's mum."

"It's nice to meet you, ma'am. I'm Scarlett, Asher's friend," Scarlett said politely.

"Please, call me Pippa. I can't stand being called ma'am. Reminds me of *my* mum, and no one wants that." My mother shuddered before she examined Scarlett with an eagle eye.

Uh-oh. I recognized that look. That was her my-baby-boy-is-

almost-thirty-and-still-hasn't-given-me-grandchildren-so-I'm-going-
to-play-matchmaker-whenever-I-can look.

I almost would've preferred she continued to sob.

"Why don't we look for—"

"Thank you for coming with Asher," my mother said, interrupting
my attempt to steer us toward another topic. "That's very kind of
you."

"It's no trouble at all. That's what friends are for."

"Indeed. Were you with him when he got the news?"

"Um…" Scarlett's smile faltered while I suppressed a grimace.
There was only one realistic reason why we'd be together this early
on a Saturday morning, but neither of us wanted to confirm it for my
mother, of all people. "Yes. We were having breakfast."

Almost true, since we'd finished breakfast by the time I got the
call.

"I see." My mother pounced on that tidbit of information like
a starving lioness on prey. "Quite early for breakfast on a weekend.
Quite a long drive from London to Holchester too."

She cast a pointed look at my outfit. I was wearing the same dress
shirt and trousers from last night's date while Scarlett was in a T-shirt
and jeans. A toddler could've put this two and two together.

"We're both morning people," Scarlett said, her voice bright.
"And the drive wasn't too bad. The roads aren't busy this time of
day."

We avoided looking at each other so we didn't simultaneously
combust from the awkwardness. Her cheeks were dark red, and I
imagined mine were a similar shade.

"I suppose not." My mother didn't sound convinced. "Now I
hope you'll forgive me for being blunt…"

Oh, fuck.

"But how long have you and Asher been friends?" My mother managed to place the verbal equivalent of air quotes around the word *friends* without changing her tone. "Because, you know, it's quite difficult for him to meet women he's *actually* interested in. He's never brought anyone home before."

"Technically, we're not—"

She cut me off again. "He's surrounded by testosterone every day, all day. I tell him, Asher, dear, it's time to meet a nice girl and settle down. You won't be a spring chicken forever, and I want to hold my grandbabies before I die. Does he listen? No." She clucked her tongue. "So you can imagine how delighted I am that you're here. Tell me, how did you meet Asher? Do you have a boyfriend? Are you interested in children anytime soon?"

Scarlett gaped at her, her eyes wide.

"Mother!" I finally interjected. "Please. Now is not the time or place for this."

Trust her to interrogate us about my love life in a hospital waiting room, hours after my father had a heart attack. No one compartmentalized their feelings better than Pippa Donovan.

"That's what you've said for the past five years," she retorted. "I'm simply making conversation. Scarlett doesn't mind, do you, dear?"

"Is Dad awake?" I switched subjects before Scarlett was forced to answer. "I'd like to see him."

"Yes." My mother's face sobered. "The doctors said he was lucky. It was a mild heart attack, and he regained consciousness soon after we arrived at the hospital. They're running tests on him now, but you should be able to see him."

"You go," Scarlett said when I glanced at her. "I'll stay with your mother."

If my mother hadn't been picturing her as her future daughter-in-law before, she sure was now. I could practically see stars pop up in her eyes as she envisioned what her future grandbabies would look like.

I didn't want to leave Scarlett alone with her—god knew what questions she'd ask when I left the room—but it would be awkward to bring Scarlett into my father's hospital room when they'd never met.

I cast an apologetic glance at Scarlett, who gave me a reassuring nod.

Luckily, I tracked down a nurse quickly, and after a bit of back and forth, they let me in to see him.

My father's room was halfway down the hall from where my mother had been sitting. He had his eyes closed when I entered, but he opened them at the sound of the door clicking shut. Tubes snaked around his torso, and a nearby monitor beeped with a steady rhythm.

Relief loosened the fist around my chest at the sound of those beeps.

He was alive.

My mother had said as much, but I'd needed to see it for myself.

"That was fast," he said as I came up beside him. His voice was a hoarse shadow of its usual boom.

"I have a lot of fast cars."

He snorted.

"How are you feeling?" I asked. I tried not to notice how small he looked in the hospital bed or how the color of his face matched the white sheets.

"I'm fine," he said with a dismissive grunt. "This whole thing is ridiculous. I should be home by now, but they insist on keeping me here for forty-eight hours. They said I need 'monitoring,' whatever that means. It's unnecessary horseshit."

"You had a heart attack over breakfast," I reminded him. "I'd say the monitoring is necessary."

"Yes, well, we can't all have healthy starts to the day, can we?"

We stared at each other. A beat of surprise passed before it dissolved into laughter, and the fist in my chest loosened another inch.

I couldn't remember the last time my father and I laughed around each other. Before Blackcastle for sure. Maybe even before I joined the Premier League.

"You drove here from London?" he asked.

I nodded.

He grunted again, which was as close to sentimental as he'd get. My father wasn't a fan of hugs, thank-yous, or emotions in general.

The monitor's beeps punctuated the renewed silence between us. Somewhere along the way, we'd lost the ability to talk to each other, and one bout of shared amusement didn't change that.

My father's eyes drifted toward the front of the room and narrowed. "Who's the girl with your mother?"

I followed his gaze to where Scarlett and my mother were talking. They'd migrated from their original spot down the hall, and we had a perfect view of them through the window.

"That's Scarlett," I said. "She's a...friend."

"Scarlett." A frown pinched between his brows. "Isn't that the name of your trainer this summer?"

Of *course* he remembered that piece of information.

"Yes," I admitted. "She's that too."

My father's attention snapped back to me. "Do all trainers hang out with their athletes at the hospital over the weekend?"

I stiffened at his tone. Whereas my mother was constantly hounding me to give her grandchildren, my father thought love and relationships were too big a distraction.

I'd agreed with him in theory, but that was before I met Scarlett.

"I'd hardly call this 'hanging out,'" I said evenly. "Like I said, we're also friends. She was with me when I got the call, and she was kind enough to accompany me here."

My father stared at me. Whatever he saw in my face had his face creasing with disbelief.

"Oh, don't tell me." He leaned his head back, his expression so pained one would think he was suffering another cardiac event. "Don't tell me you went and slept with your bloody trainer."

My shoulders locked at his visible derision. "It's not like that."

I hated how sleazy he made it sound, like I'd picked her up at the pub and brought her back to my place for a quick shag.

"The bloody hell it isn't." Anger strengthened my father's voice. "What have I told you from the start? Getting involved with anyone at this stage of your career is *not* a good idea. It'll have your head all twisted when. You. Need. Focus. Look at your last season. Number two, and that was *before* you shagged your trainer. How are you going to be number one when you're too busy thinking about getting off to play the game?"

Trust my father to rant about my performance right after a heart attack.

If he weren't lying in a hospital bed right now, I'd snap back. As it was, my jaw ached from how hard I was clenching my teeth.

Don't take the bait.

"Your focus this summer should be on improving your game *on the pitch*, not anywhere else," he growled. "If you're going to play for *that* team, you might as well win. I will *not* have a loser and a trai—" He abruptly cut himself off.

My pulse rocketed. The lights in the room seemed to flare,

whitening the edges of my vision until his face was all I saw. "And a what?"

His lips thinned in response.

"Say it, Dad." My vow to ignore his bait sank beneath a surge of adrenaline. "You will not have a loser and a traitor in your house, right?"

"I didn't say that."

"You were about to." Blood roared in my ears. It was one thing to hear strangers call me a traitor. It was another to hear my own father almost say it. "Be honest. Do you *actually* want me to win?"

"What the hell are you talking about? Of course I do."

"I'm not so sure." This wasn't the place for this conversation, but I couldn't stop the flood from consuming what was left of our civility. It was here, in this garishly lit room, with its monitors and sterile floors, that my ugliest thoughts spilled out. "I think a part of you secretly hopes I'll lose because if I lose, it'll validate what you said about how I never should've left Holchester in the first place. If I win, that means Holchester lost, and you have *never* rooted against them. So tell me, Dad. At the end of the day, if you had to choose, who will it be? Your team or your son?"

I didn't raise my voice. I didn't lose my temper. But my words reverberated through the air with an intensity that caused my father's face to flush.

Crimson washed over his skin like blood seeping into snow. The heart monitor's beeps increased in frequency until they blended into a stream of noise instead of disparate sounds.

He didn't respond. He didn't have to.

We both knew what his answer was.

Less than a minute later, the door flew open and the nurse charged in with a scowl. She scolded me thoroughly for raising my father's heart rate and promptly kicked me out.

I muttered an apology and left. My own heart slammed against my rib cage with bruising force.

If you had to choose, who will it be? Your team or your son?

Anyone who wasn't familiar with Holchester football fan culture would say it was a ridiculous question and that family was the obvious answer, but I'd seen men go to prison for beating another senseless over a missed penalty kick. Others have taken out bank loans to buy merch and follow the team around the world.

For some people, football mattered more than anything else. I had a sinking suspicion my father was one of them.

"What happened?" my mother asked when I stepped into the hall. Her worried eyes traveled from my face to my father's room and back again. She must've heard the nurse yelling at me. "What did he say to you?"

What did he say to me, not what did I say to him.

As much as she loved my father, she was well aware of his faults and our long-running dynamic.

"The usual." I didn't look at Scarlett, who stood quietly next to my mother. I was too embarrassed by the family drama. "I'm sorry, I should've kept my cool. I know how he can get, and he just had a heart attack. I shouldn't have risen to the bait."

My mother glanced at the window again. "He'll be okay." Anxiety threaded her voice, but she didn't press for more details. "I know how your father can get too." She touched my arm with a gentle hand. "Why don't you and Scarlett go to our house and freshen up? There's no use having all three of us wait around when his condition is stable. I'll stay and call you if anything changes."

"Are you sure?" It *would* be nice to change into a more day-appropriate outfit. I kept an emergency stash of clothes at my parents' house for occasions just like this.

"Yes. I need someone to bring me a change of clothes and lunch anyway. Don't make me eat hospital canteen food."

I cracked a real smile this time. "Change of clothes and lunch. Got it."

"Don't rush back," my mother warned. "I don't need you getting a speeding ticket." She gave me a gentle shove toward Scarlett. "Now go."

So we went.

CHAPTER 25

SCARLETT

I WASN'T SURE WHAT TO EXPECT FROM ASHER'S childhood home. A giant football-shaped halo, maybe, or some other sign that it once housed a future superstar.

Instead, I was greeted with a normal house that looked like every other on the block. White window frames, brick walls, a little black gate separating the front garden from the pavement.

"I'm sorry. This probably wasn't how you imagined spending your Saturday," Asher said ruefully as he unlocked the front door.

"I didn't have anything special planned, and I've never been to Holchester, so I actually have to thank you for the free trip," I said, earning myself a quick smile. I hesitated, then asked more softly, "How are you feeling?"

He didn't tell me what happened in his father's hospital room, and I didn't ask. However, the argument had clearly taken a toll on him. His eyes lacked their usual sparkle, and exhaustion darkened the grooves of his face.

I wasn't used to seeing him so subdued. The sight sent an

unexpected pang through my chest.

"When I figure it out, I'll let you know," he said with a short laugh. "Coming home is always an experience. I hope my mother didn't scare you off too badly with her interrogation."

"No, she was lovely." Pippa had startled me with her initial barrage of questions, but we had a nice chat while Asher was with his father. I could tell she truly loved her son and wanted what was best for him, even if she was a bit...intense about the grandchildren thing. "But she kept mentioning something about me and Hedy Lamarr?"

"Famous movie star from the forties," Asher said. "My mum's a big fan of classic Hollywood, and you look a lot like Hedy."

"I'll take it as a compliment." Looking like a movie star could only be a good thing, right?

"You should." His mouth quirked. "She's probably imagining little Lamarr clones running around her back garden right now."

I huffed out a laugh even as my heart tripped at the thought of having babies with him. It was *way* too early to think about that considering we hadn't even clarified our relationship status yet, but for the briefest of moments, I allowed myself to indulge in the fantasy.

The prospect of marriage and children with Asher wasn't as scary as I thought it'd be, which was worrisome in and of itself.

We'd had sex once. I was *not* going to be the person who started planning her wedding in a state of orgasm-fueled delusion, so I shoved the image of little green-eyed babies to the back of my mind as he showed me the house.

It was cozy and charmingly lived-in, with family photos strewn across various surfaces and an array of tchotchkes from France, Italy, Australia, and other holiday destinations. However, the overwhelming decor theme was *football*, especially in the den and front hall. I felt like I was walking through a Holchester FC gift shop.

"You weren't kidding when you said your dad's a Holchester fan," I said, equal parts impressed and alarmed.

Posters of the team decorated the walls, the edges curled and yellowing from age and wear. A shirt signed by the entire 2018 team was framed and displayed like the Mona Lisa at the Louvre. Photos of Asher in his Holchester kit lined the mantel along with a miniature gold football.

I noticed there were no photos of him in Blackcastle colors on display.

"Fan? More like fanatic." Asher didn't look at the mantel on our way past.

"I suppose. Either way, it seems like today's the day for home tours," I said lightly, hoping to soften the broodiness shadowing his face.

It didn't work.

"I guess so." We stopped in front of a plain wooden door toward the back of the house. "This is my childhood room. Don't make fun of it, or you'll hurt my feelings."

Something inside me loosened at the hint of his usual humor. "Oh my God. Did your parents keep it the same all these years?"

Asher's wince confirmed my suspicions.

I walked in, taking in every detail—the blue quilted duvet; the single bed pushed up against the wall beneath the window; the posters of Armstrong, Beckham, and other football greats decorating the walls.

"It's like a museum," I said, fascinated by the peek into Asher's childhood.

I could almost *see* him sitting on his bed, watching football on the telly and dreaming of the day when he was the one on the screen.

"Yeah." Asher looked around. "You know, I haven't been in here in ages. I usually stay at a hotel when I'm in town, and I never had a reason to come in when I visited my parents." A touch of nostalgia flitted through his eyes. "Ten years, and it feels like I never left."

"It must feel surreal."

"A bit." He scrubbed a hand over his face. "I'm going to change. Feel free to look around or sit anywhere."

I didn't feel comfortable snooping through his room while he was gone, so I waited on the edge of his bed until he returned. He'd ditched his earlier outfit in favor of a T-shirt and jeans, and he looked mildly more relaxed as he sat next to me.

Silence descended. It was a comfortable, companionable quiet, the kind I'd gotten used to during our drive to Holchester, but something simmered beneath the surface, waiting to break free.

"Do you remember the day of the storm?" Asher asked. "You asked why I transferred to Blackcastle. You said it couldn't have been only the money."

"Of course." I couldn't forget anything about that day if I tried. It was, in many ways, the day that'd led us to where we were now.

"You were right. I mean, the money *was* a factor, as was working with Armstrong. But the real reason was I..." He swallowed. "I needed to escape my father."

I fought a knee-jerk response and waited for him to continue at his own pace.

"I couldn't stay in the same city as him anymore," he said. "He'd pushed me to excel at the game my entire life, and I *am* grateful for it. It played a huge part in getting me to where I am now, but the further I got in my career, the more I felt like I wasn't doing it for me. I was doing it for him. Football is my life, but I was slowly losing my love for it. It terrified me. And as much as I liked my team at Holchester, I felt like I was trapped in this bubble where I couldn't breathe."

The sound of a car passing outside muffled his last word, but there was no mistaking the bleakness in his expression.

"When Frank Armstrong joined as Blackcastle's manager, I used it as an excuse to transfer," Asher said. "Still, it took me months to put in the request. If my dad wasn't so fanatic about Holchester, I wouldn't have thought twice about it. But when it comes to football, he's not my father. He's a second coach, and it was too much."

A humorless smile touched his mouth. "Before you say anything, I know what it sounds like. Rich footballer complaining about his father being too hard on him. Boo-fucking-hoo. Let me wipe my tears with my money."

"That's not what I was going to say." I shook my head. "Just because you're privileged in one way doesn't mean you can't struggle in other ways."

Yes, he was more fortunate than the majority of people in the world, but I saw where he was coming from. I'd tasted it as a dancer, but I'd never dealt with the level of scrutiny he faced every day.

The public only saw the money and glamour; they didn't see the pressures, politics, and power plays behind the scenes. They didn't see the toll those things took on someone's mental health. Rich or not, famous or not, we were all human.

"You said it took you months to put in the request. What made you bite the bullet?" I asked.

"It was the match against Chelsea last year." Asher's mouth flattened. "I scored three out of the four goals. We won. It should've been a great night, but afterward, all my father talked about was the corner I 'screwed up' and the free kick I missed. I should've been celebrating. Instead, I just wanted to scream."

A raw ache took root in my chest.

If his father wasn't recovering from a heart attack right now, I'd storm over and give him a piece of my mind.

"It wasn't anything I hadn't experienced before, but it was the straw that broke the camel's back, so to speak," Asher said. "The whole country, maybe even the whole world, has certain expectations of Asher Donovan—how I should play, who I should date, where I should fucking holiday. I can deal with that. It's what I signed up for. But I'd like a place, just one, where I don't have to be on guard. I thought family would be that place. But it isn't."

The ache intensified. It slid behind my rib cage and wound around my heart, squeezing and squeezing until it was hard to breathe.

My parents had encouraged me and Vincent to pursue our talents from a young age. They were competitive, so they constantly tried to outdo each other when I was growing up—our mother with my ballet lessons, our father with Vincent's football matches. We were the proxies in their long-distance cold war.

But at the end of the day, when I took off my pointe shoes and Vincent hung up his football boots, we were their children again. Asher didn't have that.

"If it makes you feel better," I said. "I prefer Asher to Asher Donovan."

The former was a person; the latter was a brand. I was indifferent about the brand, but I liked the person. A lot. More than I should.

He didn't respond, but his throat flexed with a visible swallow.

"You can't control what the world thinks of you," I said gently. "But you *can* control your actions, and I understand why you transferred. If I were in your shoes, I'd have done the same."

"Yeah?" His knee brushed mine when he finally shifted to face me. "I thought you liked structure."

"I do but only on my terms. I'm a hypocrite that way."

Asher's laugh scattered the cloud of melancholy, bringing a small sparkle back to his eyes and a smile to my lips. "Self-aware hypocrites are the best kind."

"Exactly. Also, anyone who gives you shit for transferring wasn't a real fan in the first place, so screw them. You don't need that negativity in your life."

His second laugh was richer and deeper than the first. "If you ever want to switch professions, you should think about being a therapist. You'd be great at it."

"No, thanks. I have enough neuroses of my own without dealing with other people's. That being said, I occasionally dole out advice when I'm feeling generous."

"So I'm one of the lucky ones."

"You are."

"Good. I'm glad." His knee brushed mine again, more purposefully this time, and butterflies erupted in my stomach. "I would hate to lose you."

The air turned thick and syrupy, so sweet I could taste it on the back of my tongue.

"As your trainer," I said.

"As my trainer," he confirmed, his knee still touching mine.

Awareness dripped into the space around us. A low buzz filled my ears, and his innocent childhood bedroom suddenly didn't seem so innocent—not when his gaze burned like a lit match against my skin and my entire body tingled from his proximity.

Drip.

Drip.

Drip.

We still hadn't discussed last night. It took a back seat to his family emergency, but—

"That's enough maudlin talk for the day." Asher finally pulled away, severing the spell. The butterflies drooped in disappointment. "Otherwise, this will be the most depressing first trip to Holchester ever."

"It's not so bad." I rubbed a discreet hand over my thigh and tried to adjust to the new mood. Our conversation vacillated so fast it gave me whiplash. "Your father is okay, and I got to visit the Asher Donovan Childhood Bedroom Museum, guided by Asher Donovan himself. Talk about VIP treatment."

"Only for you." He tilted his head toward the mattress. "As a bonus, you get to lay your head on the same pillow I slept on when I was a teen."

I wrinkled my nose. "I hope it's been washed since then. I don't need your teenage germs in my hair."

Nevertheless, I followed his lead in taking off my shoes and squeezing next to him on the mattress. It was surprisingly comfortable.

We both needed the rest after our drive, so we lay side by side on his tiny bed, our legs dangling over the edge, our arms just barely touching.

"You never talk about your childhood," I said. "Not even in interviews."

His father was the only topic he brought up from his pre-fame life. I didn't know what Asher had been like in school or whether he'd had other hobbies besides football.

I wanted to, though. The day had been filled with nuggets of information, and I was starved for more.

"You been following my interviews, darling?"

"Don't flatter yourself." I paused, then admitted grudgingly, "Maybe."

The bed shook with his soft laughter. "There's not much to talk about. I was a quiet kid, believe it or not. Life was school, family, and football. I spent most of my free time kicking a ball around in the back garden or at the park with Teddy."

"Who's Teddy?"

The ensuing silence stretched so long, I thought he hadn't heard me. I was about to repeat the question when he answered, all traces of amusement gone.

"He was my childhood best friend. We grew up next to each other. He loved football as much as I did, and he was better at it than I was."

"Stop." I found it impossible to believe that any living player could be better than Asher.

Sorry, Vincent. Yet another, albeit silent, betrayal of my brother.

But I'd worry about that later.

"It's true," Asher said. "He was better compared to how I played back then, at least. But whereas I couldn't wait to sign with a club, he refused. Said he wasn't interested in playing professionally."

"Why?"

"He was afraid. Football isn't a steady career, and he didn't want the pressures that came with it. He hated being in the spotlight. He was worried that if he failed, he'd do so publicly and humiliate himself. So instead of living his dream, he let me live it for him."

"He must be proud of your success." Proud or bitter, but I chose to give him the benefit of the doubt.

"We don't exactly talk anymore." Asher sounded distant.

I sensed there was more to the story, so I remained quiet.

I was right.

"I signed with Holchester when I was seventeen. I was so damn excited. We went out to celebrate, but I left early because I had a meeting with Holchester's manager the next morning. Teddy chose to stay, and I remember thinking, good for him. He needed to loosen up a bit, you know?" Asher's laugh sounded hollow. "We went to a pub in a seedier part of town since it was the only one that didn't ID us since we were underage. Teddy left maybe an hour after I did. He was on his way to the bus stop when he got mugged."

I sucked in a sharp breath, already dreading the conclusion to the story.

"It must've been the liquid courage, but Teddy refused to give up his wallet. He got into a fight with the mugger, who stabbed him six times and ran away. Teddy didn't even make it to the hospital."

I saw it coming, but that didn't stop my lurch of shock. *Stabbed six times*. Jesus.

"One minute, he was there. The next, he was gone. And all these years, I can't help but think...would he be alive if I'd stayed with him? If I'd insisted he leave when I did?" Asher's voice thickened. "He wouldn't have been there in the first place if it weren't for me."

"*Don't*," I said so fiercely I surprised myself. "It's not your fault. It's the mugger's fault. You didn't make him a thief, and you didn't make him commit violence. What happened is on him. Not you."

Asher released a shaky exhale.

"I know. But that doesn't change the way I feel." He turned his head a fraction, just enough to meet my eyes. "There's a part of me that feels like I owe it to him to win. Like if I don't succeed, his death would've been for nothing. It's irrational because the two have no direct correlation, but people aren't always rational, are they?"

"No," I said softly. "But not everything needs to be rational to be true."

Long-repressed emotion leaked into Asher's eyes.

That morning, he said he liked seeing the unguarded version of me. The reverse was also true.

This was the Asher the world didn't get to see. The raw, vulnerable one who hurt and *felt* like everyone else.

Part of me was glad they couldn't access this version of him. If they did, they'd break him the way they'd broken everything else, hammering and hounding until they molded him into who they wanted him to be instead of who he was.

He didn't deserve that, and they didn't deserve him.

"There goes my maudlin talk again. You asked about my childhood, and I gave you a sob story." His warm breath brushed my lips in apology. "I should take you to an ice cream shop or something so your visit isn't all doom and gloom."

"It's okay. I didn't come for the ice cream."

I came for you.

Asher swallowed hard again.

Our chests rose and fell in sync, our breaths mingling softly in the universe of unspoken words between us.

The last time we shared a bed, we'd had sex, but this was a different type of intimacy. Gentler, less tangible but no less important, and rooted in fragile, blossoming trust.

Asher tore his eyes away from mine and faced forward again. But when our hands grazed on the bed, I didn't pull away, and when I curled my pinky around his, he squeezed mine in return.

We didn't speak. We didn't need to.

Sometimes, actions were enough.

CHAPTER 26

SCARLETT

AFTER A QUICK MEAL AT HIS PARENTS' HOUSE, ASHER AND I returned to the hospital with food and a change of clothes for his mother. Thankfully, his father's condition remained stable, but we stayed for the weekend anyway.

We checked into a local luxury hotel, and their VIP services team escorted us directly to our suite without tipping off the other guests that we were there. We were both so exhausted we fell asleep almost immediately.

On Sunday, a disguised Asher took me to the famous Holchester Art Museum and a social-media-famous ice cream parlor, but we stayed at the hotel or hospital for the most part. We weren't keen on running into any paps or angry Holchester fans.

We didn't talk about his father, football, or our relationship at all after we left his parents' house. We both needed a break from the heavy topics, so we focused on TV and books instead.

"What do you mean, dinosaur erotica?" Asher's palpable shock made me giggle. "Like they have sex with dinosaurs? How is that physically possible?"

"I don't know. I haven't actually read one," I admitted. "But my favorite author recommended a book by someone called…" I squinted at my Notes app. "Wilma Pebbles? It's called *Triceratops and Threesomes*—stop laughing! And give me my phone back!"

"I have to write this down," he gasped, his shoulders shaking. He typed the author and title into his phone before handing my mobile back to me. He was laughing so hard, tears gleamed at the corners of his eyes. "Maybe I'll start a Blackcastle book club. Dinos only."

"Good. You guys need more culture anyway," I huffed, but I failed to hide a smile at the mental image of the Blackcastle team reading *Triceratops and Threesomes* together.

Now *that* would be a sight to see.

Despite my weekend stay in Holchester, I never met Asher's father. It was just as well; I didn't think I'd be able to hold back some choice words for the man.

He got discharged on Monday. Asher said an obligatory goodbye to him, and we gave his mother a lengthier farewell before we drove back to London.

The ride seemed faster this time—or maybe it was because I didn't want to leave Asher yet.

Given the situation, I'd called in sick to work and canceled our training today, which meant I wouldn't see him again until Wednesday.

"I know I said this already, but thank you for coming with me," Asher said halfway through the drive. "It helped. Truly."

"Don't mention it. That DIY sundae bar at the ice cream parlor was worth it."

His laugh warmed me more than the sunshine filtering through the windows.

We meandered in and out of conversation, letting the radio music take over when necessary until we reached London's city limits.

"Do you want me to drop you off at home?" Asher asked. His tone was casual—almost too casual.

I slid a sideways glance at him. He stared straight ahead, his pose relaxed, but a splash of tension coated the black leather interior.

Was he indirectly asking whether I wanted to continue hanging out? Would I come off as too needy if I suggested another activity for us instead of going home? Or was I overthinking a completely innocent question?

I wished I could text Carina for advice, but then it would look like I was ignoring him.

"Yes, please," I finally said. I had to change regardless. I bought a dress at the hotel's boutique yesterday, but I'd been wearing the same outfit for almost two days.

"Okay."

There. That carefully neutral tone. Was it my imagination, or was it covering up a touch of disappointment?

"But...I'm pretty hungry," I ventured. "Maybe we should grab a bite to eat first?"

"That's a good idea," he said quickly. "I know a great Indian place. It's not on the way to your flat, but I can drop you off and pick you up later if you're interested in checking it out. It's a bit too early for dinner anyway."

My heart ricocheted in my chest. That sounded awfully close to a date. "Okay."

"Okay." This time, a smile accompanied his reply.

When Asher dropped me off, we agreed to meet again in two hours. It was enough time for me to take a quick bath, indulge in some gentle yoga, and get ready.

After fifteen minutes of staring at my closet and several frantic

texts to Carina and Brooklyn, I settled on a cute top-and-skirt combo.
I'd just finished my makeup when Asher returned, freshly showered
and smelling like a delicious mix of soap and aftershave.

His appreciative gaze carved a trail up my legs and neck before
settling on my face. Little fireflies danced over my skin, lighting me
up.

"You ready?" The deep timbre of his voice ghosted down my
spine.

"Yes." I tamped down the flutters and followed him to his car,
where he pulled out a baseball cap and black-rimmed glasses.

"Disguise," he explained.

"Does that actually work?" It was so simple. It felt like Superman
disguising himself as Clark Kent with similar glasses.

"You'd be surprised. Most people don't expect to run into anyone
famous on the street, so if you're low-key enough, you can slip right
by."

"I hate to tell you this, but have you looked in a mirror?" I asked
archly. "Your face is not slipping by *anyone.*"

Even if he weren't famous, Asher was gorgeous enough to turn
heads everywhere he went.

"Is that your way of calling me good-looking?" He sounded
entirely too pleased about that.

"You know you are. Also, you get one compliment per day. Don't
try to fish for more."

"Noted." Laughter glimmered beneath his voice. "I'll wait until
midnight to fish again."

Despite my skepticism, he was right. Most people didn't spare
us a second glance when we parked and walked to the restaurant. A
group of female uni students did a double take as we passed, but I
couldn't tell whether that was because they recognized him or simply

thought he was fit. Either way, they didn't approach us.

The restaurant was packed for dinner, but we were able to snag a corner table near the kitchen. Since Asher was the expert here, I let him order for the both of us.

"Noah told me about this place," he said. "Kind of embarrassing for a Londoner to get food recs from an American, but the food is so good, I can't be mad."

"Noah?"

"Wilson. Our goalkeeper."

An image surfaced of a tall, scowly man with dirty blond hair and blue eyes. *Noah*. Of course. There weren't many Americans in the Premier League, so his signing with Blackcastle had been a big deal a few years ago.

"Are you guys close?" I ripped off a piece of naan and dipped it in chutney.

Vincent constantly partied with the team, but Asher obviously wasn't part of those nights out.

"I wouldn't say we're best friends, but I talk to him and Adil the most out of anyone at the club. Adil's one of our midfielders," he added. "They're the only ones who don't act weird around me when Vincent's there."

I could only imagine. The team's loyalties must've been split between their captain and their lead scorer.

"So who do you talk to when you need advice or have big news to share?" I asked. "Besides your family."

Asher shrugged. "Depends on the issue. If it's PR related, I talk to Sloane, my publicist. If it's football related, I talk to Coach. Noah and Adil, too. They give good advice when they're not being idiots."

"I'm not talking about business stuff," I said gently. "For example, if I hadn't been with you on Saturday, who would you have told about your father's heart attack?"

He stared at me.

The seconds ticked by with agonizing slowness until he averted his gaze. "I don't know," he said. "No one, I guess."

An iron fist squeezed my heart.

His old team hated him, his new team was wary of him, and everyone else probably either sucked up to him or wanted to use him.

I couldn't imagine how lonely that must feel. Asher was surrounded by fans and hangers-on every day, but sometimes, people felt the loneliest in a crowd.

"Well, if you ever need a sounding board, I'm here," I said. "Therapist in another life and all that."

A faint smile wisped around his mouth. "Thank you." Our server returned with our food, and Asher waited until he was gone before continuing. "If I gave you a pound every time I said those words to you, you'd drain my bank account."

"I mean, if that's what you feel called to do, I won't stop you. London rent is expensive."

His smile blossomed into a low laugh.

Pride unfolded in my chest as we dug into the food. Asher was right. It *was* delicious, and our silence as we ate was a testament to that.

I went in for seconds as my phone buzzed against my leg. It was probably Carina digging for updates or Brooklyn confirming our upcoming coffee date, but I'd text them back later.

I had something else to discuss, and we'd put it off for too long.

"So…" I snuck a peek around us to make sure no one was eavesdropping. "Should we talk about what happened on Friday?"

The look Asher gave me could've melted a glacier. "Which part?" he drawled. Velvet braided his voice.

Just like that, my mind hurtled into the past—past the hospital, past our drive to Holchester and my speech about Pluto, all the way back to when we were tangled in my bed, our bodies slick and hot against the sheets.

"You know which part," I hissed, my cheeks flaming. "I'm talking about when we, um…"

"Gave each other mind-blowing orgasms for the first time?"

"*Shhh.*" My face was hot enough to reheat any leftovers from dinner. "Do you *want* to end up in the tabloids?"

The speech I gave him for why we wouldn't work after our first kiss was rooted in truth. I didn't want the press digging into my life for dirt. I didn't want to relive the accident again, nor did I want them nitpicking everything I did and wore. The scrutiny wouldn't be as intense as if I were, say, a member of the royal family, but it would still exist, and it made my anxiety want to run screaming.

"No. I don't." Asher's expression sobered. "But you're right. We should talk about what a relationship would mean."

The clatter of plates and glasses around us filled the empty pockets of our conversation.

What, exactly, was our relationship? Were we dating now, or had Friday night been a one-time thing?

Both options twisted me with unease.

I didn't want a one-night stand, but an official relationship sounded so, well, official. I liked Asher more than I'd ever liked anyone, but my last relationship had ended in disaster, and I wasn't eager to repeat the experience.

He wasn't my ex. But I couldn't discount the little voice telling me that, no matter how well things were going in the present, they could *always* go wrong in the future.

"*Do* you want a relationship?" It was like Asher read my mind.

"Or do you want something else?"

His expression didn't change, but his eyes were sharp and cautious in the face of my silence.

"I…" I hesitated, trying to organize my thoughts into a coherent response. "I don't want to see anyone else, and I don't want you to see anyone else. But I'm also not ready for a serious relationship until we've figured out our issues with my brother, the paps, everything. I just…everything's happening so fast, and I'm…" *Scared.*

I didn't say it, but Asher must've heard it somehow anyway.

The tension that'd crawled into his shoulders when I said I wasn't ready for a serious relationship relaxed. "Fair enough. So it'll be an exclusive nonrelationship with dates. And sex. And many shared memes."

A soft puff of laughter escaped my lips. "Yes."

It was basically a real relationship in everything but name, but that was enough for now. I'd never dated someone with Asher's public profile before. I needed to know what I was getting myself into before I inadvertently got burned again.

However, I *was* glad it was exclusive. The thought of Asher with someone else made me squirm with jealousy.

"I can't control the paps," he said, bringing the conversation back to one of our main issues. "But Sloane has her ways of keeping them in line. They're more scared of her than they are of most publicists."

True. A sliver of hope entered my heart.

"And people make it work," I added optimistically. "There are lots of celebrities with non-famous partners, and *they're* not in the news every day."

"Exactly. After the initial spike, interest will wane, especially if we don't give them anything to write about."

We. That one word alleviated my worries more than anything else he could've said. *We* meant we were in this together.

I wasn't alone.

Warmth rushed to fill one of the tiny, fear-hollowed crevices in my chest.

"That being said, you'll never have full anonymity again." Asher's tone gentled. "Like you said, there are always people watching. It can be a reporter. It can be a fan. It can be a random passerby. The average person usually has enough decency not to invade our privacy, but you never know for sure. There'll be comments on online forums, social media posts, tips to the tabloids. People might make up rumors, and others will believe them even if they're blatantly false. Old friends and acquaintances will come out of the woodwork with stories, real or fake, for their fifteen minutes of fame. These are all possibilities."

The warmth dissipated, and my dinner hardened into cement sludge in my stomach. "It's like you're *trying* to scare me away," I quipped, but anxiety pitched my voice higher than normal.

I'd been in the spotlight as a prima ballerina, but that was different. I was recognized mostly by my peers and ballet enthusiasts. The general population wouldn't recognize a dancer on the street even if she was the most famous ballerina in the world.

Footballers, on the other hand? They were mainstream, especially in the UK. Especially when they played for a top club like Blackcastle. And *especially* when their name was Asher Donovan.

He'd never dated anyone for more than a few weeks at a time. The sheer novelty of our relationship (if we lasted longer than that) would drive incredible amounts of interest.

It would die down eventually, but I had to make it through the storm first.

"I'm not trying to scare you, but I'd be remiss if I didn't warn you." Asher watched me carefully, like he was afraid I'd run off and never look back.

"I know. I appreciate the warning." I inhaled a deep breath. The idea of being perceived so publicly terrified me, but I couldn't let my fears hold me back from what I wanted anymore. "We'll figure out the pap situation. However, there's a bigger issue. My brother."

Asher's entire face shuttered.

"You two have to sort out your issues for the sake of the team *and* your careers," I said. "Do you remember why we started training together in the first place? The Boss will be livid if your animosity carries over into the next season."

"The Boss?"

"Your coach. Armstrong. Vincent and I call him the Boss because, well, he's the boss. I guess it's not very original." I drew my bottom lip between my teeth. "Why do you hate each other so much anyway? It has to be more than the sponsorships or the title of greatest footballer."

If I knew *why*, then maybe I could help them mend their relationship. I didn't want my brother and exclusive non-boyfriend to hate each other.

"I don't hate him," Asher said. "I just can't stand him."

"Same thing."

"Perhaps." He leaned back, his face angled away from the rest of the diners. Luckily, the din was loud enough to muffle our conversation from potential eavesdroppers. "This career is weird. So much of it is played out in the public eye, and we're constantly pitted against each other on and off the pitch. Competitiveness is in our blood. So yes, part of our rivalry stems from the eternal battle over who's the better footballer. I can overlook that. It's par for the course." His eyes darkened. "Then the World Cup happened."

Concrete blocks settled at the pit of my stomach.

That damn World Cup. I should've known. The answer was so

obvious, but it'd happened years ago. I hadn't realized how long of a shadow it cast.

Even though Vincent had been born in London, he moved to Paris and became a French citizen when he was six, after our parents' divorce. As a result, he played for France in international tournaments.

During the last World Cup, England and France had been tied during the semifinals. A quarter of the way into the match, Vincent and Asher got into an altercation that resulted in Vincent feigning an injury and Asher getting red carded.

The loss of their star striker turned the tide against England, who'd been favored to win the cup. Instead, they lost two to four while France went on to take the tournament.

The ref got raked over the coals for his call, but it didn't matter. Side-by-side images of a triumphant Vincent hoisting the trophy and a devastated Asher walking off the pitch had dominated the news for weeks afterward.

"He faked his damn injury, and the ref didn't see it." A muscle ticked in Asher's jaw. "If it weren't for him, I'd probably have a World Cup."

I winced, unsure how to respond.

For footballers, the World Cup was the holy grail. Vincent had celebrated for *months* after France's victory. He got a lot of hate from England fans after the tournament, but as Blackcastle's captain and top defender, he also had a sizable fanbase that shielded him from the worst of the criticism. Eventually, people got over it and moved on.

Asher didn't.

"There'll be another World Cup," I said softly. "That wasn't your last chance."

"I only have so many chances." Asher's eyes flickered in the dim lighting. "It takes place every four years, and a lot can change in that time. I have maybe two more tournaments left in me, and that's not accounting for any injuries or accidents that might take me out early."

There was nothing I could say to that because it was true. Most players will never win the World Cup. It didn't matter how good an individual was; it was a team effort.

However, while this explained why Asher disliked Vincent, it didn't explain why Vincent disliked Asher so much beyond basic rivalry.

"Long story short, your brother's a dick," Asher said. "That being said, I'm not the one you have to worry about if and when he finds out about us. You know him better than I do. How do you think he'll react?"

"Um…" I gulped at scenarios playing out in my mind. None of them were ideal, to say the least. "Not well. *But* he'll listen to reason." *I think.* "He cares about his career as much as you do." *Fingers crossed he cares about it more than he dislikes you.* "He'll be angry at first, but he'll get over it." *I hope.*

Asher didn't look convinced. "He warned me away from you during one of our training sessions."

"*What?*"

"You were in the toilet." The corner of his mouth tugged up at my indignation. "He said you were off limits but I wouldn't have a shot anyway because you'd never date another footballer."

I heard the implicit question in the second half of his statement, but I ignored it.

I wasn't ready to talk about my ex yet.

"That's just like Vincent," I fumed. "He's always butting in where I don't want him to." Sure, I'd wanted nothing to do with Asher at the time, but still. Couldn't a girl make her own decisions about her love life? "He told me to stay away from Clive too."

That reminded me, I needed to follow up with him after our date. Given the way it ended, I doubted he was looking for a second date, but I liked to close all my loops.

Asher's smile morphed into a scowl. "He was right about Clive. That guy is bad news."

"Because he's a fuckboy? Vincent said the same thing. You know, you two are a lot alike," I said. "You'd probably be best friends if you didn't despise each other."

I laughed at Asher's grimace. I wasn't kidding. They *would* make good friends, but they were too hardheaded to set aside their differences and see that.

Hopefully, that'll change in the future. Until then, I could only pray and hope Vincent wouldn't lose his shit when we broke the news to him. *How* we'd do that was a problem for another day.

"So now that we've cleared the air…" I gestured around us. "Is this our first official date as an exclusive non-couple couple?"

"This is a pre-date." Asher's darkly amused stare crept under my skin, flustering me. "When I take you on our first date, you'll know."

Something hot and languid spread through my veins.

For the first time since we sat down, I wished we were eating at home instead of in a restaurant. I wanted—

"Hi. I'm terribly sorry for interrupting, but—but are you Asher Donovan?"

Our heads turned in unison toward the breathless teenage boy standing next to our table. I hadn't even heard him come up.

I witnessed Asher's transformation in real time.

His relaxed posture straightened, and his mouth stretched into a polite, camera-ready smile. Shutters rolled down over his open expression.

It was still him, but it was a shiny, guarded version of him.

"Yes," he said easily, his smile intact.

"Wow." The boy's eyes shone with star-struck wonder. "I can't believe you're here. Can I get your autograph?" He shoved a napkin and pen at Asher. "I'm a *huge* fan."

"Of course." Asher signed the napkin, and the one after that, and the one after that.

After the boy approached us, the rest of the diners realized who was eating in their midst and clamored for their turn.

The mood shifted so quickly and drastically that neither of us was ready for the onslaught. An overly enthusiastic fan nearly knocked me out of my chair in their eagerness to get to him, and I had to shield my face with a menu to avoid getting caught in the background of their pictures.

After ten minutes of chaos, the restaurant owner finally pushed through the crowd and forced everyone back to their seats. He apologized to us profusely, and then asked for a picture with Asher to hang on their wall.

Dinner was officially over.

We quickly paid and left, but the anxiety I'd pushed aside earlier resurfaced even after we made it safely to Asher's car. It wound tight in my chest, cutting off my supply of oxygen.

"I'm sorry about that." Worry passed over his face. "I honestly didn't think anyone would recognize me. But once one person does…"

"It's okay," I said with a shaky smile. "He was a teenager. They have sharklike instincts when it comes to their idols."

We didn't say what we were both thinking, which was that the restaurant had only been a taste of what was to come if the press found out about us. Fortunately, the diners had been too busy fawning over Asher to ask who I was, but it was only a matter of time.

Still, it could've been worse. I wasn't hurt (minus a few accidental elbow jabs and handbag swings), and no one caught me on camera. Even if they did, I'd live in their phone's camera roll instead of the tabloids.

In the grand scheme of things, our obstacles weren't insurmountable.

We'd talked it out, and everything would be fine.

I was sure of it.

CHAPTER 27

ASHER

Have you guys ever heard of Wilma Pebbles?

ADIL

Is she a model? She sounds hot in a Flintstones kinda way

She's an author

ADIL

Oh

ADIL

Does she model on the side?

NOAH

You're an idiot

NOAH

I never should've unblocked you

ADIL

Your life would be so boring without me and you know it

ADIL

It'd be like cardboard without glitter. Ice cream without sugar. Pizza without olives.

NOAH

WTF are you talking about?

Guys, FOCUS

And no, Wilma does NOT model on the side. But she wrote a book that sounds kinda interesting

It's called Triceratops and Threesomes

NOAH

...

ADIL

...

ADIL

Like the dinosaur?

Yeah. Apparently dinosaur erotica is a thing

NOAH

...

ADIL

...

ADIL

What the hell have you been doing in London?

ADIL

Also, do you think triceratops fuck with their horns?

NOAH WILSON LEFT THE CONVERSATION.

CHAPTER 28

SCARLETT

THE NEXT TWO WEEKS PASSED IN A WHIRLWIND OF DANCE rehearsals, training sessions, and stolen moments with Asher.

We wanted to keep our new relationship status under wraps for now, so we didn't tell anyone except Carina and Brooklyn.

However, despite tension-soaked trainings and more than a few orgasms in *both* our houses, Asher and I hadn't been on an official date yet.

Our morning trip to Kew Gardens, which I'd never visited despite being a native Londoner? Not a date.

Our late-night drinks at a secret bar followed by a tipsy walk along the Thames? Not a date.

Our weekend marathon of sex, food, and classic Hedy Lamarr movies? Not a date.

At this point, I was starting to suspect Asher didn't know the meaning of the word.

My fingers flew over my phone's keyboard as I entered the rehearsal hall at RAB. I'd added Carina and Brooklyn to the same group chat earlier that week. I was a bit nervous they wouldn't get along, but I liked Brooklyn a lot, and she was new to the city.

Carina and I usually had the same gut instincts when it came to people, and I couldn't think of a good reason why they *wouldn't* mesh.

I'd introduced them when I created the chat, so I jumped right into it.

> How do you guys feel about poker?

BROOKLYN
> Like strip poker?

CARINA
> I didn't realize this was THAT type of group chat 👀

> Very funny

> I thought we could have a girls' night at my place. Poker and drinks. What do you think?

CARINA
> I'm down. I haven't played poker in so long though, so take it easy on me

BROOKLYN
> I'd love to join as well. Just let me know when

BROOKLYN
> Don't worry. I promise not to take too much of your money ☺

"Scarlett! Good, you're here."

Tamara's voice dragged my focus away from the chat and toward the stage, where the rest of the staff was warming up. She was one of RAB's senior instructors and the rehearsal director for the showcase.

"Yvette had a last-minute doctor's appointment, so you'll have to dance in her place," she said.

My heartbeat skittered to a stop. "Dance in her place?"

"Yes." She arched her brows. "Will that be a problem?"

"No." A cold draft swept over me, peppering my arms and chest with goose bumps. "Of course not. That's—that's what I'm here for."

"Great." Tamara left to speak with the choreographer while my feet remained rooted to the ground.

My palms grew clammy as I stared at the stage. Understudies rarely danced with the whole cast during rehearsals, and I was unprepared for the sudden call to duty.

My job was to fill in during emergencies, but now that one came up, I couldn't shake off an angry swarm of nerves.

I'd practiced off to the side during rehearsals, and I'd memorized every piece of the performance. But there was a difference between practicing on my own and practicing with the cast.

This rehearsal would be my first full-length, full-cast performance since the accident. I felt like there should be a clear sign marking the milestone, like flashing neon lights or at least a heads-up call from Yvette.

Since there wasn't, I forced my feet to move across the floor, up the stairs, and onto the stage.

Warm-ups. I could do that. I've warmed up before.

My heart crowded my throat. My excitement over getting the understudy role all those weeks ago melted beneath the lights and the sideways glances from the rest of the staff.

They knew about my past. Were they waiting for me to mess up? Did they think my fall from principal dancer to understudy was pathetic?

Stop being paranoid. No one's judging you.

I took a deep breath, focused on the sliver of floor around me, and started stretching.

One. Two. Three. The silent, measured counts steadied my

breathing and calmed my heart rate. By the time I finished, the churn of anxiety had slowed to a crawl.

Tamara clapped her hands. "Okay, let's start from the top!" she said when everyone was in place.

The music started, and I didn't have time to overthink anymore.

It was move or die, so I moved.

The good thing about *Lorena* was that its choreography played to my strengths as a dancer. I hadn't performed in five years, but I'd lived and breathed ballet for sixteen years before that. My body remembered what it felt like.

After a hesitant start, I gradually flowed into the movements. Pirouettes, arabesques, grand battements...it was like saying hello to old friends I hadn't seen in a long time.

If I closed my eyes, I could almost imagine I was at Westbury, dancing for an opening-night audience.

This isn't so bad. You can do this. You—

The sudden screech of the auditorium doors opening pierced through the music. It sounded like metal screaming.

Metal. Blood. Smoke.

My veins flooded with adrenaline. My head instinctively snapped toward the entrance, ruining my choreography, but instead of the newcomer, my vision swarmed with snippets from the past.

Punctured lungs, broken ribs, shattered pelvis...

With long-term, consistent physical therapy, she'll regain normal use of her legs, but I'm afraid professional ballet is no longer a viable option...

I strongly encourage surgery. Without it, she might never dance again. Not even recreationally.

I stumbled. Sweat beaded my forehead, and the air thinned in my lungs. The stage lights were so *hot,* I couldn't think properly.

What was the next part of the choreography? Was I supposed to go left or right? How long until this damn dance was over?

My temples pounded with tension.

"Scarlett? Scarlett!"

I lifted my head, my breaths shallow.

Shit. The rest of the cast had stopped rehearsing and were staring at me, their faces painted with varying shades of concern, annoyance, and judgment.

Humiliation crawled over my skin like fire ants over broken soil.

"Are you okay?" Tamara asked. She was the one who'd called my name, and her brow pinched with worry as she ran her eyes over me. "If you're not feeling well—"

"No. I'm fine." I straightened and swallowed the bile in my throat. "I didn't hydrate enough and got dizzy, but I can finish rehearsals. I promise."

I was *not* going to quit practice. I refused to run away with my tail tucked between my legs after one misstep, and I'd never willingly quit anything I'd committed to in my life. I wasn't going to start now.

Tamara appeared dubious, but she didn't argue. We were already behind, and the other staff members looked restless.

The music started again. Thankfully, the choreography came back to me, but I never recovered from my first mistake. I either missed my cues or I was off by half a count, which threw the others off *their* counts. It was a disaster, and by the time rehearsals ended, I wanted to cry.

I slunk off the stage, my head down, but I caught snippets of my colleagues' whispered conversations.

"What a waste of an afternoon."

"I hope Yvette doesn't get injured before the showcase, or the performance will be a nightmare."

"Why did Lavinia make her an understudy? She didn't even audition."

Tears clogged my throat. I didn't blame them for being skeptical. If I were them, I'd be irritated with me too.

I was so wrapped up in my mortification, I forgot about the person who'd entered mid-rehearsal until I heard his voice.

"Scarlett."

My feet stilled.

One blink peeled the shadows away from the seats and carpet, revealing a familiar muscled frame and sculpted cheekbones. A pleat of concern creased his brow, but his eyes were soft when they landed on me.

Asher.

The auditorium had emptied out, so it was just the two of us, and the echo of my name lingered.

Scarlett.

That was all it took.

The tears climbed up my throat and tore loose with a small sob. Once the first broke free, the rest followed, filling the cavernous space with the humiliating sound of my failure.

I *hated* crying in public, but my threads of control had frayed with each minute of rehearsal. I'd reached the end of my restraint, and all it took was finding one safe shelter before I broke down.

Asher was by my side in an instant, his arms encircling me as I pressed my tear-dampened face into his chest. He didn't say a word. He just held me, his embrace so strong and steady, I was sure it could withstand even the most devastating of storms.

"I screwed up," I sobbed. "The rehearsal. I screwed it all up. I forgot the choreography, I threw everyone off, I..." A hiccup split my self-loathing in half. "I can't do it. I'm not even the principal, and I'm already making a mess of things."

Past me would've slapped present me over the words leaving my mouth. I'd believed anyone could do anything if they tried hard enough, but I was tired of *having* to try so hard.

Some days, it was a struggle just to get out of bed. I was constantly at war with my body, my emotions, and everything that should've been on my side but wasn't.

I was exhausted. All I wanted was to stay here forever, surrounded by Asher's warmth and the reassuring beats of his heart. Here, I didn't have to try. I could just…be.

"You *can* do it." Firmness underlaid his otherwise gentle tone. "This is the first time you've performed with a cast in years. Give yourself the grace to grow."

"To grow and do what? They'll never let me sub in for Yvette now," I said, my voice small. I didn't *want* to sub in for Yvette. If I fucked up during the performance the way I had in rehearsals, I'd never be able to show my face at RAB again. I'd never be able to look at *myself* in the mirror again. "I wouldn't be surprised if Lavinia calls me into her office tomorrow and takes the understudy role away from me."

My tears finally slowed to a trickle. I pulled away from Asher's chest and swiped angrily at my cheeks. "I should've practiced more, but I'm…" *I'm afraid.*

I was too embarrassed to voice the insecurity out loud.

My doctor said I could dance as long as I didn't overdo it, but I worried that I *had* to overdo it in order to master the choreography. I was rusty after years away from dancing. I did fine in the opening scene before I got distracted and everything went to hell, but could I sustain that through multiple practices and a full performance?

Surprisingly, my muscles weren't screaming after the day's

exertions, but they were fickle. They were fine one day and agonizing the next.

Even if I *could* sustain that level of performance, I had to contend with the psychological pressure of being onstage again. What if my memories sucked me back into the abyss during the showcase? What if I froze again and became a laughingstock? How could my students take me seriously if I couldn't master one performance?

Despite bouts of nostalgia for my old career, I loved my job at RAB. I'd clawed my way out of a hole of bitterness and resentment to build a new life here, and I didn't want to jeopardize it.

"If you want to practice more, we can practice more. It's not too late." Asher's thumb skimmed over my cheek and wiped away a stray tear. His eyes searched my face. "*Do* you want to practice more?"

Different responses rushed to the tip of my tongue.

Yes. No. I don't know.

No was the easy answer.

Yes was the optimistic challenge.

I don't know was the truth, so that was what I went with. "I'm probably overthinking, per usual," I said with a weak smile. Now that the tears had tapered off and I had other company besides my treacherous thoughts, it was easier to pull myself back from the brink of despair. "The chances of me dancing in Yvette's place again are slim. This was probably a one-time thing."

"Maybe, but the practices wouldn't be for anyone else. They would be for you." Asher's hand paused at the curve of my jaw. He cupped my face, his touch tender. I unconsciously leaned into him. Fatigue was settling into my bones, but the press of his skin against mine gave me enough strength to keep going. "If you're worried about overexerting yourself, I have a solution."

He always knew what I was thinking without me having to say it.

"We can incorporate your practices into my training," he said in response to the quizzical arch of my brows. "You don't have to dance the full two hours every time. We can break up the choreography into pieces. Ninety minutes for my training, thirty for yours, depending on how you're feeling. We'll be in the studio anyway. We might as well make full use of it." A roguish grin appeared. "I'm not a dancer, but I can spot you if you need me to."

A laugh cleared the rasp in my throat. "I don't think spotting means what you think it means in ballet."

Dancers used the spotting technique to maintain control and avoid dizziness during the execution of various turns. It involved finding a stationary focal point and had nothing to do with partner assistance the way it did in the gym.

"Ah, well." Asher shrugged. "Regardless, I'll be there if you need me."

I battled a wave of emotion. "Thank you. That's..." *Do not cry again. Once was enough.* "I'll think about it."

It was a good idea. It straddled the line between practice and overexertion, and I could rehearse without the pressure of my peers. It was a more palatable option than giving up.

Shame stole through me at my earlier weakness. If Asher hadn't been here, I might've admitted defeat after one bad rehearsal.

Was that the type of person I'd become? Had I grown so soft that I couldn't handle a bad day, or was I so hard on myself that I thought a bad day was the end of the world?

I didn't like either possibility.

"Actually, I don't need to think about it," I said. My resolve firmed. "You're right. We'll add my practice to our training sessions."

"Good." Asher's smile was as slow and languid as the warmth seeping under my skin. "That's my girl."

That's my girl.

Three words shouldn't have the power to undo me, but they did.

Butterflies erupted low in my stomach. They were so distracting I almost overlooked the novelty of seeing Asher at RAB again. As far as I knew, he hadn't stepped foot in the building since we changed our training location.

"What are you doing here?" I asked as we made our slow ascent up the stairs toward the exit. "We didn't have a meeting, did we?"

"No, but I had my midsummer check-in with Lavinia. It was one of Coach's requirements." Asher placed a hand on the small of my back and steered me around a box of props that someone had carelessly left in the aisle. "Don't worry. I didn't talk too much shit about you."

"Wow, thanks. I appreciate the glowing recommendation."

"Anytime." His mouth quirked. "But I also wanted to come by and see you. I wanted to give you formal notice."

I eyed him with wariness. "About what?"

"About this weekend." He pushed the door open. Thankfully, the hinges let out a squeak this time instead of a full-on metallic screech.

I racked my brain for upcoming special occasions and came up empty. "What's happening this weekend?"

Asher glanced at me again, his eyes dancing with mischief. "We're going on our first official date."

CHAPTER 29

SCARLETT

ASHER REFUSED TO TELL ME WHAT OUR DATE WOULD entail. He only gave me a dress code (nice but casual), so I spent the next four days trying to guess the activity.

My friends helped. Our new group chat was growing increasingly active, and I was relieved to see them hitting it off, virtually at least. They'd been a little hesitant with each other at first, but the texts were now flying fast and furious.

CARINA

Nice but casual is THE most generic description ever. He didn't give you more than that?

Nope. He won't even tell me which part of London it's in

BROOKLYN

Maybe it's not London

BROOKLYN

Maybe he's taking you on a weekend trip to the Cotswolds or something

> Hmmm…I don't think we're traveling anywhere, or he would've told me to pack

CARINA

> Babe, he's a multimillionaire. You don't have to pack. He can buy whatever you need once you get there

BROOKLYN

> Exactly!

> Me: You guys, please. I really don't think it's travel.

> Me: I don't want to go anywhere right now anyway. I'd prefer something more low-key

BROOKLYN

> Booooo

CARINA

> No souvenirs for us ☹

Spoiler: He did not take me to the Cotswolds. Instead, he took me to…someone's house?

"Is this a private residence?" I craned my head to take in all four stories of the redbrick behemoth before us. It was large enough to double as a hotel.

"Most days, yes. Today, it's…something else," Asher said.

"That's not vague at all."

"Sometimes, life is more fun when there's a little mystery." He laughed at my pout. "Don't worry, darling. I'll explain everything soon enough."

He knocked on the door. It opened two seconds later, revealing a tall, reedy man with silver hair and a perfectly pressed black suit. He looked like a butler straight out of central casting.

"Mr. Donovan, Ms. DuBois. Welcome." He greeted us with a small bow. "I'm Mr. Harris, the head butler. Please, follow me."

Head butler? Was there more than one?

The house's mystery deepened the further we walked. Asher said it was a private residence most days, but I didn't see any personal effects. There were only miles of gleaming marble and original oil paintings hanging in gilded frames.

Our footsteps echoed in the massive halls. Otherwise, it was silent as a mausoleum. If it weren't for Asher's reassuring presence, I would've been thoroughly creeped out.

I thought Mr. Harris might lead us to the gardens or an indoor cinema, but we stopped at the kitchen instead.

"Enjoy." He gave us another bow. "If you need anything, anything at all, please feel free to give me a ring on the intercom."

With that, he retreated, leaving us in what might have been the biggest kitchen I'd ever seen. I wasn't a culinary enthusiast, but even I was impressed by the setup. A massive kitchen island, professional-grade cookware, *three* stainless steel Sub-Zero fridges and acres of storage space...it was every chef's dream.

An inordinately handsome man with dark brown hair and hazel eyes stood in the middle of the room. He wore black pants and a crisp white shirt with the sleeves rolled up, and he oozed enough natural charm to make most women fall at his feet.

If I weren't dating Asher, I probably would've succumbed at the sight of his forearms alone.

"Seb! I didn't know you were in London." Asher sounded surprised. "I thought Gerard was going to be our instructor."

"He was, but ironically, he got food poisoning yesterday. Not from one of our restaurants, of course," the man added. He clapped a hand on Asher's shoulder in greeting before he turned to me. His smile dazzled as he held out his hand. "Sebastian Laurent." His voice contained a smooth, light trace of France, evoking images of sun-dappled vineyards and walks along the Seine.

"Scarlett. DuBois," I added as an afterthought. Were we introducing ourselves by our full names now?

"DuBois." His brows rose an inch. "Any relation to Yves DuBois?"

I smiled. "He's my great-uncle."

My grandfather's brother was a famous couturier. We didn't talk much, but he occasionally sent me a dress sample out of the blue, which was enough to earn him a spot in my good graces forever. Yves DuBois gowns weren't cheap.

"Sebastian is the chief marketing officer of the Laurent Restaurant Group," Asher said. "This is his house."

"Part-time house. I'm based in New York," Sebastian explained. "When I'm not here, I change the residence to a venue for VIP brand events and activities such as what we're doing today."

I had an inkling, but I asked anyway. "Which is...?"

"A cooking class." Asher's eyes sparkled. "You love structure, and there's nothing more structured than cooking. Look at any recipe. It's literally a step-by-step guide."

His reasoning was so unexpected yet so perfect that I couldn't help but burst into laughter.

"Step by step with room for interpretation." Sebastian smiled. "However, we'll stick to the rules today since it's your first time."

He handed us aprons and gave us a brief spiel about the guidelines and agenda. We were learning how to cook a three-course meal consisting of a salad, main course, and dessert.

"Like Asher mentioned earlier, Gerard Brazier was supposed to be your instructor today, but alas." Sebastian gave a quintessentially French shrug. "I hope you don't mind if I take over. I'm not a Michelin-starred chef, but I did attend culinary school before business school.

Family tradition," he said when my eyebrows shot up. "Our business is food. If we want to sell it, we should know everything that goes into making it."

"I don't mind at all." I tied the apron behind me. "Though this seems like something a CMO shouldn't have to do on a Saturday afternoon."

Sebastian's mouth tilted into a smile. "I've followed Asher's career since he was with Man U, so I've known him for a while. I couldn't pass up the opportunity to make him suffer a little."

I laughed while Asher rolled his eyes.

"Don't listen to him," he said. "I may not have attended culinary school, but I know my way around the kitchen."

He was right. He did—much more than me. As the class got underway, it became painfully clear that my talents did *not* include tossing salads or searing filet mignon.

Nevertheless, I had a blast. Sebastian kept us entertained with stories about previous events while Asher tried to convince me my filet mignon wasn't *that* overcooked (it was) and I tried to steal one of the raspberries for his cheesecake without him noticing (he did, but he let me have it anyway).

It was different and interactive and *fun*. I didn't feel any pressure to be "witty enough" or "charming enough"—not that I ever felt that pressure with Asher, but it was nice to spend time with him in an intimate yet casual environment.

Physical attraction and romantic feelings aside, I just liked hanging out with him. Some people drained my energy if I was around them too long, but he lit me up.

After our class, we brought our food into the dining room, which looked way too fancy for my blackened steak.

"This is where I leave you. Scarlett, it was a pleasure." Sebastian gave me a cordial cheek kiss. "Asher, I'm looking forward to next season. Here's hoping Blackcastle wins the league." He clapped Asher on the back again and flicked a glance at my plate. He barely suppressed a wince. "Please, ah, enjoy your meal. Mr. Harris will bring out the wine."

You'll need it. He was too polite to say it, but I knew what he meant. My food was a disaster.

"Here," Asher said when Sebastian left. He gestured for me to swap seats with him. "You take my meal, I'll take yours."

"No way." I didn't budge. "I'm not making you eat this."

"So you're going to eat it instead?"

"It's not that bad. The salad is edible...I think."

Asher's mouth twitched. "Okay. I'm going to say something, and I don't want you to be offended."

"Let me guess. I'm a terrible cook?"

"Well, yes. But that's not what I was going to say, although it *is* related to that." He pressed the intercom button next to the table. "Mr. Harris, can you bring in our food, please?"

My lips parted when our servers returned, this time with fresh dishes that we absolutely did not make.

"Wait. You had a backup meal this *entire time*?" I shot him an accusing glare. "You made us go through the class for nothing?"

"Not for nothing. I had hope." Asher's eyes gleamed with laughter at my outraged gasp. "I'm sorry, darling. You're beautiful, talented, and wonderful in so many ways, but ever since you told me you thought it was impossible to overcook shrimp...I figured it was better to be safe than sorry."

"That wasn't my fault! I told you the internet lied," I grumbled, but I couldn't hang onto my indignation for much longer. The meal I made *was* awful, so I was happy to have an alternative.

"I hope you had fun anyway, even if your steak didn't turn out as planned." The corner of Asher's mouth twitched again. "I figured we'd take the class for the experience and not the, ah, outcome."

My face softened. How could I stay mad when he was so bloody thoughtful all the time? "I did have fun. This was one of the best dates I've ever had."

"I'm glad." Asher paused. Swirled his wine. Then said, "One of? What dates have been better than this one?"

"Oh, you know." I flattened my mouth into a line, sealing the laugh that threatened to spill out at his obvious fishing. "There was that helicopter ride in Hawaii, and the eight-course meal on a beach in St. Lucia..."

It was total bullshit. I'd never been to Hawaii or St. Lucia, but a disgruntled Asher was too cute not to tease.

His face crumpled into a scowl, and I couldn't hold it in any longer. My laughter broke free, bouncing off the walls and rattling the silverware as I tried to rein it in.

Asher's eyes narrowed with dawning realization. "You were taking the mickey out of me."

"I'm sorry. I couldn't resist." My cheeks hurt from grinning. "I've never seen someone look so annoyed by the mention of Hawaii, but I was joking. This *is* the best date I've ever had." I gestured around us. "My ex would've never thought of something like this. He liked the flashy things. Fancy dinners, over-the-top treatment. I like those things too, in moderation, but sometimes I felt like he was doing them for the image instead of the sentiment. So this..." My mirth faded into something softer. "This was perfect."

It was probably frowned upon to talk about an ex during a date, but Asher picked up the thread and kept pulling.

"When did you two break up?" he asked.

"Five years ago." Asher's brows furrowed.

"Yeah. It was right after my accident." I took a fortifying sip of wine and debated how much to tell him. I didn't want to turn our dinner into a therapy session. I hadn't talked about Rafe in years. The only people who knew the details of our split were my family and Carina, but wasn't this what couples did? Share parts of their pasts, both the good and the bad, with each other? He'd trusted me enough to tell me about Teddy; it was only fair I tell him about Rafe.

Besides, even though we weren't an official couple, I felt more comfortable talking to Asher than anyone else I'd dated.

"We started dating when I was eighteen," I said. "He and Vincent were teammates at the time, which was how we met. We were together for three years. It was my first serious relationship, and I thought he hung the moon and stars. We even talked about getting married one day." I toyed with my wineglass, lost in recollection. "I should've known better. We were so young, and we were caught up in the fame and money. Especially him. It blinded me to things that should've been red flags. But I loved him, or at least I loved the *idea* of him, and I truly believed we would be together forever."

Sometimes, I remembered the girl I used to be, and I couldn't believe she existed in the same lifetime as me. She'd been so bright and shiny, filled with hope and stars in her eyes. Rigid when it came to her career but romantic in every other way.

Look where that'd gotten her.

"Things were going so well, I thought he was going to propose. Then…" I swallowed hard. "Then the accident happened. I was in the hospital for weeks afterward. My recovery was brutal, both physically and emotionally. Rafe couldn't handle it. He'd signed up to date the beautiful prima ballerina, not the…not that shattered version of me who was depressed and angry all the time. I had good reason to feel that way, but like I said, we were young. We weren't equipped to deal with the strain it put on our relationship. He broke up with me a month after I was discharged from the hospital, and he started dating someone else two weeks after that."

Say what you will about Rafe, but he didn't waste time.

Asher's expression hardened. His anger didn't surface often, but when it did, it transformed the entire landscape of his face, sharpening the angles and carving dark hollows beneath his cheekbones. "That *fucker*."

"It's okay." I shook my head. "Don't get me wrong. I hated him at the time, but in hindsight, it was the best thing for both of us."

Time and therapy had blunted the serrated edges of my anger. We would never be friends, but I didn't curse him every time I thought about him either.

However, his abandonment had left me with deep-seated trust issues. It also stripped the shine from our relationship, and I saw the faults that infatuation had glossed over—the arrogance, the desperation for status, the desire for me as a trophy instead of a person.

They were things I'd overlooked because I loved him, but like the saying goes, a person's true nature is revealed in the face of adversity.

Asher's lips pressed together. "He's the reason for your no-footballers rule."

I nodded. "I was so heartbroken, and football was such a big part of who he was that I conflated his shortcomings with the sport as a whole. Besides my brother, every footballer I met reminded me of him, so I swore them off altogether."

"I don't blame you. Most of us are absolute wankers," Asher admitted with a trace of a smile.

"Most are," I agreed. "But you're not."

I used to think he was. Before we were forced to spend time together in training, I'd already formed an opinion about who he was based on what Vincent told me, what I read in the press, and the mere fact that he was Asher fucking Donovan. How could someone so famous and good-looking *not* be an arrogant playboy?

But over the past few months, I'd discovered that he was so much more than the words other people used to pigeonhole him. It wasn't about what he did so much as how he made me feel—like I was safe, worthy, and cherished. Like I could share my deepest secrets and ugliest thoughts without diminishing myself in his eyes.

I expected a flippant response, but Asher's mouth sobered as he regarded me across the table.

"I try not to be," he said. "I don't always succeed, but I try."

I drew in a shallow breath. We'd barely touched our food, but my stomach was full of butterflies.

The silence stretched just long enough to end in a perfect, pinpoint period.

"Thank you for letting me ramble," I said. "I know it's probably bad etiquette to talk about an ex during a date."

"You can talk to me about anything, anytime." Asher rubbed a hand over his mouth. "You said he used to play with Vincent. Do you mind if I ask who it was?"

I hesitated for only a beat. "Rafael Pessoa."

The Brazilian striker had been Vincent's teammate at Chelsea before they both transferred. Luckily, Rafael left the Premier League for La Liga soon after our breakup, so I didn't have to worry about running into him in London.

"Pessoa?" Asher snorted. "I always knew he was an arsehole. He dives more than an Olympic swimmer."

I laughed. Rafael *did* have a penchant for feigning injuries. "Don't let him hear you say that. He hates when people call him out on it."

"I bet he does. You're better off without him. He doesn't deserve you."

Emotions jumbled in my throat. Luckily, Asher saved me from the humiliation of crying in front of him again when he reached for the intercom again.

"I do have one more surprise for you," he said. "I hope you're in the mood for a double dessert."

My brows knitted together when our servers returned and placed two cakes on the table. One was a raspberry cheesecake similar to what we'd baked during class. The second was...

I blinked, certain I was seeing wrong.

I wasn't.

"Asher." I covered my mouth with one hand. "You didn't. Tell me you didn't ask *Sebastian Laurent* to make that cake."

"No. His pastry chef made it." Asher grinned. "I wanted something memorable to cap off our evening. I hope you like it."

"Like it? I *love* it." I dragged the second plate closer so I could examine it in detail. My voice bubbled with laughter. "I'm just not sure I can eat it. It's too beautiful."

The buttercream-frosted cake was large enough for six people. A golden yellow fondant figurine of a certain cartoon dog adorned the top, next to a picture of a tiny planet. And beneath that picture, written in neat, blue frosting cursive, were three words.

Justice for Pluto.

CHAPTER 30

ASHER

I HATED TO ADMIT IT, BUT MY FATHER WAS RIGHT. I *WAS* distracted.

I just didn't care.

It was summer. I had a few weeks before the season started, I was in great shape training-wise, and I wanted to soak up every moment with Scarlett while I could.

Once the season was underway and her brother returned to town, our dynamic would change, so fuck focus. I'd worked my ass off for over a decade; I could afford a little time off.

"You're unusually quiet," Scarlett said, trailing her fingers up and down my thigh. "What are you thinking about?"

"You." I wrapped my arms around her from behind and rested my chin on her shoulder. We were lazing in her bathtub, the lavender-scented bubbles barely covering her curves as we luxuriated in the quiet evening. It was Thursday so we didn't have training, but I didn't need that as an excuse to see her anymore. "Your practices are going well. You nailed the choreography yesterday."

In addition to her Tuesday cast rehearsals, she was practicing pieces of *Lorena* on her own after our trainings.

"Do you even know what the choreography is supposed to look like?" She sounded amused.

"Yes. It's supposed to look like how you did it yesterday."

Scarlett turned her head, her face stamped with good-natured exasperation. "Asher Donovan, you are too smooth for your own good."

"Am I?" I skimmed my mouth over the curve of her shoulder and up her neck, savoring the silky-smooth feel of her skin. "Or am I just telling the truth?"

She let out a sigh of pleasure when I captured her mouth in a kiss. She tasted like sugar and strawberries, and when she slid her tongue against mine, my entire body reacted with instant, visceral *need*.

Every time we kissed felt like the first fucking time. There was always another layer to unpeel.

I bracketed her waist with my hands and turned her so she wasn't craning her neck. The friction of her body against mine sent another jolt of lust from the head of my cock to my aching balls.

"Fuck." I groaned.

The vibrations from Scarlett's laughter didn't help my situation. "You're wound tight today," she murmured. "Let's see if we can take care of that, shall we?"

She kissed me again, winding her arms around my neck and rocking against me with delicious, deliberate movements that made my brain short-circuit.

I'd always preferred showers to baths, but not anymore.

Screw showers. Baths were the best.

I cupped the back of her head, holding her steady as she ground harder against me. Another tortured groan traveled up my throat.

We didn't have condoms with us, and I didn't want to break our embrace to grab them from her bedroom. But she was so slick and soft, and she tasted so good, that if I didn't get inside her soon I—

A sharp gasp bled into our kiss—not of pleasure but of *pain*.

I instantly pulled back, my lust puddling into panic when Scarlett winced, her brow crumpling. "What's wrong? Did I hurt you?"

"No, nothing like that," she reassured me. She shifted her weight and took a deep breath. "It's this position. I got a sudden twinge in my leg. That's all."

"Fuck." I ran a hand over my face. Of *course* her tiny tub wasn't a good place for foreplay. I was usually hyperconscious of how and where we had sex in case it aggravated her chronic pain, but I'd gotten too lost in the moment. "I didn't think…"

"It's not your fault." Scarlett gave me a quick smile. "Usually it's not so bad, but it's been a long week. I'm more sensitive than usual."

"I should've thought of it," I insisted, mentally kicking myself for the oversight. "We don't have to stay here. We can move somewhere more comfortable if you need to rest."

I hated that I'd played a part in her discomfort. I'd pay any amount of money to take away her pain—not just her physical ones, but the mental and emotional ones too.

But money couldn't buy peace. I, of all people, knew that.

"Stop. This isn't on you." Scarlett's fingers skimmed over my mouth, soothing my grimace. "I *want* to have sex. I like sex. I also like this tub, and I like what we were doing in here. I just needed a little… adjustment before we continue. If I truly need to stop, I'd tell you."

I must've looked unconvinced because her mouth flattened into a stubborn line. "Don't," she said. "Promise you won't treat me like I'm a porcelain doll you're afraid you'll break. That's not what I want."

I brushed my lips over hers in the lightest of kisses. "So what do you want?"

"I want to stay here." I felt her smile more than I saw it. "I didn't pour a quarter of my fanciest bubble bath for nothing. That stuff is expensive."

Relief and humor laced my chuckle.

She's fine. Like she said, she'd tell me if she wasn't, and I didn't want to assume I knew her body better than she did. If there was one thing Scarlett couldn't stand, it was people pitying or babying her. She didn't need that. Regardless of her physical condition, she was one of the strongest people I knew.

"Then we'll stay, and I won't treat you like a porcelain doll." My lips grazed hers with each word. "I promise, I've never imagined doing to dolls the things I'm going to do to you."

My mouth curved at her sharp intake of breath.

"Turn around," I said.

She obeyed, and I waited until she'd settled into a comfortable position before I grabbed a loofah from next to the tub and dipped it in the still-warm water. I squeezed it over her shoulders, letting the foam-tipped beads drip down her back, before I rubbed them in with long, languid strokes.

Our conversation tapered into her soft sighs and the gentle splash of water as I worked my way over her body. White sudsy trails trickled down her bare skin, and she looked so beautiful and content sitting there, her limbs heavy with desire, that I could've spent the rest of my life doing this.

I'd never bathed anyone before, but the intimacy of it destroyed me more than sex. To have Scarlett trust me enough to take care of her when she was at her most naked and vulnerable...it was a gut punch in the best way possible.

After I finished lathering her back, I ran the hot water again before I moved the loofah around to her front. I glided it up her thighs and over her stomach to her chest. The water lapped against the sides of the tub with every movement, creating a rhythm that was almost hypnotic.

Steam rose from the freshly heated water and curled in lazy tendrils around us. The air was redolent with the scent of lavender and soap, and an aching tension muffled any noises that might've bled over from neighboring flats.

In that moment, we were the only people on earth.

However, my languorous exploration of her body came to a brief halt when Scarlett sank deeper against my chest and shifted in a way that rubbed directly over my cock.

Heat raced to my groin.

I gritted my teeth. I was rock-hard, but I forced myself to finish the bath without rushing. When I smoothed the loofah over her breasts, she let out a breathy sigh that made every last drop of blood head south.

"You know exactly what you're doing, don't you?" I said roughly. I underscored the question with a nip on her ear.

A shiver rippled through her. "I have no idea what you're talking about."

"No?" I ditched the sponge and cupped her breast, giving it a punishing squeeze. "Try again."

Her shiver intensified into a full-body shudder. "I don't want you to use the loofah anymore," she said, her voice thick with desire. "I want you to touch me with your hands."

"Where do you want me to touch you?" I released her breast and slid my hand over her stomach. It went taut, her muscles quivering from the light caress. "Here?"

She nodded.

"Or here?" I dipped lower to her thighs, parting them so her knees pressed against mine. I couldn't see through the layer of bubbles, but I could picture her pussy, pink and perfect and *wet*.

"*Yes*," she breathed.

"Maybe you want me to touch here instead." I trailed my fingers over her inner thigh, my knuckles just grazing her clit.

Scarlett's whimper amplified the pressure gripping my cock. I hadn't touched it, but hearing her whine with need was almost enough to make me blow.

My muscles throbbed with pent-up lust. If we hadn't been sitting, my knees might've buckled from the sheer force of my desire, but I took it slow—for now.

"You're a greedy little thing, aren't you?" I murmured when she arched her back and tried to press harder against my hand.

Instead of giving in to her insistent squirming, I took my time, my palms mapping every inch of her wet, flushed skin. I dragged them back up over her hips and stomach until I reached her breasts again. They were soft and firm, tipped with diamond-hard nipples that strained for my touch.

I rolled them between my fingers, tugging and pinching until her whimpers escalated into full-out moans. Her hips surged up, seeking friction that the water couldn't give.

"Please." Scarlett gripped my wrist and tried to guide my hand down between her legs. "Asher, *please*." A sob rent the air when I resisted.

"Patience, darling," I soothed. My lips grazed the shell of her ear. "Let me play with you first."

I kept one hand on her breast while the other continued its exploration. She shuddered and panted, so damn responsive that it took everything in me not to haul her into the bedroom and fill her up the way she was begging me to.

There'd be time for that later, after I finished what I'd started.

After an agonizing length of teasing that was as torturous for me as it was for her, I finally brushed her clit with my thumb. She was so on edge that the single, featherlight caress ripped a strangled cry from her throat.

Scarlett bucked against me hard enough to send water splashing over the side of the tub and onto the floor. Her fingers gripped the porcelain edge with bleached-white knuckles, and a series of unintelligible moans filled the room when I stroked her swollen bud.

"Oh, God." She gasped as my hands pinched and rubbed and squeezed in tandem—one on her breast, the other between her legs. My teeth scored the curve between her neck and shoulder as I fought to keep the leash of my control intact.

My cock was so hard it fucking hurt, but I pushed its demand for attention aside for now.

I increased my pace, loving the sounds of Scarlett's cries and her body's response until her body stiffened and she came with a scream.

Her orgasm rolled on and on, its ripples seemingly never-ending as she convulsed from the intensity.

I groaned against her neck, my breathing ragged. I wished I was inside her, feeling her cunt clench around my cock while she flooded me with wet heat, but this wasn't the place for that, and this wasn't about me. It was about her.

Eventually, Scarlett's orgasm subsided, and she slumped against me.

"I think I've found a new favorite way to take a bath," she said, sounding dazed.

Laughter rumbled up my throat. "Mine too." I wrapped my arms around her waist from behind and pressed a kiss to her shoulder. "We should do this after every day."

"You won't hear any arguments from me." Scarlett hummed with pleasure. "But we're not finished yet."

I sucked in a breath when she adjusted her position and sat up straighter so she could grasp me without turning around.

"Is that right?" I drawled. A low buzz filled my ears. I couldn't see what she was doing, but God, I could *feel* it. "What else did you have in mind?" My strained voice belied the casual words.

She glanced at me over her shoulder, her gray eyes sparkling with mischief. "More like what I have in hand."

"*Fuck*." The curse slipped out when she squeezed the head of my aching cock. "Scarlett…"

"Yes?" she said innocently.

I didn't answer. I *couldn't*. Every thought emptied when she slid her hands up and down my shaft, her slick palms working in tandem to yank me toward the brink. She let go occasionally to scrape her nails lightly across my balls, but I quickly lost track of her individual movements.

I was too focused on the electric heat gathering at the base of my spine. My muscles turned rigid, and I—

The jarring ring of the doorbell brought a screeching halt to my orgasm. My eyes flew open as the asshole visitor rang the bell *again* less than a second later and thoroughly killed the moment.

I hissed in aggravation when Scarlett released me fully. Who the *fuck* was here this late in the evening?

"That must be our takeaway." She looked like she was trying not to laugh as I glowered at the door. "I'm sorry, baby. I'll finish taking care of you when I get back. I don't want you scaring them off." She arched an eyebrow at the bubbles, which had cleared enough for us to see my still-raging erection beneath the water.

"The delivery guy has the worst timing ever," I growled. "Zero stars for them."

A sliver of Scarlett's laugh escaped. "Don't be mean." She climbed carefully out of the tub and belted a thick robe around herself. "I'll be right back."

I sank deeper into the tub, cursing past me for thinking takeaway was a good idea. We should've ordered it *after* our bath. That way, I wouldn't be sitting here with blue balls.

The minutes ticked by. She was taking awfully long for a quick delivery.

Concern cut a path through my grumbles and coalesced into alarm when I heard voices in the living room. Why the *hell* was the delivery guy in her flat?

I was about to bolt out of the tub when the door opened and Scarlett entered.

My relief sputtered out at the sight of her face. It was the color of parchment. "What happened? Did he—"

"*Shhh.*" She glanced over her shoulder. When she turned again, her eyes brimmed with fresh panic. "That wasn't the delivery guy. It was my brother. He's in the living room."

A boulder tumbled into my stomach as her words sank in.

Vincent was *here*, standing less than twenty feet away and separated from us by only two flimsy sets of doors while I was naked in his sister's bathtub.

Oh, fuck.

CHAPTER 31

SCARLETT

I TOLD VINCENT I WAS GETTING DRESSED, SO I COULDN'T stay in the bathroom too long. I left Asher there with strict instructions not to make a single sound, tossed on a T-shirt and leggings, and hurried back to the living room.

I hadn't wanted to leave my brother alone in case he picked up on the clues scattered around the flat—the men's shoes in the entryway, the two half-empty glasses on the kitchen counter—but I had to warn Asher so he didn't wander out looking for pizza.

"Sorry for the wait. I had to, um, find clean clothes," I said brightly, closing the bedroom door behind me. Thankfully, I'd scored one of the coveted flats with an en suite bathroom. If Asher were in the hall with only *one* door separating him from my brother...a chill shivered across my back. "You didn't tell me you'd be visiting. You were just here a few weeks ago."

"I was." Vincent stood in the middle of the living room, his arms crossed.

I gulped. *Uh-oh.* He looked furious.

"I didn't tell you I was coming for a reason," he said. An accusatory note slid beneath his words. "I didn't want to give you time to make up excuses."

Oh, fuck. Ohfuckohfuckohfuck. He knows. A bead of sweat cut a small swath down my neck.

Why did Asher and I keep putting off our Vincent strategy? We said we'd figure out a way to tell my brother, but we never brainstormed the *how* part. If we had, I might be able to respond with more than a dismayed squeak when Vincent's eyes flicked around the room and landed on the trainers by the door—specifically, the white, size nine *men's* trainers.

A muscle worked in Vincent's jaw. "Is there something you want to tell me?"

I mustered a weak smile. "I love you and you're the bestest big brother ever?"

I swore I heard a growl. "*Scarlett.*"

"Look." I held up my hands. My nerves felt like barbs punching through my skin, but we were already here. There was no use denying the obvious. "I was going to tell you, I swear. But I didn't want you to get mad and do something stupid."

"Stupid?" Vincent's eye twitched. Okay, maybe that hadn't been the best choice of words. "Like *what*?"

"Like when you told one of my dates you'd get the entire Blackcastle team to jump him if he didn't bring me home before midnight."

"He was an idiot," Vincent snapped. "What kind of person with common sense would believe that? And don't try to deflect. How long has this been going on?" He jabbed a finger toward the trainers.

"Um…" I braced myself. "A few weeks?"

"*A few weeks?*" he exploded. "Jesus, Lettie."

"It's my love life," I said defensively. "I don't have to tell you every time I date someone. Besides, I wanted to see where things went before I said anything."

"Maybe that's true, but it'd be nice to hear about it from my sister instead of the internet!"

The internet. Ice water flooded my veins. Dread grabbed my heart and slammed it against my rib cage with heavy, relentless beats.

"You…you found out about us from the internet?"

How did we miss that? Did the news break today? If so, how did Vincent get here so fast?

Then again, Paris was only a two-and-a-half-hour train ride from London, and Asher and I hadn't been on our phones all evening.

Vincent scrolled through his cell and shoved it at me. "Someone saw you guys at the Golden Wharf a few weeks ago. They posted a picture on some sports forum but it didn't make the rounds until today."

I stared at the screen, open-mouthed, because the picture he'd pulled up wasn't of me and Asher.

It was of me and Clive.

It was grainy, but our faces were clearly visible. The photographer had captured me getting out of his car while he waited with his arm out like a gentleman. We were smiling at each other like we were in love, even though I'd been hungry and he'd been distracted.

Thankfully, whoever took the photo hadn't stuck around to see us meet Asher and Ivy. If they had, I'd bet my last quid the pictures would've made the rounds *way* sooner.

Oxygen flowed more smoothly into my lungs. My brother didn't know about Asher—yet.

"Clive Hart? Seriously?" Vincent's annoyed voice brought my attention back to him. "Of all the people you could've chosen, you

chose to date *Clive Hart*? I told you he was a fuckboy and I meant it.
Don't fall for his nice-guy act, Lettie. It's broken a lot of hearts."

"I'm not dating Clive," I said, trying to wrap my head around the
new and unexpected development. I didn't know there were people so
invested in rugby players' love lives. "We went on one date. That's it."

"Then whose shoes are those?"

Fuck. I realized my mistake too late.

"Uh…" I scrambled for an excuse. "I—I have a friend from RAB
over. We were going over something for *Lorena*. You know, that
school showcase I'm an understudy for? He spilled something so he's
taking a shower."

"I don't hear the water running."

My brother was usually an idiot. *Why* did he have to be so
observant today of all days?

"I guess he's lathering," I said. "He's very, um, thorough with the
soap."

Vincent's eyes tapered in suspicion. He didn't believe me for a
second. "Are you sleeping with him? I just want to have a talk." He
started toward my bedroom.

"No!" I grabbed his arm. "I told you—he's showering."

"I can wait in your room."

"No. You are *not* going to storm in there and embarrass me."
I released him but put myself in his path, blocking him from the
door. "I'm an adult, Vince. While I appreciate your concern, I can do
whatever I want with *whoever* I want. I don't need to run it by you
first. You don't see me interrogating you about every girl you're seen
with."

"That's not the same."

"Why not? Double standard much?" I shook my head. "I know
you're worried about me and you don't want to see me get hurt, but I

promise I know what I'm doing."

"Do you?" Vincent's mask of anger fractured, revealing slivers of worry underneath. "You haven't dated anyone seriously since Rafael, and we know how that ended. You were inconsolable after the breakup. I don't want to see you in that place again. Ever. It was... fuck, Lettie. It was a scary time."

My indignation melted at his agonized expression. For all his bluster and overprotectiveness, he really did have my best interests at heart, and he was right. The early post-breakup days had been mired in darkness. Between the accident and the abrupt end of a three-year relationship, there'd been times when...

I swallowed. "I get it," I said, more softly this time. "But I'm not twenty-one anymore. Let me handle my relationships as I see fit, okay?"

Vincent stared at me for an extra beat before he let out a resigned sigh. "Fine. But if anyone fucks with you, tell me and I really will get the team to jump him." He eyed the trainers again. "So *are* you sleeping with your colleague? Who is it? Is it serious?"

"*Vincent.*"

"Just curious." He cracked a small smile. "Anyway, I didn't come all this way just to yell at you about Clive—though this conversation would be a lot longer if you really *were* dating him."

I figured as much. Vincent was as capable of yelling over the phone as he was in person. "Do you have another PR thing in the city?"

"No. Coach wanted to check in with me since I, ah, backed out of the training sessions with you and Donovan. Dad's doing fine with the nurse now, so I'm actually returning to London earlier than expected. I'm staying through the weekend, then I'll go back to Paris to wrap up loose ends. But I'll be training with you again starting the Monday after next."

I suspected there was more to the story than he was sharing, but I was too stuck on his last sentence to delve deeper. *I'll be training with you again starting the Monday after next.*

That meant Asher and I had even less time together than anticipated.

"Oh. How nice." My words squeaked with surprise. "I mean, yay! Can't wait."

If Vincent noticed my pitiable attempt to feign enthusiasm, he didn't mention it. "The upside is, I can keep an eye on Donovan. I can't stand that guy." His mouth twisted into a grimace. "At least you're not sleeping with *him.* I'm sorry, Lettie. I know it's your love life, but if he was the one in your bathroom right now, I'd smash his face into the wall."

My high-pitched laugh sounded like it was supercharged with helium. "Me and Asher? Haha. That would be something. *Anyway.*" I pushed him toward the exit. "Let's catch up later. I don't want my colleague to see you when he gets out of the shower, and—oh!"

The pizza delivery guy beamed at us when I yanked open the door. "Sorry I'm late," he said with the kind of pep only a uni student desperate for extra cash could scrounge up. "There was an accident, so traffic was a nightmare. *But* never fear! Pete's Pizza's state-of-the-art warming bag ensures your food will taste as fresh as when it left the oven."

"Great." I pushed my brother into the hall and reached for the pizza. "Thanks—"

The delivery guy cut me off with the remainder of his spiel. "Can you please confirm that you ordered one large pepperoni pizza with a side of garlic breadsticks for Ash—"

"*Yes!*" I shouted. Asher had placed the order under a pseudonym, but he'd stupidly used his real first name. "Thanks so much. Have a great day. Vince, I'll call you later. Bye!"

I grabbed the pie, waved, and slammed the door in two stunned faces.

I stood there, pulse pumping, until I heard their footsteps fade. To be safe, I peered out the window and waited until Vincent's car disappeared down the street before I turned and set the pizza on the coffee table.

"Smooth."

I jumped at the unexpected voice and whirled around, my poor heart rate spiking to the top of the roller coaster before plummeting with relief.

I placed a hand over my chest. "God, don't scare me like that."

Asher stood in my bedroom doorway, dressed and scowling. Logically, I knew he was the only other person in the flat, but my nerves were shot from dealing with my brother. Every little thing set me on edge.

"Smash my face into the wall?" Asher had obviously overheard Vincent's threat. "I'd like to see him bloody try."

"Tone down the testosterone for a moment and focus," I admonished. "Do you know how close of a call that was? If our timing had been just a little off…"

"He'd beat me up? Please. I'd wipe the floor with him." Asher snorted, but his frown released with a sigh at my warning glare. "Fine. I'll behave."

"I can't believe someone took a photo of me and Clive."

Did Clive know about the picture? I hadn't spoken to him since I thanked him for our date but politely insinuated that I wasn't open to a second one. He'd taken my rejection in stride. I didn't think he was that into me either.

"Yeah, he's a C-list celebrity at best. The public doesn't care who he dates." Asher shrugged when I made an exasperated noise. "Sorry, but it's true. I Googled it when you were talking to Vincent. The photo's on a few gossip forums, but the only news outlet that ran it is some shitty online tabloid no one reads. I'm surprised your brother even saw it."

Relief unwound the knots in my gut. "Thank God the photographer didn't see you, or this would be a different story." I tried to sort through our next steps. "Okay, so Vincent thinks I'm dating my colleague, and he'll be training with us again soon. What do we do?"

"We make sure he's not around sharp objects when we break the news to him."

"Can you be serious?"

"I am serious." But his confident smirk didn't fully reach his eyes. "I'm not looking forward to the conversation either, but despite our differences, your brother and I have one thing in common. We both care about you. That counts for something, right?"

A warm drop of pleasure dripped into my pool of anxiety. "Right. You're right," I repeated. "Maybe it won't turn out as bad as we're making it out to be. He cares enough about what your coach thinks to return to London early and continue training with you, which is good. He doesn't want a repeat of last season either."

Last season had been a disaster because Asher and Vincent butted heads, but now Asher said he was willing to let bygones be bygones. If he extended an olive branch, Vincent would have to take it. He was the team captain. His job included boosting team morale and cohesion.

He was overprotective at times, but he had my best interests at heart. If I was happy with Asher, he wouldn't begrudge me that.

"We'll discuss exactly how to tell him over pizza." Asher gave me a crooked smile. "Don't want Pete's Pizza's state-of-the-art warming bag's hard work to go to waste."

I returned his smile with a small one of my own. "Best idea you've had all day."

"Even better than the bath?"

"*Second* best idea you've had all day," I amended.

His laugh settled over me like a warm blanket on a winter night. It was so rich, so strong and comforting, that it made it easy to believe everything would turn out all right.

"I'm sorry we didn't finish our...activities earlier." I glanced down at his sweats. The past half hour had killed our moment in the bathroom.

I felt bad since he'd given me an incredible orgasm (I'll never look at my tub the same again) while I'd left him with blue balls.

"It's fine. I'm used to Vincent fucking shit up for me," Asher said sardonically. "And don't worry, darling. I have ideas for how you can make it up to me later."

Heat curled low at the velvety dip of his voice. "Do you now?"

"Mmhmm." He broke off half a breadstick and handed it to me. "Later, once your brother's stench is fully gone. It's a mood killer."

"*Asher.*"

"Sorry. I couldn't help it." He didn't sound sorry at all.

I swear, men acted like boys half the time.

"How're you feeling about the charity match this weekend?" I asked, switching subjects. "It's at three on Saturday, right?"

Asher was participating in Sport for Hope, a football fundraiser organized by a nonprofit foundation of the same name. It provided mentoring and sports opportunities for kids in high-need communities.

I'd never heard of them until he mentioned the match last week, but I was excited to see him play in person. Football matches were usually too rowdy for me, so I hadn't attended a Blackcastle match since he transferred.

"Yep. It's always a fun time." Asher hesitated. "I know Vincent is staying through the weekend, so you don't have to come if it makes things dicey."

"No way," I said stubbornly. "I'll bring the girls, and we'll make a day out of it. But I'm not missing the match."

A small smile graced his lips. The moment swirled around us for a gentle second before he cleared his throat and averted his eyes. "Speaking of the girls, are you excited for tomorrow?"

Carina, Brooklyn, and I were scheduled to have our poker-and-drinks get-together tomorrow night.

"Mmhmm. I can't wait. I need more estrogen in my life." I finished my pizza and wiped my mouth with a napkin. "Between you and my brother, I've been around way too much testosterone. I need better company before I go absolutely bat—" I cut off with a squeal when Asher tackled me to the floor.

He swallowed my laugh with a kiss, and soon, I wasn't thinking about my brother, my friends, or anything at all besides his touch.

ASHER

"We have a problem." Finley removed his hat and rubbed a hand over his bald pate, his frustration visible through the screen. "Simon injured his foot and won't be able to play tomorrow."

"*Shit*." I swallowed a longer litany of curses. "What about our backups?"

It was Friday night, and the big charity match kicked off in less than twenty-four hours. We didn't have time to recruit someone new.

Fucking Simon. If I was reckless with cars, he was reckless with everything else. I wouldn't be surprised to learn he'd injured his foot doing something stupid, like kicking a marble statue out of anger.

Finley grimaced. He was the head of Sport for Hope. I'd participated in their charity match for so many summers that I was basically a de facto advisor, and he often called me for advice when it came to marketing and recruiting players.

"We only have one backup, and his wife gave birth early last week. He's not leaving his newborn's side."

"Shit," I said again.

With Simon injured and our backup out of town, we were missing a good defender.

Sport for Hope relied on its summer fundraiser for the bulk of its annual donations. The match always sold out, but the *real* cash came from its secret benefactor. No one knew who it was, but apparently they had an odd way of calculating how much they'd donate. The number of goals scored by the winning team equaled how many times they'd match the ticket sales.

For example, if the match sold fifty thousand pounds worth of tickets and the winning team scored three goals, the donor would wire a hundred fifty thousand pounds to the charity.

It was strange, but *people* were strange.

The stipulation also meant we worked hard to recruit good players every summer. Better players usually meant more goals. Unfortunately, it was hard when the match took place during the off-season when everyone was on holiday.

"I don't suppose you know anyone who can fill in?" Finley asked. Lines of stress bracketed the sides of his mouth. "I know it's a big favor to ask at the last minute, but the new football pitch took a big chunk of our money last year. We need the extra donation match from SB." SB stood for Secret Benefactor. Not a creative nickname, but it did the job.

"I don't know." I racked my brain for possibilities. "I want to help, but most of the players I know aren't in…" I trailed off.

There was one defender who was in town and uninjured—one *very* good defender who made Simon look like an amateur (no offense to Simon).

No. My pride quashed the seed of possibility before it fully blossomed. There was no fucking way I'd ask *him* for help. I'd rather chop off my leg and serve it to him on a silver platter.

Then I looked at Finley's pleading face, and I thought of all the kids his organization helped. Teddy had been one of those kids, which was how I found out about Sport for Hope in the first place. Besides London, it had chapters in Holchester, Manchester, and Birmingham.

Before Teddy's mother remarried and his family moved next door to mine, his parents had struggled to put food on the table. Sport for Hope was the one that'd provided him with the resources to play football in a semi-professional setting for youths. Without them, we might've never bonded over the sport.

I joined the Sport for Hope tournament after Teddy died and stayed involved since. It was part atonement for my role in his death and part way to honor his memory. I couldn't screw it up.

"Forget SB," I said. "I can more than match the ticket sales."

Finley's expression crumpled into a scowl. "You say that every year, and my answer is the same every year. Absolutely not. You already do more than enough. I'm not taking advantage of you like that."

I knew he would say that, but I had to offer.

"Don't try to pull some secret shit with me either," he added. "If a big, anonymous check comes in from anyone other than SB, I'll know."

Bloody hell. Finley was stubborn as hell, but his convictions were what made him a great leader.

Pride battled guilt for dominance. Was I going to fuck over Finley and the kids because I couldn't set aside my rivalry for one weekend?

"I may know someone," I finally said. The admission tasted bitter on my tongue. "I can't guarantee he'll agree to play, but I'll ask. If he says no, we'll have to sub in Ricky."

Finley and I winced in unison. Ricky was their operations coordinator. He was a nice guy, and he played football in a local amateur league. He just wasn't good. At all.

The last time he subbed in for a player, he accidentally tripped one of his teammates and scored for the opposing team. Twice.

"Please," Finley said. "You'll have our gratitude forever."

After I ended our video call, I leaned back and stared at my office ceiling. The damn defender. I couldn't ask him directly. He'd shut me down before I opened my mouth.

I would have to go through Scarlett, which was tricky considering he didn't know about us yet. We'd decided to tell him in person together, after he officially returned to London.

But Scarlett and I had been training together all summer. It would make sense for us to develop a friendship, so her asking him a favor for me wasn't inherently suspicious.

The clock ticked toward eight.

I was running out of time.

Fuck it. I bit the bullet and called her. I hated interrupting her girls' night, but I didn't have a choice.

"Hey, I'm sorry to bother you, but I have a time-sensitive favor to ask," I said when Scarlett picked up. "Any chance you could convince your brother to play in the charity match tomorrow?"

CHAPTER 32

SCARLETT

I DIDN'T KNOW HOW, BUT I DID IT.

Well, okay, I *kind of* knew how—a guilt trip, a group photo of cute kids wearing their Sport for Hope-provided football kits, and a promise to let him choose our next four dinners in a row worked wonders in getting Vincent to sign up for the charity match.

I suspected having Asher owe him one helped as well. Knowing my brother, he'd never let Asher forget it.

Regardless, I was thrilled Vincent said yes. I knew how much the charity meant to Asher, especially given its connection to Teddy, and hopefully the match would be a first step toward my brother and my boyfriend tolerating each other.

"So Vincent wasn't suspicious of you asking a favor for Asher?" Carina followed me to our front-row seats in the bleachers. The charity match took place at a local football stadium, and it was already packed with families.

"Nope. He bought my excuse that I was the messenger and that Asher asked me to ask him because it was an emergency."

"When exactly are you going to tell him about you two?" Brooklyn took the seat on the other side of me. It didn't take much convincing to get them both to come to the match today. Carina was always down for a fun outing, and Brooklyn was apparently a football fan. "You said next week?"

"That's the plan." My stomach danced with nerves as the players filed onto the field for warm-ups.

I spotted Asher and Vincent immediately. The two teams were divided into colors, the Reds versus the Greens. Asher and Vincent both sported red kits, and the crowd's excitement reached an audible crescendo when people noticed who was on the pitch.

They studiously pretended the other didn't exist, but at least they weren't actively picking arguments with each other.

I tamped down a laugh when I noticed how they performed the exact same stretches at the exact time in the exact same manner.

Like I said, they were more alike than they cared to admit.

"God, he's even dreamier on the pitch than he is off of it." Carina sighed when Asher sank into a calf stretch. His leg muscles flexed, and half our section released similar sighs. "You're a lucky, lucky girl."

Her tone indicated she was teasing me more than anything else. She had a visual appreciation for athletes, but when it came to dating, her type ran toward the artsy, angsty segment of the male population.

"*Shhh.*" I cast a nervous glance around us. We were surrounded by parents who were more concerned with keeping foreign objects out of their toddlers' hands than with our conversation, but there were a few members of the local press lurking around. I didn't want any of them to overhear. "Lower your voice."

At least the paps weren't here. They didn't know Vincent would be playing today, and they clearly thought a charity match for kids wasn't a ripe breeding ground for scandal.

"Calling your brother to play a match with his rival-slash-your secret lover is a boss move," Brooklyn whispered. "You have balls. I respect it. You deserve a feature story in *Mode de Vie*."

Carina giggled while I fought an exasperated sigh. "I don't *want* a feature story in *Mode de Vie* or any other outlet. I just want to—"

"Bone your man all the way to Sunday and back again?" Brooklyn tossed me a devilish grin. "Understandable."

"*Totally* understandable." Carina leaned over me to give the American a high five. "You have a way with words, Brook."

"Thank you." Brooklyn beamed. "I try."

I scowled. "You know what? I'm sorry I introduced you guys. *This*"—I gestured to the both of them as they laughed at my expense— "is unacceptable."

As I predicted, Carina and Brooklyn instantly hit it off when they met in person last night. I figured they would, but part of me had worried Carina would feel weird about me introducing someone new into our tight-knit duo. However, they took to each other like ducks to water.

Unfortunately, that meant they sometimes ganged up on me, which I did *not* appreciate.

"Aw, you know we love you." Carina tossed an arm around my shoulders. "Would we be real friends if we didn't take the piss out of you for your soap opera of a life?"

"Yeah, some of our lives are boring. We have to live vicariously through you." Brooklyn crossed her legs, the picture of effortless cool with her high ponytail, gold hoops, and giant sunglasses. "The only thing that would make today more interesting is if Asher and Vincent got into a fight. *Not* that they would," she said when I blanched. "No one wants to derail a charity match for kids. It's bad press."

"Don't even put that thought out there." I eyed the pitch again.

Asher and Vincent were still ignoring each other, thank God. "It could very well happen."

"If it does, whose side would you be on?" Carina asked Brooklyn. "Team Asher or Team Vincent?"

The blond wrinkled her nose. "No team. I like the sport, not the players. They're way too full of themselves."

It was a quintessentially Brooklyn answer. We'd texted constantly since the night we met, but I still didn't know much about her. I knew she grew up in California, she was an aspiring nutritionist, and she could rock a ponytail like no other, but that was about it. She had an impressive talent for carrying on a full conversation without revealing anything about herself.

"I agree," I said. "Take it from someone who's related to one. *Way* too full of themselves."

Carina arched an eyebrow. "This coming from the girl *dating* a player."

"Well…" I caught Asher's eye when he scanned the crowd, his gaze skimming over the different sections until it found me. A thousand fluttering wings filled my chest. "He's different."

My friends let out good-natured groans, but I didn't care. The world narrowed to pools of intense green and the heat of Asher's stare. Electricity buzzed to life between us, slipping beneath my skin and setting every nerve ending on fire.

We couldn't do much with my brother and a thousand other people present, but we didn't need to. It wasn't about what we said or did; it was about what we felt.

Then, right before the teams finished their warm-ups, Asher grinned and winked. It happened so fast I would've missed it had I not already been looking at him, but it was enough. The thousand wings multiplied into a million, and I couldn't keep an answering grin off my face as the players took their places for kickoff.

When I finally looked away, my friends were staring at me with amusement.

"It's so sweet it's disgusting," Brooklyn said. "I want it."

"I don't," Carina said. "I'd never get any work done."

"So real."

I pointedly stayed out of their conversation, which petered out as the match started.

We screamed and cheered for the Reds and groaned when the Greens scored a goal. The players were a mix of top-level professionals and hobbyists. It made for an uneven match at times, but the crowd's enthusiasm and the buzzy atmosphere was so much fun that no one seemed to mind.

It was also the first match where we saw what Asher and Vincent were capable of when they weren't at each other's throats. Maybe it was the relatively low stakes or the fact they were playing for charity. Whatever it was, they played so well together that the Reds dominated the first half. The combination of Asher's offense and Vincent's defense resulted in two goals that roused the stadium into a fit of pandemonium.

Then disaster struck.

Less than a minute into the second half, one of the Reds fouled one of the Greens. The Green player crumpled to the ground, and the cheers cut off so abruptly it was like someone had pressed mute on a thousand people.

The two sides swarmed the ref, their hands gesticulating wildly as they argued with the stern-faced man. I couldn't hear what anyone was saying, but no one looked happy.

Asher and Vincent wore matching scowls, and after maybe a minute of heated discussion, the ref shook his head. He'd made his decision.

Greens got a penalty kick.

Someone helped the injured player off the pitch, and there was another small commotion when the Greens indicated they were subbing in a new player.

I squinted, trying to make out the new player's face.

When I did, my heart plummeted to my toes. A cold sensation crawled down my throat and filled my lungs.

"No fucking way." Carina verbalized my sentiments exactly. She grabbed my arm, her eyes the size of dinner plates.

I hadn't seen the sub during warm-ups. I didn't know why he was at the match or why he was in London, period, but there was no mistaking that dark hair or cocky smile.

My stomach curdled with disbelief as he jogged onto the pitch.

Of all the people who could've subbed in for the injured Green player, it had to be *him*. Rafael Pessoa. My ex-boyfriend.

Asher and Vincent's heads snapped toward him like lions sensing prey. Their bodies went rigid, and identical shadows darkened their faces.

Oh, no. Oh nononono.

"This is not good," Carina said. "This is not good at all."

Brooklyn's brow puckered. She didn't know about Rafael, so she had no clue why we were freaking out. "Why? What's wrong?"

"Well." My mouth tasted like pennies. "I think you're going to get that fight you were hoping for."

ASHER

"What is *he* doing here?" Vincent spat from his spot beside me.

I wasn't sure who he was talking to since he wasn't aware I knew about Scarlett and Rafael, but I replied with the obvious anyway.

"He's the sub."

"No shit. I meant what he's doing *here*, at the match."

They were the first words we'd exchanged all day. We'd greeted each other with stiff nods in the locker room, and I suppose I had to thank him later for agreeing to play at the last minute. However, I preferred to live in denial about that for as long as possible.

Was it mature? No.

Did I care? Also no.

I didn't have an answer for why Rafael was in London when he lived in Brazil and played in Spain, but one of the other Reds piped up with an explanation.

"I heard he's thinking of transferring back to the Premier League. Maybe he heard about the match and wanted to participate," he said.

A low growl rumbled through my chest.

I'd never been a big fan of Rafael, but after Scarlett told me about the shitty, cowardly way he broke up with her, I despised that man with every fucking fiber of my being.

Judging by Vincent's scowl, he felt the same way. He regarded the Brazilian forward with more loathing than he'd ever directed toward me.

The match resumed, cutting our conversation short, but a new tension suffocated the pitch. The first half had been for fun; this half was for vengeance.

I didn't want to win against the Greens. I wanted to *crush* them.

Unfortunately, despite his assholishness in his personal life, Rafael was a good player, and he managed to score with a header ten minutes into the half.

Frustration poured through my blood.

Rafael and I matched each other step for step for possession of the ball. I triumphed after I successfully kicked the ball away from him and caught it before another player could swoop in, but I barely had time to gloat before he fell to the ground, clutching his knee.

The ref blew his whistle, and the match paused. Boos rose from crowd.

"He tripped me," Rafael said when the ref came over to investigate. He gestured toward me, his eyes gleaming with…were those *tears*?

Jesus Christ. He should quit football and go into acting.

"That's bollocks. I didn't touch him!" I fumed.

Vincent came up beside us. "Ref, you saw that play! We all did," he argued. He pointed at Rafael. "He always pulls this crap. Like Donovan said, he didn't touch him."

Either he wanted to win enough to swallow his distaste and defend me, or he simply hated Rafael more than he hated me. Or both.

I cut a glance in his direction.

It was ironic Vincent was backing me up on this when he'd done the same thing as Rafael during the World Cup. In fact, what he did had been a million times *worse*. The difference between getting red carded in the World Cup and giving the opposing team a penalty kick during a charity match was the difference between Mount Everest and a molehill.

However, Rafael had a history of diving, a.k.a falling to the ground and/or feigning injury in order to draw a foul. Vincent only did it once—on the biggest stage possible with the worst consequences for me imaginable, but it was still once.

Sadly, our combined efforts weren't enough to convince the ref. He awarded the Greens another penalty kick. They'd missed their last one, but this time, Rafael kicked the ball firmly into the net.

The Greens were now up, three to two.

I clenched my jaw. *Goddammit.*

It was a charity match, but the stakes felt as high as those of a championship. I *refused* to let Rafael bloody Pessoa take home a win.

The mere thought caused bile to rise in my throat.

Even if he hadn't screwed Scarlett over, I would've hated him. Maybe it was my lingering bitterness from the World Cup, but I firmly believed that any player who engaged in regular diving didn't deserve a place on the pitch.

"Tough luck," Rafael said the next time we were close enough for him to shit talk without anyone else hearing. "Guess the golden boy of football isn't so golden anymore. Can't wait to follow Holchester's footsteps and kick your and DuBois's asses."

I shouldn't take the bait. Players trash talked each other all the time, and I was usually pretty good at letting their taunts roll off my back.

However, my frustration over the direction of the match and the ref's earlier calls had already reached a furious simmer. The mention of Holchester turned it into a full boil.

I might still have been able to contain it had I not glanced at the crowd and seen Scarlett in that moment. Her worried expression blended with the image of her face when she shared what'd happened with Rafael. How forlorn she'd seemed and how sad she'd sounded. She said their breakup turned out for the best, but no one liked being abandoned when they were at their lowest.

I pictured her lying in bed and in pain while he ditched her to date someone else.

I imagined how heartbroken she must've felt.

And I snapped.

Red crept into my vision. Anger burned reason into ash, and instead of brushing off Rafael's taunt, I turned and shoved him hard enough to make him stumble.

At that moment, we weren't playing a match. We were fighting for real, and I wanted nothing more than to wipe that smug smirk off his face.

A collective gasp reverberated through the stadium.

Rafael recovered and spat out something in Portuguese. He shoved me back. Vincent grabbed the back of my shirt to prevent me from punching him, but when Rafael issued another taunt that I couldn't hear, he let out a growl and released me.

Vincent swung for him and would've made contact had another Green not stepped in at the last minute. The rest of our teams jumped in, blinded by their temporary loyalty to their colors. From there, it devolved into a dirty, all-out brawl.

The crowd's shouts thundered across the pitch, drowning out a flurry of swear words and threats.

"What is your problem?" Rafael shouted.

"My problem is *you*." I had more choice words for him, none of which were appropriate for the venue, but before I could unload on him, a shrill, prolonged whistle cut through the chaos.

"Enough!" The ref shoved his way into the middle of the brawl. He'd been trying to get us under control for the past two minutes, and he'd clearly had enough.

The man's face matched the color of my kit as he glared at us, his shoulders quivering with outrage.

"This is a charity match for *kids*," he hissed. "I don't care who you are or what bad blood you have. This is a bloody disgrace. Look at them! Do you think you're setting a good example for them right now?"

I followed his finger to where a group of kids sat in the front row. They ranged from maybe six to thirteen in age, but they all wore matching Sport for Hope T-shirts and round-mouthed expressions of shock.

Shame snuffed out the hostility faster than rain over fire.

My blood pumped with the dregs of fury, but the reminder of the children's presence and why I was doing this—for the kids, yes, but also for Teddy's memory—chastised me enough to step back from Rafael.

The other players hung their heads, equally abashed.

It wasn't a regulation match so the ref couldn't red card us, but he awarded the Greens yet another penalty kick since I was the one who made first contact.

Once again, they scored. They were now up four to two.

"That smug bastard." Vincent seethed beside me. "Look at him. He thinks they're going to win."

Rafael gave us a mocking two-finger salute from across the pitch, his smirk firmly back in place.

"Over my dead body." My hand curled into a fist. "Let's take him down."

A vicious smile slashed across Vincent's face. "Best idea I've ever heard."

Like the saying goes, the enemy of my enemy was my friend. For the next thirty minutes, we were united in our hatred of Rafael, and we played like we were vying for the World Cup again—only this time, we were on the same team.

Vincent blocked a pass from Rafael to another Green. He kicked the ball to me, and I took it and ran.

The goal was a foregone conclusion. The Greens' keeper barely had time to react before the ball sank deep into the net, and the stadium erupted into cheers.

"Gooooallll!" The announcer dragged the word out over the loudspeaker.

I allowed myself a spark of triumph.

Three to four. Almost there.

"Go, Reds!" A familiar voice screamed over the crowd.

My gaze snapped to the source, and an unfettered grin spread across my face when I saw Scarlett jump from her seat between Carina and a blond whom I assumed was Brooklyn.

I'd played in front of royalty, celebrities, and heads of state, but hearing Scarlett cheer for me beat every other match a thousandfold. It wasn't even close.

She waved, her face glowing.

I almost waved back until I saw Vincent returning her greeting. He must've thought his sister was cheering for him alone.

Right. No public displays of affection allowed yet.

I shook off a twinge of disappointment and refocused on the match.

A few minutes later, Vincent blocked a goal attempt by the other team. An audible wave of appreciation rippled across the bleachers.

I hated to admit it, but the bastard really was good.

Soon, we tied with the Greens again.

Five minutes left. All we needed was one more goal.

Four minutes.

Three minutes.

I finally stole possession of the ball from Rafael. I kicked it from the left wing, and—

"*Gooooallll*!!"

The stadium shook from the force of the audience's jubilation. The Greens never recovered, the clock wound down, and we won five to four.

"Yes!" Vincent pumped his fist in the air. "That's fucking right!"

The sweet thrill of victory streaked through my veins. It was blazing hot, I was dripping sweat, and I'd lost my temper in a deeply public way, but none of that mattered.

We won. We'd raised a shit ton of money, and I got to savor Rafael's scowl as he slunk off the pitch.

It was the perfect ending to a rocky day.

I found Scarlett in the crowd again. She smiled at me, her face soft with pride and something else that made my pulse race.

Vincent was too busy signing autographs to notice, so I let myself smile back.

The noise around us dulled into an indistinguishable roar. No matter where we were or how many people surrounded us, she commanded my attention like a lighthouse in a storm.

Bright. Beautiful. Unwavering.

I started walking toward her, but a Sport for Hope employee shepherding the group of kids I saw earlier stopped me halfway.

"Hi, Asher. I'm sorry to keep you. You must be exhausted," she said apologetically. "But the kids are big fans, and they'd like a few autographs and pictures. Is that okay?"

"Of course. Today is for them." I tore my gaze away from Scarlett and smiled at the group. They were adorable. "Who wants a picture first?"

After much clamoring and excitement, I finished signing every autograph and taking every photo. By then, the stadium had emptied, but when I checked my phone, I saw a text from Scarlett saying she was by one of the side exits.

I grabbed my duffel bag and headed to meet her. As promised, she was waiting in the area between the stadium and the car park. I didn't see Vincent, Carina, or Brooklyn, but my anticipation over stealing a few moments alone with her—as well as my warm and fuzzy feelings from interacting with the kids earlier—disappeared as soon as I saw who she was talking to.

Rafael.

CHAPTER 33

SCARLETT

I DIDN'T EXPECT A CASUAL CHARITY FOOTBALL MATCH to devolve into a brawl.

I didn't expect my brother and my secret non-boyfriend boyfriend to team up against my *ex*-boyfriend (though that was satisfying to watch).

Most of all, I didn't expect said ex-boyfriend to seek me out after the match and try to hug me like he hadn't dumped me faster than yesterday's trash after my accident.

"Scarlett! It's so good to see you." He reached for me. I stepped back before he made contact. His smile faltered, but he recovered quickly. "You're here to support your brother, I see."

I responded with a tight curve of my lips. I may have released my bitterness toward him after *extensive* therapy, but that didn't mean I wanted to talk to him.

Unfortunately, I was stuck here waiting for my brother, my friends, and Asher. Carina and Brooklyn were in the loo, and Vincent and Asher were probably still signing autographs. I hadn't wanted to sit alone in the stadium like a loser, so I hung around the exit instead.

In hindsight, I should've stayed in the stadium. I didn't think Rafael would be bold enough to approach me in front of Vincent, especially after what happened on the pitch.

How did *he* escape the people clamoring for pictures and autographs? He wasn't as famous as Asher and Vincent in the UK, but he was recognizable enough.

"I just wanted to say hi," Rafael said when I didn't encourage further conversation. He swept his eyes over me, his attention lingering on my bare legs and chest. Once upon a time, I would've been flattered. Now, my skin crawled beneath his scrutiny. "You look great."

"It's been five years," I said coolly. "I've changed a lot since the last time we saw each other."

Rafael winced at my pointed tone.

"How's Vicky?" I asked even more pointedly. Vicky was the reality TV star he'd started dating almost immediately after our breakup.

"C'mon, Scar. You know I'm not with her anymore."

I *hated* when people called me Scar.

"Actually, I don't." I shrugged. "I don't keep up with news about you. Sorry."

Rafael's expression clouded. He was like Teflon when it came to certain things, but jab at his ego and his unflappability punctured faster than tires rolling over a bed of nails.

Despite my desire to get away from him as fast as possible, I couldn't resist indulging one bit of curiosity. "What are you doing here anyway?"

"I'm in London to take care of some business," he said vaguely. "An old teammate was participating in today's match and asked me to be their backup. Good thing I said yes, or they wouldn't have scored so many goals." Smugness coated his words.

Ugh. Had I really been in love with this man? What had younger me been *thinking*?

"Right," I said. "But your team lost."

Rafael's smile tightened. "Barely," he said, rubbing his jaw. "I'm guessing your brother hasn't forgiven me for what happened."

"No, which is why you should leave before he gets here."

He ignored my warning. "I saw you in the stands and wanted to talk to you alone, after the match. I was going to call you later, but since you're already here, I figured, why not?"

I kept my mouth shut and my expression neutral.

"I wanted to apologize for the way I handled things after your accident," he said after several beats of silence. "I know it's been years since we've seen each other, but you're not the only one who's changed since then. I acted like a jerk, and I'm sorry."

I couldn't have been more surprised if he'd sprouted fairy wings and started tap dancing in the middle of the breezeway.

Was Rafael Pessoa *apologizing* for something he did?

"It's great to see you looking so good," he added. "It's like the accident never happened."

A sudden, irrepressible wave of fury swamped my earlier surprise. *It's like the accident never happened*?

No wonder he was so friendly and chatty. He probably saw me and thought I would be an easy hookup now that I was back to "normal." He also probably thought that I was the same girl who'd fallen head over heels for his cocky flashiness when I'd been too young and inexperienced to know better.

What he *didn't* see were the years of surgery, therapy, and rehab I had to go through to get to where I was today. He didn't see my self-loathing spirals or the fatigue that kept me glued to my bed during my worst flare-ups. Even at that moment, when I "looked so good," I had little prickles and aches that formed an incessant hum in the background of my life.

My symptoms were invisible, but they were real.

Rafael didn't see any of that because he *hadn't been there*. He'd ditched me then had the nerve to waltz up to me five years later like all was forgiven and forgotten.

I forgave him for *me* because I didn't want to stew in a toxic pool of resentment anymore. But I certainly didn't forget.

"Actually, Rafael, the accident *did* happen." Poisonous honey dripped from my voice. "Remember when you saw me in the hospital for the first time and flinched? Remember how you told me I would feel better if I 'chose to'?" The honey congealed into cold, hard anger. "Remember when you broke up with me *after my first surgery* because you said I 'needed space' to heal on my own, then ran off to fuck the first girl you saw at the club? You framed it like you were doing me a favor when in reality, you were too much of a little shit to handle the fact that you were no longer the center of my world. You hated that I didn't make you the center of attention anymore and that you didn't have a shiny trophy to show off in public."

The color leached from Rafael's face. "That's not what—"

"I'm not finished so *don't* interrupt me." The anger snapped inside me, teeth bared and claws elongated. "For you to come up to me *five years later* and say it's like *the accident never happened* is the biggest fucking slap in the face. But you know? I shouldn't have expected anything more from you. You've always been a self-centered *dick*, and I'm sorry it took me so long to realize it. In hindsight, the only good thing you've ever done was break up with me. If you hadn't, I would've been stuck with you all this time, and that would've been a worse punishment than *any* pain or accident."

The silence that followed my rant was so deep and all-encompassing I could've heard a moth breathe.

Rafael gaped at me, his face a mottled canvas of shock, anger, and the tiniest smidge of remorse.

I'd never spoken to him like that before. I'd never spoken to *anyone* like that before, but my feelings had been pent up for years. They'd rattled inside me, repressed but unforgotten, until his appearance popped the cap off their prison.

Once they were unleashed, there was no stopping them until they'd spent every last bit of their energy.

Exhaustion settled into my bones—exhaustion, and no small amount of pride.

"We're done," I said, more calmly this time. "Don't try to contact me again."

I'd waited years to give Rafael a piece of my mind. Now that I had, I was ready to put him in my past once and for all.

Unfortunately, he was either too arrogant or too stupid to realize I wasn't joking.

He grabbed my arm when I attempted to brush past him. A sour feeling spread through my chest. "Scarlett, I was just—"

"*Don't touch her.*"

My gaze flew to the right just in time to see Asher blaze a path toward us with Vincent hot on his heels.

Oh, fuck.

Rafael dropped my arm.

Asher punched him.

And everything went to hell—again.

CHAPTER 34

ASHER

IN MY DEFENSE, THERE WERE NO KIDS AROUND THIS TIME.

Also in my defense—Rafael deserved it. If I hadn't punched him, Vincent would've. I hadn't heard him walking behind me on my way out, but when Rafael grabbed Scarlett's arm, he was right there backing me up.

I'd arrived in time to catch the tail end of her speech and know she *definitely* didn't want Rafael touching her. If there was one thing I couldn't stand, it was a guy who couldn't take a hint.

However, Vincent and I only got one punch in each before Finley stormed in out of nowhere and pulled us apart. Rafael left without pressing charges—the circumstances were too humiliating for him to contemplate making them public—and Finley dragged us back to the locker room to read us the riot act.

As appreciative as he was of our participation today, he didn't hold back on ripping us a new one over the brawl on the pitch *and* over what happened with Rafael.

A seeming eternity later, Vincent and I slunk out of the locker room, appropriately chastised.

"He was livid," Vincent said.

"Yeah. I had no idea his voice could reach that volume."

"It was impressive."

"Mmhmm." I flashed back to the satisfying crunch of my fist connecting with Rafael's face. "I don't regret it though."

A smirk broke out over Vincent's face. "Absolutely not. Pessoa's shiner? That belongs in a hall of fame."

I chuckled.

I couldn't wait for Rafael to try to explain away his black eye. His ego was probably more bruised than his face, and he deserved every second of discomfort.

You did not go around grabbing women against their will. Period.

"Thank you for protecting my sister," Vincent added stiffly. The stadium had truly emptied by now, and the only sound was our footsteps echoing against the concrete floors. "You didn't have to do that."

If you only knew.

"You're welcome." I cleared my throat. "Thank you for filling in at the last minute."

"You're welcome."

We lapsed into silence again.

We reached the exit and stood there, taking care not to look at each other while we waited for Scarlett and her friends to join us. Scarlett hadn't seemed too upset by us sucker punching her ex, but Carina and Brooklyn had showed up in time to see Finley herding us to the locker room the way a fed-up schoolteacher would herd his troublemakers to detention.

I didn't know what the girls were doing. Debriefing each other on our absolute shitshow of a day, probably.

At least we'd raised over a hundred thousand pounds for Sport for Hope (if we included SB's donation match. Five goals equaled five times the ticket sales).

Vincent tapped his foot. I checked my watch.

Awkward silence hummed.

We weren't friends, but today's match and our united front against Rafael had eased some of the animosity that usually tainted the air between us.

So what the hell did we do now?

"Did you guys get it all out of your system?" Scarlett's voice dispelled my cloud of uncertainty.

She came up beside us, flanked by a wary-looking Carina and an amused Brooklyn.

Vincent straightened beside me.

"Get what out of our system?" I asked.

"The overwhelming testosterone. You did *not* have to come up and sucker punch him like that." She leveled us with a stern look.

Vincent and I ducked our heads.

"That being said…" Scarlett's mouth twitched. "It was quite satisfying to see it happen."

Our relieved grins broke out at the same time.

"I even caught it on camera." Carina waved her phone in the air. "In case we have a bad day and need a pick-me-up."

"Oooh." Brooklyn leaned over. "Can you send it to me?"

"Totally."

"Thank you," Scarlett said quietly as her friends huddled over the video of me punching Rafael. "Both of you. Like I said, you didn't have to go all out with a punch, but I appreciate you having my back."

"Always. You're my baby sis." Vincent ruffled her hair. "Someone messes with you, they mess with me."

"*Vince.* What did I say about touching my hair?" She swatted his hand away, but a smile peeked through the creases of her annoyance.

I remained silent. I didn't want to say what I was really thinking with Vincent there, so the words crowded in my throat, straining against the leash I'd snapped around them.

I'll always have your back. Always. No matter what happens, there's nothing in this world that I won't do for you.

Scarlett's gaze brushed mine. She stilled for a fraction of a second, her lips parting like she'd heard my silent promise loud and clear.

A familiar buzz sprang to life beneath my skin—just for a second, just until Brooklyn called out Scarlett's name, but it was enough to make every dip of today's rollercoaster worth it.

"The first cab's here," Brooklyn said, checking her phone as a black car rolled up beside us. "We're celebrating at the Angry Boar."

"Great." Vincent flashed her a smile. "We can ride together. I don't believe we've met. I'm Scarlett's brother, Vincent."

"I know who you are." She didn't look up from her screen. "We're not riding together. You're riding with Asher."

Our smiles vanished in unison.

"*What?*" Our voices overlapped over our glares.

"We can't fit five in a car, so you boys are going first to snag us a prime table. We'll be right behind you," Scarlett said brightly. Carina opened the door; Scarlett pushed us inside. "See you at the pub!"

Brooklyn waggled her fingers at us. "Have fun and play nice."

We didn't get a chance to voice our outrage before Carina slammed the door shut and our driver sped off.

"What the hell just happened?" Vincent asked, his voice soaked with disbelief.

"I wish I knew." I wiped a hand over my face, torn between annoyance, amusement, and pride. "Don't ask questions. Just go along with it. Trust me, it's easier that way."

Of *course* our bloody driver got lost. London taxi drivers rarely got lost, but it was just our luck to be stuck with the one that did.

One very long, very silent car ride later, Vincent and I finally arrived at the Angry Boar. The girls had already snagged one of the few coveted booths in the back, and we had to fight our way through the crowd to reach them.

It was Saturday night, and the pub was packed. Music and alcohol flowed freely, and a few patrons had set up a makeshift dance floor next to the jukebox. Mac slung drinks behind the bar with his trademark scowl, which deepened when he saw us enter.

In fact, *everyone* noticed when we entered. Dozens of pairs of eyes followed our trek to the corner booth. If it weren't for the pub's rules, there'd be a million phones documenting this historic moment in football history.

Asher Donovan and Vincent DuBois, out on the town like best mates.

Ha. Over my dead body.

"It's about time," Brooklyn said as we took our seats on either side of the circular booth—me next to Scarlett, Vincent next to Brooklyn. Carina sat smack dab in the middle, her eyes glued to something on her phone. "Did you two enjoy your ride so much you extended it?"

"Don't push it, Blondie," Vincent said. "You're cute, but not that cute."

She smirked. "Was that why you wanted to ride with me earlier?"

"No, that was because I was already in a charitable mood and wanted to extend my generosity to you."

"Children," Scarlett murmured as Vincent and Brooklyn continued to bicker. "I'm surrounded by children."

"Don't lump me in with them," I said. "I'm a mature adult."

"Today is not the day for you to make that assertion."

I frowned. *Hmm*. Fair enough.

"How was the car ride?" Scarlett asked. "I see you're not sporting any fresh bruises, which is a good thing."

"It was fine. Quiet." I ran a lazy hand over her thigh beneath the table. Her skin heated beneath my touch, and a smile flickered over my mouth when her breath hitched. "I would've much rather been riding with you though."

"Mmhmm." She shifted, her eyes flicking over to where Brooklyn and Vincent were still bantering/flirting/whatever they were doing while Carina remained engrossed in her phone. "You were supposed to use that time to bond."

My hand stopped an inch above her knee and squeezed. Scarlett swallowed, her breath shallowing.

"He's not the one I want to bond with, darling." The soft, languid glide of my words landed with the feathery grace of a dancer. Heavy enough to impact the vibrations of the air around us, but so light it only reached the person closest to me.

"Asher." Nerves twined with breathlessness. "Not here."

I hummed in disagreement. I stroked the inside of her thigh with my thumb, loving the way it tensed and flexed.

A server approached our table, and my hand lingered on Scarlett's leg for an extra beat before I discreetly, reluctantly pulled away. Brooklyn and Vincent broke off their conversation to place their orders with the rest of us.

Beer, burgers, and chips. The dinner of champions.

Most pubs didn't have servers, but we were seated in the dining area and it was the weekend. The Angry Boar only supplemented their bar service with waiter service during the busiest nights.

"So what's your beef with Pessoa?" Vincent asked after our server left.

My glass paused halfway to my lips. "What?"

"Pessoa. Why did you shove him on the pitch? Even before he grabbed Scarlett, your vendetta seemed personal."

Carina finally looked up from her phone while Scarlett stiffened. Waves of tension rolled off her rigid shoulders and white knuckles.

I finished taking a sip of my water and used the time to think.

I didn't have a publicly known problem with Rafael. Should I respond with an edited version of the truth and admit I knew about Scarlett's past with Pessoa? Or was their relationship too intimate a part of her history for her to have shared with a casual friend?

Because that was what Vincent assumed we were after Scarlett called him about the charity match on my behalf. Casual friends.

I settled for a vague yet believable answer. "He's a wanker," I said. "And he dives too much."

Vincent snorted. "Yeah. He could win an Olympic gold medal in it."

Scarlett's tight-lipped mask splintered into a smirk, and I knew she was remembering the time when I said almost the exact same thing.

I squeezed her leg again, this time in warning.

"What about you?" I asked as she choked on her water. "Why do you hate him so much?"

Vincent hesitated and glanced at his sister before replying. "It's a personal issue, but you're right. He *is* a wanker."

Unfortunately, my estimation of him inched up another notch. We'd overheard Rafael harassing Scarlett, but he didn't know if I was privy to the details and he didn't spill them without her explicit consent. His consideration for his sister was one of the few unimpeachable facets of his personality.

"Enough football talk. It's boring," Brooklyn said when our server returned with our drinks and food. "Let's play a game. How about Truth or Dare?"

"No!" Scarlett and I shouted at the same time.

Carina coughed into her fist while Vincent's eyebrows skyrocketed.

"I mean, I don't want to do anything embarrassing in public," Scarlett said. She pinned her friend with a hard stare. "You understand. *Right*?"

The last thing we needed was to inadvertently slip up during a drinking game.

"Uh, right." Realization unfolded across Brooklyn's face. "Fine. Let's play something else." Her smile returned in all its dazzling glory. "How do you guys feel about King's Cup?"

Two hours and one deck of borrowed cards later (Brooklyn managed to charm even the uncharmable Mac into lending us the deck), we were drunk off our asses and laughing like we were longtime friends.

It was amazing how beer and the high of winning could smooth even the rockiest of histories.

"I asked around and found out how Simon injured his foot." Vincent leaned forward, his eyes gleaming. "Guess."

"He kicked a wall too hard."

"No. It's even stupider than that." He lowered his voice. "He was assembling a bookcase and the thing toppled over onto his foot. He has to miss the first few matches of the season because of *furniture*."

I burst into laughter. "Shut up."

Simon played for Liverpool, so it was easy for us to make light of his situation. Part of me sympathized because injuries were nerve-wracking, but...his came from a *bookcase*, for Christ's sake.

"I swear to God. That's what I heard." Vincent held up one hand, his grin wide.

Honestly, he wasn't that bad. He was almost tolerable.

Or maybe that was the five pints of ale talking.

I finished my current pint and caught Scarlett watching us with a small smile. We'd shuffled seats an hour ago, so she was sitting in between Carina and Brooklyn while Vincent and I remained on opposite sides of the table.

Her rosy cheeks and glittering eyes betrayed her tipsiness, but her smile was pure, authentic Scarlett.

See? Best friends, she mouthed.

I shook my head. Just because Vincent and I sort of got along when we were drunk didn't mean we were or ever would be best friends.

"That girl is looking at you like you're a fucking Sunday roast." Vincent's observation dragged my attention away from her.

I followed his gaze toward a pretty brunette sitting two tables over. She was with a group of friends, and she blushed a deep red when she noticed me staring.

"She's hot," Vincent said. "You should dance with her."

A needle of paranoia punctured my buzz. Why was he suddenly playing matchmaker? Had he seen me smile at Scarlett and this was his way of warning me away from his sister?

But when I studied him, his face contained nothing but genuine encouragement. This wasn't a subtle dig; this was his way of returning the olive branch I'd offered with the charity invite (even if that branch had been tied to my selfish reason of needing a substitute player).

Rejecting it out of hand would be rejecting his peace offering, but I sure as hell didn't want to dance with a random woman in a pub.

"I don't feel like dancing," I said lightly. "You should talk to her instead."

"I'm not the one she's eye fucking. C'mon." Vincent grinned. "Let's liven things up a bit. Brooklyn and I will join you guys."

"Excuse me." Brooklyn crossed her arms. "How did *I* get dragged into this?"

"No, really." I deliberately avoided looking at Scarlett again. "I'm not in the mood to chat someone up."

"Don't mess with me. When are you *not* in the mood to chat a hot girl up?" Vincent lifted his brow. "Do you have a secret girlfriend or something?"

Scarlett choked on her drink for the second time that day. "Sorry," she gasped. "My beer went down the wrong pipe."

Smooth, darling. Very smooth.

"What is up with you?" Vincent grabbed a napkin from the stack next to him and handed one to her. "You've been acting weird all night."

She mumbled an incoherent reply.

He'd hit the nail a little too close to the head with the "secret girlfriend" comment. I had to nip his suspicion in the bud before he thought too hard about why I'd been so protective over Scarlett earlier and why she was so antsy around me.

"You know what? You're right." I stood. "It's a celebration. Let's dance."

The music from the jukebox changed to a more upbeat song. I forced myself to approach the brunette, whose friends erupted into giggles when I introduced myself.

I chatted with them for a bit, but I couldn't bring myself to actually dance with her. Hopefully, the flirting was enough to throw Vincent off our scent.

I snuck a peek at him about five minutes into the conversation. He'd sandwiched himself between Brooklyn and Carina on the dance floor and wasn't paying me an ounce of attention.

Thank God.

My gaze traveled further across the pub until it landed on Scarlett, who watched me from the bar.

"Do you want to get out of here?" The brunette touched my arm. "My flat isn't far."

Scarlett's cheeks flushed, and she quickly glanced away.

I wished I remembered the brunette's name. I didn't, but I did let her down gently before I extricated myself from her disappointed clique.

I came up behind Scarlett, who didn't turn around even when I grazed my hand over her lower back. A thick crowd separated us from the dance floor and blocked Vincent's direct view of us.

"Done talking to the Megan Fox clone?" she asked without looking at me.

"It would appear so." I came up next to her and suppressed a smile at the sight of her adorable pout. "Jealous?"

"No. Why would I be jealous?"

"Exactly. There's no reason to be jealous, darling. I was only talking to her because Vincent was getting suspicious. You're the only one I want." I touched her back again, her warmth searing through her shirt and into my skin. She was always so contained that a part of me relished in her jealousy. To know she cared and that she wanted me as much as I wanted her—it was intoxicating. "When we leave, I'll show you exactly how much."

"Sure." Scarlett sounded indifferent, but I detected a trace of breathlessness when my palm slid from the small of her back to the curve of her waist. We were packed too tightly for anyone to notice what we were doing, and everyone was too drunk to care anyway. "Will you flirt with me as much as you did with her?"

"If you want." I lowered my head, my voice dipping into a murmur. "But what I really plan to do is strip you naked, lay you down on your bed, and tongue fuck you until you forget your own name."

Scarlett's breath stuttered to a brief halt.

"And once I've made you come all over my face..." I tightened my grip around her waist. "I'm going to pound my cock into your sweet little pussy and make you scream in that pretty way I love so much."

Her fingers curled around the edge of the bar. The blush decorating her face and chest was so intense I could practically feel the heat pouring off of it.

I straightened and spoke at my normal volume again. "Hey, Mac. Can we get some more food?" I flagged down the scowling owner before I glanced at Scarlett. My mouth curled into a small grin. "What are you in the mood for? Another burger or fish and chips?"

She made a strangled noise.

I swallowed the laugh rumbling up my throat. "I'll say fish and chips. Two, please. Thanks, Mac."

"You're diabolical," she said when he left. "You can't *say* stuff like that and then pretend nothing happened!"

"Trust me. I know it happened." My steel-hard erection was proof of that. Thank God I was standing at the bar, or I'd have some explaining to do. Hopefully, we could leave soon without making our intentions obvious. We'd stayed long enough. "I'm also serious.

I don't make promises I don't keep." Dark velvet touched my words.

Scarlett blushed again right as Vincent popped up out of fucking nowhere.

He took one look at her and frowned. "Why are you so red?" he asked. "Did you drink tequila again? Because you know you can't handle that type of alcohol. Don't think I forgot about the time you threw up over my brand-new Nintendo because you took one too many Jose Cuervo shots."

"No," she squeaked. "It's not tequila. It's just, um, really hot in here."

I coughed out a laugh, and she kicked me under the bar. Hard.

"Okay, whatever." Drunk Vincent didn't question my proximity to his sister the way Sober Vincent would've. He barely glanced at me as he grabbed another pint from Mac. "Acting weird *all night*," he muttered on his way back to the dance floor.

Scarlett and I exchanged glances.

We had to tell Vincent about us soon, but I allowed myself to enjoy the night for what it was: a celebration with friends (and a new frenemy) after a hard-earned win.

The day had been a mess almost from the start, but I couldn't deny that this was one of the best nights I'd had in a while.

It was *normal*, Scarlett was with me, and that was all I needed.

CHAPTER 35

SCARLETT

IF SOMEONE TOLD ME AT THE BEGINNING OF THE SUMMER that Asher and Vincent would spend a night drinking and hanging out together *peacefully*, I would've asked what they were smoking. The idea was absurd.

However, their brief truce on Saturday gave me hope that they could not only tolerate each other, but that they might actually be friends. They just had to set aside their pride and admit their rivalry was played out. At this point, they were holding on to their grudges for ego.

I didn't say any of that to them. They had to figure it out themselves.

Vincent returned to Paris that morning to wrap up his affairs, but he'd be back next Monday. That meant Asher and I had one week left to enjoy our alone time together—or so I thought.

"I have some news," Asher said, his face unusually somber as finished up practice.

I'd run through the first half of *Lorena's* third act after his training today. I hadn't danced in Yvette's place again during rehearsals since my disastrous debut, but I'd worked on the choreography in bits and pieces like Asher had suggested. So far, I wasn't pushing myself past my limits, and I felt pretty good about my progress.

However, my thrill at nailing the third act faded at his tone.

"Good news or bad news?" I asked warily. If it was good news, he'd look happier, but if it was bad news, he'd be more upset. Right?

"It depends on how you look at it." Asher rubbed a hand over his face. "I have to go to Japan this week. Aoki Watches is my biggest sponsor, and they want to fly me out to do some press and promo for the launch of their spring collection." A grimace crossed his face. "I got the email from my manager this morning. We were originally supposed to shoot the promos later this year, but a scheduling conflict came up and they had to shift everything last minute."

"Japan?" I sucked in a sharp breath. That wasn't a quick trip to, say, France or Italy. That was halfway across the world. "How long is the trip?"

"Three days. I leave on Wednesday."

Wednesday. That was in two days, which meant he'd be gone until Sunday. That ate up the full remainder of our time together before Vincent's return.

"Oh." I swallowed past the irrational lump in my throat. "That'll be fun."

I shouldn't be upset. It wasn't like I'd never see him again, and it was ridiculous to feel like Asher was abandoning me because it wasn't his *choice* to leave.

At the same time, it was the end of an era. This summer had changed everything—my self-esteem, my willingness to leave my comfort zone, my relationship with others and myself. It was our little bubble against reality, and I wasn't mentally ready for it to just *end* without a proper sendoff.

We had one week. I'd prepared for that. I'd *planned* for that. Now, we had two days, including today. Maybe not even that, since he probably needed to spend tomorrow packing and prepping for his trip.

Asher's face clouded at whatever he heard in my voice. "Scarlett—"

"Make sure to eat all the food for me. Ramen, sushi, matcha... and beef. Kobe beef is world famous, right? I bet their fish and steak is amazing. Will you be in Tokyo? You should visit some of the temples if you have time. They look beautiful." I prattled on, hoping the words would bulldoze over the hollow cavern in my chest. "The time difference will be killer, but if you don't FaceTime me at least once to show me the sights, I'll never forgive you. Oh, and I—"

"*Scarlett.*"

I stopped, slightly out of breath from my rambling. "Yes?"

"Come with me."

"Come with you to where?"

"To Japan."

My lips parted. Surely, he was joking. "I can't go with you to Japan!"

"Why not?"

"Because I have a job! I have practice. I have..." I floundered, trying to come up with other reasons and failing. "I can't just drop everything and fly to another continent with you. What will I tell Vincent? He'll be suspicious for sure."

"Vincent isn't here. By the time he finds out, we'll have told him about us already," Asher said calmly. "I also asked Carina about your schedule after I found out about the trip. She mentioned you had quite a few days of holiday leave you need to take before summer's end or you'll lose them. Where better to enjoy them than in Japan? With *me?*" His roguish grin matched the teasing sparkle in his eyes.

Typical Asher.

But I couldn't be mad because he was right. I hadn't taken a proper holiday in too long, and Japan *was* on my bucket list.

"I don't know." My reflection stared back at me from the studio's mirrors, its face wracked with indecision. "Leaving for Asia with less than forty-eight-hours' notice is wild."

Asher noticed the crack in my shield and pounced. "You know what they say. Spontaneity is the spice of life." His expression gentled when I didn't reply. "If you really don't want to go, you don't have to. But if you're concerned about work, Carina said she can squeeze in your holiday and find someone to cover you." As Lavinia's executive assistant, Carina was in charge of overseeing the staff's schedules. "Aoki is also flying us out on the company jet, so we don't have to worry about being spotted in the airport. I can bring a plus-one, so they'll also cover your expenses, and the Japanese press won't hound us the way the paps do here. I have a bunch of work obligations while I'm there, but I'll have free time too. We'll actually be able to enjoy ourselves without looking over our shoulders every minute of the day."

I drew my bottom lip between my teeth. That did sound nice.

Asher and I made our relationship work in London, but we spent half our time hiding out in one of our houses and the other half hoping people wouldn't see past his disguises when we were out and about. We couldn't hold hands or kiss in front of other people. Even in "safe" spaces like the Angry Boar, we were constantly on alert for eavesdroppers.

I wanted to experience what it was like to be a normal couple with him.

In the end, that was what sold me. Not the private jet, not the all-expenses-paid trip to Tokyo, but the prospect of simply spending more time with him.

"Okay," I said, torn between nerves and excitement. "Let's go to Japan."

I'd visited Asia only once in my life. My parents took Vincent and me to Disneyland Shanghai before their divorce, but I was so young I only retained vague recollections of a pink castle and the fairy-light sugariness of candy floss.

Tokyo was the polar opposite of that sweet, hazy childhood memory.

Glittering skyscrapers and giant neon signs draped across the skyline like jewels adorning a crown. The streets teemed with people, and the energy of the city pulsed with such vibrancy it seeped through our car windows and reverberated in my bones.

It was electric. It was frenetic.

It was *incredible*.

Asher's publicist Sloane met us on the tarmac when we landed. Blond, statuesque, and intimidating as hell, she issued orders and shepherded us through the city and into our penthouse hotel suite with the brusque efficiency of a four-star military general.

I didn't know what Asher told her about me, but she didn't question why her star client popped up in Japan with his summer trainer in tow.

"Here's a detailed itinerary for the next three days," she said, handing Asher a thick sheaf of stapled, color-coordinated papers. "Call time is at seven a.m. tomorrow. I'll be here at six-fifteen sharp to make sure you're awake and ready. If you need anything, call, text, or email *in that order*. If it's a true emergency, find me in my room. I'm staying in 805."

"Got it." He took the papers without looking at them. "You know, it's still early in the evening. You should hit the spa for a massage or something. My treat."

Sloane's mouth pursed. If anyone looked like they needed a massage, it was her, but she didn't acknowledge his suggestion before moving on.

"One more thing," she said. "You'll see you have several blocks of free time. They're highlighted in yellow. You are, of course, free to spend that time however you wish. *But*"—she jabbed a finger at his chest—"if I find out you've so much as stepped foot *near* a sports car while you're here, I will personally fetch a Japanese steel knife from the kitchen and castrate you with it. Scarlett is my witness. Do. You. Understand?"

She punctuated her question with additional jabs.

I hid my grin behind my fist while Asher raised his hands in surrender.

"Sports car. Japanese steel. Castration." He nodded. "Understood."

"Good." Sloane dropped her arm, took a deep breath, and smoothed a hand over her flawlessly tailored skirt suit. "Scarlett, it was lovely to meet you. Asher, *stay out of trouble*."

With that, she left. Her heels clacked against the marble floors of the suite's entryway before the door opened and closed, and silence descended once more.

"You could look a little less entertained by her threat," Asher said dryly. "Castration would be unfortunate for *both* of us."

"Yeah, but it'd be worse for you." I offered a cheeky smile. "At least I have dildos to take over the—aah!" I squealed when Asher swept me up with a growl and carried me to the bedroom. "Let me down, you Neanderthal!" I pounded a fist against his back, but I was laughing when he finally laid me down on the bed.

He hovered over me, his face creased with a mock scowl. "What were you saying about dildos?"

"That they're one of mankind's greatest inventions?" I wrapped my arms around his neck and kissed away his adorably boyish pout. "*But* they're not as good as something else I can think of."

"That's the right answer." His lips lingered on mine for a moment before he pulled back and examined me. "How was the plane ride? Do you want me to draw you a bath?"

Warmth dripped from my chest into my stomach.

"It was okay." Eleven hours was a long time to spend in the air, but the private jet's luxurious amenities prevented any bad flare-ups. The seats had pressure-relief cushions, and I could walk around and stretch my legs whenever I started getting stiff. They even had a heated massage chair onboard. "I can take a bath later. Right now, I need to eat. I'm starving."

While Asher ordered us room service, I explored our home for the next three days. The suite was twice the size of my flat in London. Its living room boasted a home theatre system and a state-of-the-art universal remote while the lavish dining room was big enough to accommodate eight. Delamonte soaps and gels lined the bathroom's double marble vanity, and a wall of one-way tinted windows provided a dazzling view of the Tokyo cityscape. There was even a grand piano and a balcony with a second dining area.

"It's nice, isn't it?" Asher came up beside me as I stared out at the sea of lights below us. "Makes me want to watch *Tokyo Drift* again. Do you think Sloane will consider that 'stepping foot near' a sports car?"

Exasperated laughter erupted from my lips. "Don't even joke about that. She will *actually* castrate you, you know, and she'll spin it into a good PR move too. She's terrifying."

He grinned. "That's why I pay her the big bucks. She puts up with a lot of shit from me."

"Mmhmm." I could only imagine. Being a celebrity publicist sounded like the most stressful job ever. "Like your car crashes over the past few years?"

I didn't ask the question with the intention of being combative. It came out soft, almost hesitant, but the ease with which it escaped proved it'd always been there, lurking beneath the layers of my denial and avoidance.

Asher's grin faded. "Yes," he said after a long pause. "Like the crashes."

We'd avoided the topic all summer, but Sloane's warning had ripped my layers to shreds and bared the ten-ton elephant in the room.

My hang-ups about cars and driving were known quantities. That was why Asher hired Earl to drive me to training every week and why he was careful to stick to the traffic rules when I was with him.

But I didn't know what he was like when I wasn't there. Was he the same guy who made headlines for destroying his Ferrari in an illegal street race with another footballer? The one whose off-pitch antics fed into the controversy of his transfer because people worried his recklessness would eventually catch up with him and screw the whole team over?

I hadn't asked because I hadn't wanted to know the answer, but the question was out there now, and there was no taking it back.

"Sloane's warning about staying away from sports cars." My next words stuck in my throat before I forced them out. "Was that a general warning, or do you still race?"

I hated doubting him, but I had to know.

Even racing in official competitions like Formula One was dangerous, and those had safety measures in place. I'd seen footage from a few illegal street races. They were the Wild West, and the likelihood of injury or arrest was even higher than in sanctioned racing.

Asher stilled, his throat bobbing with a hard swallow. Tension coated the air like oil spilled over water.

"Not often," he said. "I haven't done it in a while."

"When was the last time you raced?" I didn't want to turn our first night in Japan into an interrogation, but I'd already opened Pandora's box.

We might as well see it through to the end.

Shadows flickered in his eyes. "Earlier in the summer. Early July."

Early July.

Barbs hooked into my throat. That was more recent than I'd anticipated. It was before we officially got together, but it was around the time of our first kiss.

"Does it bother you?" Asher asked quietly. "Me racing."

"I..." I tried to wrestle my thoughts into some semblance of coherence before I answered.

I knew he loved the thrill, and I didn't want to take that away from him. But every time he got behind the wheel, he put his career and his *life* in danger. Could I really sit by and let him take that risk without pointing out the dangers? He'd been lucky so far, but all it took was one stroke of bad luck to end everything.

I knew that better than anyone.

"It worries me," I finally said. "Regular driving is dangerous enough. Accidents happen every day, but cars are an essential part of modern life. It's a risk we have to take. Street racing is more than that." My voice sank into a tremulous whisper. "I don't want you to get hurt. I don't want what happened to me to happen to you. I don't want you to lose your dreams or..." *Die.*

The word wedged in my chest and clung on with bloodied nails, like it was trying to hide from the inevitability of its own passing.

I couldn't imagine a world where Asher didn't exist—where I didn't hear his voice teasing me or see his smile beckoning me from across the room, where his heartbeats didn't sync with mine when we fell asleep and where I didn't have a constant safe harbor in the storm.

I couldn't imagine a me without him, and that terrified me more than anything else.

Tears stung the backs of my eyes.

"Scarlett." Asher sounded anguished as he pulled me into his chest. "It's okay. I'm okay. Nothing's going to happen to me."

"You don't know that." The tears trickled down my cheeks. *God, this is humiliating.* I was ruining our first night overseas together, but I couldn't stop. I'd spent years running from my fears, but the prospect of losing him was so overwhelming that I *couldn't* outrun it. It swamped me, dragging me under waves of anxiety and horrible, bloody what-ifs.

I raised my head to look at him. "I used to think I was invincible. I was young and healthy and on top of the world. I thought *nothing* could happen to me, but I was wrong." Emotion clogged my throat. "The thing is, I couldn't have prevented my accident. I was in the wrong place at the wrong time, and that's up to the universe. But street racing...you're *choosing* to put yourself in that position."

Asher's face crumpled. "Darling..."

"No." I shook my head and wiped my tears with the back of my hand. "Please let me finish. I know you love racing. I do. I don't want to discount that, and I don't want to tell you how to live your life.

But I can't wake up every day wondering if that's the day your luck runs out, and I'll get a call saying you're gone." My words cracked. "I can't lose you."

"You won't." His voice sounded thick, or maybe that was the weight in my chest talking. "You won't because I won't race anymore. I don't need it, but I need you."

Another sob bled out, formed of relief and a dozen other feelings I couldn't name.

When I was younger, my friends and I tried to guess what our future partners' professions would be. I didn't care much at the time, but I was adamant about not dating anyone in emergency services. No firefighters, no police, no one whose job involved them running headfirst into danger for a living.

In theory, a footballer should be safe, but there was nothing safe about my feelings for Asher.

Maybe I was selfish for asking him to give up something he loved. If that was the case, then so be it.

I would rather be selfish with him alive and healthy than selfless with him buried beneath the ground.

Asher tightened his hold on me. "I won't race anymore," he repeated. "I promise."

CHAPTER 36

ASHER

I SHOULD'VE FELT MORE CONFLICTED AFTER I PROMISED
Scarlett I would stop racing. Getting behind the wheel had been my
version of therapy for so long, so giving it up should've engendered
some resistance.

Maybe that'd come the next time I heard about a race or got
a message about a new Bugatti from my car guy. In the meantime,
I felt...nothing. Nothing except regret and a fierce, yearning desire
never to make Scarlett cry again.

I had no idea she felt that way about my racing, but I should've
known. Her past with cars made our conversation that first night in
Tokyo inevitable. On the bright side, it meant everything was uphill
from there.

Don't get me wrong—my schedule for the next three days was
brutal. Aoki Watches had me booked back-to-back with promo
shoots, press, meetings, and events. Sloane kept me supplied with
coffee, but the jet lag and early call times kicked my ass.

Thankfully, everything with Aoki went smoothly. The brand

was happy, Sloane was happy, and Leon was happy from his luxury apartment in London, the bastard. My business manager had somehow weaseled his way out of the grueling cross-continent trip.

Work consumed my days, but the nights were mine, and I spent them all with Scarlett.

It was during the nights that I took her to my favorite izakayas, where we stayed up late talking over drinks and snacks. We wandered through the temple precincts of Sensoji, its illuminated lanterns casting a pale orange glow over our intertwined hands, and indulged in rousing renditions of old nineties songs in one of the city's many karaoke bars (note: singing, along with cooking, was not one of Scarlett's strong suits).

Exploring Tokyo with her was a revelation.

As much as I loved London, I loved being away from the prying eyes and whispers even more.

Here, amidst the electric hustle and bustle of the biggest city in the world, we could be a normal couple. No disguises, no nerves, no hiding from paps. Just us.

My last shoot with Aoki Watches wrapped early. It was Saturday, so no one wanted to stay on set too long. While Sloane hung behind to double-check the details, I took Scarlett on a special date I'd planned with the hotel concierge's help.

I couldn't join her on her daytime tourist excursions, but I *could* make sure our last night in Tokyo was as memorable as possible.

"I hope you don't mind heights," I said, opening the door to the hotel's rooftop.

Scarlett stopped dead in her tracks. "*Asher*." Laughter and shock laced her words. "Tell me you didn't!"

She had to shout to be heard because waiting less than ten feet away, its rotors whirring, was a sleek white helicopter with the hotel's gold logo stamped on the side.

"Private sunset helicopter tour of Tokyo," I said with a grin. "Seems like a fitting way to celebrate our last night here."

I paid an arm and a leg to book the helicopter at the last minute, but it was worth every single penny to see Scarlett's enraptured expression as we soared over the city. I was so used to the luxuries in my life that I sometimes took them for granted, but experiencing them through her eyes did something to my soul.

I couldn't describe what it was, but I wanted to give her every good thing in the world.

"That's Odaiba." I pointed out the popular entertainment hub located on a man-made island in Tokyo Bay. "We were there the other night. There's Shibuya, the Tokyo Tower..."

I'd taken this flight before, so I took over our pilot's tour guide duties until we landed on our hotel's rooftop again. The staff had done an excellent job of turning it over during our twenty-minute ride.

Instead of a large, empty expanse of concrete, the rooftop now featured a gourmet candlelit dinner for two, complete with a linen tablecloth, fine china etched with a cherry blossom pattern, and portable heaters. The setup was tucked inside an alcove that protected it from being blown away by the helicopter landing.

Scarlett's jagged inhale made me smile.

I walked her to the table as the helicopter took off again to give us privacy.

The rooftop was ours for the rest of the night.

"Be honest," Scarlett said as we sat down. "Was the heli tour inspired by my joke about a similar ride over Hawaii?"

"I have no idea what you're talking about. But *hypothetically*, if it was, it's a lot better than Hawaii, isn't it?"

Amusement pulled at her lips. "You know that date didn't exist.

I was baiting you."

"I know. That's why I said hypothetically, mine's better."

Scarlett laughed and shook her head.

Our omakase dinner was prepared by Japan's top chef. There was a fourteen-month waitlist for his flagship restaurant in Osaka, but Sebastian had pulled some strings and convinced him to fly here for the weekend.

One bite proved why he had a fourteen-month waitlist. Every course, from the trio of tuna sashimi to the A5 Japanese wagyu sirloin, was exquisite.

"I'm so full, you're going to have to roll me back to our hotel room." Scarlett groaned, but that didn't stop her from eating the last bite of her green tea cheesecake. "This has spoiled me for life. I can't go back to regular takeaway after this."

"I'll make some calls and see if the chef is willing to relocate to London," I said with a laugh.

She perked up. "You think he will?"

"No, but it doesn't hurt to try."

"Don't get my hopes up like that." Scarlett sighed and took a sip of her sake. She glanced around, her expression turning wistful. Dusk had deepened into the full inkiness of night, and we were so high up that we couldn't even hear the traffic below. "It's so beautiful here. I wish we could stay longer."

Regret twinged in my gut. We were flying back tomorrow so we could make it to London before Vincent, but I wished we could stay longer too.

"We can always come back," I said. "It's only a flight away."

"I know." She toyed with her silverware. "But it won't be the same."

I remained quiet.

I knew what she meant. I felt it too—the impending curtain call on our summer, heavy velvet drapes descending to divide our lives into "us" and "us and them."

Once we told Vincent on Monday, our relationship didn't belong to just us anymore. It belonged to everyone else too. Everyone would have opinions, and we couldn't escape them if we tried.

"Before we leave, I do have something I want to talk to you about." Scarlett ran a finger over the etchings on her fork and avoided my eyes.

"Okay." I strove for a neutral expression, but I had a feeling I knew what she wanted to discuss.

We'd agreed to an exclusive non-relationship when we started dating. We basically *were* in a relationship, but she didn't want to be hemmed in by the label, so I hadn't pushed the issue.

However, if we were telling Vincent about us soon, it would make sense to redefine our status. Right?

My heart crawled into my throat while I waited for her to continue.

"I…" Scarlett finally met my eyes, her expression alive with nerves. "I know we've been dating without a real label, but it's almost the end of summer so I was thinking we could maybe make it official? It would be easier when we're explaining things to Vincent," she rushed out. "To tell him we're boyfriend and girlfriend instead of this weird *non*-boyfriend and girlfriend thing we have going on."

"Scarlett." I placed my forearms on the table and leaned forward. "Do you want us to be official because of Vincent or because you want to?"

My question hung in the charged air, held aloft by the thundering beats of my heart.

A second passed.

Two.

Then... "Because I want to."

Scarlett's soft admission dispelled the breath from my lungs. I leaned back, relief a cool balm for the knot in my gut. "Then we're official."

"Just like that."

"Just like that." I looked at her, this beautiful, incredible woman whom I never would've expected would turn my world upside down, and marveled that she was mine. The universe knew what it was doing after all. "I've been here since day one, darling. I was simply waiting for you to join me."

Scarlett's smile spread so wide and warm I felt it all the way in my bones.

"I haven't had an official boyfriend in years, so this is exciting," she said. "Does this mean you'll hold my bag and let me borrow your shirts to sleep in because men's shirts are *always* more comfortable than women's, for some reason?"

"The shirts, yes. The bag, depends. If you have as much shit in it as the day we met, then no." I raised a brow. "I'm a top athlete, you know. I have to conserve my strength."

I laughed when she kicked me under the table.

"My old therapist would be proud of me." Scarlett slid her pendant along its chain. "She said healing wasn't just about closing the door on my past. It was about allowing myself to open one for the future too. We worked a lot on my trust issues after Rafael. If it weren't for her, I'd carry a lot more resentment than I do now."

I noted the past tense of her words. "You don't see her anymore?"

She shook her head. "Some people fold therapy into their daily lifestyle, but I got to a good place. However, I know I can always call her if I need to, even if I hate asking for help."

"Really? I hadn't noticed."

"Ha ha." She rolled her eyes, but she was smiling. "My parents weren't thrilled at first. They're old school. There's this stigma around therapy in their generation, but once they saw how much it helped, they were onboard."

Curiosity wound through me.

Scarlett didn't talk about her parents much. I knew they divorced when she was young and that she had a fairly normal relationship with them, but that was it.

"How did they…"

"Deal with my accident?" she finished. "As well as they could, I suppose, but my mother was shattered. She was worried about me, obviously, but I think she was equally devastated about the end of my career. She liked having a prima ballerina daughter that she could brag about to her friends. My father moved to London for the first few months after the crash. Vincent was already here. They rallied."

"Do you resent your mother for that?"

I tried to imagine how my father would react if I got injured and couldn't play football anymore.

My blood congealed at the mental image.

I'd checked in with him a few times since his heart attack, but it was always through my mother. I hadn't spoken with him directly since the hospital. However, it didn't escape my notice that he never reached out to answer my question.

Your team or your son?

"Surprisingly, no." Thankfully, Scarlett's response drew my thoughts back to her. The last person I wanted to focus on during our last night here was my father. "I knew she felt those things, but she didn't act on them, if that makes sense. She didn't push me to try dancing again, and she was supportive when I became a teacher at RAB instead." The wind blew stray strands of hair across her face, obscuring her pensive expression. "We all have ugly feelings sometimes. It's a part of human nature. But it's what we do with them that counts."

Every time I thought she couldn't get more amazing, she proved me wrong.

"That's a mature way to look at it. I'm sure your old therapist would've been proud of that, too," I teased.

She offered a flicker of a smile. "Maybe. But can I confess something?"

"Always."

"Sometimes..." Her smile dimmed. "I get so jealous of my students that I can't breathe. I want them to be happy, and I'm truly proud of their success, but there are days when I look at them and see not only the potential they have, but the potential I *used* to have. They have their entire careers ahead of them, shiny and untarnished, while I'm a has-been. It's the wrong way to think about things, but it can be...difficult to live in the shadows when I've trained my whole life to be in the spotlight." Her cheeks reddened. "I know this makes me sound like a terrible person. I'm their teacher. I shouldn't be jealous of *teenagers*. And I don't feel that way all the time. But on bad days, it can make me spiral."

"They're human feelings," I said gently. "Like you said, they're normal, and you're not trying to sabotage your students. You're allowed to feel what you feel."

"I know. But it's easier to give advice than to take it." Scarlett played with the edges of her napkin. "Emma, one of my top students, got the role of Sugar Plum Fairy in the school's student showcase this year. She wants me to attend the opening night. The staff showcase is at the school, but the student one takes place at Westbury, and I can't bring myself to go there."

Westbury was one of the leading performing arts venues in London. I'd never attended a show there, but I passed by it all the time.

"I was on my way to perform at Westbury when the other car hit us," Scarlett said, her voice quiet. "It was also where I got my first rave review for my performance in *Swan Lake*. That review put me on the map. In many ways, Westbury is the ultimate symbol of my old life, and I haven't been able to step foot near it since the accident. It hurts too much to remember what used to be."

Her eyes were a thousand miles away, and I let the revelations of the night settle around us instead of disrupting it with an immediate response.

Sometimes, listening was a better strategy than talking.

The remnants of our dinner had long gone cold. The hours stretched toward the obscenely late half of the night, but I hung on to each minute like it was our last.

If I could've stayed on that rooftop with Scarlett forever, I would've.

"I'm sorry," she said after a long silence. "Every time we go on a date, I end up making things so depressing."

"Don't be sorry. I'm no better," I said. "Remember the time I brought you to Holchester and trauma dumped on you in my childhood bedroom? That was fun."

Her laughter chased away the melancholy and brought an answering grin to my face.

"It's not depressing to learn these things about you," I said. "I *want* to know you better. The good, the bad, and everything in between."

Scarlett's expression melted into a different, softer smile. "Asher

Donovan, I was so wrong about you at the beginning."

"Most people are. I'm even more handsome, charming, and witty than they could've imagined."

"You forgot humble."

"Obviously. That's a given."

She laughed again, and everything else we wanted to say was communicated through our long, lingering gaze across the table.

Our relationship was built on unspoken words. We'd gotten better at expressing them over the past two months, but there were still a few words that remained locked away inside me.

Three, to be exact.

I was saving them for another time, when the prospect of revealing our relationship to my brother didn't darken the horizon like a thundercloud.

For now, I simply enjoyed my last hours in Japan with Scarlett and let the future take care of itself.

CHAPTER 37

SCARLETT

THANKS TO THE TIME DIFFERENCE (JAPAN WAS EIGHT hours ahead of the UK), we left Tokyo Sunday morning and landed in London in the early afternoon.

Our late dinner, early wake-up call, and the change in time zones conspired to confuse my body about what it was supposed to be doing when, so I opted for the safe option and slept for a majority of the flight.

When we arrived in London, I went to Asher's house instead of going straight home. Vincent was joining us at training tomorrow, and I wanted to say goodbye to our studio.

It sounded stupid, but the studio had been our private little Eden for two months. It deserved a proper farewell.

"How did he react when you told him we've been training at my house this entire time?" Asher asked as I ran my hands over the smooth wood barre.

I winced. "Um, he didn't. He thinks we've been training at RAB."

Asher's eyebrows skyrocketed.

"I know, I *know*." I dropped the barre and crossed my arms, hating myself for the lies piling up around me. The mature thing would've been to tell Vincent the truth. We initially changed studios because of the paps, not because we were trying to sneak away for weekly rendezvous.

But I knew my brother. He would flip out about me coming to Asher's house three times a week, every week without telling him, and that would put him in a bad mood for when we dropped our relationship bombshell news.

I would rather rip off both bandages at the same time and contain the explosion to one instance instead of two.

Plus, a small, selfish part of me didn't want to share this space with anyone else. It was a ballet studio, but it was *our* ballet studio.

"The paps aren't hanging around RAB anymore," I said after I explained my reasoning to Asher. "And people at the school aren't going to say anything. Even if they did, they don't know I've been training you at your house. So I told Vincent to meet us at RAB tomorrow like he did for our first session."

The weight of our impending talk hooked into my stomach and dragged it down to my feet. My emotions vacillated wildly between anxiety and optimism, unsure of where to land.

Asher and Vincent were finally getting along (sort of). Our relationship news would either go *much* better than we anticipated, or it would destroy their fragile truce and bleed over into the upcoming season.

No pressure or anything.

"That makes sense." Asher leaned against the barre, looking fresh and rested despite not sleeping during our long-haul flight. His eyes pierced mine. "So this is technically our last day together in this studio."

My chest twinged. "I guess it is."

We could come down anytime we wanted, but it wouldn't be the same. I wouldn't be training him anymore, and the vibes would just be different.

"Since it's our last day..." He pushed off the wall and closed the distance between us with two lazy, pantherine steps. "Let's make it count."

Embers of heat flared to life at his suggestive drawl. The air thickened, infusing oxygen with electricity that rolled down my spine like a hot, sensual caress.

"How so?" My response sounded husky beneath the sudden crackle of attraction.

Asher's grin was pure wickedness. "We've never christened the studio."

The embers ignited into flames.

He was right. We'd spent so much time in the studio, but we'd never had sex here. It felt forbidden somehow, like we were defiling our workplace even though it was a private residence.

But it was that same forbidden undercurrent that stoked those flames higher when he gripped the back of my neck and pulled me into a kiss.

It wasn't a gentle, yearning kiss; it was hard and aggressive, almost desperate, and the deliciousness of it made my toes curl.

A moan slipped from my mouth into his. I was the good kind of dizzy, floating on lust and euphoria and everything in between.

Asher pushed me against the barre and slid my dress straps down my shoulders. I shivered, my skin pebbling from a mix of cold and desire. I wasn't wearing a bra, and my nipples were so hard they abraded the light cotton of my dress. They scraped against the material with every movement, sending jolts of heat straight to my core.

Asher broke the kiss and skimmed his mouth down my throat, his lips curving into a tiny smile when he found the wild flutter of my pulse. He lingered there, leisurely tracing his tongue over my skin before he continued his journey downward.

He tugged on my neckline as he did so, and it wasn't long before my already-slack bodice sagged around my waist.

His mouth trailed down...

Down...

Down...

Until it closed around a peaked nipple and sucked, teeth tugging and lightly grazing across the sensitive tip.

This time, my moan was closer to a strangled cry. My hand flew up and my fingers tangled in Asher's hair, both holding on and holding him close as he teased my breasts into pebbled stiffness.

I was so wet I could feel my underwear getting soaked. I squirmed, trying to get more friction between my thighs when Asher lifted his head and spun me around so I faced the wall of mirrors.

Heat consumed my face when I saw my disheveled, half-naked reflection.

"Bend over and spread your legs." Asher's rough command sent shivers streaking down my spine.

I obeyed, placing my hands on the top beam of the double barre and edging my legs apart. My pants of anticipation fogged the glass, turning my reflection into a haze of dark hair and red cheeks.

However, a needle of confusion pierced my lust when Asher walked to the sound system and turned it on.

The familiar strains of classical music filled the studio, its elegant symphony a stark contrast to the obscene image of me bending over the barre, my legs spread wide, my breasts bared, and my thighs slick with my juices.

My clit pulsed at the dichotomy.

If any of my old ballet teachers could see what we were doing in this studio...

Asher's steps echoed against the polished wood floors. He returned to his spot behind me, his gaze taking me in with such intensity that I blushed again.

"The music is in case someone from the household staff wanders downstairs." His velvety drawl slid over my skin as sure as a caress. "Wouldn't want them to hear us."

With that, he shoved my dress up around my waist, hooked his thumbs into my underwear and yanked it down, exposing the glistening evidence of my need.

"Fuck, you're *dripping*." He dragged a finger through the wetness. I whined and squirmed again, my entire body flushed. His chuckle brushed my back. "Does this turn you on, sweetheart? Getting bent over and played with while you wait for my cock?"

I was too aroused to be embarrassed. "*Yes.*"

"Hmm. I thought so." He removed his hand, ignoring my cry of protest. "You'll have to wait a little longer, but don't worry, darling." A wicked grin slashed across his face as he knelt between my legs. "I'll make it worth your while."

That was the only warning I got before his tongue touched my clit, and my world splintered into fragments of pure lust.

I cried out, my hands gripping the barre as Asher ate me out from behind. He lapped up my juices and swirled his tongue over my swollen clit before he thrust it inside me. The piano music mingled with the sounds of his tongue fucking in and out of my pussy in delicious, rapid strokes.

Firm hands manacled my thighs, holding me steady while I shook and sobbed, the pleasure so intense it brought tears to my eyes.

He released one of my thighs and rubbed his thumb over my clit. He thrust his tongue deep inside me at the same time, and that was it.

I exploded, my orgasm rocketing through me and taking possession of every single muscle while I drenched his face with my come.

He groaned, the vibrations sending mini shockwaves up my core before he pulled back and stood.

I heard the metal rasp of a zipper coming undone and the rip of foil, but I didn't get a chance to ride out the final waves of my orgasm before he was inside me, filling me up until I gasped.

I was still sensitive from our earlier activities, and the single thrust sent a second, smaller orgasm chasing after the heels of my first one.

It was my first set of back-to-back orgasms ever, and I was so lost to the sensations, the *want*, that I could only hold on tight while Asher fucked me into a state of sobbing, mindless delirium.

He was typically gentler when we had sex, but this? This was raw and hard and everything I didn't know I needed. We were swept up in the needs of the moment, our troubles drowned beneath an ocean of desire and expelled with each cry and groan. Still, despite the brutal rhythm of our coupling, he intermittently slowed down to check on me.

I appreciated the sentiment, but I was fine in this position—more than fine. And I didn't want him to hold back. I wanted him to fuck me harder.

"Right there." I gasped. "Harder, deeper...*yes*."

His balls slapped against my skin with each thrust, underscoring the speed and force of his rhythm, but it still wasn't enough. I wanted *more*.

Asher slowed again to accommodate me when I straightened, raised one leg, and stretched it out along the lower barre. I wasn't quite as flexible as I'd been before my surgeries, but the height of the barre and the way he held me alleviated any pressure that would've incited a flare-up.

It actually felt good to stretch out my leg. Most importantly, the new position allowed him to fuck me *deep*, deeper than any position we'd tried before.

"*Fuck*," Asher hissed, his body tensing at whatever sensations he felt. His skin gleamed with sweat, and his fingers dug into my hip as he drove into me again.

He quickly matched his previous pace, only it felt even better like this, with me stretched out and him buried to the hilt.

I squealed when he hit a spot he'd never hit before, and my mind blanked from sheer pleasure.

I'd never had sex like this before. Rough and unrelenting and passionate, where he fucked me like he couldn't get enough of me, and I knew for a fact that I couldn't get enough of him.

It was the kind of sex that could ruin a girl for life.

My breasts bounced wildly from the force of the pounding, and my mouth hung open, unable to speak, unable to think. I was a sweaty, dripping mess, but I didn't care.

In fact, it only spurred me on. It was so unlike me, so opposite the careful control that I exhibited in every other area of my life, that it was a turn-on.

I didn't have to be Scarlett. Instead, I could be this wanton creature who dealt in pleasure and carnality, who could slip out of herself and enter a world of fantasy.

"Look at the way you're taking my cock." Asher reached up and gripped my chin with one hand, forcing me to look at him in the mirror. To watch the way his cock plunged in and out of my drenched cunt. "Every inch buried inside you, and your pussy still can't get enough."

I whimpered, my pussy clenching around him in shameless agreement.

"So fucking tight." He lowered his head and sank his teeth into the curve between my neck and shoulder. "So fucking *mine*."

Another, more savage thrust scattered any coherence that might've formed in my short-circuiting brain.

I was nothing but a giant raw, exposed nerve. Even the brush of air against my skin was unbearable in its sensuality. Add in the dirty words, the lewd sight of him pounding into me in broad daylight, with the innocent music playing in the background...and it was too much.

The piano score hit a crescendo, and my third orgasm of the afternoon detonated from deep inside me. I screamed, waves of pleasure mushrooming from my core to engulf my entire body. My back bowed, and fresh tears pooled in the corners of my eyes as I lost all sense of space and time.

I was a thousand pieces of sensation, broken apart and put together again.

My come was still dripping down my thighs when Asher lowered my leg off the barre and turned me around. He sat me on the wooden beam and hooked my legs around his waist before he continued fucking me, his grunts growing deeper and more guttural as I convulsed around him.

I was still flying high on the last wings of my orgasm when he came with a final deep thrust. His cock twitched inside me as he groaned loudly, the lines of his face drawn tight with pure bliss.

The music was still playing as we held each other, me on the barre and him standing in front of me, our limbs intertwined in a sweaty, exhausted tangle during our come down.

"That's one way to do cardio," I panted. "Congrats, Donovan, you passed your final training test."

His hoarse laughter vibrated from my head to the tips of my toes. "I expect a gold medal commemorating the moment."

"Of course you do." I rested my head on his shoulder, closed my eyes, and breathed him in. Some people were comforted by the smell of their childhood or their mother's cooking, but I was comforted by the scent of *him*. Rich, earthy, masculine.

It was the scent of home.

"How are you feeling, darling?" Asher stroked my hair, the gentleness of his touch a complete one-eighty from the way he'd just fucked me. "That leg on the barre move…"

I giggled at the mix of awe and concern in his voice. "I'm okay. The position wasn't uncomfortable, and the lower barre helped." I lifted my head and gave him a teasing smile. "That's one of the perks of dating a dancer. We're *very* flexible."

His eyes glittered with relief and a fresh touch of heat.

"I see that. I can't believe it took us this long to use the studio *properly*." He shook his head in mock disappointment. "What have we been doing?"

"Less fun stuff, unfortunately." I sighed, drowsy but satiated. "But it's a good last day, isn't it?"

Asher's face softened. "Yeah, it is."

We held each other for a few more minutes until our breathing returned to normal and we finally, reluctantly disentangled. We turned off the music, cleaned ourselves up, and sanitized the studio, but we were still holding tight to the day while it lasted.

Because come tomorrow, everything would change.

CHAPTER 38

ASHER

THE NEXT DAY, A HEAVY SENSE OF DÉJÀ VU SLAMMED into me when I walked into Scarlett's studio at RAB for the first time in two months.

It looked exactly the same as it did my first day here, and memories resurfaced like vivid snapshots from the past.

The bag. The realization that she was the mystery girl from the pub. The shock when I found out she was also Vincent's sister.

The events felt like they happened both yesterday and a century ago.

I'd walked in resentful of my forced training and reentered head over heels for my trainer.

It was funny how one summer could change so much.

Scarlett's smile dazzled when she saw me, but it lasted only a second before her gaze drifted over my shoulder and it morphed into a more neutral version of itself.

"Vincent, you're early," she said a little too brightly.

"I dropped off my luggage and came straight here." Her brother strode in and hugged her. "Look forward to seeing what you have in store for me."

He gave me a curt nod, which I returned with a similar one of my own. Neither of us quite knew how to handle the thaw in our relationship when we were sober, so we kept a respectful distance while Scarlett turned on the music.

"It's going to be harder than the wishy-washy workouts you've been doing on your own," she said.

"*Wishy-washy*?" Vincent sounded outraged. "I have a great training regimen. Ask *Men's Health*. My interview with them was their most popular article last year!"

Second most popular. I bit back my reflexive response. *My* interview with them got a thousand more clicks than his, but antagonizing him before I told him I was dating his sister later this afternoon was probably not a smart move.

"Uh-huh." Scarlett sounded unimpressed. "Either way, you're not caught up on the type of training we've been doing all summer, so I've modified today's session to account for that. The season starts in less than two weeks, which means we only have five sessions together." She wrinkled her nose. "I'm not sure why your coach insisted on having you come back for so short a time, but it is what is. We'll start with warm-ups and then go into the resistance bands."

I knew why Coach wanted Vincent to catch the tail end of our training together, even if it was only for two weeks. He was gruff and grumpy as hell, but he was an optimist at heart. He probably thought two weeks of forced bonding was better than none.

"Also..." Scarlett drilled us with a hard stare. "The three of us haven't trained together since the beginning of summer, but my rules still apply. There will be *no* fighting or bickering in my studio. Understand?"

I offered a laconic salute. "Yes, ma'am."

Vincent smirked. "What he said."

She rolled her eyes, but a tiny sprout of optimism peeked through her professional demeanor when we transitioned into our workout without a speck of argument.

Scarlett paced the studio, studying our forms and adjusting us when necessary.

When it came to football, Vincent and I were on par with each other skills-wise. But when it came to cross-training, I had the added benefit of three months' worth of dance-based practice; he didn't.

I fought a smug smile when I breezed past our resistance and flexibility training while he struggled with the movements. The muscles we used for dance were different than those we used for football, and I'd be lying if I said I didn't relish the way he faltered.

Just because we didn't actively hate each other anymore didn't mean I should pass up an opportunity to (silently) gloat a little.

Vincent growled something in French that made Scarlett sigh. "Okay, let's take a five-minute break. Hydrate, get your heart rate down. I'm going to use the loo."

She slid a quick look at me on her way out.

Remember, be nice, it said.

I am nice, my glance responded.

We'd been careful not to make eye contact during our session in case we gave away our feelings somehow. We'd agreed to take Vincent out after training and ply him with a few beers before we dropped our bombshell on him, but I was having second thoughts.

Should we ambush him on his first day back in the city, or should we give him time to settle in first?

Silence hummed alongside the A/C as we waited for Scarlett to return.

I chugged half a bottle of water and glanced at Vincent, who was wiping his forehead with a Blackcastle-branded sweat towel.

"What are you doing after training?" I asked, breaking the ice.

"Why? You planning to ask me on a date?"

I snorted. "DuBois, I wouldn't ask you on a date if you were the last living creature on earth."

Not *this* DuBois, anyway.

"Good, because I wouldn't fucking say yes." He tossed his towel back onto his gym bag. "But I don't have plans yet."

"You fancy a pint at the Angry Boar? For subbing in at the charity match," I added gruffly. "Last weekend was to celebrate winning, so this is my official thank-you. I don't like owing people."

His smirk returned. "So you *are* asking me on a date."

"Oh, piss off. Do you want a pint or not?"

"I guess I could use one today." He patted his stomach. "Can't drink like that after the season starts."

I made a noise of agreement. We had to be much more careful with our diets during the season.

"Speaking of thank-yous…" Vincent glanced at the door. No sign of Scarlett yet. "Thanks for listening to what I said at the beginning of the summer." His voice was layered with so much reluctance it sounded like someone was forcibly dragging those words out of his mouth.

My brows bent with confusion.

"About not hitting on my sister," he clarified. "I admit, I expected to come back and see you all over her, but you've been respectful. And professional. And you punched that fucker Pessoa for touching her. So I appreciate it."

His grimace indicated how much it pained him to admit he was wrong, but it probably wasn't as distressing as my knowledge that he *wasn't* wrong.

You've been respectful. If he only knew. There'd been nothing *respectful* about what I did to Scarlett in the studio yesterday.

"Right." I coughed, hoping Vincent couldn't see the remnants of yesterday's activities stamped all over my face. "He deserved it."

I purposely didn't acknowledge the first part of his statement, but my muscles coiled with dread when Scarlett finally returned and cut our awkward conversation short.

The rest of our training passed without incident, but when Scarlett tried to bring up the Angry Boar afterward, I stopped her with a meaningful look behind her brother's back.

"I was thinking we could…" She trailed off at my wide eyes.

"We could what?" Vincent asked.

"Uh, we could bring things up a notch during our next session. I think you've got the hang of the basics now," Scarlett said.

"Sounds good," I interrupted before Vincent could ask any more questions. "Vincent and I are going to hit up the Angry Boar for a pint. Get some of that bonding time Coach wanted us to have before the season starts." I punched him in the shoulder like we were long-time mates.

He stared at me like I'd lost my mind.

I didn't blame him. I was acting wildly out of character, but I was so jumpy from our earlier talk that I acted without thinking.

If Scarlett joined us, she'd attempt to tell him about us like we'd originally planned, but I couldn't let her do that until I figured out Vincent's current headspace. Would the sentiment he expressed earlier make him more or less angry when he learned about our relationship?

Unfortunately, I wouldn't have time to explain all this to Scarlett before we got to the pub, since she'd have to ride there with her brother instead of me. It would be easier for me to talk to Vincent alone first.

"Oh! Okay. Um, have fun?" Scarlett's questioning tone revealed her confusion about why I was deviating from our original plan, but she trusted me enough not to press the issue as Vincent slung his duffel over his shoulder and said goodbye to her.

"I'll explain later," I muttered when I passed her.

"Looking forward to it," she muttered back. She glanced at her brother's retreating back. "Good luck."

If I thought a one-on-one conversation at the pub would solve my dilemma, I was dead wrong.

I figured I could ease into the possibility that I was dating his sister after a pint or two and gauge his reaction, but Vincent continued our conversation like we never stopped the instant we sat down, drinks in hand.

"I meant what I said earlier." He ran a hand through his hair. "You and I haven't always gotten along, and I was nervous about leaving you alone with her. You're arrogant, you sleep around—"

"Huh. Sounds like you could be describing yourself."

Vincent glared at me. "And I wouldn't want Scarlett dating someone like me, either," he snapped. "She's been through enough. She has a...bad history with footballers, and she doesn't need to deal with your bullshit after all that."

I couldn't resist following up. "By bad history, you mean Pessoa?"

He hesitated, then confirmed with a short nod. "I'm not going to go into the details because that's not my place, but their breakup was hard on her. I never want to see her in that dark of a place again. She's my only sister, and I'm protective of her."

My mouth thinned. *Fucking Pessoa*. I should've hit him harder when I had the chance.

"Anyway, that's why I'm sitting here," Vincent said gruffly. "I don't give a shit about thank-you drinks—no offense—but it does mean a lot to me that you protected Scarlett and that you didn't try to take advantage of my absence over the summer. So I guess…" He rubbed the back of his neck, his expression turning sheepish. "Maybe we should let bygones be bygones. Like Coach said, I don't want our issues to fuck up our next season. And as much as I dislike you, I hate Holchester even more."

"What a ringing endorsement. That truly makes me feel all warm and fuzzy."

"Oh, don't give me that bullshit. You're not my biggest fan either."

"I most definitely am not, but I also hate Holchester more, so"—I raised my glass—"the truce continues."

Vincent snorted but clinked his glass against mine.

We sipped our beer and lapsed into awkward silence once more.

We had plenty to say when we were rivals, but friendliness was a tougher bridge to cross than enmity.

"What's your problem with me anyway?" I asked, genuinely curious.

I would never forget what happened at the World Cup. Getting ejected from the biggest football tournament on the planet because of a faked injury wasn't something *any* player would ever get over, and England's subsequent loss only added to the sting. But it'd been two years since that fateful call, and I was willing to leave what happened in the past for Scarlett's sake.

Besides, I planned to kick Vincent's ass in the next World Cup.

However, that didn't explain why *he* was so against me. We competed for sponsorships and status, but so did a lot of players.

Was it because the internet constantly pitted us against each other in those "who's the better player" polls? Was it because I earned more than him? Or was it something else?

"My problem with you? Besides the fact that you're a cocky son of a bitch with a superiority complex?" Vincent asked. "You have it too easy."

I almost spat out my drink. "Excuse me?"

Have it too easy? I trained and played just as hard as he did, and I worked my ass off to get to where I was. Admittedly, I was lucky enough to grow up in a relatively stable, two-parent household, but having my father scream in my ear all the time hadn't been a walk in the park.

Besides, it wasn't like Vincent grew up in a tough household. His parents were divorced, but from what I could tell, they'd been supportive of his dreams. His father had been an engineer and his mother was a nurse, and they had enough money to pay for Scarlett's ballet lessons *and* his football training.

"I'm not talking about your work ethic." It was like Vincent could read my thoughts. "I'm talking about *you*. Asher Donovan." He gestured at me. "If any other player had pulled half the shit you've pulled, with the cars and racing, they would be radioactive. No one would touch them. You, on the other hand, got a record-breaking transfer deal and a renewed sponsorship from Aoki Watches. You're reckless, you're flashy as hell on the pitch because you can't stand not being the center of attention, and it doesn't matter because your brand is too big to fail."

I sat there, too stunned by the barrage to respond. I thought his issues with me stemmed from disparities in pay or fame, but clearly, they ran deeper than that.

Vincent was quiet for a moment before he spoke again. "Do you remember the Rocco campaign you did five years ago?"

I nodded. The sneaker campaign had been my first *major* brand sponsorship. When I received my first check from them, my eyes nearly fell out of my head.

"I was originally slated to be their brand ambassador." He flashed a bitter smile. "But I got into a fight with Pessoa after the shit he pulled with Scarlett, someone recorded it, and Rocco pulled my contract."

I vaguely remembered hearing about the fight, but it happened before our rivalry truly kicked off, and I'd glossed over the details at the time.

"Shit." I grimaced. "That sucks. I'm sorry."

I wasn't responsible for Rocco pulling his contract, but if I were him, I'd resent the person who took my place, too.

Now, I understood why my transfer bothered him so much. I got into trouble and got rewarded; he got into trouble and got penalized. Granted, we were at a different level of fame five years ago—Rocco might've let the fight slide if it'd happened today—but feelings were feelings.

Vincent shrugged. "What's done is done. My Nike contract later soothed the burn." His mouth curled into a smirk. "Besides, I was Rocco's first choice."

"Oh, piss off." But instead of being annoyed, I felt the tentative tendrils of understanding snake around us, softening some of our hard-baked bitterness.

For two people entrenched in a career where ego and reputation ruled the day, that wasn't a small feat.

"But like I said, that's water under the bridge." Vincent laughed. "I'm just glad nothing happened between you and my sister, or we'd be having a different conversation. I can get past work-related problems, but family? That's another issue."

My short-lived relief solidified into ice. *Scarlett*. Letting go of our past resentments was all well and good, but our biggest obstacle for a friendly relationship continued to simmer in the background like a volcano waiting to erupt.

"Anyway, I'm glad we had this talk. Coach will be happy too." This time, Vincent was the one who raised his glass. "You ready to kick Holchester's ass this season?"

I forced a smile and tapped my glass against his. "Absolutely."

"We can't tell him yet."

Scarlett stared at me from my phone screen. I didn't want to risk going over to her house after Vincent and I left the Angry Boar, so I'd video called her instead and explained why I changed our plans earlier. "What do you mean?"

"I mean, we have to rethink our strategy for breaking the news." I rubbed a hand over my face. "You should've heard him. He mentioned *multiple* times how much he appreciated me not making a move on you while he was gone. That's one of the main reasons he's willing to bury the hatchet. If we tell him now, he'll feel like a fool, which means he'll probably take the news even worse than we thought."

"Maybe he won't," Scarlett said hopefully. "Maybe he'll take it *better* now that he doesn't think you're the devil."

I raised an eyebrow.

"Ugh. You're right." She dropped her head into her hand. "I don't believe this. We were nervous about telling him because he didn't like you, and now we can't tell him because he *does* like you. I swear, the universe hates us."

"We can still tell him. We just have to adjust our timing," I said.

"2075 should be an auspicious year."

"*Asher*."

"I know, I know." I sighed, conflicted.

On one hand, we could stick with our original strategy and deal with the fallout as it came. That would give Vincent time to calm down before the pre-season started.

On the other hand, I doubted two weeks would be enough of a buffer period for him to get over the news. He would start the season with fresh hatred of me, which wouldn't be good for *anyone* involved.

Old me would've chosen option one, but I was trying to be more thoughtful and less reckless about the decisions I made. I couldn't jump into a situation headfirst and expect everything would work out in my favor. I had to think of the consequences.

I also wasn't stupid enough to call Coach's bluff. He would absolutely condemn us to the bench if he felt like we weren't working together well enough, and I hadn't worked this hard to sit on the sidelines during what I was starting to think of as my redemption season. If I didn't bring home a trophy come May and prove my critics wrong, I might as well pack up my boots and call it a day.

Plus—and I would never admit this out loud—my truce with Vincent had lifted a huge weight off my shoulders. Clashing with someone on my own team took a lot of energy, and I needed every spare ounce of it if I wanted to beat Holchester.

"Maybe we can tell him during the holidays," I said. "The spirit of giving and all that."

Scarlett gave me a dubious look. "You want to tell him halfway through the season *and* ruin his Christmas?"

"Well, not when you put it *that* way."

We sat in silence as we attempted to workshop a new strategy.

It didn't work.

"Maybe it's because it's so late, but my brain is mush," Scarlett said. "We can table this for now, but is it really better to tell Vincent after the season starts than before? What if he finds out before we're ready? He'll be even more upset if he hears about us from someone else."

"I don't know." I tipped my head and stared at the ceiling, wishing it contained the solutions to our problems. "I really don't know."

CHAPTER 39

SCARLETT

TURN. TURN. PLIÉ. STEP BACK.

I was practicing for *Lorena* alone in my studio. I went through the motions well enough, but I found it hard to focus the way I should.

Asher and I never figured out a new strategy for telling Vincent. At this point, we were winging it and hoping the right moment would come up in conversation, which wasn't really a strategy at all, but it was all we had.

Thankfully, Vincent didn't suspect a thing. After his Angry Boar outing with Asher, the two developed a wary but burgeoning...well, friendship might be too strong a word. It was more like a friendly acquaintanceship.

Whatever it was, it meant the rest of our training sessions passed by smoothly. I'd hyped up the drama of Vincent's return so much in my mind that the ease with which he transitioned back into our lives was almost unsettling.

However, as the days wound down toward the start of the season, my anxiety took flight again.

Everyone would be back in London, which meant more eyes on us and more opportunities to get caught. I understood and even agreed with Asher's reasoning for postponing our Big Talk with my brother, but my mind couldn't stop chasing down every scenario where things might go wrong.

What if someone captured a photo of us on the street and uploaded it online the way they did with Clive and me?

What if Vincent ran into Clive himself and the rugby player exposed us? I hadn't talked to him since I told him we wouldn't work after our double date, but I knew he and Asher didn't get along.

What if Vincent found out about the private ballet studio or our trip to Japan? I managed to keep the Asia trip a secret from my brother because it was so short, and I'd blamed my delayed replies to his texts on my busy schedule. But all it took was one slip-up or errant picture on the internet to blow our cover.

Part of me wished Asher and I had been honest from the start, but it was too late. We were stuck in a web of our own design.

My worries and disjointed thoughts jumbled in my head. I was so distracted that I missed two counts and stumbled when I tried to correct myself.

"Dammit!" The curse slipped out on a bed of frustration.

I stopped, rested my forearms on the barre, and placed my head on them as I tried to reorient myself.

I couldn't tack on my extra practices to Asher and Vincent's training for obvious reasons, so I'd rehearsed alone since my brother's return. Asher offered the use of his private studio in the evenings anyway, but I was too paranoid to sneak over to his house.

I'd been doing so well over the summer. However, without Asher there, I was making more mistakes. Losing focus. Questioning myself.

The noticeable change in the quality of my rehearsals added

another layer of anxiety.

What if he was the secret ingredient? Could I perform in front of a crowd without him next to me, encouraging me?

My stomach cramped.

No. As much as I lov—liked Asher, I refused to make my success dependent on another person.

I didn't care if I was practicing as an understudy and that I'd probably never get the chance to perform onstage. I was going to nail this bloody dance on my own.

I gritted my teeth against the slow creep of exhaustion and forced myself to stand again. I had ten minutes left in the ballet's final act. I could finish it.

My body might hate me for it later, but I would hate myself more if I gave up now. It was easier to soothe physical pains than it was emotional ones, especially if they were self-inflicted.

My old therapist and doctors said my determination to push myself to my limits was toxic and unhealthy. They were right; it *was*, which was why I didn't advocate my choices to others. I wouldn't want anyone else to override their body's warning signs the way I did mine.

But that was them and this was me. I was hard-wired for competition, which included competing against myself.

I had to win, so I pushed.

And it worked.

I restarted from where I'd stumbled and made it through to the end without botching the choreography.

I held the final position for two beats before my legs gave out and I half sank, half collapsed on the floor. Bile rose in my throat; I was either going to throw up, pass out, or both.

My muscles trembled as I tried to breathe through a white-hot blaze of pain. It engulfed my body, scalding my arms, shoulders, and legs and sinking so deep into my bones that every joint ached. A migraine pounded behind my temple, and the room seemed to tilt as I struggled to get my bearings.

Tears prickled my eyes.

I hadn't had this terrible of a flare-up in a long, long time. I knew it was a likely outcome given how hard I'd exerted myself over the past few weeks, but I hadn't expected to crumple so suddenly and viciously.

My emergency packet of pain pills beckoned from my bag. They were just out of arm's reach.

I pulled my legs up to my chest and rested my head on my knees. It helped with the dizziness, but not the pain.

Every muscle screamed, but...*but*.

I'd finished the choreography. And I'd nailed it the second time around.

Inhale, exhale.

One, two, three, four...

By the time I reached a hundred, my tears had dried. When I reached two hundred, the needle-sharp pain had dulled into a steady ache.

Thank God I didn't have classes for the rest of the afternoon. I didn't want my students to walk in and find me curled up on the floor, crying.

I'd purposely scheduled my rehearsals for the end of the day, when I was supposed to be working on my lesson plans, but I could do that at home.

Eventually, the pain and nausea faded enough for me to raise my head. The world returned in bits and pieces, starting with the intermittent buzz of my phone.

I checked and saw I had two new messages from Carina, both sent ten minutes ago.

CARINA

Lavinia wants to see you

CARINA

I think it has to do with the staff showcase 👀

A groan swelled in my throat.

The last thing I wanted was to talk to the director in my current state, but I didn't have a choice.

I took one last deep breath and dragged myself to my feet. Pins and needles shot through my leg. I had to pause and wait until they subsided before I shuffled to Lavinia's office.

Carina's eyes widened when she saw me. "Are you okay?"

"Do I look that bad?" I joked, but my voice came out hoarse and weak.

"No. You just…here." She fished a wet wipe out of her purse and handed it to me. "For your makeup."

One glance in the mirror hanging on the wall revealed my tear-smudged eyeliner and mascara tracks. *Crap.*

I quickly fixed myself and gave Carina a wan thanks.

"No problem. Good luck in there." Her concerned stare followed me until I entered Lavinia's office and shut the door behind me.

Per usual, the director cut straight to the chase.

"I'm sorry for the last-minute summons, but I figured I should tell you sooner than later." If she noticed my shaky state from behind her desk, she didn't comment on it. "Yvette is no longer a member of the RAB staff. Therefore, she can no longer play the role of Lorena. You'll have to take over as the lead in the staff showcase."

The announcement was so sudden, so unexpected, that my shock temporarily outpaced my fatigue. "She resigned?"

Yvette and I didn't interact much, but she was a long-time employee of RAB. I couldn't imagine her quitting in the middle of the school year, especially when she'd been cast as the lead in the staff showcase.

"Not exactly." Lavinia's mouth pursed with displeasure. "It has come to my attention that she was responsible for a certain... disturbance at our school earlier this summer."

Disturbance? There hadn't been any disturbances at RAB except for...

The paparazzi.

My jaw hit the ground. *Yvette* was the one who'd tipped the paps off about Asher? *Why?*

"I've been investigating the source of the leak that led to the disturbance," Lavinia continued, deftly alluding to the situation without outright saying what it was. "I do not take kindly to trespassers, nor do I condone *any* actions that jeopardize the safety and privacy of our students and staff. I can't share details, but since you were one of the directly affected parties, I *can* tell you that Yvette's involvement was substantial enough to warrant her departure."

My head spun, but this time, it had nothing to do with overexertion. "Do you know why she did it?"

The director's elegant shrug indicated she didn't particularly care. Punishment had been meted out, and that was what mattered.

"Money makes people do strange things." She examined me, her expression shifting from distaste to inquisitiveness. "Will taking over her role be an issue?"

I'd been so caught off guard by the Yvette revelation that I'd glossed over the reason Lavinia called me in here.

She wanted me to take over as the lead in *Lorena*.

Me.

The lead.

Not an understudy waiting in the wings, but the star attraction, the one who everyone would be watching.

She couldn't have picked a worse time to tell me if she'd tried.

My tongue took on the taste and texture of the Sahara. I opened my mouth, but no words rushed to my rescue.

I sat there, pinned like a bug beneath Lavinia's stare while my body quaked from the aftermath of my rehearsal.

Performing again in theory was one thing. Actually doing it was another.

I pushed myself in practice for *me*. I wanted to prove to *myself* that I could do it, but I'd always operated within the safe confines of my understudy role.

Yvette's departure shattered those confines and exposed me to the terror of putting myself out there again. I remembered how badly I'd screwed up my first and, so far, only rehearsal with the cast. How hard I'd had to push just to get through today's thirty-minute practice.

It didn't matter that I'd gotten through a majority of my practices without incident. It only took one bad night to screw things up, and since the December staff showcase was a one-time performance, I didn't *get* a second chance. I needed to be perfect.

Panic drenched my palms with cold sweat.

"Scarlett?" Lavinia prompted.

"Yes. I mean, no. I mean…" I winced when her eyebrows arched. "That won't be a problem."

"Good. I'll let the rest of the cast know. Tamara will reach out with more details." Lavinia peered at me over her glasses. "I expect cast rehearsals will go smoothly in the future."

Judging by her tone, she knew about my screw-up earlier this summer.

I wanted to sink through the floor and die, but I forced a bright smile. "Yes. I won't let you down."

I left her office in a daze. Carina was on a toilet break when I got out, but instead of waiting for her, I returned to my studio and called the only person who could calm the nausea roiling my stomach.

"Hi, darling." Asher's voice flowed over the line. "Miss me already?"

My smile wobbled. "Actually, yes. How's your first day back?"

Today was the official start of Blackcastle's pre-season training. It was our first Monday apart in months, and I felt his absence like a gaping hole in my chest.

"It was good, but Vincent and I have a meeting with Coach in ten. We'll see how that goes."

"Hey, you two are finally getting along. He should be happy."

"He should." I heard male laughter and chatter in the background. He must be in the changing room. "But I'm guessing you didn't call me in the middle of work to discuss football."

"No," I admitted. I told him about my conversation with Lavinia but not about my flare-up after practice. I didn't want Asher to freak out or get distracted. I could handle this on my own.

"Wow." He whistled when I finished. "What a way to start the week."

"I know." I stared at my pale, disheveled reflection in the studio's mirrors. I was still riding the carousel of dizziness, but Asher's voice kept me grounded enough to get through the conversation without shaking.

"How do you feel about being the lead?" A note of caution crept through his words.

"What *don't* I feel? Nervous, terrified, nauseous, a little excited. I honestly haven't processed it yet." I leaned my head back against the wall. "Ask me again in seventy-two hours."

He laughed. "You got it."

"Anyway, I just wanted to call and tell you. If I waited until tonight, I might've combusted, but I don't want to keep you any longer." I dreaded hanging up, but I couldn't use him as a security blanket forever. "Good luck with your meeting."

"Thanks." I heard the smile in his voice. "And Scarlett? For what it's worth, I think you'll kill it as Lorena."

My lips tipped up, but they slowly flattened again after I ended our call.

Asher, Vincent, Yvette, Emma, the showcase, the pain, the threat of the paparazzi...all the loose threads in my life, big and small, swirled inside me. They tangled together and formed a rope in my chest, pulling tighter and tighter until it nearly cut off my supply of oxygen.

Sometimes, merely existing took too much energy, so I closed my eyes and tried to breathe.

At that moment, it was all I could do.

CHAPTER 40

ASHER

I ENDED MY CALL WITH SCARLETT AND TOSSED MY PHONE in my gym bag right as Adil bounded over to me and Noah, whose locker was next to mine.

"There they are! My fellow Blackcastle baddies!" He clapped one hand on each of our shoulders. "Missed me?"

"Like a toddler misses a rash," Noah muttered, but he didn't shake off the midfielder's greeting.

"So you *did* miss me." Adil appeared unfazed by the goalie's lackluster enthusiasm. "New season, boys. We're back, and we're going to *crush* those Holchester bastards! And everyone else," he added as an afterthought.

"You got that right." I bumped my fist against his in agreement, but my mind lingered on Scarlett. She sounded a little off during our call. Perhaps it was her nerves over the Yvette and showcase situation. She had complicated feelings about performing in public again, and the sudden promotion from understudy to lead couldn't be easy.

I made a note to check in with her again once I was home.

I changed shirts while Adil regaled us with tales of his summer at home. The locker room crackled with the back-to-school energy of a new season, and laughter and teasing banter filled the air as the players caught up with each other for the first time in months.

"I can't wait to see them on the pitch again." Adil rubbed his hands. "Bocci better watch his fucking back."

The mention of my old teammate filled my mouth with the taste of copper. It was the taste for competition. For redemption. For vengeance.

We *almost* swept the league last season, and this was our chance to vindicate ourselves. Since Vincent and I set aside our differences, there was nothing stopping us from taking the number one title come May.

Coach entered the locker room. "DuBois! Donovan!" he barked. He jerked his head toward his office. "Get in here."

A chorus of taunting *oohs* swelled as Vincent and I stopped what we were doing and walked toward him, our expressions identically wary.

"In trouble already? That's a record," Samson joked. The Nigerian winger laughed when Vincent gave him a light shove on his way past.

"Next time you want to make a joke, make sure you can complete a forty-five-minute run without heaving like you're in labor first," he called over his shoulder.

The first day of pre-season was always the toughest as players transitioned from a summer of food and holiday back to work.

Another chorus of *oohs* mingled with jeers as Samson shook his head. "Low blow, captain!" he yelled after us. "Low blow!"

I smirked, but my amusement quickly faded when we arrived at Coach's office. He shut the door, and once again, déjà vu permeated my senses as Vincent and I settled into our seats.

Coach sank into his chair opposite us and steepled his fingers beneath his chin.

The clock ticked.

The air-conditioner hummed.

The muffled noises from the locker room emphasized the tension dripping around us.

Vincent and I shifted in our seats.

If Coach was employing some sort of psychological warfare tactic to make us uncomfortable as fuck, it was working.

After what felt like an eternity of interminable silence, his eagle eyes zeroed in on Vincent. "DuBois, your father alright?"

"Yes, sir."

"I'm glad to hear that." Coach leaned forward. "If I ever find out you trumped up a family emergency to get out of something *I* assigned to you, I'll have you running interval sprints until you develop a bloody intimate relationship with the nearest rubbish bin. Understand?"

Vincent swallowed. "Yes, sir."

My snicker died halfway when Coach turned his attention to me.

"This is a new season. A fresh start," he said. "I'll chalk last season's problems up to growing pains, but your petty antics end here and now. You may not have spent the summer together like I'd planned"—he cast another glare at Vincent, who slid a few inches down in his seat—"but that's not an excuse for picking up where you left off. I expect you to behave like more than adults; I expect you to behave like *champions*. If that's going to be a problem, you need to tell me right bloody now." His eyes glinted with warning. "*Is* it going to be a problem?"

"No, sir," we chorused.

"Donovan and I have come to an understanding," Vincent added. "So you don't have to worry about us."

Coach's thick brows beetled with skepticism. "Is that so?"

"Yes." I picked up on Vincent's thread. "We've learned from last season's mistakes."

"It won't happen again," Vincent said.

"We are fully prepared to work together to destroy—to beat Holchester. And everyone else," I went on, echoing Adil's earlier addendum.

Coach's eyes tapered into suspicious slits. "Good," he finally said. "I assume this *understanding* started with the Sport for Hope charity match?"

Our mouths formed identical O's of surprise. He knew about my long-time involvement with the non-profit, but how did he know about Vincent?

"I read the local papers, and I have spies everywhere." The curve of Coach's mouth would've resembled a smile if he wasn't allergic to smiling. "I heard about your brawl with Pessoa and the Greens too." The curve vanished. "He's a wanker, but don't pull any of that shit during one of my matches, or—"

Someone knocked on the door, interrupting what I was sure would've been another flinch-inducing threat.

Vincent and I exchanged glances. Who would dare interrupt one of Coach's meetings?

Coach's brows bent further until they formed a single line across his forehead. "Come in," he snapped.

The door opened, and Greely, our assistant coach, popped his head in like he was afraid Coach would chew off his limbs if he allowed them past the threshold. "Sir, your daughter's here. She's waiting in the hall."

"Tell her I'll be out in a minute." Greely left, and Coach glared at us again. He did that a lot. "I have other business to attend to, but

I trust you won't do anything to jeopardize this beautiful, budding friendship of yours."

We shook our heads in unison even as my unease rattled in my veins.

I was going to take a wild guess and assume dating Vincent's sister fell under Coach's "anything" clause.

Vincent and I didn't breathe until he dismissed us and left to meet his daughter. I guess he didn't care about leaving us alone in his office—not that we were dumb enough to snoop through his stuff. We valued our lives.

"Christ. I felt like I was a student getting called into the headmaster's office again," Vincent muttered on our way out.

We'd given Coach plenty of lead time so we didn't have to walk next to him. The man was inspiring but also, frankly, terrifying.

"You're not the only one," I muttered back. "I'm surprised he didn't put us in detention and make us scrub the floors."

"Don't give him any ideas."

I snorted.

When we re-entered the main locker room, it was empty. However, a flurry of whispers led us around the corner to the exit, where the rest of the team was huddled around the little window in the door.

"What's going on?" I asked.

"Have you ever seen Coach's daughter?" Adil turned, his eyes gleaming. "She's *here*."

"So?" Vincent yawned. "What's the big deal?"

"I heard she's joining the team staff," Samson said. I didn't know how, but he always found out about team-related breaking news first. "She'll be interning with Jones."

Jones was Blackcastle's lead performance nutritionist.

"Big deal. We get new interns all the time. She's not special just because she's Coach's daughter." Vincent sounded unimpressed. "You all better get back to the locker room before Coach sees you, or he'll make us do horseshoe runs again."

A collective shudder rippled through the group, but that wasn't a big enough threat to make them disperse.

"Dude. Samson forgot the most important part." Adil walked over and placed his hands on Vincent's shoulders with great solemnity. "Coach's daughter is *hot*."

That got his attention.

I shook my head as Vincent pushed his way toward the window, but curiosity got the better of me as well. None of us had ever seen Coach's daughter. I knew she lived with his ex-wife and that she was his only child, but that was about it.

I didn't care that she was hot, but I *was* curious about what Frank Armstrong's daughter looked like.

I squeezed next to Vincent and peered out the window. Coach's back faced us, obscuring most of her body. After a minute or so, he shifted, revealing long blond hair, hazel eyes, and a heart-shaped face.

My jaw dropped.

Beside me, Vincent went rigid, his breath expelling in a similar rush of shock.

Because it turned out we *had* seen Coach's daughter before. Not only that, we'd drank and partied with her.

We turned to each other, our expressions identical masks of disbelief while Coach continued to talk to Brooklyn.

The first thing I did when I left training was call Scarlett again. She had no idea Brooklyn was Coach's daughter, but she didn't sound particularly upset about it.

"I *knew* she was hiding something," she said. "It makes sense. She does want to go into nutrition, and if I were Frank Armstrong's daughter, I wouldn't run around telling people either. I barely acknowledge being Vincent's sister."

"For good reason," I told her.

She laughed, but like our conversation earlier, it sounded a bit forced. However, when I offered to drop by her house or have Earl pick her up for a rendezvous at mine, she declined, saying she was tired from rehearsals and wanted to nap.

I didn't push it. She sounded like herself again the next day, so I took her explanation at face value.

The grueling demands of the pre-season soon dominated my attention, and the novelty of discovering Brooklyn's relation to Coach quickly evaporated as we swept through the friendlies and the real season kicked off several weeks later.

We won our matches easily, but we hadn't faced any heavy hitters yet. The real test would be our match against Holchester in two weeks.

Still, that didn't mean we passed up the opportunity to celebrate beating Wentworth in our first official match of the season.

What I really wanted was to celebrate with Scarlett, whom I barely got to see these days. Between my club obligations and her adjusted rehearsal schedule, we spoke on the phone more often than we did in person. I was spoiled after a summer of having her mostly to myself, and I was desperate for alone time with her.

Nevertheless, I couldn't say no to the first team outing of the season, which was how I found myself packed into the Angry Boar with the rest of the Blackcastle team.

"Captain buys the first round," Adil announced after we placed our orders at the bar—beer for those who indulged, water or soda for those who didn't. "It's tradition."

Vincent narrowed his eyes. "Since when?"

"Since now."

"Interesting," Vincent said. "You know, I seem to recall you never picked up a single tab *last* season…"

"Hey, I entertain with my wit and humor. You can't put a price on that," Adil said defensively. "Speaking of which, I have a team bonding idea, and it's all thanks to Donovan."

Every head swung toward me.

I shrugged, as confused as they were.

"I read the book you recommended." Adil reached into his pocket and brandished a small paperback featuring a colorful cover of a half-naked redhead and two massive, scaly reptiles. "*Triceratops and Threesomes*. Hey, it was *good*!" he shouted over an outburst of laughter and jeers.

"Bruv, what are you reading?"

"Are those *dinosaurs*?"

"What kind of kinky shit are you into?"

"Donovan." Samson crossed his arms, his mouth twitching. "Explain."

I almost told them the truth until I remembered Scarlett was the one who'd introduced me to the title. I hadn't read it, but I did not want to explain why Vincent's sister was the one giving me erotic book recommendations.

"I saw it in a bookstore," I lied. "It looked…interesting, so I shared it with Adil and Noah."

"Don't look at me," Noah said when everyone swiveled to stare at him. "I was an unwilling recipient of the information."

"You were in a bookstore? You mean, you can read?" Stevens, one of the other forwards, cracked.

I crumpled a napkin and tossed it at him. It hit him square in the face. "Bugger off, Stevens. You don't even know how to do your own laundry."

His face fell. "I told you it was the machine's fault! That high-tech shit is bloody confusing."

"*Excuse me*, but let's get back to the topic at hand!" Adil raised his voice. "Anyway, as I was saying, I have a team bonding idea. We should create a Blackcastle book club where—"

More jeers drowned out his voice.

"Where we read a different erotic book every month!" he shouted. "It'll be fun!"

A book club? That was *my* idea! Granted, I'd been joking at the time, but still. Let it be known that I thought of it first.

However, the rest of the team was not onboard.

"*Fun*?"

"You have a strange idea of fun."

"No bloody way!"

"You don't have to join if you don't want to," Adil said with great dignity. "But it *will* be fun, and you'll miss out on some great books. Now, who's in?" He looked around.

Silence.

"Come on, guys," he wheedled. "This is way more interesting than partying every weekend."

"That's because you don't drink," Stevens said.

"Exactly." Adil's smile wilted as the team remained silent. "Seriously? *No one* wants to join?"

Bloody hell. I was going to regret this later, but… "I'm in."

I was the one who inadvertently got us into the mess. I might as well see it through.

His face brightened again, and he shot me a grateful look.

"Me too," Vincent said, surprising the shit out of me. "I'm the captain. Team morale is part of my job."

"Great!" Adil's smile returned to full wattage. "I always *knew* you two had a good taste. Who else is interested?"

There was another beat of silence.

"I'll observe." Noah's quiet rumble shocked me even more than Vincent's participation. "But I'm not reading about dinosaur threesomes."

"Fine." Adil sounded delighted. "You can be our mascot and bring snacks."

Noah's scowl expressed how *not* delighted he was with the assignment. However, his participation, combined with my and Vincent's approval, led the rest of the team to join in trickles and then a wave.

Soon, almost every person agreed to join the book club, though I could tell some didn't think we were seriously going to read dino erotica every month.

We grabbed our drinks and crowded around various tables and booths. The atmosphere was the most relaxed I'd felt since I joined Blackcastle. Everyone was less on edge now that Vincent and I had called a truce, and our victory that afternoon added an extra lift to our spirits.

This was what I'd missed. I loved the sport, but I loved the camaraderie and brotherhood of being part of a team too.

It's nice...until you fuck it up, a voice sang inside my head.

The revelation about my relationship with Scarlett was a guillotine waiting to fall. At this point, I was deep in denial and taking my interactions with Vincent day by day.

Who knows? Maybe we could keep our secret from him until Vincent and I were both retired and I invited him to our wedding. He couldn't kill us at our own wedding, could he?

"You good?" Noah asked while half the team left to argue over what song to play next at the jukebox.

"Yeah." I flashed a quick smile. "Just thinking about the Holchester match coming up."

He didn't look convinced.

The gruff goalie was the quietest, most subdued member of the team, but he was also the most observant. He had to be, considering he was raising an eleven-year-old on his own. That couldn't be easy.

"I'm glad you and DuBois made up," he said. "I guess Coach's summer plan worked, even if you only had two weeks of training together."

The beer turned sour at the back of my tongue.

"I guess so." I avoided Noah's eyes. "I was the one who messed up last season. I don't want that to happen again."

The jangle of bells above the door cut our conversation short, and a noticeable hush fell over the pub when several members of Holchester's team walked in.

I stiffened, my fingers curling tight around my pint glass. Noah straightened as well while the other Blackcastle players glared at the newcomers like they were intruding on our turf—which, in my mind, they were.

The Angry Boar was open to the public, but London was our city (yes, I only moved here at the beginning of the year, but I already thought of it as home). Holchester was only here because they had a match against Arsenal earlier that day.

Tension brewed into a toxic storm. Even the other patrons were on high alert.

Mac and his triplet bouncers looked like they were ready to throw fists at the first sign of trouble, but that didn't stop Bocci, Lyle, and the other Holchester players from approaching me.

"Look who it is." Lyle's smile didn't reach his eyes. "Judas himself."

Once, we'd been friends. I'd bailed him out of sticky situations, and he'd thrown a surprise birthday party for me at my favorite club in Holchester. It was wild to think that a standard team transfer could've ruined our relationship so thoroughly, but to him it wasn't a standard transfer. I'd left mid-season to join their biggest rival without so much as a heads-up, and that was on me.

But it'd been almost a year, and I was tired of their taunts. They needed to get the bloody hell over it.

"I'm starting to think you fancy me, what with the special nickname and all," I drawled without standing. They didn't deserve that acknowledgment. "Did you seek me out at my favorite pub too? I'm flattered."

His face reddened. "I don't fancy traitors," he snapped. "But it's nice to see you getting so chummy with Blackcastle. You've truly turned, haven't you?"

"They're my team," I snapped back, my pretense of fake congeniality gone. "And they're not the ones who hung effigies of me in front of Holchester pubs."

Non-sports fans would never understand it, but there was nothing like a Holchester football fan who felt like they'd been wronged.

"We can't be held accountable for the public's actions." Bocci shrugged. "It's not our fault they hate you so much."

My jaw clenched. I should've been used to it, but after all this time, the sentiment still stung. I could try explaining it to people, but until they lived through it, no one quite understood what it was like to have a city that once adored you turn on you at the drop of a hat.

They felt betrayed by me, but I felt betrayed by them too. Their loyalty truly was transactional.

It made sense, but it hurt all the same.

"Get the fuck out of here." Vincent came up behind Bocci, his face creased with a scowl. "You want to drink, drink, but leave my team the hell alone. Are you so petty you can't get over a bloody transfer?"

"Oh, we don't care about the transfer," Bocci said. "It proved we didn't need him because guess which one of our teams is the reigning league champion?" A nasty grin split his face. "Not yours."

The tension thickened into a stifling weight.

Vincent's face darkened, and even Noah let out a warning rumble beside me.

"Hold on to your glory while you can, because it won't last long." Vincent bared his teeth in a semblance of a smile. "I look forward to beating you at our next match."

Bocci smirked. "You think *you* can beat us?"

"I don't think. I *know*." Vincent spat something in French.

Bocci was Italian, but whatever Vincent said was similar enough to his language that he understood it. He snarled out a response, but I stood and stepped in between them before Vincent did something stupid that would get us tossed out of the pub.

"Back off," I warned. I itched to slam my fist into Bocci's smug face, but I was trying real bloody hard to play by the rules this season. I wasn't going to mess up my shot at a championship for anyone. "You know Mac's rules."

"How sweet. You're defending your new best mate," Lyle sneered. "Don't come back to Holchester, Donovan. You're not welcome. Even your own *father* doesn't want you there anymore."

My hands instinctively curled into fists. Anger chased after my strained calm and torched it into ashes.

I'd told Lyle about my relationship with my father when we were friends, and now he was using it to bait me?

Fuck. That.

"I can come back anytime I want, *Artie*," I said, using his much-hated nickname. Arthur Lyle, or Artie for short. "Remember that wide-open shot you missed during our season final against Chelsea? An amateur goalie could've knocked that ball right back at you. If I hadn't covered your ass, we would've lost that match. Or how about the way you fumbled the first half of the season opener against Tottenham? There's a reason you weren't tapped to play for the national team, and you should be fucking glad I don't *want* to go back to Holchester. If I did, you can kiss your playing time goodbye because guess what? You're not. That. Bloody. Good."

Lyle was good enough to play in the Premier League, but compared to other forwards at the same level, he was merely okay, and he knew it.

It was a sore subject for him, which explained why he reacted so quickly and thoughtlessly.

His face flushed scarlet, and he pushed me hard enough that I stumbled back into Vincent. "Fuck you, Donovan!"

A snarl ripped up my throat. I almost retaliated, but I held back when I saw the triplets bearing down on us.

Mac got to us before they did. "Out!" His grizzled beard trembled with outrage. "All of you!"

Shouts of protest erupted from both teams.

"C'mon, Mac!"

"They started it!"

"We didn't touch them!"

"I don't want to hear it!" he growled. "You know the rules. *No fighting*. I don't care how rich or famous you are. You." He pointed at Lyle. "Show your face in here again, and I'll have the triplets knock your ass out the door. The rest of you, take it outside. I will *not* have you in here arguing and disturbing the rest of my customers. Argue with me, and I'll ban you for life. Now get out!"

We snapped our mouths shut and skulked out the back exit since we didn't want to attract attention from the hordes of tourists streaming past the front entrance.

One of the triplets slammed the door in our faces, leaving us in an alleyway next to the dumpster.

"Nice bloody job," Bocci spat. "You got us kicked out before we even got a drink."

"How is this our fault?" Adil's normally good-natured face flashed with anger. "*You* were the ones who instigated things first!"

Fresh arguments exploded between the two sides again.

Meanwhile, I focused on Bocci and Lyle, who led the Holchester hate campaign against me.

"You can argue all you want now, but we'll see who the real winner is during our match," I said. "Reigning champions doesn't mean you'll *stay* champions."

"Yeah?" Bocci's dark eyes gleamed with malice. "How about we put some money on it? A race after our match. You and me. We won't be bound by rules like we are on the pitch, and the winner of the match gets a five-second head start."

The others' arguments petered out.

Meanwhile, the wind died, throwing the alley into eerie silence. Summer heat and the suffocating reek of rubbish crawled into my lungs.

A race. I hadn't raced since I beat Clive over the summer.

Bocci and I used to compete for fun when I lived in Holchester, but that was then. This was now.

Any competition we had going forward, whether it was on the pitch or in the streets, wouldn't be for fun. We would go for the jugular.

"Why so quiet, Donovan?" Bocci taunted. "I thought you loved racing. Too scared you'll lose to take me up on the offer?"

Adrenaline pounded in my ears. I wanted to wipe the smug smirk off his face as much as I wanted to win the league, but I'd promised Scarlett I was done.

I won't race anymore. I promise.

My teammates' curious stares drilled into my cheek. I hadn't told them I'd retired from street racing, so I didn't blame them for being confused.

"Look at him," Lyle said. "He *is* scared. He'll lose the match, and he'll lose the race. There's no shame admitting it, Donovan. You gotta know when to call it quits."

The other Holchester players snickered.

Pride reared its ugly head, demanding action. A punch, a kick, an accepted challenge that'd shut them up and leave them eating dust in two weeks.

I wanted to feel the vibrations of the car and hear the triumphant roar of the engine as I sped past the finish line first.

Only the memory of Scarlett's tears stopped me.

I can't wake up every day wondering if that's the day your luck runs out, and I'll get a call saying you're gone. I can't lose you.

I swallowed the ball of rage in my throat.

My pride wasn't worth breaking my promise to her.

"I'm not going to jeopardize my career to satisfy *your* insecurities," I said coldly. "We don't need a race to determine who's better. We'll find out on the pitch soon." My smile could've frozen lava. "And Bocci? You've won *one* race against me ever, and that was because I let you win. I felt bad for you. That won't happen again. So I wouldn't be so quick to challenge others in something you're clearly not adept at."

I left him sputtering in the alley with the rest of the Holchester team.

My teammates followed me, their voices overlapping as they consoled me and talked amongst themselves.

Despite leaving with the last word, my heart continued to race from the confrontation. Blood roared in my ears as I tried to push the image of Bocci's gloating smirk out of my head.

I did the right thing by not rising to his bait.

Now, I just had to make bloody sure I beat him in two weeks' time.

CHAPTER 41

SCARLETT

ON THE BRIGHT SIDE, MY SUBSEQUENT CAST REHEARSALS for *Lorena* went a lot better than my first attempt. I could practically see Tamara unclenching her butt cheeks after every practice, and I didn't hear any more mutters from the rest of the staff.

On the not-so-bright side, I ached *all the time*. They weren't intense, debilitating aches like the day I learned about Yvette, but they weren't easily dismissed either.

No matter how many baths I took, massages I got, or Pilates sessions I indulged in, the pain was always there. It was so incessant and all-consuming that, on the morning of the Holchester match, four days after a particularly grueling rehearsal, I reached for my emergency packet.

If I didn't, I wouldn't be able to get through today's match, and I *had* to be there for Asher. It was Blackcastle versus Holchester. I couldn't miss it. However, the thought of sitting in Markovic Stadium for two plus hours without help made my body revolt, so I took a pain pill and prayed it would be enough.

I was already pushing myself too hard with the extra practices on top of cast rehearsals. I knew that. But the staff showcase wasn't *just* a staff showcase. It was my redemption to myself, and the pressure to nail the performance was worse than when I'd danced at the Royal Opera with the actual royal family in attendance.

I just needed to hold out for another two and a half months. After that, I could rest.

"Scarlett, do you want another drink?" Brooklyn's voice brought me out of my thoughts. "We have time for another round or two before I have to be at the stadium. Gotta support Dad and all that."

I spun around, my heart ricocheting in my chest. "What?"

"Another drink," she repeated as she entered the kitchen. "I can do a virgin mojito or a virgin daiquiri. Up to you."

"Mojito. Please." I forced a smile.

I'd kept my escalating fatigue and discomfort a secret from my friends and Asher. I didn't want them to worry when they were already under so much stress—Asher with the new season, Brooklyn with her internship, and Carina with her endless second job search.

If only keeping secrets wasn't as exhausting as practice.

"I still can't believe you're Frank Armstrong's daughter and that you *hid* it from us." Carina came in behind Brooklyn with an empty glass and a plate of crisps. "But you got us VIP seats for the match, so you're forgiven. All hail nepotism."

Brooklyn laughed.

We were pre-gaming at my flat before the match this afternoon. It was too early to drink (though some would argue it was *never* too early to drink), so we'd whipped up mocktails and noshed on several meals' worth of snacks.

"Sorry again for not telling you guys earlier," Brooklyn said, a tinge of guilt coloring her voice. "But people get kind of weird when they find out who my father is. They think they can use me to get access to the players or something even though I've never met half of them before my internship." Brooklyn wrinkled her nose. "I guess I should've known that wouldn't be a problem with you guys, given your ties to Asher and Vincent."

"Don't feel bad. I understand." I tried to ignore the prickles of pain in my leg. "I'm the same way about Vincent."

I was taken aback when I first learned about Brooklyn's family tie to Blackcastle, but I wasn't mad at her for not divulging the information. We hadn't known each other for that long, and I hadn't asked about her background. When I did bring it up, she easily confirmed the truth, so I didn't bear her any ill will.

The prickles intensified.

I sat down at the kitchen table, trying to pay attention to my friends' conversation while simultaneously trying not to throw up. I felt a little lightheaded, though that might be from the drinks.

Brooklyn *said* they were mocktails, but I wouldn't put it past her to slip a splash of rum into the glasses.

I scrolled through my phone for a distraction and pulled up my last set of messages with Asher.

> Good luck with the match today

> Can't wait to see you kick ass on the pitch ❤

ASHER

> Can't wait to see you, period

ASHER

> We'll celebrate later tonight. Just the two of us ☺

A bubble of anticipation floated past my aches. Asher and I didn't see each other in person as often as we did over the summer, but we exchanged daily texts and calls. It was almost as good as face-to-face interactions.

Almost.

Despite the exhaustion weighing on my limbs, I was excited to spend some time alone with him tonight. He always recharged me.

"Maybe I should become a Premier League intern," Carina mused. "But I'm guessing internships don't pay much."

"Afraid not," Brooklyn said apologetically. "But if you need someone to whip up a personalized nutrition plan, I'm your girl." She handed me my alcohol-free mojito and glanced at the clock. "*Shit*. I didn't realize it was so late already. I have to go. Traffic is going to be killer because of the match."

"Ugh, I have to go too. I have a tutoring session in half an hour." In the absence of a steady side gig, Carina occasionally tutored secondary school students in maths. "Scarlett, we'll see you at the match later?"

"Yep." I forced myself to stand and help as we piled the empty glasses and dishes into the sink. The prickles shot up to my hips and down to my toes. "You guys go ahead. I'll take care of the dishes later."

Brooklyn frowned. "Are you sure?"

I nodded. I loved my friends, but I *needed* to lie down as soon as possible. My energy was running dangerously low, and it was barely noon.

It was a testament to my acting skills that they didn't question me or pick up on the sweat drenching my back.

After they left, I collapsed into a chair again. It didn't seem like the pain pill was working. If it was, why did I—

Someone knocked on the door.

"Scarlett?" Brooklyn's voice drifted through the cheap wood. "I'm so sorry, but I think I left my bag in the kitchen. Can I grab it?"

A headache crept from the base of my skull up to my temples.

I scanned the kitchen until my eyes snagged on the purple tote sitting on the chair across from mine.

"Coming!" I yelled. My voice sounded unnaturally scratchy.

I blinked away the spots in my vision and grabbed her bag. I walked out of the kitchen and into the living room, my steps sluggish. My flat had never seemed so endless.

I faltered beneath a wave of wooziness, but I shook it off and soldiered on. I just needed to make it to the door and hand Brooklyn her bag. Then I could lie down, close my eyes, and *breathe*.

It was a sound plan in theory, and it almost succeeded—that was, until my body decided it'd had enough of my plans and mutinied.

It seemed to happen in slow motion.

The bag slipped from my grasp.

My legs buckled.

My vision blurred.

And I crashed to the floor, my mind stretching out the fall so long it almost seemed graceful.

Somewhere in the distance, I heard renewed pounding on the door and a voice infused with panic. "Scarlett, what was that noise? Are you okay? Scarlett!"

I wanted to reply, but I was so tired, and my mind was too jumbled.

The only thing I could do was give in to gravity and—

A fresh spear of pain lanced through my head. I'd hit something on my way down.

I *felt* it, the impact reverberating and amplifying and consuming until there was nothing left except agony and exhaustion and finally, blissfully, oblivion.

CHAPTER 42

ASHER

I SPENT THE MORNING OF THE HOLCHESTER MATCH prepping my go-to match day meal—a high-carb, high-protein mix of whole grain pasta, grilled chicken, and salad with a hard-boiled egg on the side—and listening to my pregame playlist.

I never worked out the day of a match, but mental preparation was as important as physical conditioning. Over the years, I'd curated my playlist to include only the songs that motivated and calmed me in equal measure.

It looped back to the first song as I tossed my lucky boots into my playing kit. I hadn't played in them since the halfway line goal that put me on the map, but I carried them with me to every match. Call me superstitious, but I credited many of the impossible goals I'd made to their help.

They were the boots that started it all, and they were going to take me all the way to a World Cup championship.

A thrill of anticipation streaked through my blood. It wasn't match time yet, but I couldn't wait to wipe the smirks off Bocci's and

Lyle's faces when we crushed them today. Our team was stronger and more cohesive than ever, and if we played our cards right, we'd be hoisting the Premier League trophy at the end of the season.

Holchester may be the reigning champions, but that would only make the taste of victory that much sweeter.

I glanced at my watch. *Fuck.* I needed to leave soon if I wanted to avoid traffic and get to the stadium in time.

I grabbed my playing kit and headed to the entryway. I'd just locked the door behind me when my phone rang. I didn't recognize the number, so I let it roll to voicemail.

Bloody telemarketers. How did they get my unlisted number?

I made a mental note to ask Sloane to double check if my private contact information was leaked anywhere. Stalkers were real, and I didn't want random people blowing up my phone with weird calls.

I made it to my car when my phone rang again. And again. And again. All from the same number.

A slice of worry wedged into my chest. Telemarketers didn't usually call this many times in a row from the same number, did they?

It could be an emergency, and someone I knew was calling from a stranger's phone. Was it my mother? Did my father have a heart attack again? I hadn't talked to him in the past two months. My mother said he was doing fine during our calls, but anything could happen.

I was in a time crunch, but I answered the call anyway.

"Hello?" I tucked the phone between my ear and shoulder as I tossed my duffel into the passenger seat.

I climbed into the driver's side, my chest tightening with worry.

"Asher, it's Brooklyn." The strain in her voice had me straightening immediately. The worry compounded, spreading from my chest to my throat. "I tried calling Vincent, but his phone's off, and I—"

"What happened?" I demanded. I didn't have time for a detailed breakdown of what she did before she called me.

Brooklyn wouldn't reach out this close to match time unless something was terribly wrong.

My mind spun gruesome images of Scarlett lying somewhere, injured or...

Bile climbed up my throat.

When Brooklyn didn't answer immediately, I clutched the steering wheel with impatient white knuckles. *"What's wrong?"*

"It's Scarlett." Her voice sounded tiny and far-off beneath the sudden thunder of my pulse. "She's in the hospital."

The drive from my house to the hospital should've taken forty minutes.

I made it there in twenty flat.

I might've followed the traffic rules or I might've broken them. I had no bloody clue. The entire drive was a blur, propelled by panic and the echo of Brooklyn's words.

She's in the hospital.

She didn't give me details other than Scarlett collapsed at home. Luckily, she'd been with her at the time and called 999.

She said Scarlett wasn't in life-threatening danger, but that didn't ease the knots in my chest. I barely breathed until I reached the hospital, but I still had the presence of mind to alert Sloane about the situation.

For once, she didn't warn me about "staying out of trouble." She simply said she would take care of everything on her end, including calling Coach and the hospital, and that she was on standby for new developments.

When I arrived, a waiting staff member ushered me in through a side exit and up to Scarlett's floor. I wasn't family, but apparently she was conscious and gave them permission to let me see her.

She's conscious, which means she's okay.

She's okay.

She's okay.

The mantra thudded in rhythm with my pulse.

Conscious wasn't dead. It didn't mean she was doing bloody cartwheels, but at least she was alive.

After a seeming eternity, the lift doors pinged open. I sprinted into the hall, leaving my escort behind. I didn't need them to tell me which room Scarlett was in; I could see Carina and Brooklyn standing outside, their faces pale with worry.

Carina opened her mouth, but I didn't wait to hear what she had to say before I barreled into the hospital room.

I didn't care if that was rude. I *needed* to see Scarlett with my own eyes, or I would fucking combust.

The door shut behind me. I came to an abrupt halt, my chest heaving as I stared at her.

She lay half propped up in the bed, her body swaddled in a loose white hospital gown that was almost the same shade as her pale, waxen complexion. She was hooked up to several machines, and gauze dressing covered half her forehead.

She blinked in visible shock when she saw me. "Asher?" Her voice was barely audible.

My lungs twisted, cutting off the free flow of oxygen.

"Hi, darling." I swallowed as I approached her bedside. "Next time you want to get a hold of me, a call would suffice, yeah?"

Scarlett's smile was a shadow of its usual self.

The vise in my chest constricted further. I'd seen her tired, I'd seen her in pain after a flare-up, but I'd never seen her look *this* fragile and exhausted. She was always so vibrant and full of life, and the evidence of her mortality instilled a bone-deep terror in me.

"You know me. I like a little drama." She coughed. "How did you find out I was here?"

"Brooklyn called me. She tried calling your brother too, but his phone was off."

Did they get through to him? Did he know his sister was in the hospital, or was Coach holding off on telling him until after the match? He should be at the stadium by now, but if he *did* know what happened, he'd be here. Vincent's care for Scarlett was one of the things I'd never questioned about him.

"He always turns his phone off before a match. Said it's too distracting," Scarlett murmured.

I smoothed her hair back from her forehead, careful not to exert too much pressure lest I aggravate her injury. "What happened?"

"Nothing. I got dizzy and hit my head."

"That's not nothing." My hand lingered over the gauze. "How much does it hurt?" I asked quietly.

Not just the injury, but *everything*.

Her silence said more than words could.

Jagged shards raked through my insides. My heart felt like cracked glass, its pieces held together only by the sound of Scarlett's breaths.

I *hated* this. I hated the asshole whose car rammed into hers, I hated that medical technology wasn't advanced enough to take away her pain, and most of all, I hated how helpless I was.

Despite all my money and all my fame, I couldn't do a thing.

"It's not too bad." Her voice grew fainter. "I pushed a little too hard during rehearsals, that's all. I'll be fine after some rest."

My shoulders stiffened.

Her feelings toward the showcase ran deeper than the mere act of performance, and I had to tread carefully with what I said next.

"The showcase is in December," I reminded her gently. "You have two months of rehearsals left."

Based on the stubborn jut of her chin, I knew it was a lost cause before she even responded. "I'll be more careful in the future. I can make it to December."

Frustration swelled. She was already killing herself to prove she could make it through rehearsals like everyone else. I couldn't bear the thought of seeing her go through two more months of this.

Her collapse wasn't the result of one bad day; it had to be an accumulation of them. I wasn't sure what hurt more—the fact that she hid it from me or the fact that I hadn't been there to notice.

My schedule was always packed during the season, and we'd been prepared to spend more time apart than over the summer, but dammit, I should've *been* there.

"I'll always take care of you." I cupped her cheek, my chest aching. "But promise me you'll also take care of yourself."

Scarlett's eyes gleamed with emotion, and she responded with the tiniest of nods.

"I'll leave so you can get some rest." I leaned down and brushed her lips with mine. If I had the choice, I'd stay by her side until she was discharged, but that would only distract her. She needed to sleep. "I'll be outside if you need me."

I stood and turned to leave.

"Wait. I just saw the time." Scarlett's voice gained a modicum of strength along with panic. "*Your match*. You have to go. It's starting in—"

"I'm not going." I'd already instructed Sloane to call Coach and tell him what happened. He would give me absolute hell for it later, but I'd deal with that when the time came.

"What?" Her eyes widened. "But it's against Holchester. It's... Asher. You *have* to go. I'm fine." She coughed again, her breathing growing labored. "There's no point in you staying here when I'm sleeping."

"There is a point." My jaw tightened. "When Brooklyn called and told me you were in the hospital...there are no words to describe how I felt. It was like the world had collapsed and buried me beneath its rubble. And even though she told me you were alive and that you weren't in serious danger, I couldn't think, couldn't even fucking *breathe* until I saw it with my own two eyes." I shook my head, my throat taut with emotion. "If I left now and went to the match, it wouldn't matter. I'd spend the entire time thinking about you. I'd be a liability more than anything else."

Prior to Scarlett, I would've crawled through a sea of broken glass before I missed a match. Football was the most important thing in my life. It always had been, and I thought it always would be.

But I'd finally found something—some*one*—that I cared about more.

It didn't matter that I'd spent weeks anticipating today's match against Holchester or that my pride was on the line. It didn't matter that Coach was probably furious with me and that the fans would be too.

Scarlett was more important than all of that, and I couldn't, *wouldn't* leave her side as long as she was here.

A tear slipped down her cheek. "I'm sorry," she said, her voice small.

My heart squeezed for the millionth time that day. "Don't be sorry, darling." I rubbed the tear away with my thumb. "It's not your fault."

"But—"

"No. I *chose* to come here, and I chose to stay here. Do not feel guilty about me missing the match. That's my problem to deal with. You just focus on resting so we can get you out of here as soon as possible. I'd hate to subject you to hospital food for longer than necessary."

Scarlett's laugh came out as a wisp of a sound, but it was enough for me.

Our conversation must've spent her energy because she didn't protest further. Her eyes fluttered closed, and I waited until her breathing settled into a steady rhythm before I stepped into the hall.

Brooklyn and Carina were huddled over the former's phone, wearing identical masks of apprehension.

They raised their heads when they heard the door open, and my temporary relief from seeing Scarlett morphed into fresh concern.

"What's going on?" I asked.

They exchanged glances.

"I hate to be the bearer of bad news twice in one day, but…" Brooklyn handed me her phone. "You should see this."

I took it, and my skin immediately went ice-cold.

Someone had captured a video of me arriving at the hospital and sprinting toward the entrance. Going through the side was more private than going through the front, but I guess it still wasn't private enough.

Whoever took the video had uploaded it to social media seven minutes ago, and it already had over fifty thousand views and hundreds of comments.

Once the paps picked up on this, it wouldn't take them long to figure out who I was here to see. After that, it'd take an even shorter leap for them to connect the dots of our relationship.

I'd missed a huge match against Holchester for her. There was only one reason why I'd do that.

"I'm sorry," Carina said. She must've come to the same conclusions I had. "Let us know if there's anything we can do."

"No. It's..." I scrubbed a hand over my face. "No. We'll deal with it. It'll be fine. Thank you."

It's not fine. I batted away the voice that told me our secret, the secret Scarlett and I had worked so hard to keep for so long, would soon be out of the bag in the most public way possible.

One thing at a time.

The news hadn't broken *yet*. Until then, I needed to call Sloane—a quick scan of my messages revealed she'd already seen the video— then call Coach, then find the doctor and figure out a way to make Scarlett's recovery more comfortable.

I didn't know how long she needed to stay at the hospital, but she bloody sure wasn't staying in that small, sad room for longer than a night.

I made my calls in a quiet corner near Scarlett's room. Sloane was, as expected, on top of the impending relationship leak. She wasn't thrilled about the timing or the circumstances, but I think she was just glad I wasn't making headlines for racing anymore.

My call to Coach went to voicemail. I wasn't surprised since warm-ups for the match had already started, but I needed to apologize to him in my own words, so I left a short message. He could be livid with me in person later.

Finally, I spoke with the doctor, who said Scarlett could be discharged as soon as tomorrow if her condition remained steady.

That was a relief, but I was already worrying about next week's rehearsal. And the week after that. And the week after that. Would Lavinia let her remain the lead if she found out about the hospitalization? With Yvette gone, she didn't have other options for the Lorena role, but I couldn't see the stern, rule-abiding director letting what happened today slide. She wasn't warm and fuzzy, but she cared about her staff's well-being.

My head pounded with a million worries stacked on top of each other.

While Scarlett slept, I kept an eye on both the news and the match. Thankfully, we were up by one, but I was more focused on the brief close-ups of Vincent's face than the actual gameplay.

I tried to read his expressions and figure out if he knew about Scarlett yet. The video of me at the hospital had been uploaded when the players were already on the pitch, so I doubted he was aware of that. But had he turned on his phone or spoken with Coach before the match?

It was impossible to tell since Vincent always looked like a moody son of a bitch during a match.

Coach, on the other hand, was visibly angry. If he clenched his jaw any harder during the few camera shots of him, he'd shatter a molar. Gallagher, my sub, was doing a damn good job, but it didn't matter.

There'd be hell to pay for my last-minute decision to skip the match later. It was technically a personal emergency, but since no one was dead or dying, I doubted he'd sympathize much.

"Asher, go get something to eat," Brooklyn said. "Scarlett's still asleep. She's not going to, I don't know, roll over and fall onto the floor."

"We'll keep an eye on her," Carina added.

I nearly protested, but we were all tired and hungry and cranky after hours in the hospital. I didn't want to get into an argument with Scarlett's friends, but I would also rather chew off my hand than eat the cafeteria food.

Instead, I ducked into the loo and bought a pack of pretzels and water on my way back. I ate them next to the vending machine, grateful for the energy boost.

When I returned to the hall outside Scarlett's room, only Brooklyn was there. She jumped up when she saw me.

"Any new developments while I was gone?" I asked.

I didn't expect her to say yes, but a nervous expression crossed her face at my question.

"Well, Carina's in the bathroom, and Scarlett's awake again."

"Already?" She'd looked so exhausted when I talked to her that I expected her to sleep through the night. Did something happen? Was she in so much pain she couldn't sleep?

"Yes. But, um, you might not want to go in there," Brooklyn said when I moved toward the door.

It was too late. I'd already cracked it open.

"Why…" My words died in my throat.

Because Scarlett wasn't alone. Standing beside her bed, his back to me, was Vincent. I'd recognize that buzz cut and number four kit anywhere. He must've come straight from the match.

He turned, his face darkening when he saw me.

Fuck. I hadn't seen any news about me and Scarlett yet, but considering I'd missed my most anticipated match of the season so far to be by her side, I guess he'd pieced the puzzle together faster than the paps.

I held up my hands as he stormed toward me. "Vincent, I—"

I didn't get a chance to finish my sentence before he hauled his fist back and slammed it into my face.

CHAPTER 43

SCARLETT

IT TURNED OUT HOSPITALS FROWNED UPON FISTFIGHTS breaking out on their premises, especially when one of their patients tried to hobble out of bed and stop it.

I wasn't stupid enough to try and throw myself into the middle of Vincent and Asher's fight, but I needed to do *something*. God knew I didn't have the strength to yell like I normally would.

Unfortunately, I also didn't have the strength to sit up straight, much less walk anywhere. My head made it about four inches above my pillow before sheer fatigue dragged it back down.

"Stop." The word scraped up my throat. "*Stop.*"

Neither of them heard me over their grunts, curses, and the sound of fists striking flesh.

Once Vincent threw the first punch, all bets were off. Asher had retaliated, and now the two of them were grappling five feet from me like Neanderthals without impulse control.

A migraine blossomed at the base of my skull.

Rest and medical attention had soothed the worst of my pain, but

I still hurt all over, and my head throbbed where I'd hit it against the corner of my coffee table. Thankfully, the angle at which I fell meant I'd only suffered a flesh wound and mild concussion; it could've been much worse, all things considered.

However, seeing two of the people I cared about most beat each other up in my hospital room was *not* conducive to a speedy recovery.

"You bastard!" Vincent swung at Asher again. "You lied to me!"

"We were going to tell you." Asher ducked the hit. "*This* is why we didn't!"

"You—"

The door swung open again, cutting off Vincent's response. The doctor rushed in, followed by Carina, Brooklyn, and one of the nurses.

Screams, shouts, and swear words flew through the air with abandon.

I wanted to scream with them. I wanted to stand, yell, do anything except be an observer of my own life, but I couldn't summon the strength.

The migraine spread to my eyes, my temples, my jaw. *Everywhere.*

"*Enough!*" My doctor finally wrestled the situation under control. Her eyes flashed with fury. "Everyone, *out.*"

"But—"

"You can't—"

"She doesn't—"

"I don't want to hear it! I have a patient resting in here"—she pointed at me—"and you are in here *fist fighting?* You should be glad I don't call security. Now get *out!*" For such a kind-looking old lady, Dr. Ambani had one hell of a set of pipes.

It was as if a fog had cleared, and they realized I was in the room for the first time since Asher opened the door.

Vincent and Asher swung toward me with stricken expressions.

Guilt etched horrified lines across their faces, but the doctor didn't give them an opportunity to apologize.

She jabbed her finger toward the door, and they shuffled out, their heads hanging in shame.

I tried to say something before they left, but the words didn't make it past my lips.

I'd sapped the remainder of my energy talking to Asher and then Vincent when they first arrived. It was a miracle I could keep my eyes open.

Dr. Ambani and the nurse bustled to my side. There was poking and prodding and low murmurs exchanged between them, but I couldn't make out what they were saying.

A host of sentiments crowded my throat.

I wanted to tell Asher how touched I was that he'd skipped the match for me and that everything would be okay. Our secret was out, which meant the worst had passed.

I wanted to apologize to Vincent for keeping our relationship from him and reassure him that he didn't have to worry about me. That this wasn't a Rafael 2.0 situation and that I was happier with Asher than I'd ever been.

I wanted to remind them not to let today ruin their fragile truce because they were so much better as friends than as enemies.

I wanted to say a lot of things, but they would have to wait.

My grasp on consciousness slipped. Steel anchors dragged my eyelids closed, and darkness descended, shutting out the rest of the world.

ASHER

I let Vincent have the first punch, but after that, the gloves were off. I felt guilty about lying to him, but I didn't feel guilty enough about it to serve as his docile punching bag.

By the time the doctor kicked us out of the room, we were both worse for wear. A cut on my lip dripped blood into my mouth, and a dark bruise mottled his jaw.

I was ashamed of fighting with him when Scarlett was lying right there, but when Vincent swung at me, my fight or flight had kicked in and blacked out everything except self-defense.

Dr. Ambani and the nurse stayed in the room while we glared at each other in the hall.

It was either a slow day or the hospital staff had been warned not to linger near us because the corridor was empty save for two nurses at the far end. There was no one around to eavesdrop or record us except Carina and Brooklyn, who appeared shell-shocked by the rapid escalation in events.

Vincent's fists clenched and unclenched. "How long has this been going on?"

By *this*, I assumed he meant my relationship with Scarlett.

The truth was already out. I might as well tell him the *whole* truth. "Since July."

"*July*?" I swore I saw steam billowing from his ears in clouds of unchecked anger. "You've been sneaking around together behind my back for *almost three months*?"

"Like I said, we didn't tell you because we knew you would react like this." Frustration snapped its teeth, lending my words more bite than I'd intended. I should give Vincent more grace considering he had to deal with the double whammy bombshell of our relationship and his sister's hospitalization, but I was too stressed and worn-out to give a damn. "For the record, we didn't *want* to date or keep it a secret from you after you returned to London. It sort of just…happened."

It was a lame excuse, but this wasn't the time nor place to explain the intricacies of the past three months.

Vincent didn't appear to be listening anyway. His attention had dropped to my trainers (I never wore my cleats to the stadium before a match). Disbelief bloomed across his face. "Were *you* the guy in my sister's shower when I dropped by her flat over the summer?"

Fuck.

"Technically," I said with great caution. "I was in the bath."

"Christ!" A resulting string of French swear words echoed in the sterile hallway. "She told me it was someone from RAB!"

I cleared my throat. "Also technically, I *was* someone from RAB. At least for the summer."

Vincent's eye twitched. He looked like he wanted to swing at me again, but a sharp voice interjected.

"Stop it!" Brooklyn stepped between us. She and Carina had been observing so quietly from the sidelines I almost forgot they were there. "*Look* at you two. Grown men acting like children in a hospital, of all places. Are you not ashamed?"

Crimson streaked across the tops of Vincent's cheekbones. "Don't—"

"Don't what? Call you out on your bullshit?" She crossed her arms, her face the picture of stubbornness. He was at least a foot taller than her, but she appeared to tower over him even as she glared up at him. "Your *sister* is lying in there"—she pointed at the closed door to Scarlett's room—"trying to rest, and one of the first things you do when you arrive is start a fucking brawl in her hospital room. She's stressed enough. She doesn't need her brother and her boyfriend making things worse. And you."

Brooklyn whirled around to jab a finger at me. "*You* should've known better than to indulge Vincent's bullshit. There's a difference between self-defense and actively engaging in a fistfight. No *wonder* my dad gets so grumpy when either of you comes up in conversation. I'm surprised you haven't driven him into an early grave yet considering he has to deal with your selfish, childish antics every day!"

You could've heard a pin drop in the silence.

We gaped at her, too stunned about getting dressed down by someone half our size to respond immediately. Behind her, Carina smirked, looking like she was enjoying our discomfort a little too much.

But Brooklyn wasn't wrong. We *were* acting selfish and childish. The doctor had pretty much said the same thing, but the way Brooklyn laid it out struck home.

We were so caught up in our pride and our need to win this stupid argument that we hadn't considered how our actions would affect Scarlett.

A fresh wave of guilt doused the testosterone in the hall, leaving me cold and shame faced. Across from me, Vincent shoved his hands into his pockets, his face red.

If I really wanted to get technical, I was the one at fault for convincing Scarlett to delay telling Vincent about us. His anger was understandable, but when he came at me, my knee-jerk instinct had been to go on offense.

"*We* are going to stay here and keep an eye on Scarlett." Brooklyn gestured to herself and Carina. "You two talk it out somewhere else. I don't want your negative vibes poisoning this area."

"Yeah?" Vincent's eyes narrowed. He obviously didn't appreciate getting bossed around. "How are you going to make us leave?"

Her smile dripped with sugar. "Stay and find out."

They stood toe to toe, their expressions stamped with defiance. The air sparked with challenge, but after a tense, drawn-out stare down, Vincent jerked his gaze away from her and stormed down the hall. He didn't say a word as he left.

"That's what I thought." Brooklyn arched an eyebrow at me. "Your turn, lover boy."

I didn't argue—I owed her for telling me about Scarlett's hospitalization and for slapping some sense into us, figuratively speaking.

I headed down the hall after Vincent, and we walked in silence until we reached a quiet alcove next to the vending machines. The bulky black boxes blocked us from view of the main hall and afforded us a small degree of privacy.

We leaned side by side against the wall, our bodies vibrating with lingering resentment.

"I can't believe you're dating my sister." Vincent stared straight ahead, his jaw grinding. "I *knew* you would try to pull that shit while I was gone. I was a fool to think otherwise. I never should've left her alone with you."

"You think I *wanted* this to happen when I first found out who she was? She's a DuBois. I thought you all sucked."

Vincent snorted.

"I told you, none of this was planned," I said. "It just happened."

"Right. You just *happened* to fall into bed with my sister." He turned to face me, his cheekbones taut with suspicion. "Did you do it to get back at me? So you could rub your relationship in my face?"

My temper ignited again. "First, we didn't just *fall into bed*. Second, not everything is about you," I snapped. "If I wanted to rub it in your face, I would've told you the second you were back in London. Hell, I would've sent a carrier pigeon to break the news to you while you were gone. *That* would make sense. Trying to hide it from you doesn't. Of course, I can't blame you for not connecting those dots considering your brain is the size of a peanut and your common sense is floating at the bottom of the Seine somewhere."

Vincent's nostrils flared. "Fuck you!"

"Fuck *you*!" I was so tired of his shit. I felt bad about fighting with him in front of Scarlett, but she wasn't here right now. "You might think the world revolves around you, but Scarlett is her own person. She confides in you because she respects you—God knows why—and she cares about you, not because she *has* to. And I think you're doing her a great bloody disservice to insinuate I'm only interested in her because she's your sister and not because she's incredible on her own. She's smart, beautiful, talented, funny…believe me when I say her relation to you is her biggest con." I paused. "That and her cooking."

Vincent stared at me, at a loss for words.

Several beats passed before he finally responded. "She is a shit cook," he muttered. "That's why we always order takeaway when we eat together."

I allowed myself a tiny scoff as we lapsed into another brooding silence.

My pulse pounded from the force of my rant, but now that I'd gotten it off my chest, I could think more clearly. Our arguments were great for blowing off steam, but they weren't getting us anywhere because they didn't address the root of the issue.

"Look," I said. "I know I'm not your first choice when it comes to boyfriends for Scarlett—"

"You're not my second, third, or fourth choice either."

I ignored his petulant grumble and continued. "But I care about her more than anyone else in the world, and I don't want you to blame her for any of this. She hated lying to you, but she was so worried about your career that she didn't want to just drop the news on you."

Vincent's brows drew together. "What the hell does your

relationship have to do with my career?"

"She was worried that if you found out, it would make things worse between us and affect our game. She knows what Coach said about benching us if we couldn't work together. She didn't want to add to the problem."

He huffed out a long breath. "Right."

The initial thoughtless, instinct-driven flames of our wrath had died down, leaving us drained. Brooklyn had basically sent us to time-out, but we'd needed it.

"I don't doubt you care about her," Vincent said. "The fact you skipped a match against *Holchester* to be with her proves that. But this isn't about your feelings toward her. It's about honesty. You both lied to me." His mouth pressed into a thin line. "When we were at the Angry Boar after the charity match, you let me go on and on about how I appreciate you not hitting on her, and you didn't say a fucking thing."

"I know." Guilt seeped through me. "I'm sorry."

It was my first time apologizing to Vincent. It was easier than I thought it would be because I meant it. If I were in his shoes, I'd be upset too.

"We were going to tell you the week you returned to London," I said. "But you and I were starting to get along, and after your speech at the Angry Boar, I was even more worried that you wouldn't...handle the news well. I was the one who convinced Scarlett to postpone our talk. I didn't want to ruin our truce so close to the start of the season."

Looking back, we could've handled the situation better. *Communicated* better. But these things were clearer in hindsight, and it was hard to make the right decision in the moment.

"You should've just told me," Vincent growled. "I'm the captain of our team. I care about the season and about winning as much as you do, if not more. I would've handled it *better* if you told me to my face like a man instead of letting me figure it out myself while my sister's in the fucking hospital."

"I should've," I admitted. "But it's too late for that now."

He let out another snort. "You think?"

More silence.

The hum of the vending machines buzzed through the air, muffling the faint voices and footsteps from the main hall.

"Did we win?" I asked after several minutes of wordlessness. "The match." I hadn't checked the final score before he showed up.

Vincent shook his head. "Draw. Two-two."

"Fuck."

"Yeah."

We exhaled our frustrations with twin sighs.

"Coach is absolutely furious with you, by the way." Vincent sounded far too happy about that. "He's going to flay you alive the next time he sees you."

I grimaced. I foresaw a lot of punishing runs in my future, but I didn't care. Much.

"That's fine," I said. "I'll survive."

"You always do." A trace of bitterness ran beneath Vincent's voice and reminded me of his reasons for not liking me. "You're like Teflon."

"Trust me." I flashed back to the thousands of awful messages I received after I announced my transfer to Blackcastle. "I'm not as invincible as you think."

"Maybe not, but let me think you are. It's easier to hate you again that way." He rubbed a hand over his mouth. "No matter what I did, I was always compared to you. We don't even play the same position, yet there you were, always mentioned in the same breath as me when

I know I couldn't have gotten away with half the shit you did."

"If it makes you feel better," I said after a long pause. "You have a World Cup, and I don't."

Vincent barked out a short laugh. "It does, actually."

As recently as yesterday, I wouldn't have dreamed of joking about the World Cup. Seeing victory slip from my grasp during the last tournament would *always* be one of the defining moments of my life and career. I would never forget it.

But my earlier fight with Vincent allowed me to vent some of that pent-up anger, and our truce the past few weeks had softened the jagged edges of my resentment. He'd stood up for me against Bocci and Lyle, and like it or not, we were on the same team. Even if we weren't, I'd have to interact with him regularly because of Scarlett.

All that made the World Cup incident easier to swallow. It really was time to put it behind us—but that didn't mean I wasn't going to get my revenge the next time we played against each other.

"Don't worry, though," I said. "That'll change in two years."

The next World Cup was bearing down fast. Qualifiers for Europe started in the spring, and I could already *taste* the thrill. There was no way England wouldn't make it into the tournament. Our national team was the best it'd been in over a decade.

"We'll see about that," Vincent scoffed, but his words lacked bite. This time, he was the one who paused before continuing. "I'm not proud of what I did. If I could go back, I would've done things different, but the past is the past. We can't change it."

I closed my eyes. Old memories resurfaced, as vivid as if they were happening right at that moment.

The shrill of the whistle. The cheers and boos of the crowd. The smell of grass and sweat, and my sheer, utter disbelief when the ref whipped out a red card.

It was the closest I'd come to punching someone on the pitch in my entire career.

Every time I trained, every time someone criticized me and I thought I couldn't keep going, I relived that moment. I channeled my grievances and used them as fuel not only to be better, but to be the *best*. And it worked.

The red card had affected the trajectory of my career in many ways, and as much as I'd despised Vincent for it, not all of the consequences had been bad. It'd pushed me to where I was today.

"No, we can't change the past," I said. "The same way Scarlett and I can't go back and tell you before today. But what's done is done. There's no use dwelling on it."

Honestly, I was relieved our relationship was out in the open. The circumstances of the reveal weren't great, and Vincent's first response had been less than ideal. However, we'd needed that fight. We had too much bad blood for it to be smoothed over with words.

Vincent blew out a deep sigh. "No. I guess not."

We didn't say anything else. Instead, we took the moment to simply sit and acknowledge the closing of one long, rocky chapter in our shared history.

Coach, Holchester, the paps, the public's inevitable discovery of my relationship with Scarlett and the ensuing fallout...that was the future.

The future would always be there, but today, we'd finally laid the past to rest.

CHAPTER 44

SCARLETT

THE HOSPITAL KEPT ME OVERNIGHT AND DISCHARGED me the next evening.

That same night, an hour before I was discharged, news of my relationship with Asher broke.

Football superstar ditches match for his hospitalized girlfriend!

The thin line between love and hate: Asher Donovan revealed to be dating his biggest rival's sister!

Who is Scarlett DuBois, Asher Donovan's secret girlfriend?

It was pure chaos. My phone blew up with so many calls and texts that the battery couldn't handle it, and it died before I made it home. Paps swarmed the hospital, hoping for a money shot, a sound bite, or even better, a video of Asher with me.

Fortunately, Sloane had flown in from New York last night to deal with the situation on the ground. She, along with hospital security, was able to usher us out a side exit and into a discreet black SUV without anyone stopping us.

A familiar man with salt-and-pepper hair waited in the driver's seat.

"Good evening, miss." Earl smiled at me in the rearview mirror, but his eyes were filled with concern.

"Good evening, Earl." I mustered a half-hearted smile in response. I was happy to see him again, but it was hard to scrounge up much enthusiasm when my life had careened off the rails in the past hour.

The lingering consequences of my collapse didn't help. Thanks to plenty of rest and medical attention, my pain wasn't as debilitating as it was yesterday, but it was still *there*. It was in my muscles, my joints, and my bones—and in certain moments, it felt like it was in my very soul, tearing me apart from the inside out.

Dr. Ambani wanted to keep me in the hospital for an extra day, but I'd insisted on going home. I wanted the comfort of my flat, and there wasn't anything more they could do for me that I couldn't do at home.

Sloane stood next to the open car door, blocking me and Asher from the view of any passersby.

"Earl's taking you both to the Ashworth," she said, naming one of London's top luxury hotels. "I have to deal with the paps first, but I'll be in the car behind you. I've already briefed the hotel staff. When you arrive, the general manager and security will personally escort you to your suite."

"Wait." My heart climbed into my throat. "Why are we going to a hotel? I thought I was going home."

I didn't want to sleep in another strange bed.

"You can't go home. The place is swarming with press," Sloane said crisply. "So is Asher's house. The best thing you can do is lie low in a place where they can't find you. The Ashworth is the most discreet hotel in the city. They'll keep your presence a secret."

I flinched at the mental image of paps overrunning my quiet, tranquil neighborhood. It was my safe haven, and knowing that its sanctity had been breached felt more violating than any picture or video they could've snapped.

"It'll only be for the night," Asher said, ignoring Sloane's sharp glance. "We'll get you home tomorrow."

"*If* the situation improves," she caveated. "I've contacted a security company that'll assess the situation and implement measures as necessary, but that'll take time. I'll see you later at the hotel." She closed the door before we could ask more questions.

The cramps worsened. "How bad is it?" I asked as Earl pulled away from the curb.

I'd purposely avoided clicking on the links friends, coworkers, and random acquaintances had sent me since the news broke, but curiosity gnawed at my insides.

Asher hesitated. "It's not *too* bad," he said carefully. "Right now, it's mostly fact-based stories—if you define 'fact' loosely. Who you are, how we started dating, my history with Vincent. That sort of thing."

"But?"

"But it's early," he said with no small amount of reluctance. "The news just broke. I don't know what narrative the tabloids will spin in the upcoming weeks and months. They could tire of us before it gets really bad, or…"

"It could actually get really bad," I finished. I'd seen the way they tore public figures apart in the past. The thought of them doing the same to us made me want to throw up. "I can't believe we live in a world where people are *that* invested in others' relationships."

"A lot of people are deeply invested in a lot of strange things." Asher squeezed my hand. "Luckily, I have the best publicist to guide us through it."

"The scariest one too."

"That's why she's the best."

This time, my smile inched a tad higher. Having Sloane on our team did make me feel better. She was a professional. She knew what to do, right?

Fatigue weighed heavy on my limbs. I'd slept for nearly sixteen hours straight, but I was still groggy and prone to fits of exhaustion.

However, I clung to consciousness the best I could. I had a feeling this would be my last truly peaceful moment alone with Asher for a while.

"How's the public taking your absence from yesterday's match?" I asked.

Given the fanaticism of certain fans and the bitter rivalry between Blackcastle and Holchester, I dreaded their reaction to Asher skipping the match.

"Ironically, they seem to be taking it better now that they know *why* I missed the match," Asher said, his tone wry. "Of course, there's a vocal minority that's furious with me, but a majority of the internet thinks what I did is romantic."

"It *is* romantic." I reached between us and laced my fingers through his. His warmth traveled up my arm and settled in the vicinity of my heart. "But I'm sorry you missed it. I know how much it meant to you."

"I'm not," he said simply. "It doesn't mean as much as being with you."

Emotion tangled in my chest. I didn't trust myself to respond with words, so I squeezed his hand and looked out the window while I gathered my composure.

We had to pass by the hospital entrance to reach the main road. The SUV's tinted windows prevented anyone from seeing in, but that didn't stop the skitter of chills down my spine when I saw the crowd of paparazzi near the entrance. Armed with giant camera lenses and an air of rabid anticipation, they reminded me of an angry mob on the verge of hysteria.

And they were all there because of *us*.

Asher Donovan dating his biggest rival's sister would've been a story.

Asher Donovan having a secret relationship with his biggest rival's sister *and* skipping the first major match of the season to run to her hospital bedside? That was a sensation.

Bile sloshed in my stomach. I tore my eyes away from the spectacle and refocused on Asher.

"Have you talked to your parents?" I asked in an attempt to take my mind off the scrutiny awaiting us. I'd received a dozen voicemails from both my mother and father. I imagine his parents were equally concerned. However, based on what he'd told me about his father, the elder Donovan was probably more upset about his skipped match than anything else.

"Not yet." A grimace tugged at his lips. "That's an issue for tomorrow."

"At least you and Vincent made up." I tried to look for a silver lining. "If I'd known a few punches was all it took to heal your relationship, I would've tossed you two into a ring myself ages ago."

I'd hated their fight while it was happening, but it turned out for the best. I'm glad *one* good thing came out of this craptastic weekend.

Vincent wasn't here to see me off because Sloane pointed out that we needed *less* attention, not more. The fewer famous faces hanging around the hospital, the better.

"What can I say?" Asher's grimace morphed into a small smile. "Men are simple creatures."

"You mean Neanderthals."

"Basically."

We finally left the hospital grounds and pulled into traffic. Yellow from the streetlights and red from the surrounding taillights blurred into a giant, jumbled stream that matched the chaos of my thoughts.

The paps didn't know we were gone yet, but they would soon. After that...

This was the moment that'd kept me awake at night before Asher and I started dating. The moment when my life changed and was no longer my own.

It was one of the many reasons I'd been hesitant to get involved with him, but he'd proved time and again that none of those reasons mattered. My life hadn't truly been my own since I met him, and if I had to do it all over again, I wouldn't change a thing.

However, that didn't mean I wasn't scared of what was coming. It wasn't the scrutiny that unnerved me; it was the uncertainty.

Would the press paint us as heroes or villains? How deep into my life would they dig? Would they limit their attention to me, or would they go after everyone I worked and interacted with?

"Don't worry, darling." It was like Asher could read my mind. "We'll get through it together."

I nodded and swallowed the lump in my throat.

We'd spent the better part of the summer preparing for the storm. Well, the storm was here, and he was right: we'd get through it together.

We didn't have another choice.

When we arrived at the hotel, we made it to our suite without incident.

Sloane had sent someone to bring me extra clothes and essentials from my flat, so I wasn't stuck wearing the same outfit for God knew how long.

While Asher showered and I waited for my belongings to arrive, I called my parents back. I finally had the energy to talk to them, and I didn't want to compound their worries by being radio silent.

I checked in with my father first. He must've been waiting for my call because he picked up on the first ring when it usually took me several tries to reach him (he was a big believer in digital detoxes).

"Scarlett." His worried voice flowed over the line and made my eyes prickle with emotion. I hadn't realized how long it'd been since we actually *talked*. "How are you, *ma chérie*?"

"I'm fine. I just got out of the hospital." I explained the situation to him. "We're staying at the hotel until things with the press die down."

"The press." My father made a disgusted noise. His opinion of the press hovered just above his opinion of politicians (whom he despised) and below his opinion of fast food (which he considered an abomination). "The press are vultures," he said, switching fully to French. "It is their job to be as horrid as possible to get clicks. Don't listen to a thing they say."

"I'll try not to." I forced a smile even though he couldn't see me. "How are you feeling? Is your hip still bothering you?"

"It's okay now, but you know, it was so terrible over the summer." My father heaved a huge sigh, and despite the circumstances, my smile turned genuine. Jean-Paul DuBois was nothing if not dramatic. "Luckily, your brother was here to help, or I would've been stuck with the nurse by myself. Can you imagine? Me, alone with a stranger twenty-four-seven in *my* house? Bah!"

"Really?" I leaned deeper against the headboard. "Vincent said you quite liked the nurse after a while."

"What? He said what?" My father sounded flustered. "Don't listen to your brother. He should focus more on taking care of you and not about whether I *like* my nurse. That's what he's there for."

"He's here to play football, Dad, not take care of me," I said, glancing at the bathroom door. Asher was still in the shower. "I don't need taking care of. I'm an adult."

"An adult who was hospitalized and now has her picture all over the news." I flinched, and my father sighed again when I didn't answer. "I'm sorry if I sound harsh, *ma chérie,* but you must understand why I worry."

My throat clogged at way his voice softened. In his eyes, I was still his little girl, but he couldn't soothe all my hurts with a hug and a kiss anymore. That time had passed, and we both knew it.

"I understand, and I know I've made mistakes," I said. "But I'm fixing them. Don't worry too much about me, okay?"

"It's in a parent's nature to worry." Nevertheless, my father didn't press the subject. "If the attention gets to be too much, or if you need a break from the city, you can always come and stay with me. Paris is better than London, anyway."

Another smile flickered over my mouth. "Thank you. I'll visit you soon. Just…just not now, okay?" I couldn't run away to France and pretend my problems didn't exist, no matter how much I wanted to.

We spoke for another few minutes before I hung up, took a deep breath, and called my mother. As expected, she was beside herself.

"Oh, sweetheart," she said after I gave her the same summary I gave my father. She sounded like she'd been crying. "I know how much the showcase means to you, and you *know* how thrilled I am that you're dancing again, but you have to take care of yourself. I'm not in London anymore to watch over you, and I just…" I could practically hear her shaking her head as she sniffled. "I don't want you to hurt yourself again."

"Trust me. I've learned my lesson," I said. I hated making her worry, but I also hated how everyone in my family infantilized me sometimes. "I know better than to push myself that hard in the future."

There was a long silence before my mother spoke again. "Are you sure you want to stay in the showcase? Perhaps it would be better if…" She trailed off, but her sentiment was clear.

I sat up straighter, my heartbeat quickening. My mother had always been my biggest supporter when it came to ballet. She'd been devastated when my doctors said I'd never dance professionally again, and I knew part of her secretly hoped I'd make some sort of miraculous recovery so my career could pick up where I'd left off.

For her to suggest I pull out of the showcase…she really *was* worried. I should've known when she didn't even bring up Asher. Normally, my love life was at the forefront of her mind.

"I'm sure," I said, my voice firm. "It's only a few months away. I can do this. I have to."

If I quit, all my hard work would've been for nothing. I would've been *hospitalized* for nothing. I refused to let that happen, especially when there was so much riding on my performance. I needed to prove to myself I could do it, if only for one last time.

"Alright." My mother must've heard the determination in my voice because she didn't argue. However, her sigh contained a multitude of worries. "Just *promise* me you'll take better care of yourself, okay?"

"I will," I said as the bathroom door opened and Asher stepped out. I gave him a small smile, which he returned. "I promise."

ASHER

To say Coach was angry was like saying Mount Etna got a little spicy sometimes. He was, to put it simply, livid.

It was the Monday after the Holchester match. Scarlett and I were still camped out in the Ashworth's presidential suite, and when I'd arrived at Blackcastle's training grounds, the paps were already out in full force. I'd have to pull MI5-worthy maneuvers after practice to ensure they didn't tail me back to the hotel.

However, I'd rather deal with the paparazzi than endure Coach's wrath.

I didn't know a face could turn so many shades of red in so little time, but he proved my previous understanding of biology wrong. When it reached a particularly fascinating hue of magenta, I worried I'd have to add killing my coach to the list of grievances certain members of the public had against me.

"You do *not* skip matches to see your girlfriend!" The vein in his temple throbbed so furiously I half expected it to pop out, reach across the table, and strangle me. "Of all the bloody *stupid*, reckless things you've done, that has to take the fucking cake!"

"She was in the hospital." I defended myself as much as I dared. I understood why he was upset, but it wasn't like I'd skipped the match to frolic on the beach. I had a good reason. "I got the call right before the match, and I had to make a split-second decision. If it was your daughter in the hospital, wouldn't you have done the same thing?"

I wanted to snatch back the last sentence before it even left my mouth. Coach was extremely protective of Brooklyn, and referencing her in any way while he was in a rage was probably not my best idea.

A thundercloud darkened his face. "*What* did you just say?"

I blanched. "I mean, it was an emergency, sir," I amended. "I'm sorry I missed the match, but I wouldn't have done it unless it was important."

Thankfully, none of the tabloids had reported on the reason for Scarlett's hospitalization. To me, the reason was important, but I suspected Coach didn't think it was serious since she'd been discharged after an overnight stay. Hell, he wouldn't consider anything short of near-death serious. However, he couldn't *prove* it.

Judging by the tic in his jaw, he'd come to the same conclusion, but he wasn't happy about it.

"Next time," he said. "*You* call me, and *you* tell me what the bloody hell is happening. I don't want to hear it from your fancy-ass publicist."

Was that it? Was he about to let me off the hook?

I held my breath. "Yes, sir."

"Now." Coach's glare pinned me like a flailing bug to my chair. *Shit*. Not off the hook after all. "Can you explain why *both* my captain and my lead striker walked into practice today looking like they lost a round in an MMA fight?"

I forced myself not to touch my cut lip. The paps had, of course, caught wind of our injuries when we arrived at the training grounds. They were probably spinning salacious tales about our fight over Scarlett at that very moment.

They wouldn't be wrong, but I wasn't going to regale Coach with the ugly details from Saturday.

"Vincent and I had a misunderstanding that...escalated over the weekend, but we sorted it out. I promise it won't happen again. Sir," I added quickly.

"It better not." The vein in Coach's temple pulsed again. "I'll let it slide for now, but if I catch one bloody whiff of dissent between you two today or any other day, I won't be so lenient. Now get the hell out of here and join your teammates in training. You've missed enough work this past week."

Relief flooded my veins. He wasn't benching me or making me, I don't know, scrub the stadium with a toothbrush. *Thank God.* "Yes, sir."

The meeting had gone far better than I'd anticipated, but I hightailed it out of there before he changed his mind.

I only missed warm-ups and the first five minutes of training, so it didn't take me long to catch up.

The rest of the team didn't hold my absence on Saturday against me—they had wives, girlfriends, and beloved family members too; they understood—but I could tell by their stares that they were curious about Scarlett and my meeting with Coach.

"What happened?" Adil pounced during our first break. "What did Coach say?"

The other players drifted over, their ears perked as I summarized our conversation.

"You're lucky, mate." Stevens slapped me on the shoulder. "If the match had been a loss and not a draw…"

Shudders rippled through the group. If we'd lost, I'd be six feet under the pitch instead of standing on it.

I'd watched a replay of the match. We'd played well, but so had Holchester. They didn't have any megastars in their current lineup— Bocci was the closest they had to one—but they were incredibly cohesive. That was their biggest strength and our biggest weakness.

Hopefully, that changed this season. We were already playing better together now that Vincent and I had patched things up, but we had room to improve.

"Forget the match," Samson said. "I want to hear about your secret girlfriend. *DuBois*'s sister?" He whistled. "Ballsy. Very ballsy."

Heads swung between me and Vincent, who was walking toward us from the water station.

I was not in the mood to discuss my love life with anyone right now. Luckily, Vincent cut in before I had to respond.

"Is this training or is this a gossip session?" he asked pointedly. "We're not here to discuss our personal lives unless you want to tell us about the girl you hooked up with during our last away match."

The rest of the team laughed and elbowed an embarrassed-looking Samson. He'd brought a girl back to the hotel but refused to tell any of us who she was, which was unusual for him. He was typically an (over)sharer.

"Man, Captain, why do you have to always do me like that?" he said with a shake of his head.

Vincent grinned. "You make it too easy."

We didn't get a chance to speak further. Greely shouted at us to gather for our next set of conditioning drills, and our good-natured teasing immediately morphed into concentration.

Our assistant coach was running today's training. He was usually nicer than Coach, but he ran us ragged. By the time practice ended, no one had the energy to do more than shuffle into the locker room for a hot shower and a change of clothes.

"Thanks for running interference earlier," I told Vincent. We'd finished cleaning up around the same time, and I fell into step with him as we walked toward the car park. "When the guys were asking about Scarlett."

He lifted a shoulder. "She's my sister. I don't want those idiots thinking about her in *any* romantic way." He side-eyed me. "Too fucking late for you, though."

I smirked.

"How is she?" Vincent asked. "I talked to her on the phone last night. She says she's fine, but you know her. She'll say she's fine even if she's forced to run a marathon barefoot over hot coals."

"I know." Scarlett's stubborn resilience was one of her most admirable and most worrying traits. "She's feeling better. Still lethargic and in pain sometimes, but she's taking the week off work to fully recover." It'd been her idea, which gave me a measure of relief. She wasn't pushing herself to jump straight back into work. "She has a call with Lavinia today to discuss the tabloid and showcase situations."

The paps were staked out at RAB again, but Scarlett was most nervous about the showcase. She worried that Lavinia would pull her as the lead.

I had conflicted feelings about the issue. I wanted Scarlett to get the chance to shine, but the thought of her enduring two more months of rehearsals made me break out in a cold sweat.

There was only so much the human body could take.

"Good. I'm glad she really is feeling better." Vincent sounded relieved. We turned the corner toward the final set of exit doors. "What about the pap situation? They've been hounding me too, but not as much as you two."

"I hired a team. They're securing our houses." My place already had a high-tech security system, but it wouldn't hurt to shore up its defenses. "Once they're done, we'll move back home."

We couldn't stay at a hotel forever, and Scarlett was getting antsy.

"It'll blow over." Vincent seemed like he was trying to convince himself more than me. "The paps have short attention spans. They'll find a new target soon and move on. But I swear..." His face clouded. "If *any* of them hurts Scarlett in any way, I will fuck them up."

"I'll be right there with you."

Despite our history of differences, the only thing we'd always agreed on was protecting Scarlett.

He gave a short nod of acknowledgment. "You mind if I drop by the hotel later to see her? I'll be careful."

Sloane wouldn't like it. She was so serious about our lockdown she came up with a convoluted strategy to make sure the paps didn't follow me from training to the hotel. I had to go home first, wait an hour, then sneak out back to meet Earl—who would, of course, be driving a different decoy car every time.

I *could* stay at my house, but that would mean leaving Scarlett alone in the hotel since her flat wasn't as secure as mine. There was no way in hell I'd do that, so Plan Decoy it was.

"Yeah," I said. Sloane would rip me a new one later, but Vincent was Scarlett's brother. I wasn't going to keep him from her. "Just make sure not to drive your bloody Lambo."

"I won't—what the hell?" Vincent stopped halfway through the car park. The club's security must've kicked the paps out because there was no press in sight, but the players who'd left before us were gathered in a half circle around one of the parking spaces. "What are you guys looking at?"

The group's unintelligible mutters ceased. They glanced back at us, their expressions colored with varying shades of surprise, nerves, and pity.

A few shifted uncomfortably, but no one answered. Instead, they parted, creating a clear path between us and the hunter green convertible parked in the space.

That was my car.

A mounting sense of dread hooked into my stomach.

I walked past my teammates and stopped next to the driver's side door, where I immediately saw what they'd been gawking at.

My dread solidified into cold, hard ice because there was one word—one *name*—scratched into the side of my favorite vintage Jaguar.

Judas.

CHAPTER 45

ASHER

NOTHING BROUGHT A TEAM TOGETHER LIKE AN ATTACK
from another team.

It didn't take a rocket scientist to figure out the keyed car was
Holchester's handiwork. People might think professional footballers
were above such juvenile antics, but they weren't. The *Judas* scratched
into the hunter green paint was proof of that.

They were the only ones with the means and motive. If the
incident happened in Holchester, I would've been more circumspect,
but in London? It couldn't have been anyone else.

They called me *Judas* consistently, and they'd played Chelsea over
the weekend, so they were in the city through Monday. I didn't know
how they did it without anyone noticing—unfortunately, my car had
been parked in one of the CCTV cameras' blind spots—but it didn't
matter. What mattered was that they did it.

Even though it was my car, the rest of the club took it as a personal
affront. Even Coach was angry, and I wasn't his favorite person at the
moment.

The fact that Holchester came to *our* training grounds and vandalized *our* property was an act of war, so we waited. We waited until they were back in town two weeks later to play against Arsenal before we confronted them.

That night, Vincent, Noah, Adil, and several other players joined me at the Angry Boar, where the Holchester team always hung out after a London match.

Mac had banned Lyle after he shoved me, so he was nowhere in sight. However, Bocci was playing billiards with another player when we arrived. The other player saw us first and nudged his captain, who straightened and turned.

A slow grin spread over Bocci's face. "Look who it is. Donovan finally shows his face. I thought I'd have to track you down after you ran away from our last match like a coward."

I let his taunt roll off me. Everyone in the UK—hell, everyone in the *world*—knew the real reason behind my absence from the Holchester match.

My relationship with Scarlett had been prime tabloid fodder for the past two weeks. Every news website, every magazine, every bloody celebrity podcast was talking about us. Scarlett could barely enter RAB without getting accosted by the paps. People were stopping her on the streets for photos, and she'd had to private her social media after it got inundated with follows and comments (not all of them pleasant). She handled the onslaught of attention as well as she could given the circumstances, but it was taking a toll on both of us.

All that to say, Bocci was full of shit when he insinuated that I was too scared to play against him. He was trying to get a rise out of me, and I wouldn't give him the satisfaction.

"I'm not having this discussion with you here," I said icily. I flicked my gaze at Mac, who looked like he was seconds away from kicking us out, fight or not. "Meet me outside unless you want to join Lyle in...hmm, where *is* he? Eating pizza alone in his hotel room, I imagine."

Bocci narrowed his eyes, but he didn't want to suffer Lyle's exiled fate any more than I did. He followed me into the alley behind the pub, our teams trailing after us.

The other patrons tried and failed to pretend they weren't eavesdropping, but I heard them buzz with excitement before we fully exited the establishment.

The minute the door shut, I grabbed Bocci by the front of his shirt and slammed him up against the wall. The other Holchester players immediately bristled and moved toward us, but my teammates blocked them.

The two sides glared at each other, drenched in the threat of violence swirling through the air.

Summer heat had given way to an early fall chill, but the alley reeked of rubbish all the same.

"What you did to my car." I tightened my grip on Bocci's shirt. "I knew you were bullies, but I didn't know you were petty criminals too."

"I don't know what you're talking about." Bocci sounded unfazed by his current predicament, but his eyes glittered with loathing. "We live in different cities, Donovan. Do you think you're so important that we'd risk our careers to play whatever prank you accused us of playing?"

"You're the only people who could've done it," I growled. "*Judas*, your favorite nickname for me. Who else would carve that into the side of my Jag?"

A shadow of what looked like true surprise flashed across Bocci's face before he laughed. "Hate to break it to you, Donovan, but there are plenty of people who call you that, and plenty more who despise you enough to key one of your precious cars. You can't use us as a scapegoat for everything."

"It's not about scapegoating; it's about honor. You want to attack me? Have the balls to do it to my face. This sneaky sabotage is the work of a coward."

Bocci's smile vanished. "You want to talk about honor? How about we talk about *loyalty*?" he hissed.

My temper reared its head again, fangs bared and ready to strike. "It's a *transfer*, and it's been nine bloody months! Get over it!"

"You know it's not about the fucking transfer!" he shouted back. "You can transfer whenever the hell you want. It's a reality of the league. But to blindside us and ditch us mid-season for *Blackcastle*?" He spat on the ground. "You didn't give us any heads-up. One day, you were with us, and the next, you were against us. *That's* cowardice."

The air thickened into toxic sludge.

No one moved. No one so much as breathed, but the tension was so palpable I could taste its bitterness at the back of my tongue.

Bocci hadn't said anything I didn't already know. I *knew* I should've told them first, but I'd been afraid the news would get back to my father and he'd talk me out of it before I signed the contract.

I understood why my old team felt betrayed, but again—it'd been nine fucking months. I hadn't killed one of their family members or instigated a hate campaign toward them with Blackcastle. They were holding onto something that should've been old news long ago, and *none* of that was a good enough reason for what they did.

It wasn't about the property itself; it was about the principle behind it. The lack of respect and good sportsmanship.

"I apologized," I growled. "The minute the news came out, I *apologized* for not telling you earlier. This grudge is unnecessary, as was your fucking stunt with my car."

Bocci's lips thinned. He didn't acknowledge what I said.

Fresh irritation streaked through me, but I refused to get into another fight. Not when I was already on shaky ground with Coach and the paps were breathing down my neck. Anything I did would be blown ten times out of proportion given the current scrutiny I was under.

My teeth ground together, but after a serious moment of contemplating whether I could punch him once and get away with it—it wasn't worth it—I released Bocci and stepped back.

However, the tension didn't dissipate. If anything, it intensified.

"You want straight talk? I'll do you one better," Bocci said. "Race me. Let's end this *grudge* once and for all. You win, we back off. We'll still talk trash on the pitch, but you'll never hear another word about Judas or your transfer from us again. If I win…" A dark gleam entered his eyes. "That Jag of yours is mine—after you've fixed it up, of course."

That bloody bastard.

He didn't want the car. He wanted a symbol for his victory. He wanted proof that he was better than me in some way. Every time he drove that car, he'd feel a kick of triumph at beating me.

It was too bad for him that was never going to fucking happen.

My fists curled. It took every ounce of willpower not to take him up on his challenge and make him eat his words. I wanted to see his expression when he lost so badly that my blood burned with it.

But racing would be worse than another fistfight, and I'd promised Scarlett I wouldn't do it…no matter how much I wanted to.

"What's the matter?" Bocci arched an eyebrow, his expression turning mocking. "Got cold feet again? Going to chicken out the way you did for our match?"

I bit my tongue so hard the faint taste of copper filled my mouth.

My pride roared at me to *say* something. To prove him wrong.

I stormed in here with my team, ready to confront Bocci, and what did I have to show for it? A few useless words? If I wasn't going to fight him and I wasn't going to race him, why was I even here? I might as well have stayed home and fumed from a distance.

You promised Scarlett. A voice warned me away from the ledge.

Scarlett doesn't have to know. Another, more insidious voice slithered into my ears, promising retribution with impunity. *It's one race. That's all.*

"You didn't take me up on my challenge the first time. Now you're running scared a second time." Bocci tsked in mock disappointment. "You've lost your touch, Donovan. It's only a matter of time before everyone else finds out you're not the perfect golden boy you portray yourself as. You say we've been holding on to our grudge for too long, and maybe we have. But I offered you a chance to end this feud once and for all, and *you're* the one who declined." He nodded at the silent players gathered around us. "We have plenty of witnesses who can vouch for that."

My heart slammed against my ribcage with bruising force. Bocci's taunting words tangled with snippets from my past, filling my head with unwanted memories.

You'll never amount to anything.

Football is a ridiculous dream.

Dammit, Asher, you're not trying *hard enough! Do you want to be second best forever?*

Promise me you'll play for both of us. You have what it takes to be the greatest footballer in the world. Don't let this opportunity go to waste.

You've lost your touch, Donovan.

Your team or your son?

My old teachers, my father, Teddy...their fragmented voices sank their claws into reason and ripped it to shreds, making me bleed pure emotion in the dark alleyway.

Do it.

Don't do it.

Walk away.

You can't let him have the last word.

The last gasp of rationality died beneath the roar of blood in my ears.

I'd spent the better part of a year taking the high road. I'd endured the taunts and the hate messages silently, without retaliation, but I was *sick* of taking the high road.

Bocci and my old team said they valued loyalty, but they were really bullies. They dragged their resentment out because having a target made them feel good. Unless I put them in their place, they'd continue their campaign of harassment until I snapped or they got bored.

I hadn't made it this far in my career by being passive and waiting for things to happen to me. This was *my* life and *my* reputation. It was time I retook control of them.

"I'm not scared of anything or anyone, Bocci, much less you," I drawled, my smile a blade of white in the dark. "You want to race? Fine. Let's race right now."

Word of the last-minute competition spread like wildfire through a certain segment of the city's street racing community.

I didn't know who alerted them to the event, but when we arrived at our designated meetup spot in north London—the same spot where I'd raced against Clive and won—there were around two dozen people waiting for us. Most of them were athletes.

Simon was there. So was Clive himself, who I hadn't seen since our double date. He'd shown up with his rugby buddies, and they watched Bocci and me exit our cars to make the rounds with quiet anticipation.

I greeted them with nothing more than a short nod. I still didn't like Clive, and I hadn't forgiven him for dragging Scarlett into the middle of our spat over the summer. He looked like he hadn't forgiven me for denting his ego, either.

He clapped Bocci on the back and said something that made the other man laugh. There was no question who he was rooting for to win tonight's race.

Noah came up beside me after I finished saying hi to Simon, who was back in the game now that his foot was fully healed.

"Are you sure this is a good idea?" he said quietly. "You're still on thin ice with Coach. If he finds out…"

"He's not going to find out." Adrenaline streaked through my veins, dulling my sense of danger. Coach, the paps, the slim but ever-present possibility of crashing—they didn't exist at that moment. All that existed was the shining lure of victory. "I can't back down after I agreed to the race. You know that."

Noah frowned, his expression troubled. He didn't attempt to talk me out of the race again, but he hung back from the rest of the crowd, clearly uneasy as shouts and laughter rang through the air.

I was surprised he was here at all. He was usually home with his daughter at this time, but he recently hired a new nanny, so maybe he had more freedom to stay out late.

Bocci hadn't finished making his rounds.

I let him take his time. In half an hour or so, he wouldn't be so happy.

"Asher."

I turned at the sound of Vincent's voice. He stood between me and my car, his face half cast in shadows.

He didn't know about my promise to his sister, and I didn't tell him. I couldn't dwell on that right now. Not when we were a heartbeat away from the race.

Vincent dipped his chin in a cursory nod. "Good luck."

I nodded back, and that was that. Nothing else needed to be said.

Two minutes later, the race finally started.

Bocci and I climbed into our cars—his Lamborghini versus my trusty Bugatti. He lived in Holchester but owned a house in London, and he kept part of his auto collection in the city.

We drove to the designated starting point on the main street.

I gripped the steering wheel, my body alive with nerves and anticipation.

A small voice screamed that this was a bad idea and I should back out before it was too late, but it was *already* too late. Like I told Noah, I couldn't back out now—not without doing irreparable damage to my reputation.

This face-off with Bocci had been months in the making. In hindsight, it was foolish of me to assume we could settle our differences through a polite, regulated match on the pitch. It had to be something grittier. More personal.

Scarlett's face floated at the edges of my consciousness, but for the first time since we started dating, I pushed it aside.

I hated breaking my promise to her, but I wasn't racing tonight for an unnecessary thrill. I *needed* to do this. It was the only way for me to close the door on this chapter of my past.

I'm sorry, darling.

My grip tightened on the wheel.

All I had to do was win this one last race. After that, I was truly done.

Simon had offered to count us down, and the revs of our engines drowned out everything except the next few seconds.

Three.

Two.

One.

The flag came down, and we were off.

CHAPTER 46

SCARLETT

I HATED THE PAPARAZZI WITH A BURNING, ACIDIC PASSION.

I thought I hated them when they first ambushed me and Asher at RAB, but that didn't compare to the loathing I had for them now.

They were *everywhere*—at the school, in front of my house, at the local café Carina and I used to frequent every weekend before it became a press hellscape because apparently, people wanted to see Asher Donovan's girlfriend drink tea and scarf down scones.

It'd been two weeks since news broke of our relationship and one week since we checked out of the Ashworth. Thankfully, the security team Asher hired did a good job of keeping the paps at bay around my building, but I drew the line at having a bodyguard shadow my every move.

I already lacked privacy in the public eye; I didn't need to lose it at home either.

"Look on the bright side." Carina smeared another glop of plain yogurt onto my face. "At least they haven't said anything nasty about you. Most of the coverage has been pretty positive."

Carina, Brooklyn, and I were having an at-home spa night at Brooklyn's flat. It was our first girls' night since my hospitalization, and we were keeping it low-key so 1) we didn't have to deal with strangers, and 2) I didn't risk overexerting myself.

I'd more or less recovered from my collapse, but I had to be very careful about how and where I spent my energy.

"They've been positive *so far*," I said. "But you know how the press is. They're more fickle than the weather. Plus, it's not just the press that's a problem."

While the tabloids had been surprisingly restrained in their coverage, there was a certain vocal segment of the internet who was upset because they thought I'd "stolen" Asher from them. I tried to block anyone malicious who'd slipped through before I privated my social media, but I'd learned quickly not to look at my message requests folder. It was wild in there.

"This will all blow over soon," Brooklyn said optimistically. She sat in the armchair opposite the couch, her own face lathered with honey. "I heard a certain movie star couple is on the brink of divorce. Once that battle erupts, everyone will move on."

That seemed to be my mantra these days. *Everyone will move on.*

"I hope so," I said.

I'd never been involved in *any* sort of celebrity scandal. Despite my brother's public profile, I stayed out of the limelight, so to have complete strangers scrutinizing every aspect of my life was disconcerting, to say the least.

Everyone had an opinion on my looks, my clothes, my diet, and whether a ballet teacher was "good enough" for England's star athlete. They hounded my brother too, given his famous rivalry with Asher, but I received the brunt of the scrutiny. Even Asher didn't get as much attention as I currently did.

I was the unknown quantity, the shiny new thing they could pick apart and dissect. I loathed it.

"Is your mum still threatening to move in with you until this all blows over?" Carina asked. She reached for the bowl of cucumber slices and slapped two of them over her eyes.

"More or less, but I've convinced her to stay in Birmingham for now. It wouldn't do anyone any good to have my mother running around, trying to plan our hypothetical wedding while dodging the paps."

My parents weren't thrilled with the endless press coverage, especially my father, who considered any public attention unwanted attention. My mother was cautious, but she was also over the moon about the fact that I was *finally* dating someone. I was sure she already had a scrapbook filled with cake suggestions and lace samples tucked in her bedside drawer.

Ironically, hospital fistfight aside, my brother was the one taking my new relationship most in stride. I'd apologized for lying to him, and he'd assured me he was over it, but I still felt a bit guilty.

"Too bad. I would've *loved* to see your mother take on the paps." Brooklyn laughed when I kicked my foot against hers. "I mean, she has to come to London eventually, right? For the staff showcase?"

I winced. If my mother was over the moon about Asher, she was *ecstatic* after I told her I was dancing the lead in *Lorena*.

I was still conflicted about performing in front of her and, well, everyone else, but at least Lavinia hadn't kicked me out of the showcase.

The director had been furious when she found out I'd collapsed because I hadn't listened to my body and pushed myself too hard, too fast. After a twenty-minute lecture on the importance of proper self-care for dancers, she threatened to kick me out of the show altogether and bring in a last-minute replacement for Lorena. It was a risky move, considering the show was in only two months, but she'd been *that* furious.

Luckily, after much begging and cajoling, I convinced her to keep me on as long as I produced a doctor's note every week clearing me for rehearsals. I'd learned my lesson. I got plenty of rest during my non-rehearsal days, and I'd started seeing a physical therapist weekly again to ensure my body got the care it needed.

So far, so good.

Asher even bought me a new custom heated mattress that was specially designed for people with chronic pain. I'd balked when I first looked up the price, but it helped so much I stopped resisting.

Speaking of Asher...

I checked my phone. I texted him half an hour ago to see how his night out with his team was going, but he hadn't responded yet. He was usually quick to reply, but I assumed he was too caught up in whatever they were doing.

A smile touched my lips. I hoped he was having a good time. He didn't say it, but I knew he wanted a stronger sense of camaraderie with his teammates.

"So we all agree that the paps are annoying and invasive, *but* you have to admit, what Asher did was pretty romantic," Carina said as I put my phone away. She removed the cucumber slices to look at me. "No wonder the public is eating it up. The nation's star footballer ditching a big match so he could race to your bedside after you got hurt? *Swoon*. It's the stuff movies are made of. Not that we wanted you to get hurt," she added hastily. "But you get what I mean."

"She's right." Brooklyn stretched her arms over her head. "You snagged one of the few good footballers. You must've accumulated a shit ton of good karma in your past life."

I laughed. I still felt a little guilty that he'd skipped the match for me, but my giddiness outweighed the guilt. When was the last time someone cared about me enough to put me first?

Never. Rafael certainly hadn't done it, nor had any of my boyfriends before him.

Now that Asher and I were public, it was like a weight had been lifted off our relationship. Previously, that weight had anchored me to earth with chains of worry and anxiety.

Now…now, there was nothing to keep me from free falling into a place I'd sworn I would never visit again. No harness, no safety net.

I thought it would be scary, but it was exhilarating because I knew who'd be waiting at the bottom. I trusted him to catch me.

He always did.

"Look how hard you're blushing," Carina teased. "I think our girl is in deep."

"*Stop*." My face flamed hotter, but I couldn't hold back a grin. Despite my grumblings, the headaches and drama of the past two weeks were worth it if it meant Asher and I could date openly once all this was over. Sloane had left London to deal with another client crisis, but she'd advised us not to give the paps any more fodder for now. So far, we'd stuck to her plan, but one day, we wouldn't have to hide in our houses anymore.

However, I didn't want to spend the night talking about myself, so I attempted to steer the conversation in another direction. "Speaking of footballers, how's the internship going?" I asked Brooklyn.

"It's great." Her face lit up. "Jones, the lead nutritionist, is a total powerhouse and I'm learning so much."

"If you're looking for another paid intern, let me know." Carina sighed. "My barista gig is *not* working out."

She'd taken a weekend job at our local café. Unfortunately, she was great at drinking specialty lattes but not at making them. I took one sip of her lavender latte the other week and almost spat it right back out. I'd endured out of pure love for my best friend and the ability to chug a hot drink without breathing.

Needless to say, Carina's future at Peggy's Place looked bleak.

"Are you interested in nutrition?" Brooklyn asked.

Carina wrinkled her nose. "I'm interested in food. Does that count?"

The blond managed to laugh and wince at the same time. "It's a start, but I'm not sure our internship coordinator would agree…"

While my friends brainstormed other potential side gigs—including but not limited to museum tour guide, social media influencer, and greeting card designer—I closed my eyes and savored how *normal* this felt.

Normal was in scarce supply these days, and I'd take it whenever I could.

I reluctantly cracked an eye open again when my phone pinged with a news alert. I spent the first few days after the hospital trying to ignore any and all articles about me, but I'd since come to the conclusion that it was better to stay on top of the news rather than behind it.

I'd set an alert for both my and Asher's names. Luckily, most of the "news" so far was neutral or flat-out ridiculous (according to one tabloid, we engaged in regular BDSM swing parties at an underground sex club. That version of me sounded like a badass, but my body could never).

However, when I checked the alert, it wasn't another fluff piece about what I wore that week or speculation regarding how Vincent *really* felt about us dating.

It was…

The warmth leached from my body.

No. This was a joke. It must be an article from one of those satirical news websites because it *couldn't* be real. I refused to believe it.

My friends must've picked up on my mood shift because their conversation abruptly petered out.

"Scarlett? What's wrong?" Carina asked. Her voice sounded like it was coming from far away.

I didn't answer. I couldn't.

All I could do was stare at the words on my phone screen while lead ingots piled up in my lungs, strangling the flow of oxygen.

I kept waiting for the letters to rearrange themselves into a new sentence, one I could accept, but the headline remained the same.

BREAKING: Asher Donovan rushed to hospital after car crash in north London.

CHAPTER 47

SCARLETT

THE IRONY OF ME RACING TO THE HOSPITAL FOR ASHER after he'd done the same for me two weeks ago wasn't lost on me, but I didn't dwell on the parallels of our situation.

I was too busy trying not to hyperventilate and lose my ever-loving mind.

Brooklyn floored it through the streets of central London while Carina monitored the news for any developments (none so far). They'd sprung into action immediately when they found out what happened, and I was so dazed I didn't even have the energy to fret over Brooklyn's driving.

My stomach sloshed with each jerk and stop. I was *this* close to throwing up, but if I threw up, I'd slow us down.

I couldn't slow us down. Not when every minute counted.

The news reported which hospital Asher was at, but the articles were so light on details that my imagination grabbed the blank spaces and drenched them with gruesome images.

Asher broken. Asher burned. Asher...

My dinner resurfaced in my throat. I curled my fingers around the edge of my seat and clung on for sanity until we reached the hospital.

One. Two—A small hiccup interrupted my attempts to breathe. I clutched the seat tighter and fought another sob.

Three.

Four.

The second Brooklyn parked, I flung open the door and sprinted toward the entrance. Carina shouted something, but I couldn't hear her over the noise.

The crowd…God, if I thought the press turnout when I left the hospital had been wild, the sheer number of paps here tonight was mind-boggling. It made what I'd had to deal with so far look like quaint family gatherings in my nan's backyard.

"Look! It's Scarlett!" One of them spotted me, and the rest descended like vultures on fresh spoils.

"Scarlett, do you know how Asher's doing?"

"What are your thoughts on the crash?"

"Are his injuries serious?"

"Scarlett!"

"*Scarlett*!"

They closed in around me in a seething, undulating ocean of black. Cameras flashed every other second, nearly blinding me, and my nausea intensified into a form of vertigo.

"Get out of my way!" I shouted, but my voice was lost in the cacophony. I tried to push through the crowd, but there were too many of them.

Panic and claustrophobia squeezed my lungs. The world spun. I had to get through. I *needed* to get through before he—if he—

Dots danced before my eyes.

Breathe. I need to breathe. I need to—

"She said to get *out of the fucking way*!" Brooklyn's audible anger swelled above the noise.

I heard several shouts of surprise followed by a pained grunt before firm hands grabbed both my arms and dragged me out of the viper's pit.

Cool air replaced stifling heat.

The dots gradually receded, and I sucked in a gasp of fresh oxygen so quickly it devolved into a coughing fit.

We stopped inside the hospital lobby. Someone handed me a bottle of water, and I gulped half of it down gratefully.

"Better?" Carina asked when I finished and wiped my mouth with the back of my hand.

I nodded, too drained to scrounge up a coherent reply. "I need to find Asher." Fresh panic swamped my temporary bout of relief.

"I'm on it." Brooklyn released my other arm and marched straight up to the front desk. It took some convincing, but the incessant press coverage of me finally came in handy when one of the nurses recognized me as Asher's girlfriend.

They refused to give me an update on his condition, but they allowed me to go up to the VIP floor with my friends and a security escort.

The lift seemed to take forever. No one spoke, and I couldn't stop shaking from the arctic cold stealing through my body.

I was desperate to see Asher, but I dreaded it as well. What condition was he in? Why wouldn't the nurse tell me? If he was fine, she would've told me, right?

The lights stabbed at my eyes. Why was the lift *so* slow? If I had to be stuck in this steel cage for another second, I was going to scream.

I jabbed at the button again and again like that would somehow make it go faster. Our security escort opened his mouth, but he closed it when Brooklyn sent a scathing glare in his direction.

Finally, blessedly, we arrived on our floor. The doors slid open, and I dashed out without waiting for him or my friends.

They could find me later. In a hospital, one second could mean the difference between life and death.

Startled nurses and staff jumped out of the way to avoid colliding with me as I raced through the hall, frantically searching for Asher's room. Luckily, there were only a handful of suites on the VIP floor, and I found his around the corner, at the very end of the corridor.

A familiar dark-haired figure sat opposite the door.

He raised his head, his eyes widening when he saw me. He stood right as I reached him.

"Vincent." My brother's name fell out as a half sob, half plea. I grabbed his arm, my heart a twisted mess behind my ribcage. I didn't want to ask, but I had to know. I had to prepare myself. "The nurse wouldn't—is he—"

"He's okay. Plenty scratched up, but okay." Vincent gently loosened my death grip and squeezed my hand, his face pale but his voice steady. "They're still running tests on him, but he's alive and relatively unharmed."

My knees buckled with relief.

Alive. He's alive. The word rang in my ears.

A small, morbid part of me had been so convinced I'd arrive and find Asher gone that Vincent's reassurance refused to sink in. It floated around the edges of my consciousness, suspended by an irrational fear that my brother had somehow gotten it wrong and Asher was actually steps away from death.

"They wouldn't allow all the guys in here, so I offered to stay and keep everyone updated." Vincent scrubbed a hand over his face. Exhaustion smudged the skin beneath his eyes. "I should've called you earlier, but I lost my phone on the way to the hospital. Once I got here, things were so chaotic that it slipped my mind. I was just catching my breath when you showed up."

"You were with him when it happened?" My lower lip trembled. "What *exactly* happened?"

Had Vincent been in the passenger seat? If so, why was he completely unharmed while Asher was "plenty scratched up"? Asher hadn't told me what the team was doing for its guys' night out, but alcohol, testosterone, and cars were often a volatile mix. Had he been driving drunk?

A wisp of unease ate away at my relief.

Vincent hesitated. "You should talk to him when the doctors are done." He glanced over my shoulder, and I turned to see Carina, Brooklyn, and my security escort speeding toward us.

Our escort stopped at the end of the hall when he saw I was with Vincent. My friends came up beside me and said hi to my brother, their voices muted.

Meanwhile, I stared at the closed door to Asher's hospital room, willing it to open.

If I could only see him, I'd put my pesky worries to rest. Vincent said he was fine, so he was *fine*. His well-being was the most important thing, not the cause of the crash.

Still, the unease lingered until the doctor and nurse finally stepped out and gave me the all clear to see him.

"We'll be here if you need us," Carina said, squeezing my arm.

I nodded, my heart wobbling as I walked into the hospital suite.

I'd seen the inside of a hospital more times in the past four months than I had in years, and I was sick of it. Sick of the smell, sick of the way the nurses' shoes squeaked against the linoleum floors, sick of the oppressive cloud of anticipatory dread that drifted through the hallways like a deathly specter.

However, any negative feelings I had toward the space vanished at the sight of Asher sitting, alive and whole, less than five feet away. Like Vincent warned, he was scratched up with cuts and bruises, but he was *there*.

Tears stung the backs of my eyes.

"Hi, darling." His mouth tipped up at the corner. "I wish you would've called and told me you were coming first. I'm not looking my best at the moment."

The tears spilled down my cheeks as I choked out a noise of half anger, half amusement. "Asher Donovan, now is *not* the time to make jokes."

His face softened. "I know. I'm sorry." He opened his arms. "Come here."

He didn't have to ask twice. I was by his side in an instant, my face pressed into his neck while he held me tight. Sobs wracked my body as the tears fell in a constant rain.

BREAKING: Asher Donovan rushed to hospital after car crash in north London.

I didn't have proper words to describe the emotions that engulfed me when I first saw the headline. I'd *never* experienced such cold, visceral terror, not even when I sat in the back of a taxi and saw another car barreling toward me at sixty miles an hour.

If I died, I had the relief of oblivion. I wouldn't experience pain or sadness; I would simply be *gone*.

But if someone I loved died, I'd have to live without them forever. The pain of that would eclipse anything else I'd ever felt—especially if that someone was Asher.

Because I didn't just love him; I was *in love* with him. I was so in love with him that the thought of him dying made *me* want to die.

The realization struck me with the force of a bullet, and the sentiment was so foreign, so all-consuming, that I had no idea how to handle it.

So I let the excess emotion pour out through my eyes and throat, filling the room with the intensity of my sobs.

"Don't cry." Asher kissed the top of my head, his voice strained. "It's okay, darling. I'm okay."

"Did the doctors...can you..."

"I can still play football." He picked up on my unfinished question. Short of death, his worst nightmare would've been a career-ending injury. "I have a concussion, multiple lacerations, and a sprained ankle, so I'll have to sit out a couple of matches. They're still waiting on some test results, but the doctor is confident I'll be fully healed in a few weeks."

I finally gathered enough composure to straighten and lift my head. I sniffled and swiped at my swollen eyes. I must have looked like a mess, but I didn't care. I was beyond the point of embarrassment.

"Good. I'm glad you're okay because I thought...there was a moment when..." My voice caught.

Asher's eyes softened further. "I'm okay," he repeated. "I promise."

I nodded and wiped my cheeks again. "What happened?" I hiccupped. "Did someone hit you?"

I wished I could spend the entirety of our time hugging and kissing and ignoring the events of the night, but until I knew what caused the crash, my imagination would continue running wild.

Asher hesitated. "In a way, yes," he said. He wasn't smiling anymore.

The human brain hated ambiguity. It was designed to fill in the blanks, and his vague answer gave it ample room to spin wild theories.

Was *he* the one who hit the other car? Were its occupants lying somewhere else in the building, grievously injured?

Something thick and ugly oozed through my veins. *No.* I refused to doubt him. Asher was a careful driver when he wasn't racing, and if he *had* harmed someone else, he would be sick over it. He wouldn't be this calm.

Nevertheless, the mere prospect ripped open a portal in my imagination and tossed me back in time.

One second, I was in the hospital with Asher. The next, I was transported back to five years ago, when I awoke in a room very similar to this one and heard a faint murmur of voices discussing my situation.

Punctured lungs, broken ribs, shattered pelvis.

She might never dance again. Not even recreationally.

Her injuries are severe, but she's lucky...could've died...

The world swung sideways as past and present blended into a nauseating stew.

Did someone hit you?

In a way, yes.

I placed a hand atop a nearby machine, steadying myself. "What do you mean, 'in a way?'"

The answer was probably innocuous. When it came to cars, there were many technicalities that prevented accidents from being black and white.

However, I recognized the emotion seeping into Asher's expression. It wasn't innocuous.

It was guilt.

Why would he feel...

The breath stalled in my lungs. He hadn't hit someone else's car. I sensed it in my gut.

But if he hadn't done that, then there was only one reason for the guilt shining in his eyes.

Icy talons raked down my spine. *Don't say it,* I silently begged. *Please don't say it.*

"I was racing," he said quietly. "Against someone from my old team. He was behind, but halfway through the race, when we were rounding a bend, he purposely rammed into me. My car went over the guardrail and crashed through a fence."

My nausea returned with a vengeance.

I was racing.

The confession clattered to the floor and rolled to my feet like a live grenade. My earlier relief exploded into fragments of images— Asher behind the wheel, two sports cars hurtling through the dark streets with reckless abandon, the impact of one slamming into the other the way a car had slammed into my taxi half a decade ago. Only this time, it wasn't an accident; it was planned. Malicious.

The fragments splintered further, detailing the flip of the car as it careened over the railing and the scrape of twisted metal against its hood.

I squeezed my eyes shut.

"I didn't do it for the thrill." Asher's voice hoarsened, turning the sentiment into an excuse rather than an explanation.

He told me about what Holchester did to his favorite car and how he confronted them at the Angry Boar. He told me about Bocci's racing proposal and how he'd promised they would let bygones be bygones if Asher won.

Technically, I heard what he was saying. Part of me even understood his reasoning. But the actual words took a backseat to the phantom screech of tires and promises from the past.

I won't race anymore. I promise.

Memories of my accident mixed with Asher's crash and our first night in Japan. They twisted and turned, drilling into my brain with ruthless determination.

"It was my one chance to put the bad blood with Holchester to rest." Asher's voice sounded as if it was coming from underwater. "I didn't…"

The rest of his sentence was eclipsed by the war raging inside me.

I *knew* he had a history of racing. I *knew* he'd crashed cars before. I even knew he'd raced right before we got together because he told me he had. That was what'd led to our conversation and his promise in Japan in the first place.

But the knowledge and the terror that came with it had always seemed abstract, like a parent worrying about someone kidnapping their child or a surfer worrying about a shark attack. The threat was present, but it wasn't *there* because I'd never witnessed the consequences.

Now I had.

Asher was lucky enough to have escaped serious injury, but it could've easily gone the other way. I could be in a morgue right now instead of the hospital, and the realization that he'd put himself in this situation when he was fully aware of the danger made me go cold all over.

"You promised you wouldn't race again." The words came out thick and swollen, like I'd tried to pack a lifetime's worth of emotion into nine syllables.

The beeps from the monitor thundered in the ensuing silence.

Asher's hands fisted the sheets, his face leached of color. "I know."

The soft acknowledgment shattered something deep inside me.

I should be grateful he was alive—and I *was*. No matter how many promises he broke, there would never be a version of me that didn't care whether he lived or died.

But I couldn't look at him without imagining what *could've* happened, and I couldn't imagine what could've happened without feeling sick.

This was about more than the race or even a broken promise. It was about who Asher was at his core. He was a good person, and I *loved* who he was, but he also possessed a streak of impulsive recklessness that verged on self-destructive.

If he destroyed himself, he destroyed me, and once upon a time, I'd vowed never to put myself in a position where a man would have that type of power over me ever again.

Except I had, and he did, and that was on me.

"I'm so sorry, Scarlett." Asher's eyes were bleak beneath the fluorescent lights. "I swear, I didn't mean to break my promise. The last time I saw Bocci, he challenged me to a race, and I refused. Today..." He swallowed. "My emotions got the better of me. But it was going to be—it *is*—the last time. I'll never race again."

I wanted to believe him so badly that I ached with it, but he'd said the same thing once before, and here we were.

However, this wasn't the place or time for this conversation. He was injured, the paparazzi were frothing at the mouth downstairs, and our friends were right outside in the hall. Plus, I was exhausted from tonight's wild swings in emotion. I couldn't think clearly, and I didn't have the bandwidth to sort through my muddled thoughts.

"I'm glad you're okay," I said. A weight pressed on my chest and strangled my supply of oxygen. "Really, I am. But I can't—I need—" His face blurred as the weight pressed harder.

I wanted to spend the night by his side and pretend everything was okay until we could have a proper conversation. But because of the paps, I had to "pretend" every time I stepped out the door, and I couldn't do it tonight—not with Asher, the only person I'd never had to put on a fake face for.

I wouldn't be of any consolation to him in my current state anyway. The specter of his race would hang over us, casting a shadow over everything we said and did.

I tried to put my thoughts into words, but nothing came out. There was only the sound of my breaths and the monitors beeping.

I took a small step back without thinking.

"Scarlett." I *felt* Asher's agony more than I heard it. It traveled through my entire body and reverberated in my bones, making them ache worse than any flare-up.

I hated that I was the cause of it when he'd been hurt enough that night, and I hated that I couldn't comfort him even more.

We all have ugly feelings sometimes. It's a part of human nature. But it's what we do with them that counts.

I was drowning in those ugly feelings, and I needed to get out of here before I said or did something I regretted.

"I need air." I turned so I didn't have to see the devastation etched into his face. "I'm sorry. I have to—I just need some space. To breathe."

I ducked my head and rushed out, the world a blur of pale linoleum and alarmed voices as I barreled past my brother and friends.

I couldn't draw in air fast enough or deep enough to sate the strain in my lungs. I hadn't had a full-blown panic attack in years, but I was on the verge of relapsing.

However, I still possessed enough presence of mind not to rush downstairs and straight into the arms of the paps, so I rushed to the nearest lavatory and locked myself into the corner cubicle.

I made it just in time for my earlier nausea to overtake me.

I fell to my knees, leaned over the toilet, and threw up the entirety of that day's meals. Tears pooled in my eyes as the gag-inducing sound of my own retching filled the empty room.

My throat burned so terribly I was sure I wouldn't be able to speak after this. Even so, a tiny voice inside my head tried to convince me I was overreacting. It was one race. One promise he'd broken out of the dozens he'd kept.

But every chain reaction started somewhere, and I worried tonight was only the beginning.

I was in love with someone who didn't love himself, and I didn't know where that left me. Where that left us.

I kneeled there in the restroom, vomiting until I was empty and out of tears to cry. I heard people come and go, but the memory of Asher's confession was my only consistent company.

I was racing.

I knew three words would have the power to change our relationship.

I just hadn't expected it to be those three.

CHAPTER 48

SCARLETT

I SLEPT AT THE HOSPITAL THAT NIGHT. I DIDN'T SEE ASHER again, but I couldn't bring myself to leave while he was there, so I curled up in the waiting area instead.

After a futile attempt to convince me to go home, Vincent convinced one of the nurses (a huge Blackcastle fan) to let me grab a few hours of rest on the staff break room's sofa instead.

I left the next morning for work, but I made Vincent promise to update me if there were any changes to Asher's condition.

Thankfully, there weren't.

The hospital discharged him four days after the crash. In that time, the tabloids had a bloody field day. Details about his race trickled out in bits and pieces at first, then suddenly turned into a deluge.

Asher had allegedly been racing against Enzo Bocci, Holchester's captain. The articles used "allegedly" because there was no concrete proof they were racing. The circumstances pointed to a race, but no witnesses came forward to corroborate the suspicion, and no cameras caught them in the act.

However, several people spotted Asher and Bocci arguing at the Angry Boar a few hours before the crash, and Bocci was apparently being investigated for his role in Asher's accident. He was suspended until the investigation was complete. Due to his injuries, Asher was also officially out of the game for at least the next three weeks.

The world of football was in tumult, but it didn't compare to my inner chaos.

It was Monday, exactly nine days since the crash and five days since Asher left the hospital. I hadn't seen or talked to him since I visited him that first night. I suspected he was trying to give me space like I'd asked. I appreciated it because I wouldn't know what to say if I saw him; at the same time, enduring his absence was like being starved of air.

So, instead of dwelling on the dull pain in my chest, I threw myself into work. Nothing repressed important feelings like a packed schedule and a class full of students.

Unfortunately, every workday had to end.

"Excellent job, everyone." My smile stretched like plastic across my face as my students packed up their belongings. "I'll see you on Wednesday for our next lesson."

I didn't say what I really wanted to say. *Stay. Don't leave me with myself.*

Their company provided a sanctuary from my emotions, but they were my last class of the day, and I couldn't hold them. I could only watch as they trickled out of the studio and took my hopes of distraction with them—all of them, that was, except for one.

"Ms. DuBois, are you okay?" Emma asked. She was always the first to show up and the last to leave. She was also shockingly observant for a seventeen-year-old. "You look a little pale. I can get the nurse if you're not feeling well."

"No." I forced a smile. "It's been a long day, that's all. Don't worry about me. Go enjoy your evening."

Instead of leaving, she lingered, her expression conflicted.

I paused wiping down the barre. "Is there something you'd like to discuss?"

"Well, I don't want to push you or anything, but I was wondering if you'll be able to attend the student showcase after all," she said shyly. "My parents wanted to save a seat for you next to them if you do come. They're really grateful for all that you've done for me. I never would've gotten the role without your guidance."

Guilt squeezed my lungs.

I didn't want to crush her hopes, but between the press and Asher, I'd reached the end of my emotional rope. I didn't have enough left in me to deal with my complicated feelings toward Westbury.

"I'm sorry, Emma." I let her down as gently as possible. "I won't be able to attend opening night. I have a...prior commitment, but I'll make sure to watch the replay."

Her face fell for a second before she smoothed it with a valiant smile. "I understand. I'll see you on Wednesday."

I watched her leave, feeling like the worst, most selfish human being in the world.

Just one more cherry on top of the shit sundae that's my life.

The paps were even more relentless after the crash, and my parents had been blowing up my phone nonstop. My father was somewhat sheltered since he lived in Paris, but the paps had taken to harassing my mother too. She came home one day to find one of them rummaging through her rubbish bin, and she almost called the police on him before he ran away.

Between that and the accident, she was feeling much less warm and fuzzy about Asher these days.

Maybe it was karma for all the secrets I'd kept over the summer. I should've—

"Hi."

My fight or flight kicked in before my senses fully registered the unexpected voice.

I whirled around, sure I'd see another pap who'd stolen onto the grounds. They were glued to the street outside RAB's gates like leeches to their host.

But it wasn't a pap.

It was someone so much worse.

My heart folded in on itself. I might not know what I wanted to say to him, but after a week apart, I drank him in like a parched nomad at an oasis.

Asher's broad shoulders and strong, sculpted frame filled the doorway. He looked handsome as ever, even with his cuts and bruises, but his face was lined with exhaustion and his eyes were missing their usual spark.

And yet, his effect was still devastating.

Seeing him in person had the same impact as being struck with a wrecking ball. It knocked the breath straight out of my lungs and smashed a huge dent in the cool, calm facade I'd spent a week cultivating.

"What are you doing here?" To my relief, my voice sounded steady—not at all like the ragged heartbeats that threatened to break out of my chest.

"I needed to see you." Those green eyes met mine. I loved and hated how they pierced through me, like they could see straight through my shields to the vulnerable, conflicted girl underneath. "Just to make sure you're okay."

My heartbeat wobbled. "You're the one who was in a car crash recently. I should be saying that to you." But I wasn't because I was a coward, and I'd avoided him with dogged determination since the hospital. "It's good to see you on your feet again."

"We both know I'm not talking about the crash." He stepped into the studio, eradicating my attempt at a polite, informal conversation. He favored his left leg because of his ankle sprain, but he covered it up so gracefully I wouldn't have noticed had I not been so attuned to his every movement. "We should talk."

Every molecule in the air sparked to life.

"About what?" I stalled.

I wasn't ready to talk. If we talked, then I'd have to confront the state of our relationship, and I'd much rather live in denial.

Limbo was better than hell.

Asher stopped less than two feet away. "About us."

His rough, raw voice rushed over me.

As upset as I was about him breaking his promise and endangering his life, I couldn't pretend I didn't care about him.

That was the problem.

I cared *too* much. I cared too much and he didn't care enough, and I was afraid we'd never bridge that gap.

"I miss you," he said softly.

A stray tear escaped and scalded my cheek. "Don't."

"It's the truth." Asher's throat flexed. "I didn't reach out sooner because I knew you needed space after what I told you, but I can't stay away from you for too long. Even a week felt like hell." His eyes searched mine for something I wasn't sure I could give. "I know you're upset with me. I know I fucked up. But I meant it when I said that was the last time. You have to believe me."

I dragged a deep breath into my lungs. It burned like the air itself was on fire.

"I'm going to ask you a question, and I want you to be honest with me." I kept my gaze on his, my heart galloping with sickening speed. "Pretend you can go back to that night, except this time Bocci never hits your car and the race finishes smoothly. Knowing that, would you still say yes to the race?"

Asher's split second of hesitation told me all I needed to know.

The room blurred as my heart cleaved in half. Pain leaked through the crevice, seeping into my veins and solidifying into cold, hard clarity.

"It's not about the race or even the promise." Every word scraped like rusted nails against tender flesh on their way out, but I forced myself to continue. "It's about the pattern. It's about compulsively choosing to do something that leads to self-harm. You said the race was the only way to settle things with Holchester, but what about all the times before that? You've crashed before. We talked about it in Japan. You understand the danger, and you know how"—my voice broke—"you know how it would kill me if anything happened to you."

Asher didn't respond, but the rise and fall of his chest quickened like he couldn't quite get enough air into his lungs.

"Do you know how I felt when I first saw the news? There was a period of time when I was convinced you were *dead*, and it tore me apart." Another tear spilled down my cheek and salted my tongue. "You say that was the last time, but what happens when someone challenges you again or your emotion gets the better of you?"

"It won't." A thread of panic infused his response. "The race with Bocci really *was* the last time. I…" He faltered.

"Promise?" I finished with a sad smile. "If there's one thing I've learned, it's that actions speak louder than words. I want to believe you, Asher. I really do. Because I…" *I love you*. The words hovered on the tip of my tongue before I swallowed them. They went down like jagged pills. "I care about you, and that's why I can't—I can't be with you." The realization tore at me with vicious claws, making me stumble and turning my voice into a shredded version of itself. "I can't stand by and watch you self-destruct."

I couldn't force him to change nor did I want to. The change had to come from *him*, but if I stayed knowing he was still on that path of self-destruction, I would be silently condoning his actions.

I loved him too much to do that.

Asher went deathly still. He stared at me, his eyes a firestorm of emotion that scorched every inch of bare skin. "Are you breaking up with me?" The shock, the *pain* in his voice was so raw that it almost undid me.

"I…" *Just say it. Finish what you've started.* "I'll always care about you," I repeated. I sounded like a broken record, but I was too exhausted and drained to scrounge for new turns of phrase. "But until you exhibit the same care for yourself, we can't be together. It's not…I…it's not possible."

The tears were falling fast and hard now. I tried to wipe them away, but there were too many of them, and my efforts were futile.

So I let them fall silently, though their release did nothing to ease the suffocating pressure in my chest.

Asher hadn't moved. He hardly breathed. If it weren't for the tiniest tremor of his muscles, I would've thought him a statue, frozen in disbelief.

"Scarlett." When he finally spoke, his voice cracked on my name. The two halves of my heart splintered into a thousand more pieces. "Don't do this. Not after everything we've been through."

"I'm sorry." I held on to the barre for strength, but it felt cold and impersonal—an indifferent observer to my suffering. "I've made up my mind."

"You said you cared about me, and I care about you. More than anything else in this world." A rough plea hoarsened his words. "Please, darling. I know I broke my promise once, but I'll never do it again. Not when I know it means losing you."

It would be so easy to give in. To collapse into his arms and let him sweep us away from this excruciating torment.

On the surface, his reasoning made sense. Why *shouldn't* we be together? There was nothing holding us back now but ourselves.

Except we were often our own biggest obstacles, and if I papered over our issues now, they would only fester and grow in the future.

"That's the problem," I said, my voice just above a whisper. "I can't be the only reason you don't race anymore. The fact you don't understand that is why I...why we need space."

"Scarlett." This time, my name wasn't a plea; it was a prayer.

Asher reached for me, but I instinctively pulled away. I was already treading a shaky line; if he touched me, it would be over.

My lungs knotted into a messy tangle. I couldn't be near him. Not right now. I needed...he needed...

Oxygen thinned, making me lightheaded.

"Please leave," I begged. His response might not have been a plea, but mine was.

Asher remained silent. I could barely see past my veil of tears, but I could *feel* his anguish.

It seeped through my defenses like acid, eating through resolve and determination to reach the vulnerabilities shielded beneath.

I forced myself to harden against the offense. "Do you remember the favor you owe me? When I agreed to watch the horror movie that first night I slept over at your house?"

Asher's breaths were heavy and ragged in the otherwise silent studio. "Don't."

"I'm calling it in now." I hated tainting that night with today's poison, but I had no choice. "Please go."

My last sentence was nearly inaudible.

For a second, I thought he wouldn't leave, but Asher kept his word.

"If you need me," he said, so softly and rawly I almost didn't hear him. "I'm here."

Then he left, taking his warmth and promises with him.

I waited until the sound of his footsteps faded before I sank onto the floor and pulled my knees to my chest. I buried my face in my elbow and finally gave in to my grief.

It gushed up, bitter and acrid, to pour out of my throat in silent, heaving sobs. My shoulders shook, and the tears flowed so endlessly that I was sure I wouldn't survive this. I couldn't have that much moisture left. I would simply dry up and wither away into a husk of my former self.

I wasn't a stranger to pain. I lived with it every day, and some days were worse than others.

But I'd never experienced pain like this—like thousands of metal teeth were gnawing through my ribcage, tearing flesh and bone into shreds. When they reached their bounty—the beating, vulnerable organ responsible for their existence—they feasted on it, mangling it beyond recognition.

Soon, even my sobs hurt, but I could no more stop them than I could stop the agony marching through my chest.

This wasn't the pain of my muscles rebelling or my body protesting against overexertion. It wasn't even the despair I fell into after Rafael left. I thought I'd loved him at the time, but what I felt for him was mere infatuation compared to what I felt for Asher.

No. This? This inescapable, indescribable torment?

This was the pain of my heart truly breaking for the first time in my life.

CHAPTER 49

ASHER

I DIDN'T BELIEVE IN GHOSTS. I WAS SUPERSTITIOUS ABOUT my pre-match rituals—see: my lucky boots and listening to my playlist in the exact order in which I'd arranged the songs, no skips or replays—but I didn't believe in the existence of spiritual beings or haunted houses.

I changed my mind after Scarlett broke up with me.

A week had passed since I left her studio, but everywhere I turned, there she was, haunting me. Every little thing reminded me of her— the light strains of classical music piping through a lift, the entire horror movie genre, even the fucking color pink because she'd worn it so much during our trainings.

There were certain rooms I couldn't even enter, like the screening room and the ballet studio, because she was so present, so *there*, that stepping into them was akin to reaching inside my chest and tearing my heart in half.

My house had turned into a mausoleum of memories, and I couldn't stand the sight of it. I couldn't even use football as an escape because I was benched while I healed from my injuries.

Thankfully, after a week of absolute hell, my doctor gave me the go-ahead to return to training. My exercises had to be modified to account for my sprains and strains, but I was healthy enough to hit the gym while the rest of the team suffered through pain shuttles and alternating box sprints.

It wasn't much of a distraction, but it was better than nothing.

One.

I tried to focus on counting my dumbbell press reps instead of the echo of Scarlett's voice. *I can't stand by and watch you self-destruct.*

My chest clenched, fraying my concentration.

I gritted my teeth and pushed through it.

Two.

Her tear-streaked face swam past my vision, evidence that our breakup devastated her as much as it did me, and that was what killed me the most.

She was out there somewhere hurting, and I couldn't comfort her because I was the *cause* of her hurt. Me and my stupid, selfish, short-sighted actions.

I swallowed a lump of regret in my throat, but another sprang up immediately to take its place.

There was no relief from my guilt, not even in the sanctuary of the gym.

Three.

Sweat poured down my face and stung my eyes. I'd worked out for close to an hour already, but I still hadn't purged the nausea roiling my stomach.

Four.

The sound of my phone ringing snuck past the music playing on low in my ears. It wasn't Scarlett; I'd set a different ringtone for her so

I'd know if she called. She never did.

It was probably my mother again, fretting over the crash and the tabloids. It might even be my father, calling to scream at me about a host of things. They'd visited me while I was in the hospital, but they hadn't stayed in London long.

My mother wanted to keep me company until I was fully healed, but I convinced her my injuries were minor (half true) and that she couldn't take extended time off from her job as a teacher (definitely true).

She must've said something to my father before they came to the hospital because he'd held his tongue, though I could see the scathing sentiments swimming in his eyes.

It was why I avoided most of their calls these days. I was already falling apart; I didn't have the additional mental or emotional energy to argue with them. My mother would want me to talk to my father, and my father...well, he was who he was.

I closed my eyes and let the music drown out my phone.

Ten reps.

Fifteen.

Twenty.

Twenty-five.

I went beyond the planned reps for this set, but I was afraid that if I stopped, I'd be left alone with my thoughts.

So I kept going.

"Donovan."

Sometime between twenty-five and thirty, a familiar voice interrupted my determined count.

I dropped the dumbbells and paused my music. "Aren't you supposed to be in training?"

"I'm heading there now. I had to talk to Coach first." Noah stood in the doorway to the gym, dressed in his practice kit and gloves.

My eyebrows hiked up. Noah always toed the line and *never* got into trouble. What did he have to talk to Coach about that couldn't wait until after practice?

His stoic expression didn't offer any hints, though a touch of sympathy entered his eyes when he jerked a thumb over his shoulder. "He wants to see you next," he said. "As soon as possible."

Dread coiled around my gut. It was my first day back on the training grounds since the crash. I'd spent the morning meeting with the team's head of rehabilitation and physiotherapy, which meant this would also be my first time talking to Coach in person since I was discharged.

He'd visited me in the hospital, but our conversation had been limited to logistics and my physical well-being.

I had a feeling today's meeting would be less genial.

"Got it. Thanks." I stood, pulled my earphones out, and shoved them in my pocket. I took my sweet time placing the dumbbells back on the rack and wiping down the equipment I'd used, but I could only stall so long.

"Good luck." Noah clapped a hand on my back as I passed him.

I nodded my thanks.

I headed toward Coach's office, apprehension slowing me down as much as my ankle. It'd healed quite a bit over the past week, but it hadn't returned to full fighting form yet.

I knocked on the door and entered at his brusque *come in*. I sank into my usual chair—pretty sad that I *had* a usual chair, now that I thought about it— and tried to read his expression as I did so.

I'd expected him to be red-faced and raging, but he was silent and impassive—which was almost worse. I'd rather know what he was feeling than have to guess.

"Do you know why I signed you?"

His question caught me so off guard it took several beats for me to answer. "Because you wanted to shore up your attacking frontline and bring home the club's first Premier League title in a decade."

Blackcastle hadn't placed first in the Premier League since legendary forward Jamie Defoe retired ten years ago. It boasted an excellent defense, but historically, its attacks weren't strong enough to beat the likes of Holchester.

Coach grunted at my response. "That's part of it, but there are a number of great strikers in the league—and they're a hell of lot less expensive than you are."

I stayed quiet, unsure where he was going with this.

"I got a lot of pushback when I first brought your name up to the transfer committee," he said. "You're a once-in-a-lifetime player, there's no doubt about that. In fact, you're one of the *most* talented players I've coached since I became a club manager. But you're also hot-headed, reckless, and have a tendency to prioritize your personal grievances over what's good for the team."

Heat seared my face. "Coach—"

"I'm not done." His mouth pursed. "You think I didn't know about your racing habit or your rivalry with DuBois before I paid two hundred fifty *million* bloody pounds to bring you to Markovic Stadium? Everyone knew, and that's why the rest of the committee resisted so hard. They thought I was mad for even considering you." He shook his head. "I had to *fight* for you, Donovan. It doesn't matter how many hat tricks you've pulled off or how many Ballons d'Or you've won. A reckless player is a dangerous player, and the committee was adamant that we couldn't afford to be distracted by your scandals when we're trying to win the league."

I swallowed. We'd never discussed the logistics behind my transfer.

I had no idea he'd encountered so much resistance on my behalf. "But you didn't agree with them, sir?"

"Not at the time. Do you want to know why?" Coach's eyes drilled into me. "Because the fire that fuels your recklessness is the same fire that differentiates the greats from the legends. Like I said, there are a lot of great strikers. But they don't have the same hunger you have. They want to win; you want to break records. They're satisfied with maximizing their potential; you're not because you don't think there *is* a cap to your potential. If you could channel *all* that fire onto the pitch without letting your pride and petty squabbles get in the way, you'd be unstoppable. I convinced the committee that was possible. I told them that, with a little guidance, you'd understand what was at stake and pull it together." True disappointment colored his words. "You've let me down."

I strangled the edge of my seat with white knuckles. *You've let me down.* I'd heard that sentiment plenty of times in my life, including from my father, but the calm, matter-of-fact manner in which Coach delivered it stung harder than any heated words or shouts.

If my breakup with Scarlett was the worst conversation of my life, this was a strong contender for second place.

The growing weight of guilt pressed in from all sides, making me want to melt into the floor and disappear forever.

"I know you have a complicated relationship with your old team, and Bocci has a reputation for being an instigator," Coach said. "However, I'd hoped that you would've learned to control your impulses better. The authorities don't have the evidence they need to implicate anyone in a crime, but you and I both know what really happened the night of the crash."

The specter of my mistake reared its ugly head again, like a beast who kept regenerating no matter how many times I tried to kill it.

"You got lucky, but everyone's luck runs out some time. The question is, will you have pulled your head out of your ass before it does." Coach didn't sound upset, merely exhausted. "The committee said you're too rash. That you take your youth and talent for granted and that you don't respect the consequences of your actions as much as you should. So far, you're proving them right. Being a great footballer is about more than skills and drive. It's about focus. It's about teamwork. It's about the discipline and self-control to *stop and think* before you act. Emotion is a powerful motivator, but it can also be your greatest enemy."

My next swallow felt like I was forcing nails down my throat. "I am disciplined. I *will* be disciplined. I'm done fighting with Holchester off the pitch, and you won't see me behind the wheel of a car during a race ever again, sir."

I'd promised Scarlett the same thing, but like Scarlett, Coach didn't look convinced.

"Are you?" He regarded me with naked skepticism. "Discipline is a mental exercise, Donovan. Physically, you excel at the game, but mindset is as important as any of the conditioning drills that Greely is running out there. And right now, your mind is a mess. No, it's true." He cut me off when I opened my mouth in protest. "You may not see it, but I know my players, and I've watched you especially closely since you joined my club. Now, I'm no psychologist, but even I can see that something is driving those *stupid*, impulsive decisions of yours. It's not Holchester and it's not DuBois. Until you figure out what it is and deal with it, you'll never find the discipline you need to achieve your goals—or to work with the team."

Cold unease crawled under my skin. Coach's words were both vague and ominous—the worst combination.

"The doctors and our rehab team say you'll be fully healed and cleared to play in two weeks, but you'll be off the pitch longer than that." Coach sighed. "I'm benching you until further notice."

"*What*?" I nearly shot out of my chair. "Coach, you can't—" I stopped when I noticed his tired frown.

He didn't want this any more than I did. Benching me indefinitely was a *huge* gamble. Between the price of my transfer and the fact that I was their lead attacker, my absence would cause chaos. Any time Blackcastle lost a match, they would blame him for not putting me in.

Coach was going to get shredded by the public and the club's executive committee—they hadn't paid millions of pounds for me to sit on the sidelines—but he felt strongly enough about the situation to risk that outcome.

I sank back into my chair and tamped down my knee-jerk indignation. He had every right to bench me. He'd given me plenty of warnings regarding my behavior, and I'd ignored him.

He would be a terrible coach if he *didn't* discipline me.

"Prove to me you can think before acting first and that you have a handle on your impulsiveness. Once you do that, I'll allow you back on the pitch." He nodded at the door. "Now get back to training. Just because you're benched doesn't mean you can slack off."

"Yes, sir," I said quietly.

I walked out, my ears ringing with condemnation.

It's about the pattern. It's about compulsively choosing to do something that leads to self-harm.

Something is driving those stupid, *impulsive decisions of yours.*

I can't stand by and watch you self-destruct.

Do you remember the favor you owe me? Please go.

My head pounded from the tumult of voices swarming my brain. They overlapped and blended together, their collective volume rising to a point where I could no longer hear my steps against the concrete floor or the anxious hammer of my pulse.

Scarlett, football, my control over my own bloody life...everyone and everything I loved was slipping through my fingers.

If I didn't get my shit together soon, I'd lose everything I'd worked so hard for.

Permanently.

CHAPTER 50

ASHER

THAT WEEKEND, BLACKCASTLE PLAYED TOTTENHAM AND did just fine without me. They squeaked out a miraculous goal in the last minute, but a win was a win, and as happy as I was for them—for us—I couldn't stop something unpleasant from slithering through my veins.

It was like my absence didn't mean anything.

Like I didn't matter.

The dark cloud that'd followed me since the crash grew heavier, and I begged off celebrating with the team afterward. It wasn't like I'd contributed to their victory.

Maybe if Teddy were alive or I had another best friend, I'd have an outlet to vent the sickly emotions coiling inside me. Since I didn't, I was forced to drown in them alone.

"I can't believe you're pulling a Noah on us," Adil said when I told him I was going home. Noah rarely came out with us after a match.

However, even the ever-persistent Adil didn't push me to join their revelry. The team had been walking on eggshells around me since the crash and my breakup with Scarlett. I hadn't confirmed it myself, but they must've noticed how I clammed up when she came up in conversation and grilled Vincent about it instead.

It was mortifying—I hated being the object of pity—but at least they had my back. No one gave me shit about what happened with Bocci. Many of them had been present for the race, and they'd wanted to make him eat his words as much as I had.

"Anyway, enjoy your night off. I'll see you on Monday." Adil slapped a hand on my shoulder. Neither of us mentioned that I didn't have nights *on* anymore since Coach benched me. "Take it easy, Donovan."

I forced a smile and nodded as the team piled into their cars for a night at the Angry Boar. Noah had gone home, and Vincent was noticeably absent. Maybe he was already at the pub. We hadn't talked much the past few weeks, and I suspected he was avoiding me given my broken relationship with Scarlett.

It was for the best. I couldn't look at him without thinking about her, and I couldn't think about her without feeling like someone had jammed a sword through my gut.

I drove straight home from the stadium and cut a direct path to the kitchen. Thankfully, my security team had succeeded in scaring off the paps that used to lurk around my house, so I didn't have to worry about them on top of everything else.

Yes, I was wallowing.

No, I didn't give a shit.

I grabbed a glass bottle of Coke from the fridge and popped the cap off. Normally, I didn't indulge in much alcohol or soda during the season, but since I was benched for the foreseeable future, I allowed myself a cheat drink—or two, or three.

I leaned against the counter and took a swig, my eyes sweeping dispassionately across the giant kitchen until the copper gleam of cookware caught my eye and a flood of memories assaulted me.

I thought you were an intruder.

Why would you think that?

I came downstairs for a snack and saw the light from the kitchen. I didn't realize…

That I might've gotten the same idea?

My mouth curved at the recollection of Scarlett wielding a frying pan like a weapon before reality intruded and flattened it again.

That night seemed like a lifetime ago.

She might never step foot inside my house, much less my kitchen, again.

The taste of the soda staled on my tongue, but I finished the rest of the bottle and forced myself not to call her like a pathetic ex desperate for a second chance—which I *was*, but I had enough dignity left not to broadcast it so loudly.

I did not, however, have enough dignity to stay away entirely. I visited her favorite café every weekend, hoping for a glimpse of her, but she was never there. She'd stopped going weeks ago because of the paps, but I thought…

It doesn't matter what you think. She doesn't want anything to do with you until you figure your shit out.

My stomach knotted itself into a ball of frustration. I'd promised her and Coach I wouldn't race again, but how could I *prove* it? It was impossible to prove a negative.

Plus, I still didn't know what Coach meant when he said something was driving my impulsiveness. If it wasn't my pride or hot-headedness, as he called it, what the hell was it?

My phone rang.

My heart leapt, and for a wild, hopeful moment, I thought it might be *her*. Then I registered the ringtone, and my heart plummeted again.

Not her.

A quick glance at the screen revealed it was my father. I promptly sent the call to voicemail.

If I was avoiding him before, I was hell-bent on not talking to him now that news of my indefinite suspension had leaked. As predicted, Blackcastle fans were in an uproar, though today's victory had soothed their anger somewhat.

That wouldn't matter to my father. In fact, it probably made him *more* angry. I was supposed to be indispensable, and if I wasn't, then I was clearly doing something wrong.

I reached for a second bottle when the phone rang again, and I sent it to voicemail. Again. If it was an emergency, he would've left a message after his first call. He hadn't, so I assumed he simply wanted to yell at me and make me feel like shit. What else was new?

Between my suspension, the car crash, and the media circus around my relationship with Scarlett, he had plenty to vent about. But I'd taken enough verbal beatings this month, and I wasn't interested in serving as his punching bag tonight.

I took my drink into the living room.

The house felt unbearably cold and lonely these days, but it was my only feasible sanctuary. I couldn't go out in public without risking my privacy. I couldn't go to my parents' house without facing, well, my parents. And I didn't have the privilege of staying at Scarlett's flat anymore.

Remorse swelled in my throat. I was surrounded by the best luxuries money could buy, but I would give it all up for the chance to see her again.

I care about you. I care about you so much, and that's why I can't be with you.

Perhaps I was delusional, but I could've sworn she was about to use another word before she settled on "care about." A word with four letters that began with the letter L.

I wasn't sure whether that would've made things better or worse, though I couldn't imagine feeling worse than I did at that moment.

My phone rang again.

And again.

And again.

Finally, I couldn't take it anymore. I picked up, but I didn't even get the chance to speak before my father's gruff voice filled the line.

"About time you picked up," he snapped. "Open your gates."

I shot up straight. "What?"

"I said, open your bloody gates." His voice deepened into an irritated grumble. "The taxi driver is getting impatient and so am I."

I checked my home security app, which allowed me to surveil various sections of the estate from my phone. Sure enough, a black cab idled outside the gates. I could just make out my father's scowl through the back window.

Fuck. My pulse sputtered.

My father showing up in London unannounced wasn't on my bingo card for the night. Since he was here, I had no choice but to let him in.

I opened the gates and waited for him by the front door. Every inch of my body, from my skin to my bones, was saturated with dread.

The cab dropped him off right in front of the door and sped off.

My father walked toward me, his cane gleaming under the house lights. It'd been months since his heart attack, but according to my mother, he got winded easily, so his doctor had suggested the regular use of a walking aid.

"Dad." I greeted him stiffly.

"Asher." He looked a little haggard, but his stare was as piercing as ever.

We didn't exchange another word as I led him to the living room. Tension sprouted between us like weeds through cracks in the pavement. It tangled around our ankles, making me feel like a prisoner in my own home.

This was my father's first time visiting my house in London. He didn't look particularly impressed even though the mansion was about fifty times bigger and more expensive than my childhood home. In fact, he looked almost annoyed by the display of wealth.

When we reached the living room, we settled on separate sofas, as far away from each other as possible.

"Where's Mum?" I asked, breaking the silence. He wouldn't leave Holchester without her.

"She's at the hotel. She wanted to come, but I told her I wanted to talk to you alone first." He sounded deceptively calm. "I didn't want her to be here when I asked you what the *bloody hell you're doing!*"

I went rigid at the sudden but not unexpected escalation in his temper. Honestly, I was surprised it'd taken him this long to march to my house and read me the riot act.

He glared at me, flaying me alive with his anger.

I glared back, my muscles taut. I'll admit, I'd made my fair share of mistakes this year, but I wasn't a kid anymore. I wasn't going to let him ambush me in my own fucking house.

"I'm not in the mood, Dad," I said, striving for calm. "If you came to yell at me for the crash or getting suspended, you're out of luck. I already got the talk from Coach. I don't need it from you, too."

His face reddened further. "You think I came all this way because you got *benched*? Boy, if I wanted to yell at you about that, I could've called you on the phone and saved myself the train and hotel money. And no, I don't give a shit that you've been avoiding my calls. I would've found a way." His eyes flashed. "I'm here because I want you to look me in the fucking eye and tell me *why* you're sitting on your ass at home when you should be proving to those vultures out there"—he thrust a finger toward the entryway—"that you're Asher fucking Donovan for a reason. Have you seen what they're saying about you? Are you going to take it lying down?"

My jaw clenched.

The tabloids were relentless in their coverage. They were dragging Coach through the mud for suspending me, but they were howling at me too for putting myself in a position to *be* benched.

It was a lose-lose situation for everyone except fucking Bocci, who'd gotten off scot-free after the "investigation" into what happened the night of the crash yielded no actionable results.

"How?" I snapped, my temper igniting. "The tabloids are uncontrollable, and Coach benched me because he thinks something is *driving my impulsiveness,* whatever the hell that means. I assume he wants me to figure out why I feel compelled to race, even though I said I wouldn't do it again. I have no desire. But how am I supposed to prove I'm *not* going to do something?"

"By showing him why he signed you in the first place!" My father stamped his cane against the floor. "Have I taught you nothing? When life throws you obstacles, you either obliterate them or you find a way around them. You don't bloody wait for the universe to haul them out of the way for you. You think those parasite paps sit around waiting for a photo to fall into their laps? I don't *fucking* think so. You can't prove you're *not* going to do something, but you can bloody well do more than drown in self-pity!"

My hands fisted. He wasn't wrong; I *was* drowning in self-pity. However, I couldn't figure out how to pull myself out of the deep end without exposing myself to worse elements—like whatever was causing me to engage in the self-destructive behavior Scarlett accused me of.

But I wasn't going to admit any of that to my father. I was wound tight from weeks of pent-up emotion, and I was spoiling for a fight.

"You should be happy," I said. "You don't have to watch your son play against—instead of for—Holchester anymore. Isn't that what you wanted?"

My father's nostrils flared. "What I *wanted*? You think I *want* a son who gets sidelined and fucking lambasted by the press because he can't keep his emotions under control?"

"No, you want one who wins, but only if it's for your team," I shot back. "Tell me. Have you attended a single one of my matches since I transferred to Blackcastle? Have you ever called just to *talk* to me like I was your son instead of using it as an opportunity to criticize everything I did on the pitch?"

"For fuck's sake, what do you want me to do?" he shouted. "Coddle you like you're a fucking baby? You can't improve if all I do is pat you on the head and say *good job* every time you kick the bloody ball!"

"I'm not asking you to coddle me. I'm asking you to act like my father and not my bloody coach!" The emotions exploded past the dam I'd spent years constructing and poured through my mouth, flooding the room with a lifetime's worth of resentment. It wasn't just the past month, and it wasn't just my father.

It was *everything*. Scarlett, Coach, Teddy, Vincent, my critics and my fans, my triumphs and my mistakes. Sometimes, the weight of it all was so great I couldn't breathe.

My home was supposed to be my haven, and I didn't even have that.

"I have a coach already. I don't need a second one," I said, unable to keep the furious tremor out of my voice. "What I *need* is a family, and you took that from me!"

My father and I glared at each other, our chests heaving from the force of our anger.

We'd tiptoed around this conversation our entire lives. Our argument in the hospital had revealed a slice of it, but this? This had been decades in the making.

"You think I *took* your idea of a family from you?" my father spit out. "I'm not trying to be your fucking coach! I'm trying to make you into what you've always wanted to be: the greatest footballer in the world. What kind of father would I be if I didn't push you to your full potential?"

"One who cares about his *son* more than his team." We'd circled back to square one, but we'd never really left. "If you were trying to help me achieve my goals, you would've kept the same energy after I transferred to Blackcastle. But you didn't, did you? You could only focus on how I betrayed you and Holchester by switching teams. You couldn't even congratulate me when we won a match. Not once."

He stared at me, his hand clenched tight around his cane.

I expected him to bluster and yell some more, but to my surprise, he seemed to deflate before my eyes. The anger drained from his face and body, making him look smaller and older than he had minutes ago.

"I'm not saying I act perfectly all the time," he growled. "Was I upset when you transferred to Blackcastle without telling me first? Of course. Holchester wasn't *my* team. It was *our* team. When you were a kid, they were all you talked about. We went to every match together. We strategized how to get you a spot in the club. I thought you loved them."

In the face of his unexpected calm, my anger leaked out too, leaving a hollow cave in my gut.

"I did, but we can't stay in the same place forever, even if we love it. We have to grow." I swallowed. "I didn't tell you beforehand because I was afraid you'd somehow convince me to stay before the paperwork went through. I *needed* to leave Holchester to become my own person. I couldn't do that with you in my ear all the time. I couldn't make a single move or celebrate a single win without you disparaging me. I can take criticism, but not if it's the only thing I hear."

My father's mouth formed a thin slash across his face. "Your mother always said I was too harsh on you about football, and maybe I was. But I didn't push you to win for me. I did it for you."

"Bullshit." We may be having a civil conversation, but I wasn't stupid.

"Think what you want, but it's true," he snapped. "You *need* that title, son. You need the validation. You were so afraid of proving your critics right that it would've killed you to fail, especially after Teddy died. So I didn't let you. And look at you now." He nodded at the trophies and medals and expensive gadgets surrounding us. "Do you think you would've made it this far if I hadn't pushed you from the start?"

I didn't believe him. I didn't *want* to believe him.

I'd spent so long constructing my narrative for our relationship that to alter any piece of it would mean altering my worldview, and that was unthinkable.

But I heard the whisper of truth in his words, and even if it wasn't the whole truth, it was more than I'd expected.

My father sighed, his face softening again. "You were inconsolable after Teddy died," he said. I flinched. We hadn't talked about Teddy since I was a teenager, and I preferred it that way. Some memories were better left in the past. "You blamed yourself for what happened to him. The night after his funeral, you took my car and stayed out all night. Your mother and I were frantic with worry. But you finally came home at four in the morning, smelling like ale and cigarettes. You couldn't imagine…" His voice trailed off. "It was like you had a death wish and you were punishing yourself for surviving when he didn't."

My breath stuttered beneath the blow of my surprise. "I don't remember that."

Honestly, the days and weeks after Teddy's death were a blur. I either blacked out or repressed them, but my father's words dredged up a vague recollection of cheap beer and the rev of the engine as I floored it through dark, empty streets.

"I don't suppose you would, but it's not something a parent forgets." My father's jaw ticked. "We grounded you. Yelled at you. Lectured you. But I could tell the only thing that kept you going during that time was football. You were doubly determined to succeed for yourself *and* for Teddy. So I focused on that. I pushed everything out of the way and made it the only thing you thought about."

An overwhelming pressure spread from the base of my skull to my temples. I couldn't parse truth from fiction anymore, and I suspected he was making his motives sound more pure than they were.

However, he was right about one thing—Teddy's death and the role I played in it had sent me into a dark spiral. Football saved me, but…

Something is driving those stupid, impulsive decisions of yours.

It was like you had a death wish and you were punishing yourself for surviving when he didn't.

My heart stopped for a beat.

No. It couldn't be that simple, could it?

"You can believe me or not. It doesn't matter. What's past is past," my father said, dragging my attention back to me. "But I came here to remind you of that boy who would've done *anything* to sit where you're sitting right now. Do you think teenage you would've come this far only to squander his dreams on a few stupid, bloody mistakes? He would've *fought* to play again."

He stood, leaning heavily on his cane as he did so. "I can't make you do anything you don't want to do, though Lord knows I've tried. But think about what I've said tonight. Think about what you're tossing away if you don't pull your head out of your ass soon." He stumped toward the door. "I'll see myself out. It's late, and if I don't get back to the hotel soon, your mother will have my hide."

I almost let him leave without further comment, but there was one more unresolved issue hanging over us.

I stopped him just before he reached the doorway. "You never answered my question from the hospital."

Your team or your son?

I needed to hear him say it.

My father looked back at me, his face unreadable. "The team will always be there," he said. "But I only have one son."

Then he left, and I was alone in the silence once again.

CHAPTER 51

ASHER

MY FATHER'S WORDS ECHOED IN MY HEAD LONG AFTER he left, especially what he said about Teddy and my death wish.

Was that really the reason behind my compulsion to race? It seemed absurd. I *enjoyed* racing, and it didn't make sense for his death to be the reason behind my self-destructive behavior. It'd driven me to succeed, not to sabotage myself.

But the thrill I got from racing was the thrill of cheating death, so maybe...

My headache intensified. It was too late for this. I needed sleep first. Then I could figure out what to do with the revelations from my father's surprise intervention tomorrow.

Unfortunately, the night had other plans for me when, less than an hour after he left, someone else showed up at my gates.

Disbelief cut through me when I saw who it was. "You've *got* to be kidding me."

I was tempted to leave him outside, but I caved and opened the gates again. What was one more visitor? Hell, maybe I should ask the London Philharmonic to come over for a concert and then set up sleeping bags for all the paps to camp out in my living room.

Maybe the universe was doing me a favor by trying to distract me from thoughts of Scarlett—or maybe it was trying to punish me by making me deal with my father *and* the person who reminded me most of her within the span of one hour.

I opened the front door to Vincent's scowling face.

A bolt of irritation darted through me. He showed up at my house uninvited and had the nerve to look annoyed?

Typical Vincent.

"What are you doing here?" I asked. "Did someone put out a broadcast telling London I'm having an open house tonight or something?"

Given the way my week was going, I wouldn't be surprised.

"We need to talk." He shoved past me into the foyer. He was still wearing his kit from that afternoon's match, which didn't improve my mood.

Not only did he remind me of his sister, but he reminded me of my suspension. At that moment, he was the symbol of everything I'd lost, and I almost decked him for it.

I didn't.

One, that wouldn't solve my problems; it would compound them. Two, my issues weren't his fault, though I wished they were. It was easier to blame others for my misfortunes than myself.

"I don't want to talk." Nevertheless, I slammed the door closed in case there was a pap lurking out there with a long-range night lens or whatever they used to spy on their unsuspecting victims. I trusted my security team, but one could never be too careful. "If this is about your sister..."

I couldn't bring myself to say Scarlett's name. It hurt too much.

"It's not. I'm not here as Scarlett's brother." I flinched even as Vincent continued without so much as a *hello, it's lovely to see you.* "I'm here as your captain, and I'm telling you to *get your shit together.*"

Oh, for fuck's sake. Was it Kick Asher While He's Down Day and no one told me? Why was everyone barging into *my* bloody house to yell at me? "I already—"

"You see those?" He pointed at the medals displayed inside a glass case in the hall. "If you want another one, you need to get your head out of your ass. So you're suspended and your girlfriend broke up with you. Boo-fucking-hoo."

My shoulders stiffened. "You said this wasn't about Scar—about her."

"It's not. It's about the way you're acting *because* of her," Vincent snapped. "You want to be the greatest footballer in the world, yet you can't hold it together after one breakup. Let's say you get back together. What happens if you get into a fight before a match? What happens if she breaks up with you again before the World Cup?"

"I—"

"You've been moping like a teenager for a *week*, and it's time you got over it." He barreled over my response. "Now I'm going to say this once—and if you tell anyone, I'll fucking deny it—but we need you back on the pitch. Team morale is down, and we can't keep up our streak without you. We *barely* won against Tottenham. Most importantly, you need to get your shit together and figure out a way to win Scarlett back. For some reason I can't fathom, she still has feelings for you, and frankly, I'm sick of seeing her mope around too."

I stared at him, stunned into silence for the second time that night.

I couldn't believe Vincent DuBois, of all people, was giving me a pep talk. A harsh and annoying one, but a pep talk nonetheless.

Either he'd conspired with my father on tonight's double attack, or the universe had determined I needed that much of a kick in the ass to get my shit together.

I suspected it was the latter.

The shock of the night's events cleared some of the daze I'd been walking around in for the past two weeks.

It pained me greatly to admit it, but my father and Vincent were both right. I prided myself on my drive and determination, but I'd displayed neither since Scarlett ran out of my hospital room the night of the crash.

Why was I sitting around waiting for inspiration to strike instead of *fighting* for her and for my spot back on the pitch? I kept thinking it was impossible to prove a negative, but was it really?

Even if it was, I'd achieved the impossible before. I could do it again.

For Scarlett, I could do anything.

Clarity dissolved the rest of my daze, allowing Vincent's words to fully sink in. "She's moping around?"

He gave me an exasperated look. "Out of everything I said, *that* was your takeaway? And yes, she is, unfortunately, moping."

My heart skipped a beat. I hated the thought of Scarlett being sad, but moping was good. Moping meant she hadn't moved on.

Our issue wasn't a lack of feelings for each other, but Vincent's confirmation was the fuel I needed.

"You know, you could've saved half your speech," I told him. "My father was just here. He also told me to get off my ass and fight, so you're a little late with that."

Vincent frowned. "Seriously? I have more to say. I rehearsed on the ride here."

"Save it. I got the message."

"Oh. Well, that's good then." He looked uncertain now that his original plan had been thwarted. "So, what are you going to do about it?"

My mind spun as it formed and discarded dozens of strategies.

I had to prove to Scarlett that I wasn't the same reckless hothead who'd raced Bocci that night.

In order to do that, I needed to take concrete action. Do something that would highlight how serious I was about changing. *What can I...*

My heart stopped for a second before it kicked into double time.

I got it.

"I have a plan," I said in response to Vincent's question. "But I need the team's help."

The next afternoon, the entire Blackcastle football club piled into my house for an "unofficial team meeting."

They bitched and moaned about the last-minute summons, the long drive, and the imposition on their day off, but every single member showed up.

An embarrassing twinge of emotion scoured my throat as I surveyed the crowded living room. I would never say it aloud because they'd give me never-ending shit about it, but the fact they were giving up part of their Sunday for me when I hadn't given them any details about this meeting's topic meant a hell of a lot.

One of the things I loved most about football was the brotherhood. I'd lost that after I left Holchester, but I was tentatively hopeful that I'd found it again.

"So what's this mystery meeting about?" Samson asked, stretching his arms and legs with a yawn. "It better be something good. I'm missing a Sunday roast for this."

"Are we finally starting our book club?" Adil straightened, his eyes gleaming with excitement. "Wilma Pebbles has a new book coming out soon. It should be our featured read."

Ever since he read that Triceratops book, he'd been obsessed with Wilma Pebbles.

The rest of the team laughed and jeered, though several members looked intrigued. Stevens tossed a throw pillow at him. Adil easily caught it.

"Don't forget you all agreed to join the book club," he reminded them. "I'm adding everyone to the group chat once I've sorted out the logistics."

"You mean you haven't sorted them out yet?" Gallagher snorted. "What kind of club admin *are* you?"

"The kind who'll put you on cleanup duty if you don't show me more respect."

"Yeah? I'd like to see you enforce *that* rule—hey! Watch the hair!" Gallagher protested when Adil threw the pillow at him.

Beside me, Vincent rubbed his temple and shook his head.

This was why I didn't want to be team captain. Corralling a group of footballers was harder than herding a litter of hyperactive puppies.

"This is *not* a book club meeting," he said. "This is a strategy meeting. It has to do with our newest team member."

The other players quieted, their eyes roving between us with open curiosity. They were still getting used to Vincent and me working together instead of arguing, but they were fully on board with the new dynamic. Last season's tension hadn't been fun for anyone.

"Did you two finally kiss and make up?" Elliott, a midfielder, called from his seat next to the fireplace. "Are our parents not divorced anymore?"

Laughter erupted around the room.

"Excuse me." Vincent looked insulted. "I've been your captain for years. *He* only transferred in this year." He jerked his thumb at me. "We are not on the same level. There's only one parent here, and it's me."

"Sure," I said. "You can be the annoying parent. I'll be the fun older brother."

He glared at me, but the expression lacked heat. "Are you going to continue taking the piss, or are you going to explain to everyone why they're here?"

Right. As much as I enjoyed humbling his ego, we had more important matters to discuss.

I faced the team again. "First, before we get to the reason why we're all here, I want to apologize," I said. The sentiment had been weighing on me for a while, and I needed to get it off my chest. "I know things have been difficult for various reasons since I joined the club. Some of it is due to external circumstances, but some of it is because of me. Because of my temper, my recklessness—"

"Your huge ego," Vincent said.

"My *pride*," I said, ignoring him. "All of these things have contributed to a tumultuous start to the season. I dragged you guys into my fight with Holchester when I shouldn't have, and now we're all paying for it."

I looked around the room at everyone's somber faces. For once, they weren't cracking jokes or goofing off. We had a rocky start, but we'd been through a lot together. I was grateful to have them by my side, and I wasn't going to let them down again.

"However, that's going to change because I'm committed to Blackcastle, and I'm sure as hell committed to making sure we bring home the trophy at the end of the season."

Loud cheers greeted my words. I waited until they died down before I continued. "I'll convince Coach to put me back in the game.

When he does, know that I'll be fighting for *all* of us on the pitch. This isn't about me; it's about the team. And together, we're going to *kick the other teams' asses.*"

Another raucous round of cheers erupted.

"Hear, hear!"

"*Fuck* Holchester!"

"Blackcastle for the fucking win!" Elliott pounded on the table for emphasis.

"Alright, settle down," Vincent called like the buzzkill he is, but he was smiling. "We'll have plenty of time to talk football later. Let's get down to business." He gave me a pointed look.

The guys quieted, clearly curious about where this was going.

I paused to collect my thought before speaking again. "As some of you may know, Scarlett and I recently broke up."

"Yeah, I heard. You and DuBois's sister." Stevens clucked his tongue. "Shit luck, man. She was a hot—" He cut off abruptly when Vincent and I both pinned him with dark glares. "Uh, I mean, she seems like a lovely woman. I'm sorry. Please continue."

I let his impertinence slide—this time.

"As I was saying, Scarlett and I broke up, but I've gathered you here because I would like to request your help with the situation."

The team exchanged puzzled glances.

"I don't understand," Samson said. "How can we help?"

"And why do we need to meet in person for it?" Gallagher yawned. "This could've been an email."

"No, it couldn't," Vincent said. "You'll see when Asher explains step number one."

Gallagher frowned. "Step number one of what?"

I smiled a genuine smile for the first time in two weeks. "Of our latest playbook: Win Scarlett Back."

CHAPTER 52

SCARLETT

"CAN I ASK YOU A QUESTION?" EMMA LINGERED AFTER class again, her face stamped with nerves. "It's not about the student showcase. Not exactly."

"Of course." I turned off the music and faced her. Some instructors preferred using a live pianist for their lessons, but I liked the freedom to pause and replay without relying on another person to pick up on my cues. "What is it?"

Emma shifted her weight from foot to foot. I waited patiently, my curiosity pricking its ears up at her long silence. She was usually more direct.

"How did you deal with the pressure of performing?" she finally asked, her cheeks reddening. "I mean, knowing that all eyes will be on you and that people will catch any mistake you make onstage. Did it get inside your head? Make you...make you not want the role anymore?"

Sympathy swam in my chest. "Is this about *The Nutcracker?*"

She hesitated for a moment before she nodded, her expression miserable. "I know it's a school showcase and not, like, a performance for the king or anything, but it's the biggest role I've had yet. I don't want to mess it up. I *know* I can do it, but the closer we get to opening night, the more I'm dreading it. There are all these voices in my head telling me I'm not good enough to do it justice, and I can't get them out." Emma's chin wobbled. "What if they're still there on opening night and mess up my performance? All my friends and family will be there. I don't want to make a muck of things."

The sympathy deepened and mixed with an iota of shame. She sounded so young and uncertain that it cast my previous, deeply buried feelings of envy toward her in an even uglier light.

I'd had my reasons for feeling the way I had, but I was an adult and she was a teenager—an extremely talented one, but a teenager, nonetheless. I'd been in her shoes once, and I understood exactly where she was coming from.

"It wasn't easy," I admitted in response to her question. "There were shows where I was so nervous I wanted to throw up backstage. I don't think that ever truly goes away. Even the greatest dancers get nervous before a big performance sometimes. It's *normal*, so don't feel like you're not good enough because you have those feelings. In fact, imposter syndrome is often a sign of greatness."

Emma frowned. "How?"

"It's proof you're setting high standards for yourself and that you're not satisfied with being simply *good enough*," I said. "If we think we're perfect and there's nothing we can improve on, we'll never grow. If there's no growth, we stagnate. And greatness doesn't come from stagnation; it comes from progress."

The words were meant for Emma, but saying them aloud struck a chord deep inside me.

I'd lived in a form of stasis since my accident. Asher had shaken it up and forced me outside my comfort zone, but there was still a part of me that resisted it because I didn't *want* to grow. The status quo was stagnation, but it was also predictable. Safe. And that part of me was clinging to the spindly branches of a long-dead tree instead of embracing the seeds of a new beginning.

It was a hard truth, and not one I'd expected to confront on an otherwise ordinary Wednesday afternoon. But it was often the ordinary days that surprised us most.

I took a deep breath and pushed my realization to the side for future reflection. Now wasn't the time to get in my own head. God knew I'd done *that* enough the past few weeks.

"As for the performance aspect, you can only do your best," I said in response to the second part of Emma's question. "I can't promise that everything will be perfect. No one can guarantee that. But I've seen you perform, and I know how hard you work in class. You are one of my *best* students, and I have full faith that you'll do the Sugar Plum Fairy justice."

A tiny smile peeked past her nerves. "Thank you."

"You're welcome." I returned her smile. "If it makes you feel better, I've found that even when the mind is anxious, the body remembers. The minute I got onstage, my worries melted away because I *let* them. I didn't try to hold on to the fear. I just let go and allowed the muscle memory to take over."

"That makes sense." Emma blew out a sigh. She didn't seem fully convinced, but she looked less anxious than she had at the start of our conversation. "I've done it before, but the stakes haven't been this high, you know?"

"I know. They'll keep getting higher, but your experience and resilience will grow alongside them."

"Growth, not stagnation."

"Exactly."

"Thank you, Ms. DuBois." She shifted her weight again, looking embarrassed. "I'm sorry I keep bothering you after class, but this was really helpful. Truly. I'm glad I'm not alone in feeling those things."

"Trust me, you're never alone, and you aren't bothering me." I meant it. I'd been in her shoes, and I understood that pressure. "I'm always here if you want to talk, whether it's about the performance or business aspect of ballet."

Emma beamed her thanks, her face positively glowing.

After she left, I cleaned up the studio, my mind scattered across a dozen different topics.

We were less than two months away from both the student and staff showcases. I hadn't joined the latter expecting it to affect my views of the former, but it had.

Sometime between getting my understudy role and my conversation with Emma today, my jealousy toward her star turn in *The Nutcracker* had gradually faded. Maybe it was because my own rehearsals reminded me of how physically and mentally taxing the lead role could be, or maybe it was because I finally had an outlet for the restlessness that'd plagued me since my accident. Whatever it was, it was liberating to be free from those particular ugly feelings.

It helped that practice had gone smoothly since my hospitalization. I took care of myself the best I could, both at home and at work. Tamara and I also collaborated on a modified rehearsal process that included time limits, frequent breaks, and a more moderate pace. Thankfully, the rest of the staff were fully on board, and I hadn't had any major flare-ups since the modifications were made.

Looking back, I was embarrassed that I'd pushed myself to the point where I had to go to the hospital. My desire for perfection and the unrealistic standard I held myself to nearly destroyed me. I'd been too reckless with my body, and I—

I froze as the words reverberated through my head.

Too reckless.

My heart twisted.

I'd done such a good job of *not* thinking about Asher today. Since I woke up that morning, he'd only crossed my mind five times, which was leagues better than the days when he consumed my thoughts entirely from dawn until dusk.

However, the echo of my earlier self-reflection yanked him back to the forefront of my mind—the sight of him standing in the studio doorway, the torment in his voice when I broke up with him, the sound of his footsteps disappearing into the distance.

The memories tugged on the knot in my chest, yanking it tighter.

Too reckless.

I'd accused Asher of being too reckless and endangering himself, but hadn't I done the same when I refused to listen to my body's demands? Granted, my situation was less likely to culminate in an immediate, fiery death, but the principle was the same.

Unease filtered through my veins.

Was I being a hypocrite and punishing him for something that I myself was guilty of?

It's not really *the same,* a pragmatic voice in my head reasoned. *You didn't make any promises to him regarding dance. You don't have a history of endangering yourself or others. You pushed yourself too hard, that's all.*

Maybe the situations aren't the same, but the principle is, another voice countered.

Oh, shut up.

You shut up.

My head pounded from the internal squabble raging inside me. Hearing voices was a bad sign, and hearing them bicker was even worse.

I really needed to call my old therapist again. I'd already been contemplating it after my hospitalization, but the past few weeks had cinched the decision for me. I thought I'd gotten to a good place after years of weekly sessions with her, but obviously, I still had work to do—for both my professional life and personal life.

Two weeks had passed since my breakup with Asher. I thought the bruising ache of his absence would fade, but it only strengthened by the day. I couldn't turn on the TV or pass by a newsstand without seeing photos of his face plastered everywhere. I couldn't even walk through my flat without seeing his face or hearing his laugh.

In the short time I'd known him, he'd ingrained himself into my life so thoroughly that I couldn't imagine living it without him. Trying to do so had been…difficult. And my new concerns about whether I'd unfairly set him up on a pedestal even I couldn't reach didn't make it easier.

I finished wiping down the barre and tossed the used wipes into the rubbish bin.

Did it *matter* if I was being hypocritical? That didn't change the reality of our situation. It wouldn't make Asher any less self-destructive or susceptible to danger. Unless he—

"Scarlett." Carina poked her head into the studio, interrupting my rambling thoughts. Her face was flushed, and her eyes glittered with excitement. "You need to get downstairs *right now*."

"Why? Is it the paps again?" They hadn't caught wind of my breakup with Asher yet, but it was only a matter of time.

Carina shook her head, looking almost awed. "You have to see it for yourself."

CHAPTER 53

SCARLETT

"I SAW THEM ON THE SECURITY CAMERAS," CARINA SAID breathlessly as we exited the building. "I had to tell you."

"Saw who..." My question trailed off when we reached the car park.

I stopped.

Inhaled.

And *stared*.

Logically, I understood what my eyes were seeing, but my brain couldn't fully process the spectacle.

Because staring back at me, their faces stamped with near-identical grins, was the entire Blackcastle football club. Every single one of them stood next to a different sports car like they were salesmen at a luxury auto show.

Well, *almost* every one of them.

My heart stopped when the two players in the middle parted, revealing a familiar head of dark hair and emerald eyes.

How...what...

My brain sputtered, at a loss for words, as Asher walked past his teammates and toward me. His mouth curved into a small smile. "Hi, darling."

It was a simple greeting. Two words, which I'd heard plenty of times before. It shouldn't have elicited such an instant, visceral reaction—but it did.

Every nerve ending sparked like live wires in the rain. Warmth sluiced through my body as my heartbeat slowed, trying to draw the moment out as long as possible.

Hi, darling. The only words that always made me feel like I was coming home.

They urged me to run up to him and throw my arms around his neck. To bury my face in his chest and listen to his heartbeat as proof that he was alive and *here*.

The compulsion was so strong, I actually took a tiny step forward before reason prevailed and I stopped myself.

Instead, I swallowed past the growing lump in my throat and gestured at the cars lined up behind him. "What's this?"

It took all my remaining willpower not to falter as Asher closed the distance between us.

One step.

Two steps.

Three.

On and on until he came to a halt less than two feet from me— close enough for his scent to steal into my lungs and for his warmth to wrap around me like a blanket on a snowy winter night.

A shiver ghosted across my skin.

"I'll explain in a second." Asher's voice pitched low enough for only my ears. "The last time we talked, you accused me of being too reckless and self-destructive. I didn't want to admit it then, but I've had time to reflect on my actions and the reasons behind them, and you were right." A cloud passed overhead, throwing the sculpted angles of his face into shadow. "I didn't race despite the danger; I raced *because* of it. I loved the adrenaline. I loved the thrill of competing against death and winning. But recently, after a few…talks with other close people in my life, I realized that wasn't the only reason."

Asher swallowed before continuing. "When he suspended me, Coach said I lacked discipline because something deeper was driving the impulsiveness that made me do stupid things like race against Bocci. It wasn't Holchester. It wasn't my pride or my desire to be great. It was something else, and I couldn't figure out what it was. Then my father showed up over the weekend"—his smile returned at my jerk of surprise—"yeah, I was shocked too. But he showed up and we had a long talk. He mentioned my behavior after Teddy died and how it seemed like I had a death wish at the time. That was when it hit me. I never truly reconciled my guilt over Teddy's death. I was drawn to the danger of racing because I was trying to punish myself for what happened. Because part of me believed I should've been the one who died that night, not him."

His raw confession hit me with the force of a physical blow. "Asher…"

"I'm not trying to make you feel sorry for me so you'll forgive me," he said. "I know it's not an excuse for the way I've behaved, but it's the truth. Like I mentioned earlier, I've had a lot of time to reflect these past two weeks, and I realized something else. Whenever I thought about racing in the past, I got an adrenaline rush. I couldn't wait to get behind the wheel and see how far it would take me. But when I think about it now, the only thing I feel is regret. Even if I hadn't had the Teddy revelation, I would've felt the same way because racing is what lost me the one thing—the one *person*—I care about most in the world. You."

Unshed tears sprang up in my eyes. I tried to speak, but it was impossible. *Breathing* was impossible. So I could only stand there, my eyes burning and my chest aching, while he slowly but systematically destroyed the defenses I'd built around my heart.

"My whole life, I focused on football and winning. That was it," Asher said, a touch of vulnerability softening his voice. "Then you came along and shattered every preconception I had of who I was and what I wanted. You made me reevaluate my life and want to be a better person—not just for you but for me."

One of the tears escaped and scalded my cheek. I was dimly aware that Carina was still there, and his teammates, and whoever else happened to pass by at the moment, but I didn't care.

At that moment, no one else mattered except us.

"I can't fully reconcile the impact Teddy's death had on me overnight, but I think acknowledging it is a good first step. I don't want to be the guy who lets his past and his pride drive him to reckless decisions anymore," Asher said. "I don't want to hurt myself or the people I care about for some short-lived high. Most of all, I don't want to ruin my chances of spending as many days with you as possible because I love you. More than football, more than racing, more than anything else in this universe—Pluto included."

A half laugh, half sob tore past my throat. More tears fell, but I didn't bother trying to stop them.

Asher's acknowledgment of my silly Pluto rant over the summer and how much the little planet meant to me in this particular moment was so perfect, so *him* that it made my heart squeeze.

"I love *you*," he repeated, his words thick with emotion. "I'm so fucking in love with you, darling, and the only reckless thing I want to do is explore how deep this rabbit hole goes with you. Together."

I laughed again, my own voice embarrassingly watery. "It goes pretty deep, I imagine."

He smiled. "I think so."

I love you. My body sang with those words, but before I could respond or acknowledge that sentiment with something more than tears, Asher stepped to the side.

"However, I know words are cheap, so I asked the guys to come and give me a hand." He gestured at the cars. "This is my entire car collection. I've bequeathed one vehicle to every member of the team."

My pulse drummed in my ears. I'd been so distracted by the team's appearance earlier that I hadn't paid attention to the cars themselves.

The Porsche. The Bugatti. The *Jaguar*.

All familiar sights from Asher's garage, all in someone else's hands now.

"Tell me you didn't," I breathed. That was millions of pounds in luxury vehicles.

Money aside, Asher *loved* his cars. Even if he didn't race, that didn't mean he had to give up his collection.

"I know we haven't met, but you're my favorite person *ever*," the player standing next to the Porsche called out. I recognized him as Samson Agbo, one of the club's wingers. "I got this baby for free." He slapped the shiny black hood with affection.

"I got the Lambo!" Adil jangled his keys with a triumphant grin. "Thanks for breaking up with him, Scarlett. You should do it more often."

The other players laughed while Asher glared at him.

I scanned the lineup until my eyes fell on Vincent, who leaned against the side of a vintage hunter green Jaguar convertible. Asher's favorite. The one he said Holchester defaced and that kickstarted this whole mess.

Whoever he'd hired to restore the paint had done an immaculate job because there was no trace of a single scratch.

Vincent nodded when our gazes met. It was a small gesture, but I heard him loud and clear.

I had his full blessing to rekindle my relationship with Asher if I wanted.

Fresh emotion gushed into my throat.

I faced Asher again, trying to piece my wayward thoughts into a coherent response. There were so many important things I wanted to say that they eluded my grasp altogether, so I fell back on the first thing that came to mind. "If you gave away all your cars, what are you going to drive?"

His face broke out into a grin as he pointed out the car next to the Jaguar. The saloon was so bland and nondescript it'd blended into the surrounding gray cement until he directed my attention to it.

"That one," he said, sounding proud. "It was voted the safest car in the world this year. Four-wheel antilock braking system, forward-collision warning system, front and rear head protection...who needs to go from zero to sixty in two point three seconds when you have adaptive cruise control?"

The wind carried my startled laugh through the car park. "I have no idea what any of that means, but it sounds...safe."

"Very safe." Asher's expression sobered. He turned his back to the team, shielding me from their eyes as his voice dipped again. "I wanted to show how serious I was about changing. I can't make up for what I did, but I can do everything in my power to ensure it never happens again. And I'm so fucking sorry for putting you through—"

I cut him off with a kiss.

In the absence of suitable words, I let my actions do the talking. My fingers delved into his hair, and after a split second of surprised hesitation, he kissed me back, his mouth melting against mine with such exquisite intimacy that I felt it in every molecule of my body.

My mind hazed, and despite the October chill, warmth suffused my skin.

Kissing Asher again after nearly two weeks of deprivation was like breaking through the surface of water after hours of icy submersion. Every sense crystallized with poignant detail—the sensual firmness of his lips, the hint of spice in his aftershave, the strength of his hand as it cupped my face.

I barely heard the team's whistles and catcalls as I gave in to the sweet headiness of the moment.

I couldn't guarantee that Asher wouldn't revert to his old habits down the road, but I trusted him. I saw the conviction in his eyes and heard it in his voice. Even if I hadn't, the fact he was willing to give up his beloved car collection told me everything I needed to know.

Plus, if there was one thing I'd learned over the past four months, it was the importance of showing grace—both to myself and to others.

We couldn't change the past. We could only shape the future, and I wanted a future with him. Together.

I pulled back just enough for us to catch our breaths. "Remember what you said earlier?"

"About the antilock braking system?"

"*No.*" I released a tiny sigh of exasperation alongside my smile. "You said you loved me."

He slid his palm down to the nape of my neck. Its heat burned deliciously into my skin. "I said I love you more than anything else in the universe, including Pluto," he corrected teasingly. "Don't dilute the poetry of my words."

"I did that on purpose. I didn't want to sound repetitive because what I really want to say is that I love you too." My voice softened.

"More than anything else in the universe, including Pluto."

I'd held back on telling him for so long that releasing the words into the world was its own kind of liberation.

Asher's breath stuttered for half a beat. He hadn't pressured me to return the sentiment earlier, nor did he seem to expect it, and that only made me love him more.

He wasn't perfect, but he was perfect for me.

"I missed you," I whispered. My tears had dried, but the emotion remained, swelling and rising behind my ribcage. "So much."

As upset as I'd been, I'd missed him so fiercely during every second of our separation that he'd haunted my dreams more nights than I cared to admit.

Asher brushed his thumb over my cheek, his touch unbearably tender. "I missed you too, darling."

"Just promise me one thing."

"Anything."

"Take the Jag back from Vincent. He'll be insufferable with it."

As much as I appreciated Asher's commitment to change, I wasn't going to make him give up his favorite car. It suited him; the saloon didn't.

Asher laughed, his eyes glittering in the late afternoon sunlight. "Done."

Then he lowered his head and covered his mouth with mine, and everything—the cars, the people, the catcalls from his teammates—melted away again.

ASHER

"Donovan!" Coach barked. "Get your ass in here." He disappeared back inside his office.

I ignored the team's heckling and finished pulling my shirt over my head. "That's getting old," I said, giving Elliott a light shove as I walked toward Coach's office. "Find a new schtick."

"We'll find a new schtick when you stop getting in trouble." Elliot snickered. "How many times have you been called into Coach's office this season? And it's only November."

"New betting pool!" Adil shouted. "Fifty quid says Donovan gets called in there *at least* two more times before the holidays."

I shook my head as the rest of the team rushed to place their bets. *Idiots.*

However, I couldn't summon true annoyance toward them. It'd been two weeks since Scarlett and I got back together, and I hadn't been able to stop grinning since. I owed the team for their help (even if their "help" simply involved taking my cars off my hands and driving them to RAB), so I let their good-natured taunts slide.

I entered Coach's office for what felt like the umpteenth time that season and waited for him to speak.

My injuries were fully healed and I was training with the rest of the team on the pitch again, but I was still benched. Unfortunately, it was harder to convince Coach I'd changed than it was Scarlett.

I doubted telling him I loved him and snogging him in front of the team would help.

Coach's eyes slitted like he could hear my thoughts and he was *not* happy about them. "So," he said. "I heard you got back together with your girlfriend."

My mouth fell open before I snapped it shut again. Of all the topics I thought he'd want to discuss, my love life wasn't one of them.

Not to mention...how the hell did he know about me and Scarlett?

"My daughter is friends with your girlfriend," Coach said, answering my unspoken question. "She talks. So do they." His jerked his chin toward the door, his face crumpled with a scowl. "Can't tell whether I'm running a team of professional athletes or an episode of bloody *Gossip Girl* at times."

Add Coach knowing what *Gossip Girl* was to the second shocker of the day.

"Yes, Scarlett and I are back together, sir," I said, unsure where this was leading.

"Does she know what an idiot she's dating?"

"Yes, sir, and she loves me anyway."

Coach's mouth twitched in the closest approximation of a smile I'd seen from him since his hat trick in 1995. When he noticed my answering smile, his expression morphed back into a scowl. "I also heard you gave away your fancy car collection."

"Most of it, sir. Except for one." I'd retrieved the Jaguar from a protesting Vincent the day after Scarlett and I made up. He pelted me with all sorts of English and French swear words, but he eventually gave up the keys with an angry grumble.

I was helping Scarlett plan a big birthday party for him next month, so hopefully that made up for it.

"You sad about it?" Coach asked.

I shook my head. "The cars were material things. I loved them, but I don't need them anymore."

I was working through my lingering guilt over Teddy's death with Myles, the club's psychologist. However, just knowing the reason behind why I acted the way I did helped me curb my worst impulses.

My emotions still got the better of me sometimes, but I didn't vent them by punching someone or speeding in a supercar.

It was progress.

Coach grunted in reluctant approval. "You've worked hard in training, even while you were injured." He examined me, his eyes shrewd. "What are your thoughts on Saturday's match?"

I grimaced. Over the weekend, Blackcastle lost its second consecutive match. It'd been a home match, which stung even more.

"We were strong in the first half, but the attack line lagged in the second half," I said honestly. "We weren't as aggressive as we should've been, and our hesitation cost us at least one goal."

Coach grunted again. "You've been a headache for me since you joined the team, Donovan, and I've seen your face in my office more times than I care to count. If I really wanted to teach you a lesson, I'd keep you benched through the holidays and into the new year. I don't give a damn what the public says."

I swallowed, my blood going cold at his words. "I understand."

"However." He leaned forward and tented his hands beneath his chin. "You and DuBois are finally acting like adults toward each other. You've demonstrated a concrete willingness to *listen* and change and, while he obviously can't share details, Myles says you're making good progress in your sessions. So I am inclined to think that maybe you've already learned your lesson."

My heart sped up, but I maintained a neutral expression while I waited for him to finish. I didn't want to jinx anything.

"I'm putting you back in for next week's match. Consider it a trial. We'll see where we go from there." Coach scowled. "However, if you so much as get a speeding ticket under my watch, you're going straight back to the bench. Am I clear?"

Overwhelming relief rushed into every cell of my body. *I'm fucking back*. I couldn't wait to tell Scarlett and the team.

"Yes, sir." My grin could've powered the entirety of Markovic Stadium on its own. "You won't regret it. I promise."

CHAPTER 54

SCARLETT

THE NIGHT OF THE WINTER STUDENT SHOWCASE DAWNED bright and cold.

My coat warded off the worst of the chill, but a gust of wind snuck past the layer of wool to claw at my bones anyway.

I shivered, half grateful and half apprehensive that we would be inside soon.

I hadn't told Emma I was coming. I wanted it to be a surprise, but I was second-guessing my appearance with every step.

Asher's gloved hand squeezed mine. "You ready?" he asked, his voice quiet.

I took a deep breath and nodded. "As ready as I'll ever be."

We were already here. It was too late to turn back.

Nevertheless, the air evacuated from my lungs when we turned the corner and Westbury's famous neoclassical facade burst into view.

It loomed ahead, its grand columns and ornate gilding illuminated by the soft glow of neighboring lampposts. The marble steps teemed with people dressed in suits and gowns, and several professional photographers snapped pictures of the arriving attendees like it was a red-carpet event.

For RAB, it *was* a red-carpet event. Most attendees were friends and family of the students, but there were also alumni and dance company representatives present. The school made a limited number of tickets available to the public, and those were snatched up by true ballet aficionados.

It was going to be a spectacular night—if I could get past the rattle of nerves in my chest.

"Breathe," Asher said as we approached the steps. "We can leave any time you want."

This time, I was the one who squeezed his hand in silent thanks.

"We're not leaving." My resolve pushed past the nerves and hardened into determination. "We came here for Emma, and we're staying for her."

After several lengthy discussions, I became Emma's official mentor last month. I'd never mentored anyone before, but I *loved* my new role. Teaching students dance techniques was one thing; guiding them in their career was another.

The latter was so much more fulfilling than I expected, and I *wanted* to see her perform live. She'd worked so hard for the role. I didn't want to be so weak and selfish that I wouldn't even try to set aside my own hang-ups to support her on the biggest night of her career so far.

So here I was, mouth dry and heart racing as Asher showed our tickets to the staff.

Several people did a double take when they saw him, but they were polite enough to keep a respectful distance, and we entered the theatre with no issues.

Thankfully, we didn't have to deal with the paps hounding us anymore either. After weeks of endless coverage and clickbait articles, they finally got bored and moved on to the messy movie star divorce Brooklyn predicted earlier in the fall.

They still popped up now and then because Asher was Asher, but compared to the circus of our early days, we were enjoying relative peace.

"I've never been here before." Asher sounded impressed as he took in our opulent surroundings. "It's beautiful."

My throat clogged at the familiar sweep of marble stairs and soaring windows.

"It is," I said softly. "It hasn't changed at all."

He glanced at me, his gaze assessing. He didn't condescend me by asking if I was okay, but I could feel his concern as we walked up the stairs toward the main auditorium.

Surprisingly, I really *was* okay.

I thought walking through the halls of Westbury again would be overwhelming, but other than my initial shock of nerves and nostalgia, I felt nothing except anticipation for Emma's performance.

For years, I'd built the theatre up to be this monstrous symbol of my old life, but it was just a building. The small man to the great Wizard of Oz of my imagination. The only power it held was what I gave it, and I'd reconciled with my past enough to not give it any power at all.

In another lifetime, I'd be backstage right now, preparing for another performance as the star of the show.

Tonight, I was merely one of hundreds of attendees who'd shown up to support the next generation of dancers.

And I was more than okay with that.

"Asher! Is that you?"

Our heads turned at the same time. A beautiful redhead

approached us in the hall with a tall, handsome Asian man in tow. Her face split into a wide smile.

"It *is* you! I haven't seen you in ages. How are you?" She hugged Asher and turned to me, her eyes sparkling with mischief. "And you, the girl who snagged the infamous Asher Donovan. It's nice to finally meet you in person."

I smiled back and returned the sentiment. We only just met, but she exuded an infectious energy that was impossible to resist.

Asher laughed. "Scarlett, this is Jules, an old friend of mine."

"And this is Josh, my boyfriend," Jules added, gesturing at the man beside her.

"It's great to meet you." Josh gave me a warm smile that revealed a devastating set of dimples. However, his smile visibly cooled when he glanced at Asher. "Donovan."

Asher looked like he was trying not to laugh. "Josh. Always a pleasure."

"We were on our way to our seats when I spotted you. I *told* him it was you, but he insisted it wasn't. See?" Jules elbowed Josh in the side. "I was right."

"You were." He didn't sound particularly thrilled.

Josh slid an arm around Jules's waist and glared at Asher while we chatted during our wait for curtains up.

It turned out the American couple was on holiday from D.C. Asher met them at Queen Bridget's wedding a couple of years ago (I still couldn't believe he'd been a guest at *the* royal wedding of the century), and they'd kept in touch since.

Well, he and Jules kept in touch. I could tell by Josh's scowl that he was not an Asher fan.

Jules was a lawyer, and a London member of her firm had a daughter who was performing in the showcase. He'd bought tickets for every employee who wanted to attend, including those who were visiting from out of town.

"I've never been to a ballet, so I figured, why not?" Jules shrugged. "Anyway, it looks like the show's about to start, so I don't want to keep you any longer. I just wanted to say hi." She lowered her voice. "And Asher, I heard about your situation from our litigation team. I know I don't practice that area of law, but if you need help, let me know anyway." She raised her voice to normal volume again. "Enjoy the show! It was great running into you."

We said our goodbyes, and I waited until they were out of earshot before I arched an eyebrow at a sheepish-looking Asher. "What situation was she talking about?"

He placed his hand on the small of my back and guided me toward our seats in the front row. "I was going to tell you later, but I finally found out who vandalized my car," he admitted. "It wasn't Bocci or anyone from Holchester. It was Clive."

I stopped dead in my tracks. "*What*? Clive as in the rugby player? The one I went on a date with?"

Asher nodded. "Ivy called to tell me last week. Apparently, they rekindled their relationship after our double date. She heard about the car incident from Poppy, who heard about it from one the players, and she stumbled on a bunch of pictures Clive took of my car after he keyed it. The idiot was dumb enough to leave incriminating evidence lying around. He wanted a trophy, I guess." He shook his head. "She asked him about it, and he confessed. His ego still couldn't get over the fact that I beat him during last summer's race, though admittedly, I hadn't been too gracious a winner at the time."

My head spun as we resumed walking again.

"That's *wild*." Clive had seemed so nice when I met him at Neon, though he'd raised several red flags during our date. I hadn't talked to him since then, so finding out he was the culprit behind the vandalization was a shock. "Did you confront him?"

"Almost." A muscle ticked in Asher's jaw. "I thought about it, but it wasn't worth the trouble. The car is fixed, I survived the crash, and Ivy broke up with him over what he did. I did consult with my lawyers, which was how Jules found out about it, but I don't want a legal battle. Karma will take care of him." A wicked smile stole across his lips. "I did see that he lost his last three rugby matches. Took quite a hit during the last one, too, and is out for the foreseeable future with a broken leg. So karma works fast."

"Asher Donovan taking the high road?" I teased. "You really have grown."

We didn't get a chance to talk more before Emma's parents showed up. Our seats were next to theirs, and they showered us with effusive greetings when they saw us.

"Glad to have you at Blackcastle, by the way," Emma's father said, shaking Asher's hand. "I've been a fan of yours even when you were at Holchester. I think this year is our year."

Asher smiled. "I think so too."

We quieted as the lights dimmed and the show started.

Emma's eyes lit up when she saw me, but that was all the reaction she allowed herself before she sank fully into the role of Sugar Plum Fairy.

As I predicted, she nailed her performance. When she glided across the stage, the picture of serene grace, I didn't feel a single ounce of envy—only pride and the liberating peace that came with laying the ghosts of my past to rest at last.

In the week leading up to the staff showcase, I hoped that, like

Westbury, it would prove less daunting than I imagined.

So far, I was conflicted.

The performance took place exactly one week after the student one. The backstage area was a zoo as everyone scrambled to finish prepping, and judging by the noise that seeped through the thick velvet curtains, it was a full house tonight.

"How are you feeling?" Tamara asked. She sounded calm, but the pinch in her brow betrayed her nerves.

"Not too bad." I smoothed a hand over my costume and tried to steady the wild patter of my heartbeat. "I can't believe it's here."

"It does sneak up on you, doesn't it?" She smiled. "You've been great during rehearsal, so don't worry. Everything will be fine."

Neither of us mentioned my disastrous *first* rehearsal. That was in the past, and we'd come a long way since then.

"Thank you," I said. "For everything."

She'd been hard on me during the first rehearsal, but since then, she'd gone above and beyond to accommodate my needs. If it weren't for her, the past few months would've been torturous.

"Don't get sentimental on me," Tamara said crisply, but there was a small twinkle in her eyes. "If you really want to thank me, go out there and show them how it's done."

"I'll try. I mean, I will," I amended.

"Good."

Another dancer called her away soon after, and I waited until she left before I braved a peek around the curtain. My heart trembled at the size of the crowd packing the auditorium, but it gradually steadied as more and more familiar faces came into view.

I spotted Asher front and center with Vincent, Carina, Brooklyn, and my parents, who sat on either end of the row so they could avoid talking to each other. My father had fully recovered from his injury over the summer, and he'd brought his (ex) home nurse as his date. That had to rankle my mother, who'd shown up solo. I'd bet my last quid she'd take up with some studly young gardener to spite my father within the next month.

Emma and her parents sat in the row behind them, atwitter with excitement. There were even a few Blackcastle players sprinkled throughout the audience, including Noah, Adil, Samson, and Gallagher.

I inhaled a deep breath and allowed myself a moment to take it all in—the lights, the people, the ripple of anticipation coursing through the air.

This wasn't my dazzling star turn as a promising young ingénue. My performance wouldn't be reviewed in *The Guardian* or have an encore at Westbury the following night. I would never be that dancer again, and—for the first time since my accident—I was at peace with it.

That chapter of my life had closed, but this time, I could close it on my own terms.

"Alright, everyone!" Tamara clapped to get our attention. "Five minutes till showtime."

This is it.

Nerves fluttered through me.

Four minutes.

The air took on a surreal, hazy quality. After months of rehearsals, anxieties, and self-doubt, it was hard to believe the moment had arrived.

Three minutes.

I pictured the people waiting on the other side of the curtain. There were strangers, yes, but there were also people there for *me*. People who loved me, supported me, and would never judge me no matter how well or how poorly I performed. They were my rocks, and thinking about them quelled some of my nerves.

Two minutes.

A strange calm descended as everyone settled into their places. Of course I wanted to dazzle onstage, but at the end of the night, it wasn't about the perfect performance. It was about the fact that I was here at all.

For years, I'd avoided participating in the showcase because I was scared I wouldn't live up to who I used to be. I'd finally faced those fears and learned to appreciate my body in all its forms.

I had to scratch and claw my way toward this moment, but I made it. I was *here*, and that was an accomplishment in and of itself.

One minute.

That being said, I wouldn't be me if I didn't pour my heart out on that stage. This performance was my swan song, and I was going to try my damn hardest to do it the justice it deserved.

The remainder of my nerves dissolved into a soft smile.

Showtime.

The curtains rose.

The music started.

And I danced.

CHAPTER 55

ASHER

TWO MONTHS LATER

"SINCE IT'S OUR SIX-MONTH ANNIVERSARY, I COULD technically *make* you tell me where we're going," Scarlett said. "I'll say it's my anniversary gift. You can't deny me that, can you?"

"Nice try, darling, but if you waste your gift asking me about the surprise, you won't get the surprise itself," I said, amused. "And trust me. You'll want the surprise."

"This is torture," she grumbled, but I heard the curiosity in her voice, even if I couldn't see it in her eyes.

I'd secured a silk blindfold over them before we left my house and remained steadfast against her attempts to make me crack. I hadn't spent months planning tonight's date to ruin it at the last minute.

Our footsteps echoed against the marble floors as I guided her through the entryway and up the lift. Our destination was on the third floor, and I wasn't going to risk taking her up three flights of stairs when she was blindfolded.

"Ooh, a lift." Scarlett perked up at the sound of the doors sliding closed. "So we're probably *not* going to a restaurant unless it's one of the ones in the Shard or something. Are we in a hotel? Museum? Harrods?"

I stifled a laugh. "None of the above. Stop trying to guess, darling. You won't get it."

"Well, now I take that as a challenge."

Of course she would. Her competitiveness was one of the things I loved about her.

But, as predicted, Scarlett couldn't guess correctly before we arrived. I wouldn't have either if I were in her shoes. It wasn't a place most people could access, and if Sebastian hadn't helped, I couldn't have pulled this off.

"You can stop guessing." I grinned and placed a hand on the small of her back, bringing her to a halt in front of a set of arched double doors. "We're here."

A thread of nerves wove through my anticipation as I removed her blindfold and slipped it into my pocket. Tonight was a big night—it'd been six months since our date in Tokyo, when we'd agreed to make our relationship official—and I'd taken a risk by adding a little...flair to the traditional anniversary dinner.

But the greater the risk, the greater the reward, and Scarlett deserved something more special than just a fancy dinner.

Scarlett blinked, her eyes presumably adjusting to the light after nearly an hour of being blindfolded. She glanced around the marble hall with its museum-quality paintings and priceless antique vases. Despite its opulence, it gave no hint as to the purpose or location of the building.

"Where are we?" she asked, her face a mosaic of confusion and intrigue.

My nerves sparked brighter as I reached for the gilded handles and opened the double doors. I stepped aside so she could enter, and my grin returned at her audible intake of breath.

"Scarlett," I said. "Welcome to the Valhalla Club library."

The Valhalla Club was an ultra-exclusive society for the world's wealthiest and most powerful. It had chapters in every major city, and its London branch occupied one of the most splendid mansions in all of England. Every room looked like it belonged in Buckingham Palace, but the library?

The library was the most magnificent of them all.

I walked in after Scarlett and let the doors close with a quiet *whoosh* behind us. It was my second visit—the first had been when Sebastian brought me for a walk-through of the space so I could plan tonight's date—but the interior never failed to awe me.

Soaring three stories to a massive, elaborately painted ceiling, the library was a wonderland of golden frescoes and leather-bound books. Crystal chandeliers cast the room in amber-hued light, and the main floor featured seven alcoves that separated the library's impressive collection by category. A sweeping staircase spiraled up to the second and third floors, its steps cushioned with the same rich emerald carpet as the rest of the room.

Beside me, Scarlett took it all in with visible awe. "This is the most *beautiful* room I've ever seen," she breathed. "How did you..."

"Sebastian is a member, and he was happy to do me a favor— especially after Blackcastle's recent wins." The Laurent heir belonged to the New York branch, but as a descendant of one of Valhalla's founding families, he held more sway than many of its other members. "But the library isn't the surprise. It's who's here."

I took her hand and pulled her toward one of the seven alcoves.

Her brow furrowed in obvious confusion as to why I would invite a third party to our anniversary night. "Who's..." Her sentence trailed off again when we reached the alcove and she saw who was inside.

"No." Scarlett stopped dead in her tracks. "Asher. *You didn't.*"

Relief and amusement washed away the remnants of my nerves at her stunned expression. "You've always wanted to meet her. I figured tonight would be a good time, especially since she just released a new book."

Inside the alcove, a striking woman with purple-black hair paused her conversation with her partner and rose from her seat behind a small table. A pile of books was stacked neatly on its polished surface. "Hi!" Her smile dazzled. "You must be Scarlett. I'm Isabella. Are you a hugger? I'm a hugger."

Scarlett made a strangled noise when Isabella Valencia, her favorite author, came around the table to greet her with a big hug.

"Asher tells me it's your six-month anniversary." Isabella pulled back, her eyes sparkling. "Congratulations. It's a big milestone."

"I—well, I mean, yes." Scarlett finally found her voice. "Hi. I'm a *big* fan. I loved your latest book."

"Oh, I'm glad! Thank you so much." Isabella's smile widened with genuine warmth. "Before we get to the signing, I want you to meet Kai, my fiancé."

She winked at her partner, who stood next to the table with a wry smile.

He and Scarlett exchanged greetings before Scarlett's gaze coasted to the stack of books on the table. "Wait. Signing?"

I took over explaining. "Isabella hasn't done a UK tour yet, but I figured a personal meet and greet would be more fun than standing in line for hours anyway." I gestured at the books. "I had special editions made of all her titles so she could sign them for you in person."

I'd found a printer who could bind personal copies in hardcover with all the bells and whistles—foiling, fancy formatting, and a bunch of other features that went over my head but that the printer insisted Scarlett would love.

Judging by the glossy sheen that brightened Scarlett's eyes, he'd been right. She opened her mouth, but nothing came out.

"When Asher emailed me about doing this, it was a no-brainer," Isabella said, rescuing Scarlett from her speechlessness. "I didn't care that I had to fly here from New York. His idea was the most romantic thing I've ever heard."

Behind her, Kai frowned, looking insulted.

"Come." Isabella hooked her arm through Scarlett's and led her to the table. "Let's get these books signed for you so you can enjoy the rest of your anniversary night with Asher. Which story is your favorite so far?"

While the women chatted, I went and stood next to Kai. We'd never interacted before, but I recognized him from various news stories as Kai Young, the CEO of a major media conglomerate. They owned dozens of news outlets in the UK, including *Match* and *Sports UK*.

"It's great of you to accompany Isabella here," I said in an attempt to make conversation. "My team would've taken good care of her, but I think it's lovely that you took the time to come with her."

Not a lot of billionaire chief executives would take time away from work to join their fiancée for a personal book signing. Most of them wouldn't do that for a *full* book tour.

I'd offered to pay for Isabella's entire trip to London, but she insisted that wasn't necessary since Kai owned a house in the city anyway.

"Yes, well, she's my *fiancée*." His tone was polite, but he placed an oddly aggressive emphasis on the last word. "I'm always happy to support her."

My other attempts to start a nice chat also failed, so I eventually fell into silence and contented myself with watching Scarlett.

My mouth tipped up at her excitement as she talked to Isabella. She'd lost her earlier shyness and was gushing about a plot twist in one of the author's earlier works, her face bright with animation.

When the signing finished and Isabella hugged her again, I thought Scarlett would dissolve into a cloud of sparkles and smiles.

It made my fucking heart sing. We hadn't officially exchanged gifts yet (though the special edition books were my anniversary presents to her), but she didn't even need to give me anything. Seeing her that happy had already made my night.

"I know this is going to sound tacky, but before we leave, do you mind if I get a photo and a few autographs?" Isabella asked me, her tone apologetic. "My friends and I are big fans, and they'd *kill* me if I came back without your signature."

Kai's frown deepened.

"Of course. It's the least I could do," I said easily.

"Great! Kai, can you take the pictures?" She shoved her phone at her fiancé. "I'd love one with Scarlett too."

I signed a few pages in her notebook for her, and we took turns grouping up for the photos—me with Isabella, then Scarlett with Isabella, followed by one of the three of us together. Isabella also insisted on taking photos of me and Scarlett to "document our night."

Kai did the honors. I heard he was quite nice and gentlemanly compared to other CEOs, but he didn't look very nice and gentlemanly to me. He looked like he wanted to roast me alive, especially during my photo with Isabella—the one *she'd asked for.*

Jesus. What had I ever done to him?

Fortunately, I made it through the photo session intact, and Isabella and Kai left after wishing us happy anniversary again. The library doors closed, and Scarlett and I were alone once more.

"I can't believe you set up a private signing with Isabella Valencia." Scarlett still looked dazed from the encounter. "How long did it take you to plan this?"

"About two and a half months. I didn't have to work too hard to convince her. Like she said, she was happy to do it."

"Lucky she's your fan," Scarlett teased. "Though I don't think I can say the same for Kai. He kept glaring at you for some reason."

"Maybe he's not a Blackcastle supporter." I shrugged. "Though apparently, I don't poll well amongst engaged or married men between the ages of twenty-five and fifty. I'm not sure why."

"Their loss." She twined her arms around my neck. "I think you're pretty great."

"*Pretty* great?"

"*Exceptionally* great," she amended. "Better?"

"Much." I gave her a soft kiss. "Happy anniversary, darling."

"Happy anniversary." She sighed dreamily against my mouth. "I could stay here forever. This library is the stuff of dreams."

"Our dinner reservations aren't for another hour." I'd booked us a private room at Valhalla's onsite restaurant. "But I can think of a few ways to pass that time..." My mouth moved to the delicate shell of her ear. "Without leaving the library."

Scarlett's breath quickened. "Here?" she squeaked, clearly picking up on the suggestiveness of my tone. "What if someone comes in?"

"They won't. The library is reserved for us tonight." I gave her earlobe a gentle nip before my voice hardened. "Now turn around, bend over, and spread your legs."

The air flickered, throwing our lighthearted teasing into the dark, murky waters of lust.

Scarlett's face flushed, but she obeyed without protest. A visible shiver ran through her body as she bent over the table and parted her legs. Her arm brushed the stack of freshly signed books, which I relocated to a nearby couch before grabbing one of the throw pillows.

I tucked the pillow beneath her hips and leaned forward, covering her body with mine. "Do you trust me?"

She nodded, but her shallow breaths morphed into a hitch of surprise when I retrieved the blindfold from my pocket and slowly slipped it over her eyes again.

A low whine escaped her throat when I stood and stepped back.

"Shhh," I murmured. "I'll take care of you soon." I pushed her dress up around her hips, my nostrils flaring in appreciation at her visible arousal.

I skimmed my fingers over the lust-dampened silk—just lightly enough to make her squirm and whine again. She pushed her hips back at me in an obvious bid for more friction, but I held firm and let myself explore leisurely for another minute despite the growing tightness in my trousers.

We had time, and I wanted to savor this moment. It wasn't just about the sex—it was about the fact that she trusted me enough to let go. To hand over the reins of control and let me take us where I wanted because she knew I would never hurt her. Her trust was more intoxicating than any sexual act.

That being said…when I initiate something, I *always* see it through.

"Please," Scarlett panted. "No more teasing."

"I thought you liked my teasing." I traced my fingers over the lace edge of her underwear and chuckled at her adorable little growl of frustration.

"Asher Donovan, if you don't—*oh fuck*." Her words cut off with a gasp and a swear when I yanked her underwear down with a sharp tug and pushed a finger inside her.

She was already so wet it was like sliding through silk, and when I worked a second finger into her, she barely resisted. Instead, her hips bucked, and a loud moan fell out when I reached around with my other hand and pressed my thumb against her clit.

The sight, sound, *smell* of her sent a shock of heat through my system as I built up a rhythm. The air swirled with the heady sweetness of her arousal, and my cock throbbed with painful need.

My heavy breaths mixed with her moans and the filthy, slippery sound of my fingers thrusting in and out of her. I kept my thumb on her clit while I finger fucked her from behind, faster and deeper, drawing her moans out into cries that lit up every nerve ending of my body.

The blindfold and temporary loss of one of her senses must've heightened the pleasure for her because her muscles went rigid only a few minutes in. Her pants deepened, and I could tell she was on the brink of orgasming when I pulled my hand away from her.

Scarlett's hoarse sound of protest died at the sound of my zipper sliding down and the crinkle of foil. By the time I rolled the condom over my eager, aching cock, she'd tensed again, her body practically quivering with anticipation.

I nudged her entrance with the tip of my cock. "Hold on to the desk," I ordered.

She did as I asked, her fingers curling around the edge just in time for me to bury myself inside her with one hard thrust. She moaned again as I bent over her and braced my hands against the desk on either side of her.

"How hard do you want me to fuck you, Scarlett?" My soft question belied the insistent, insatiable heat gathered at the base of my spine. I wanted to pound into her and hear her scream, to see her claw at the desk and come apart around my cock, but I wanted to *hear* her say it first.

My lips grazed her cheek, and I felt a shiver ripple through her body.

She didn't answer, but she let out a whimper when my hand came up to grasp her chin. "How hard?" I repeated.

"Hard," she whispered, her cheeks heating beneath my mouth.

"I can't hear you, darling." I pushed myself a little deeper inside her—no more than a centimeter, but it was enough to make her hips buck again.

"*Hard*." Her knuckles whitened. "I want you to fuck me hard. *Please*." The last word came out as a sob.

I groaned. God, I could never say no to, nor get enough of, her.

I released her chin, braced my hand against the desk again—and fucked her exactly the way she wanted. Hard and rough, my balls slapping against her skin with every thrust, her screams and moans driving me faster, *deeper* until she came with a half-cry, half-sob.

Her cunt rippled, squeezing and releasing my cock in a way that pulled a blinding orgasm out of me mere seconds later. My vision whitened, and the world devolved into pure static beneath an exquisite, almost agonizing wave of pleasure.

Scarlett and I lay there, panting, until our breaths returned to normal and I could move my limbs again.

I removed her blindfold, helped her up, and cleaned us both with the handkerchief I brought with me. I tossed the used condom and soiled cloth into the box the special edition books had been delivered in and made a mental note to place the entire box in the trash before we left.

When I finished, I caught a glimpse of Scarlett's deep blush before she buried her face in my chest. "I can't go to dinner like this," she said, her voice muffled. "I look…"

"Like you've been fucked thoroughly?" I chuckled when she

lifted her head to glare at me, the color of her cheeks deepening from pale rose to beet red.

"*Asher*."

"You still look beautiful. You're just a little more...ruffled." I smoothed a strand of hair back from her forehead. "If it makes you feel better, I booked us a private room. No one will be looking at us."

"Except the servers."

"I'm sure they've seen worse, and we can clean up before dinner. The spa here has showers and toiletries we can use."

Her jaw dropped. "Seriously? Why didn't you lead with that?"

"Because you were too adorable when you thought I was going to make you walk into the restaurant smelling like sex."

"You're *diabolical*." But her words lacked heat, and her eyes shone with so much love it arrowed straight into my chest. "I'll let it slide this time since you gave me a private signing with Isabella Valencia *and* an orgasm. This might be the best anniversary ever."

"Best anniversary ever *so far*," I corrected.

Scarlett laughed. "You are one of a kind, Asher Donovan." She stood on tiptoes and gave me a soft kiss. "I love you."

"I love you, too." I kissed her back, my heart giving a heavy thump of agreement. "More than anything else in this world."

I didn't always appreciate the way other people said my full name—like I was a brand and a commodity instead of a person.

But when Scarlett said it, she said it like she saw every piece of me—the good and the bad—and she loved me because of, not despite, the different facets of my character.

I'd been surrounded by money and fame for most of my adult life. But this, right here, with Scarlett happy and content in my arms?

This was all I truly needed.

EPILOGUE #1

ASHER

ADIL

Welcome to the Blackcastle Book Club's official group chat!

Seriously? You put a picture from The Land Before Time as the group's profile picture?

ADIL

Why not? It's a good movie

STEVENS

Dude, that's so wrong. It's a children's film, and we're reading about dinosaurs boning

ADIL

It's a good thing we're not making them read the books, isn't it?

ADIL

But fine, I see your point

ADIL

I wanted to keep it a surprise, but since you insist on policing my admin decisions, I've changed the picture to the cover of this month's book club pick

ADIL

Gentlemen, prepare yourselves for **drumroll please** Shagging the Spinosaurus!

VINCENT

We already guessed that was the book of the month. We saw you reading it the other day

Aren't you supposed to read it with the rest of the club? Why are you reading it early?

STEVENS

Yeah, that's CHEATING

ADIL

It's called vetting. Also, I'm the admin. I can do what I want

SAMSON

I tried looking for it at the bookstore yesterday and couldn't find it. Donovan, what was the name of the store you went to?

Uh...I don't remember. Just some shop I stumbled on in the city. I'm sure you can buy the book online

GALLAGHER

I don't understand. How do you shag a spinosaurus?

STEVENS

The same way you shag a triceratops and a T-rex, genius

GALLAGHER

Oh, you sound so bloody confident. Are you speaking from experience?

ADIL

Gentlemen, let's get back on track! This is a book club, not a fight club

ADIL

Our first official meeting is on Wednesday. I want everyone to come prepared with at least one discussion question

GALLAGHER

Dibs on the 'how do you shag a spinosaurus' question

ADIL

You can't ask that. It has to be a THOUGHTFUL question

VINCENT

How thoughtful do you want us to be? We're literally reading about dinosaurs fucking

And humans

If you forget them, that's human erasure

VINCENT

Fuck off, Donovan

Asher: Spoken like someone who doesn't have the IQ to come up with a good question

VINCENT

Yeah? Let's wait until Wednesday and see. I bet my question will be better than yours

You're on. May the better questioner win

ADIL

Okayyy. Moving on.

ADIL

Noah, since you refuse to participate in the LITERARY side of our club, you're in charge of snacks

NOAH

Fine

ADIL

I'm thinking we could do a themed event with dinosaur crackers

ADIL

Do you think they make custom spinosaurus ones?

SAMSON

So we're going to eat the little dude while we read about him getting it on? That's so wrong

STEVENS

Poor Spiny. He deserves better

ADIL

It was an IDEA. I don't see you guys coming up with anything better

GALLAGHER

How about jungle juice to stay with the dinosaur theme?

VINCENT

Dinosaurs didn't live in the jungle

GALLAGHER

How do you know? Were you there?

Lol

VINCENT

Don't talk to your captain like that

GALLAGHER

You're our football captain. You're not the president of this book club

GALLAGHER

Also, I just looked it up and they did live in jungles, so you're wrong

SAMSON

Wait, we have a president?

ADIL

Yes, it's me

ADIL

Anyway

ADIL

Noah, can you call the dinosaur cracker company and ask them for custom spinosaurus snacks?

ADIL

Hello?

ADIL

Noah?

NOAH WILSON LEFT THE CONVERSATION.

EPILOGUE #2

ASHER

THIRTY SECONDS OF ADDED TIME LEFT ON THE CLOCK.

Sweat coated my skin and dripped into my eyes. A ceaseless, deafening roar rolled through the stadium as fans shouted for someone, anyone on their side to score.

It was our final match of the season. Once again, we were playing Holchester; once again, we were tied, and once again, we needed a win to take home the trophy.

The déjà vu was so strong it permeated the air and etched lines of determination across every Blackcastle player's face. We'd let last season's Premier League title slip through our fingers, but we would rather die than give Holchester another victory.

Not in our bloody stadium, in our city, surrounded by our fans.

Bocci broke through our defense and attempted a goal. My heart stopped in denial only to pick up again when Vincent streaked in at the last minute with a spectacular block.

He kicked the ball to Elliott, who tried to run upfield with it but faced strong resistance from Holchester. Instead of wasting time by fighting, he passed the ball back to Vincent, who took it and ran.

Fifteen seconds left.

My blood thundered in my ears, and I tracked Vincent like an eagle as he sprinted along the sideline.

Come on, come on, come on…

I silently urged him to run faster even as I kept an eye on the opposing team as well. This was our last play. Either it worked or it didn't—and it *had* to work.

Ten seconds left.

Vincent finally paused and, without so much as a beat of hesitation, delivered a sumptuous cross so smoothly that Holchester's defense was still scrambling when I raced in to meet it.

Five seconds.

I didn't think. I acted on instinct and met the ball with a clean, simple header.

The noise that rocked the stadium swelled beneath my skin and filled my lungs as I joined seventy thousand people in watching the ball sail toward the goal in seeming slow motion.

Four.

Holchester's keeper dived.

Three.

His fingers grazed the ball, but they didn't find purchase.

Two.

The ball sank into the back of the net.

One.

A moment of pure silence.

Then the stadium erupted, its roar so deafening that my teeth and bones rattled from the sheer force of it. It built and built, climbing higher and higher, until the very ground seemed to shake beneath the jubilation of tens of thousands of fans celebrating Blackcastle's first

Premier league victory in ten years.

I stood there, too stunned to move until my team swarmed me with hugs and cheers.

"We won!" Samson shouted, shaking my shoulders. "We fucking won!"

"We bloody did it! Take that, wankers!" Gallagher yelled, flipping the bird toward the Holchester players at the other end of the pitch.

Not very sportsmanlike, but who cared?

We won. *We won.*

Exhilaration shattered shock's hold on me.

I finally joined in the celebrations, my heart full to bursting as I hugged and clapped my teammates on the back.

After all the shit we'd been through and all the obstacles we'd faced, we were bringing home the trophy.

Christ, it felt good—more than good. It was euphoric.

Laughter rumbled through my chest when the team hoisted me and Vincent on their shoulders. From this vantage point, I spotted our exultant club staff on the sidelines with Coach, who wore his first real smile since 1995.

"Good thing you didn't screw that up!" Vincent shouted over the noise. His face gleamed with a mix of perspiration and elation. "If you had, I would've banished you from the team myself."

"Like you have the power!" I shouted back. I flipped him off, laughing again when the team set us down and Vincent attacked me with a bear hug.

"Fuck you, Donovan!" he yelled in my ear. But he was grinning.

We all were.

Well, all of us except Holchester, whose members skulked off the pitch with their heads down. Bocci shot me a baleful glare on his way out. He was already in hot water with Holchester execs after he got caught street racing last month. His arrest had resulted in a hefty fine and a twelve-month driving ban, and there were rumors his stay on the team was dependent on him leading them to another league title this year.

I didn't know what would happen to him now, and I didn't care. I was focused on finding someone more important.

Vincent went off to sing our team's anthem with Adil and Stevens while I scanned the stadium.

Finding her should've been impossible given how many people were jumping and running about, but I spotted her almost immediately.

Even if there were seven hundred thousand instead of seventy thousand people here, I would've found her just as easily because a part of me would always be connected to a part of her.

Scarlett sat on the north side with Carina, Brooklyn...and my parents.

My heart stopped for the second time that day. I blinked to make sure I was seeing correctly, but there was no mistaking my mother's curly dark hair and my father's grizzled beard.

They hadn't said a *word* about attending today's match, but there they were, decked out in Blackcastle gear—even my father.

My mother beamed and waved when she saw me looking. My father didn't smile *or* wave, but his short nod was the most affirmation I'd gotten from him since I transferred.

I doubted we would ever have a "normal" father-son relationship, but it had improved incrementally since his surprise visit to kick my ass into gear during the fall. Plus, the fact that he was here today in *Blackcastle* colors? That meant more than anything else he could've done.

I swallowed the emotion in my throat—if I teared up on the pitch, I would never live it down—and refocused on Scarlett.

She grinned and blew me a kiss with one hand. Her other hand carried a sign that said *Kick Holchester's ass from here to Pluto* in huge, bright purple letters.

I burst into laughter. God, I loved that woman.

I winked and blew her a kiss back.

It was cheesy as fuck, but I didn't care how many people groaned or how many front pages it would land on tomorrow.

I meant it with all my heart.

SCARLETT

"Do you think the logo was always there or he had someone install it after you guys won?" I asked, staring at the giant Blackcastle logo etched into the foyer floor.

Asher laughed. "I have no idea. This is my first time here. I've never even met Markovic before."

It was the week after Blackcastle's historic league win—the first under Coach Frank Armstrong *and* the first under its current owner Vuk Markovic—and Markovic had invited the entire club for a celebration at his mansion outside London.

Either he'd been extremely confident about the team's ability to win or he spent an inordinate amount of money to host such a lavish party on such short notice.

He could certainly afford it. The billionaire CEO possessed a higher net worth than some small European countries. He lived in New York but owned multiple interests in the UK, including Markovic Stadium, and he was notoriously reclusive. According to the internet, he rarely, if ever, spoke in public.

Given his reputation, I was surprised he was hosting such an elaborate party, but winning the Premier League *was* a big deal. As the team owner, he had to thank the players somehow.

"It's about time you two showed up." Vincent appeared out of seemingly nowhere. Like the rest of the men, he wore a tuxedo to fit in with the black-tie theme. "I can't believe you made me the early one out of our trio. Do you have any idea what that'll do to my 'fashionably late' reputation?"

I patted his shoulder with a comforting hand. "Punctuality is a good thing. Embrace it."

"We would've gotten here earlier, but we got distracted," Asher added, swiping two pieces of baked shrimp toast off a passing server's platter. He handed me one and popped the other in his mouth.

My brother visibly gagged. "Don't *ever* say stuff like that in front of me again. I'm going to be sick."

Asher raised an eyebrow. He chewed and swallowed before saying casually, "I was talking about the injured bird we saved from the side of the road. What were *you* talking about?"

I laughed and nudged Asher gently with my elbow. "Stop teasing him. You two play nice while I say hi to Brooklyn."

My friend stood on the other side of the domed entryway, talking to another Blackcastle staff member.

The foyer represented only a sliver of the Markovic estate, which was vast enough to fit multiple football pitches with room left over for an American baseball field or two, but it was still five times as big as my flat. The aforementioned gold stallion team logo gleamed against an expanse of pale green marble while chandeliers dripped with heavy, teardrop-shaped crystals above.

It would probably take me ten minutes just to reach Brooklyn, especially given how many people were here. Besides the Blackcastle team and their dates, I spotted a few celebrities and socialites—including Polina, the model I'd caught kissing Asher over the summer.

She came with Gallagher, but judging by the way she kept scanning the room, she was on the lookout for someone else.

"I'll say hi to Brooklyn with you." Vincent moved to follow me before I stopped him with a hand on his chest.

"Don't even think about it," I warned.

"Think about what?" He was the picture of innocence.

"She is *not* going to go for you. Even if she did, her father wouldn't. The Boss will literally murder you with his bare hands if you so much as breathe wrong near her."

"Please. I don't have a death wish," Vincent said. "I just want to talk to her because I lent her the latest Isabella Valencia book and I want it back."

My brother did *not* read thrillers. "You don't own..." My eyes narrowed. "Wait. You mean *my* Isabella Valencia book? The one I haven't read yet? I was looking all over for it the other day!"

Vincent shrugged, having the grace to look sheepish.

Unbelievable. This was like the Adele vinyl situation *all over again.*

"Anyway, I'm not interested in her like that," he said. "I admit, I was intrigued when I first met her, but she's annoying."

"Because she's the one woman not related to you who doesn't fall all over you? And Carina doesn't count. She's basically your de facto sister."

"*No.* It's because she's annoying."

"You used to think Asher was annoying, and now you're best friends."

Vincent's mouth curled. "Best friends is pushing it. We tolerate each other."

"I'm standing right here," Asher interjected. "But he's right. We tolerate each other for the team and for *you.* That's it."

"Uh-huh." They tolerated each other so much they were going to watch the upcoming Nate Reynolds movie *without me*, but whatever. I wasn't bitter or anything. "Sure. Well, tolerate each other while I say hi to Brooklyn—*alone*."

I left them to bicker with each other while I joined my friend next to one of the Picassos. The other staff member had left, leaving her by herself.

"I don't know how you do it," she said. She must've been watching my interaction with Asher and Vincent. "Dealing with those two together is like dealing with children."

"Tell me about it." I hugged her hello. "You look great."

"So do you." Brooklyn grinned. "It's too bad Carina couldn't come. This place is wild. Did you know there's a shooting range in the back garden?"

"No. How did *you* know that?"

"People tell me things." She shrugged. Her gaze coasted over my shoulder, and her eyes widened—with appreciation or apprehension, I couldn't tell. "Speaking of people...look who's here."

I turned as the lively chatter in the foyer faded into silence and the only sound was the clack of shoes against marble.

He emerged from the shadows of another room and stopped at the edge of the crowd. I recognized him from my internet sleuthing immediately.

Vuk Markovic.

I thought his photos were intimidating, but they didn't do him justice. In person, he was downright terrifying. It wasn't his size or the vicious scar bisecting his face into two icy halves. It wasn't the unsmiling mouth, the burn marks around his throat, or those pale blue, almost colorless eyes.

It was the sense of danger he emitted, like a predator dressed in sheep's clothing. Even in a custom ten-thousand-pound tux, he didn't look like a CEO. He looked like someone who would calmly and efficiently dismember you with his bare hands if you crossed him.

A chill skittered down my spine when those unsettling eyes brushed over me, but they didn't pause. They simply skimmed over me like I didn't exist.

He scanned the room without a hint of emotion. It seemed like he was searching for someone, but whoever it was must not have been there because his mouth thinned with displeasure.

An older woman came up beside him and whispered something in his ear. He nodded and walked toward the Boss, breaking the spell of silence that had descended upon his arrival.

The room released a collectively held breath, and chatter picked up again.

"I guess he's not going to give a thank-you speech," I said wryly.

"He's hot."

My head snapped toward her. "Who? *Markovic?*"

"Yeah. In a scary, I-might-kill-you-after-I-fuck-you sort of way. But it works. What?" she said defensively when I arched my eyebrows. "I have a thing for bad boys."

"Sometimes, you worry me."

"I always do," she said with more cheer than the situation warranted. She glanced over my shoulder again, a small smile creeping onto her face. "But I think you'll feel much better soon."

"What—"

"I hate to interrupt, but do you mind if I steal Scarlett away?" Asher's smooth voice interjected along with a hand on my hip. "I have something important I need to show her."

Brooklyn smirked. "I'm sure you do."

Heat scalded my face. "Get your mind out of the gutter."

"Nah. It's a fun place to be, but I can take a hint." She winked at us on her way to say hi to Adil. "Have fun."

"What's this important thing you need to show me?" I asked Asher suspiciously as he led me around the edge of the entryway toward the main part of the house. "It's not your dick, is it?"

His chuckle rose over the din, teasing my senses. "Not necessarily, but if you *want* to see it…"

My blush deepened. "I've seen it plenty. I don't need—what are you doing?" I squealed out a laugh when Asher pulled me into a dark room off the foyer and locked the door behind us.

"Stealing some time alone with my girlfriend." He lifted me onto one of the side tables and stepped in between my legs. "I'm tired of sharing you with other people."

"We were apart for ten minutes max, and we see each other every day."

I officially moved into Asher's house last month after the lease on my flat expired. It was a huge step, but it was also a natural progression of our relationship.

"True," he conceded. "But ten minutes is too long, and every day isn't enough."

"You're impossible," I said with another laugh. "Even so, Mr. Markovic is going to be very upset if he finds out we're desecrating his…" My voice trailed off for a second, and my breath hitched when Asher's hand slid up my leg. "Whatever this room is."

Drawing room? Living room? Sitting room? My muddled brain noticed chairs and tables, but the bulk of my attention had diverted toward the graze of Asher's fingers against my thigh.

"I just won Mr. Markovic his first Premier League title in a decade." Asher lowered his head, his velvety murmur making me shiver. "I think he'll give me some grace."

My resistance gradually melted like snow beneath the sun as he feathered kisses along my jaw.

"I don't know," I breathed. "He seems pretty unforgiving. Do you think he's..." I swallowed as Asher's hand found the lace edge of my knickers. "Um, do you think he's actually in business or..." I gasped, my words dissolving into a burst of pleasure when he slipped his fingers beneath the lace and found my slick arousal.

Asher kissed his way back up to my mouth. "Scarlett?"

"Yes?"

"I don't want to talk about Markovic, or anything else, right now."

Heat fluttered between my legs. "So what do you want to do instead?"

His grin was pure wickedness in the dark.

"Why tell you..." he drawled, sinking to his knees. "When I could show you?"

Those were the last words we exchanged for the next half hour.

I had no idea if people were looking for us or if Markovic would be upset about us defiling his drawing/living/sitting room.

If they were, and he was, we'd deal with it together. We always did.

For now, I allowed myself to abandon my worries and sink into the pleasure of the moment.

The past was the past, and the future was unpredictable.

But the present? It belonged to us, and I wouldn't have it any other way.

Can't get enough of Asher and Scarlett? Download their bonus epilogue for free at anahuang.com/bonus-scenes

* * *

Thank you for reading *The Striker*! If you enjoyed this book, I would be grateful if you could leave a review on the platform(s) of your choice.

Reviews are like tips for authors, and every one helps!

xo, Ana

P.S. Want to discuss my books and other fun shenanigans with like-minded readers? Join my exclusive reader group Ana's Twisted Squad!

KEEP IN TOUCH WITH ANA HUANG

Reader Group:
facebook.com/groups/anastwistedsquad

Newsletter:
anahuang.com/newsletter

Website:
anahuang.com

Bookbub:
bookbub.com/profile/ana-huang

Instagram:
instagram.com/authoranahuang

TikTok:
tiktok.com/@authoranahuang

Goodreads:
goodreads.com/anahuang

ACKNOWLEDGMENTS

This was the official start of my sports romance era, so first, I want to thank you, the reader, for coming on this journey with me.

Starting a new series is always daunting, but I had so much fun exploring the London branch of the Anaverse, and I hope you loved Asher and Scarlett as much as I did.

You are the reason I do what I do, and I'm so grateful to have you by my side as we dive into this world of footballers and fame together.

I also want to thank everyone who made this literary foray across the pond possible.

Becca—Our process changes with every book, but whether it's a three-hour Zoom call or a sleepover at my house, it always ends with magic. Thank you for being a great editor and an even better friend.

Brittney, Rebecca, and Salma—We've been through multiple books together at this point, and I hope we'll be there for many more!

Paige, Emma, and Ellie—Your feedback on the chronic pain representation, British geography and culture, and Premier League football were invaluable. Who knew Axe was called Lynx in the UK? Not me before this book. Thank you for helping me make this story shine.

Jess, Malia, Jessie, Chelsea, and Tori— My wonderful beta readers. Thank you for all your notes and suggestions. They truly helped me bring Asher and Scarlett's romance to the next level.

Britt—Thank you, as always, for your eagle eye and for dealing with my tight deadlines. You're a rockstar!

Ali and Khush—Where would I be without your football

expertise? Thank you for answering my questions more thoroughly than any Google search.

Cat—Several months of DMs, purple-toned dreams, and stress-induced freakouts later, we made it! Thank you for sticking by me through this (very) long process, and thank you for the stunning cover. ILY.

Christa, Madison, and the rest of the team at Bloom—We have another series out in the world! Your enthusiasm and dedication always make me smile, and I'm so excited for this chapter of our partnership.

Ellie and the Piatkus team—The Anaverse is now in London! Thank you for your help with the Britishisms and all that you do.

Kimberly, Aimee, and the Brower Literary team—Thank you for all that you do behind the scenes. You make this wild career so much smoother. I appreciate you!

Much love,
Ana